Alex, Approximately

Alex, Approximately

Jenn Bennett

Simon Pulse

NEW YORK   LONDON   TORONTO   SYDNEY   NEW DELHI

SIMON PULSE
An imprint of Simon & Schuster Children's Publishing Division
1230 Avenue of the Americas, New York, New York 10020
First Simon Pulse hardcover edition April 2017
Text copyright © 2017 by Jenn Bennett
Jacket front and back photograph copyright © 2017 by svetikd/Getty Images
Jacket spine and flaps photograph copyright © 2017 by leetatee/Thinkstock
All rights reserved, including the right of reproduction in whole or in part in any form.
SIMON PULSE and colophon are registered trademarks of Simon & Schuster, Inc.
For information about special discounts for bulk purchases,
please contact Simon & Schuster Special Sales at 1-866-506-1949
or business@simonandschuster.com.
The Simon & Schuster Speakers Bureau can bring authors to your live event.
For more information or to book an event contact the Simon & Schuster Speakers Bureau
at 1-866-248-3049 or visit our website at www.simonspeakers.com.
Jacket designed by Regina Flath
Interior designed by Hilary Zarycky
The text of this book was set in Adobe Garamond.
Manufactured in the United States of America
2 4 6 8 10 9 7 5 3 1
This book has been cataloged with the Library of Congress.
ISBN 978-1-4814-7877-9 (hc)
ISBN 978-1-4814-7879-3 (eBook)

For the evaders, avoiders, dodgers, and side-steppers.
You probably have a good reason for hiding.
May you work through it and find your inner lion.

Alex, Approximately

LUMIÈRE FILM FANATICS COMMUNITY
PRIVATE MESSAGES>ALEX>ARCHIVED

@alex: They just announced the summer schedule for free films on the beach to kick off the annual film festival. Guess which Hitchcock they're showing? North by Northwest!

@mink: Seriously?! Hate you. But I already saw NxNW on the big screen last year, so . . .

@alex: Doesn't count. Beach movies are cooler. It's like a drive-in without the car exhaust. And who doesn't want to watch a chase sequence across Mount Rushmore while you dip your toes in the sand? Here's an idea. Tell your dad you want to visit him in June and we can go see it together.

@mink: Not a beach girl, remember?

@alex: You've never been to a real one. East Coast beaches are trash beaches.

@mink: ALL beaches are trash beaches. *peeks at film festival schedule* Besides, if I WERE going to visit my dad, I'd rather come the final week of the festival and see all those Georges Méliès films they're showing . . . INDOORS. As in: sand free.

@alex: --------> THIS IS ME FREAKING OUT. (Are you serious?! Please be serious. We could actually meet in real life?)

@mink: I don't know.

@alex: If you're serious, then come and see North by Northwest with me. Outside on the beach, as nature intended.

@mink: Films shouldn't be seen outdoors, but okay. If I come, we'll meet at North by Northwest on the beach.

@alex: It's a date!

@mink: Whoa, hold your horses. I said *if* I fly out to California to visit my dad. I'm just dreaming. It will probably never happen. . . .

"I don't think I caught your name."
—Cary Grant, *North by Northwest* (1959)

I

He could be any one of these people.

After all, I don't know what Alex looks like. I don't even know his real name. I mean, we've been talking online for months now, so I know things that matter. He's smart and sweet and funny, and we've both just finished our junior year. We share the same obsession—old movies. We both like being alone.

If these were the only things we had in common, I wouldn't be freaking out right now. But Alex lives in the same town as my dad, and that makes things . . . complicated.

Because now that I'm descending a Central California airport escalator in Alex's general vicinity, watching strangers drift in the opposite direction, endless possibilities duke it out inside my head. Is Alex short? Tall? Does he chew too loud or have some irritating catchphrase? Does he pick his nose in public? Has he had his arms replaced with bionic tentacles? (Note to self: not a deal breaker.)

So, yeah. Meeting real-life Alex could be great, but it could also be one big awkward disappointment. Which is why I'm not really sure if I want to know anything more about him.

Look, I don't do confrontation well. Or ever, really. What I'm doing now, moving across the country one week after my seventeenth birthday to live with my dad, is not an act of bravery. It's a masterpiece of avoidance. My name is Bailey Rydell, and I'm a habitual evader.

When my mom traded my dad for Nate Catlin of Catlin Law LLC—I swear to all things holy, that's how he introduces himself—I didn't choose to live with her instead of Dad because of all the things she promised: new clothes, a car of my own, a trip to Europe. Heady stuff, sure, but none of it mattered. (Or even happened. Just saying.) I only stayed with her because I was embarrassed for my dad, and the thought of having to deal with him while he faced his new postdump life was too much for me to handle. Not because I don't care about him either. Just the opposite, actually.

But a lot changes in a year, and now that Mom and Nate are fighting constantly, it's time for me to exit the picture. That's the thing about being an evader. You have to be flexible and know when to bail before it all gets weird. Better for everyone, really. I'm a giver.

My plane landed half an hour ago, but I'm taking a circuitous route to what I hope is the backside of baggage claim, where my dad is supposed to pick me up. The key to avoiding uncomfortable situations is a preemptive strike: make sure you see them first. And before you accuse me of being a coward, think again. It's not easy being this screwed up. It takes planning and sharp reflexes. A devious mind. My mom says I'd make a great pickpocket, because I can disappear faster than you can say, *Where's my wallet?* The Artful Dodger, right here.

And right there is my father. Artful Dodger, senior. Like I said, it's been a year since I've seen him, and the dark-headed man standing under a slanted beam of early afternoon sunlight is different than I remember. In better shape, sure, but that's no surprise. I've cheered on his new gym-crafted body every week as he showed off his arms during our Sunday-night video calls. And the darker hair wasn't new either; God knows I've teased him about dyeing away the gray in an attempt to slice off the last few years of his forties.

But as I stealthily scope him out while hiding behind a sunny CALIFORNIA DREAMERS! sign, I realize that the one thing I didn't expect was for my dad to be so . . . happy.

Maybe this wouldn't be too painful, after all. Deep breath.

A grin splits his face when I duck out of my hiding spot.

"Mink," he says, calling me by my silly adolescent nickname.

I don't really mind, because he's the only one who calls me that in real life, and everyone else in baggage claim is too busy greeting their own familial strangers to pay any attention to us. Before I can avoid it, he reels me in and hugs me so hard my ribs crack.

We both tear up a little. I swallow the constriction in my throat and force myself to calm down.

"Jesus, Bailey." He looks me over shyly. "You're practically grown."

"You can introduce me as your sister if it makes you look younger in front of your geekazoid sci-fi friends," I joke in an attempt to diffuse the awkwardness, poking the robot on his *Forbidden Planet* T-shirt.

"Never. You're my greatest achievement."

Ugh. I'm embarrassed that I'm so easily wooed by this, and I can't think of a witty comeback. I end up sighing a couple of times.

His fingers tremble as he tucks bleached platinum-blond strands of my long Lana Turner pin-curl waves behind my ear. "I'm so glad you're here. You are staying, right? You didn't change your mind on the flight?"

"If you think I'm going to willingly walk back into that MMA fight they call a marriage, you don't know me at all."

He does a terrible job at hiding his giddy triumph, and I can't help but smile back. He hugs me again, but it's okay now. The worst part of our uncomfortable meet-and-greet is over.

"Let's collect your stuff. Everyone on your flight has already claimed theirs, so it shouldn't be too hard to find," he says, gesturing with a knowing dart of his eyes toward the luggage carousels, one brow cocked.

Oops. Should've known. Can't dodge a dodger.

Having grown up on the East Coast, I'd never been farther

west than a single school trip to Chicago, so it's strange to step into bright sunlight and look up at such a big, überblue sky. It seems flatter out here without all the dense mid-Atlantic treetops blocking out the skyline—so flat, I can see mountain foothills girding the entire Silicon Valley horizon. I'd flown into San Jose, the nearest airport and actual big city, so we have a forty-five-minute drive to my dad's new house on the coast. Not a hardship, especially when I see we'll be cruising in a glossy blue muscle car with the sunroof wide open.

My father is a CPA. He used to drive the most boring car in the world. California has changed that, I suppose. What else has changed?

"Is this your midlife-crisis car?" I ask when he opens the trunk to stow my luggage.

He chuckles. It totally is. "Get in," he says, checking the screen on his phone. "And please text your mother that you didn't die in a fiery plane crash so she'll stop bugging me."

"Aye, aye, Captain Pete."

"Goofball."

"Weirdo."

He nudges me with his shoulder, and I nudge back, and just like that, we're falling back into our old routine. Thank God. His new (old) car smells like the stuff that neat freaks spray on leather, and there's no accounting paperwork stuffed in the floorboards, so I'm getting the posh treatment. As he revs up the crazy-loud engine, I turn on my phone for the first time since I've landed.

Texts from Mom: four. I answer her in the most bare-bones way possible while we leave the airport parking garage. I'm finally coming down from the shock of what I've done—holy crap, I just moved across the country. I remind myself that it's not a big deal. After all, I already switched schools a few months ago, thanks to Nate LLC and Mom moving us from New Jersey to Washington, DC, which basically means I didn't have a notable friend investment in DC to leave behind. And I haven't really dated anyone since my dad left, so no boyfriend investment either. But when I check the nonemergency notifications on my phone, I see a reply on the film app from Alex and get nervous all over again about being in the same town.

@alex: Is it wrong to hate someone who used to be your best friend? Please talk me down from planning his funeral. Again.

I send a quick reply—

@mink: You should just leave town and make new friends. Less blood to clean up.

If I look past any reservations I may have, I can admit it's pretty thrilling to think that Alex has no idea I'm even here. Then again, he's never really known exactly where I've been. He thinks I still live in New Jersey, because I never bothered to change my profile online when we moved to DC.

When Alex first asked me to come out here and see *North by Northwest* with him, I wasn't sure what to think. It's not exactly the kind of movie you ask a girl out to see when you're trying to win her heart—not *most* girls, anyway. Considered one of Alfred Hitchcock's greatest films, it stars Cary Grant and Eva Marie Saint, and it's a thriller about mistaken identity. It starts in New York and ends up out West, as Cary Grant is pursued to Mount Rushmore in one of the most iconic scenes in movie history. But now every time I think about seeing it, I picture myself as the seductive Eva Marie Saint and Alex as Cary Grant, and we're falling madly in love, despite the fact that we barely know each other. And sure, I know that's a fantasy, and reality could be so much weirder, which is why I have a plan: secretly track down Alex before *North by Northwest* plays at the summer film festival.

I didn't say it was a good plan. Or an easy plan. But it's better than an awkward meet-up with someone who looks great on paper, but in real life, may crush my dreams. So I'm doing this the Artful Dodger way—from a safe distance, where neither of us can get hurt. I have a lot of experience with bad strangers. It's best this way, trust me.

"Is that him?" Dad asks.

I quickly pocket my phone. "Who?"

"What's-his-face. Your film-buff soul mate."

I've barely told Dad anything about Alex. I mean, he knows Alex lives in this area and even jokingly dangled this fact as bait to come out here when I finally decided I couldn't handle living with Mom and Nate anymore.

"He's contemplating murder," I tell Dad. "So I'll probably meet him in a dark alley tonight and jump into his unmarked van. That should be fine, right?"

An undercurrent of tension twitches between us, just for a second. He knows I'm only teasing, that I would never take that kind of risk, not after what happened to our family four years ago. But that's in the past, and Dad and I are all about the future now. Nothing but sunshine and palm trees ahead.

He snorts. "If he's got a van, don't expect to be able to track it down." Crap. Does he know I've entertained that idea? "Everyone's got vans where we're headed."

"Creepy molester vans?"

"More like hippie vans. You'll see. Coronado Cove is different."

And he shows me why after we turn off the interstate—sorry, the "freeway," as Dad informs me they're called out here. Once the location of a historical California mission, Coronado Cove is now a bustling tourist town between San Francisco and Big Sur. Twenty thousand residents, and twice as many tourists. They come for three things: the redwood forest, the private nude beach, and the surfing.

Oh, yes: I said redwood forest.

They come for one other thing, and I'd be seeing that up close and personal soon enough, which makes my stomach hurt to think about. So I don't. Not right now. Because the town is even prettier than it was in the photos Dad sent. Hilly, cypress-lined streets. Spanish-style stucco buildings with terra-cotta tile roofs. Smoky purple mountains in the distance. And then we hit Gold Avenue, a two-lane twisting road that hugs the curving coast, and I finally see it: the Pacific Ocean.

Alex was right. East Coast beaches are trash beaches. This . . . is stunning.

"It's so blue," I say, realizing how dumb I sound but unable to think of a better description of the bright aquamarine water breaking toward the sand. I can even smell it from the car. It's salty and clean, and unlike the beach back home, which has that iodine, boiled-metal stench, it doesn't make me want to roll up the window.

"I told you, didn't I? It's paradise out here," Dad says. "Everything is going to be better now. I promise, Mink."

I turn to him and smile, wanting to believe he might be right. And then his head whips toward the windshield and we screech to a stop.

My seat belt feels like a metal rod slapping across my chest as I jerk forward and brace my hands on the dash. Brief pain shoots through my mouth and I taste copper. The high-pitched squeal that comes out of me, I realize, is entirely too loud and dramatic; apart from my biting my own tongue, no one's hurt, not even the car.

"You okay?" Dad asks.

More embarrassed than anything else, I nod before turning my attention to the cause of our near wreck: two teen boys in the middle of the street. They both look like walking advertisements for coconut tanning oil—tousled sun-lightened hair, board shorts, and lean muscles. One dark, one light. But the towheaded one is mad as hell and pounds the hood of the car with his fists.

"Watch where you're going, dickwad," he shouts, pointing to a colorful hand-painted wooden sign of a line of surfers marching their boards through an Abbey Road–looking crosswalk. The top says: WELCOME TO CORONADO COVE. The bottom reads: BE KIND—GIVE SURFERS RIGHT-OF-WAY.

Umm, yeah, no. The sign is nowhere near official, and even if it were, there's no real crosswalk on the street and this white-haired shirtless dude doesn't have a board. But no way am I saying that, because (A) I just screamed like a 1950s housewife, and (B) I don't do confrontation. Especially not with a boy who looks like he's just inhaled a pipeful of something cooked up in a dirty trailer.

His brown-haired buddy has the decency to be wearing a shirt while jaywalking. On top of that, he's ridiculously good-looking (ten points) and trying to pull his jerky friend out of the road (twenty points). And as he does, I get a quick view of a nasty, jagged line of dark-pink scars that curves from the sleeve of his weathered T-shirt down to a bright red watch on his wrist, like someone had to Frankenstein his arm back together a long time ago; maybe this isn't his first time dragging his friend out of the road. He looks as embarrassed as I feel, sitting here with all these cars honking behind us, and while he wrestles his friend back, he holds up a hand to my dad and says, "Sorry, man."

Dad politely waves and waits until they're both clear before cautiously stepping on the gas again. *Go faster, for the love of slugs.* I press my sore tongue against the inside of my teeth, testing the spot where I bit it. And as the drugged-out blond dude continues to scream at us, the boy with the scarred arm stares at me, wind blowing his wild, sun-streaked curls to one side. For a second, I hold my breath and stare back at him, and then he slides out of my view.

Red and blue lights briefly flash in the oncoming lane. Great. Is this kind of thing considered an accident here? Apparently not, because the police car crawls past us. I turn around in my seat to see a female cop with dark purple shades stick her arm out the window and point a warning at the two boys.

"Surfers," Dad says under his breath like it's the filthiest swear-word in the world. And as the cop and the boys disappear behind us along the golden stretch of sand, I can't help but worry that Dad might have exaggerated about paradise.

LUMIÈRE FILM FANATICS COMMUNITY
PRIVATE MESSAGES>ALEX>ARCHIVED

@alex: Busy tonight?

@mink: Just homework.

@alex: Wanna do a watch-along of The Big Lebowski? You can stream it.

@mink: *blink* Who is this? Did some random frat boy take over your account?

@alex: It's a GOOD MOVIE. It's classic Coen Brothers, and you loved O Brother, Where Art Thou?. Come on . . . it'll be fun. Don't be a movie snob.

@mink: I'm not a movie snob. I'm a FILM snob.

@alex: And yet I still like you. . . . Don't leave me hanging here, all bored and lonely, while I'm waiting for you to get up the courage to beg your parents for plane tickets to fly out to California so that you can watch North by Northwest on the beach with a lovable fellow film geek. I'm giving you puppy eyes right now.

@mink: Gee, drop hints, much?

@alex: You noticed? *grin* Come on. Watch it with me. I have to work late tonight.

@mink: You watch movies at work?

@alex: When it's not busy. Believe me, I'm still doing a better job than my coworker, a.k.a. the human blunt. I don't think he's ever NOT been high at work.

@mink: Oh, you deviant Californians. *shakes head*

@alex: Do we have a date? You can do your homework while we watch. I'll even help. What other excuses do you have? Let me shoot them down now: you can wash your hair during the opening credits, we can hit play after you eat dinner, and if your boyfriend doesn't like the idea of you watching a movie with someone online, he's an idiot, and you should break up with him, pronto. Now, what do you say?

@mink: Well, you're in luck, if you pick another movie. My hair is clean, I usually eat dinner around eight, and I'm currently single. Not that it matters.

@alex: Huh. Me too. Not that it matters. . . .

2

I'd seen my dad's new digs during our video chats, but it was strange to experience in person. Tucked away on a quiet, shady street that bordered a redwood forest, it was more cabin than house, with a stone fireplace downstairs and two small bedrooms upstairs. It used to be a vacation rental, so luckily I had my own bathroom.

The coolest part about the house was the screened-in back porch, which not only had a hammock, but was also built around a redwood tree that grew in the middle of it, straight through the roof. However, it was what sat outside that porch in the driveway that jangled my nerves every time I looked at it: a bright turquoise, vintage Vespa scooter with a leopard-print seat.

Scooter.

Mine.

Me on a scooter.

Whaaa?

Its small engine and tiny whitewall tires could only get up to forty mph, but its 1960s bones had been fully restored.

"It's your getaway vehicle," Dad had said proudly when he brought me out back to show it to me the first time. "I knew you had to have something to get to work this summer. And you can drive yourself to school in the fall. You don't even need a special license."

"It's crazy," I'd told him. And gorgeous. But crazy. I worried I'd stand out.

"There are hundreds of these things in town," he argued. "It was either this or a van, but since you won't need to haul around surfboards, I thought this was better."

"It's very Artful Dodger," I admitted.

"You can pretend you're Audrey Hepburn in *Roman Holiday*."

God, he really knew how to sell me. I'd seen that movie a dozen times, and he knew it. "I do like the retro leopard-print seat."

And matching helmet. I therefore christened the scooter Baby, as a nod to one of my all-time favorite films, *Bringing Up Baby*—a 1930s screwball comedy starring Cary Grant and Katharine Hepburn as a mismatched pair who become entangled by a pet leopard, Baby. Once I'd decided on the name, I committed. No going back now. It was mine. Dad taught me how to use it—I rode it up and down his street a million times after dinner—and I would eventually find the nerve to ride it around town, come hell or high water or drugged-out jaywalking surfers.

Dad apologizes for having to work the next day, but I don't mind. I spend the day unpacking and driving my scooter around between jet-lagged naps on the porch hammock. I message Alex a few times, but keeping up the illusion of what I'm doing with my summer is a lot harder than I thought it would be. Maybe it will be easier once I've gotten my sea legs here.

After my day of rest and a night with Dad playing The Settlers of Catan, our favorite board game, I'm forced to put my new-found independence to the test. Finding a summer job was one of my misgivings about coming out here, but Dad pulled some strings. That sounded fine enough when I was back in DC. Now that I'm here, I'm sort of regretting that I agreed to it. Too late to back out, though. "The summer tourist season waits for no one," my father cheerfully tells me when I complain.

Dad wakes me up super early when he goes to work, but I accidentally fall back asleep. When I wake again, I'm running late, so I get dressed in a tizzy and rush out the door. One thing I didn't expect when I moved out here is all the morning coastal fog. It clings to the redwoods like a lacy gray blanket, keeping things cool until midmorning, when the sun burns it away. Sure, the fog has a certain quiet allure, but now that I have to navigate a scooter through my dad's wooded neighborhood, where it's occa-sionally hanging low and reaching through branches like fingers, it's not my favorite thing in the world.

Armed with a map and a knot in my stomach the size of Russia, I face the fog and drive Baby into town. Dad already showed me the way in his car, but I still repeat the directions in my head over and over at every stop sign. It isn't even nine a.m. yet, so most of the streets are clear until I get to the dreaded Gold Avenue. Where I'm going is only a few blocks down this curvy, traffic-clogged road, but I have to drive past the boardwalk (Ferris wheel, loud music, miniature golf), watch out for tourists crossing the road to get to the beach after blimping out at the Pancake Shack for breakfast—which smells a-m-a-z-i-n-g, by the way—and OH MY GOD, where did all these skaters come from?

Just when I'm about to die of some kind of stress-related brain strain, I see the cliffs rising up along the coast at the end of the boardwalk and a sign: THE CAVERN PALACE.

My summer job.

I slow Baby with a squeeze of the hand brakes and turn into the employee driveway. To the right is the main road that leads up the cliff to the guest parking lot, which is empty today. "The Cave," as Dad tells me the locals call it, is closed for training and some sort of outdoor fumigation, which I can smell from here, because it stinks to high heaven. Tomorrow is the official start of the summer tourist season, so today is orientation for new seasonal employees. This includes me.

Dad did some accounting work for the Cave, and he knows the general manager. That's how he got me the job. Otherwise, I doubt they would have been impressed with my limited résumé, which includes exactly one summer of babysitting and several months of after-school law paperwork filing in New Jersey.

But that's all in the past. Because even though I'm so nervous I could upchuck all over Baby's pretty 1960s speedometer right now, I'm actually sort of excited to work here. I like museums. A lot.

This is what I've learned about the Cave online: Vivian and Jay Davenport got rich during the first world war when they came down from San Francisco to purchase this property for a beach getaway and found thirteen million dollars in gold coins hidden inside a cave in the cliffs. The eccentric couple used their found fortune to build a hundred-room sprawling mansion on the beach, right over the entrance to the cave, and filled it with exotic antiques, curios, and oddities collected on trips around the world. They threw crazy booze-filled parties in the 1920s and '30s, inviting rich people from San Francisco to mingle with Hollywood starlets. In the early 1950s, everything ended in tragedy when Vivian shot and killed Jay before committing suicide. After the mansion sat vacant for twenty years, their kids decided they could put the house to better use by opening it up to the public as a tourist attraction.

Okay, so, yeah, the house is definitely kooky and weird, and half of the so-called collection isn't real, but there's supposedly some Golden Age Hollywood memorabilia housed inside. And, hey, working here has got to be way better than filing court documents.

A row of hedges hides the employee lot tucked behind one of the mansion's wings. I manage to park Baby in a space near another scooter without wrecking anything—go me!—and then pop the center stand and run a chain lock through the back tire to secure it. My helmet squeezes inside the bin under the locking seat; I'm good to go.

I didn't know what was considered an appropriate outfit for orientation, so I'm wearing a vintage 1950s sundress with a light cardigan over it. My Lana Turner pin curls seem to have survived the ride, and my makeup's still good. However, when I see a couple of other people walking in a side door wearing flip-flops and shorts, I feel completely overdressed. But it's too late now, so I follow them inside.

This looks to be a back hallway with offices and a break room. A bored woman sits behind a podium inside the door. The people I followed inside are nowhere to be seen, but another girl is stopped at the podium.

"Name?" the bored woman asks.

The girl is petite, about my age, with dark brown skin and cropped black hair. She's also overdressed like me, so I feel a little better. "Grace Achebe," she says in the tiniest, high-pitched voice I've ever heard in my life. She's got a strong English accent. Her tone is so soft, the woman behind the podium makes her repeat her name. Twice.

She finally gets checked off the list and handed a file folder of new-hire paperwork before being instructed to enter the break room. I get the same treatment when it's my turn. Looks to be twenty or more people filling out paperwork already. Since there aren't any empty tables, I sit at Grace's.

She whispers, "You haven't worked here before either?"

"No. I'm new," I say, and then add, "in town."

She glances at my file. "Oh. We're the same age. Brightsea or Oakdale? Or private?"

It takes me a second to realize what she means. "I'll start at Brightsea in the fall."

"Twins," she says with a big smile, pointing to the education line on her application. After another new hire passes by, she shares more information about this place. "They hire, like, twenty-five people every summer. I've heard it's boring but easy. Better than cleaning up pink cotton candy puke at the boardwalk."

Can't argue with that. I've already filled out the main application online, but they've given us a handbook and a bunch of other weird forms to sign. Confidentiality agreements. Random drug-testing permission. Pledges not to use the museum Wi-Fi to view weird porn. Warnings about stealing uniforms.

Grace is as befuddled as I am.

"Competing business?" she murmurs, looking at something we have to sign, promising not to take a similar job within sixty miles of Coronado Cove for three months after ending employment here. "What do they consider a similar job? Is this even legal?"

"Probably not," I whisper back, thinking of Nate LLC constantly spouting off legal advice to my mom, like she wasn't a lawyer herself.

"We-e-ell, this is not legally my signature," she says in her pretty English accent, making a vague, wavy scribble on the form as she waggles her brows at me. "And if they don't give me enough hours, I am heading straight to the nearest cave mansion within sixty miles."

I don't mean to laugh so loud, and everyone looks up, so I quickly quash the giggles and we both finish our paperwork. After we hand it in, we're both assigned a locker and given the ugliest vests I've ever seen in my life. They're the color of rotting jack-o'-lanterns. We don't have to wear them for orientation, but we do have to wear HELLO, MY NAME IS . . . stickers. And when everyone is done slapping them onto their chests, we're herded down the employee hall, through a steel door (with a sign reminding us to smile), and into the main lobby.

It's huge, and our footfalls bounce around the rock walls as we all crane our necks, looking around. The entrance to the cave is at the back of the lobby, and all the stalagmites and -tites are lit with orange lights, which only ups the creep factor. We're led across the expansive lobby past a circular information desk, a gift shop that looks like it was transported from 1890s London, and a sunken lounge area filled with couches that might have been stolen from the set of *The Brady Bunch* . . . all of which are the exact color of our ugly vests. I'm sensing a theme.

"Good morning, seasonal new hires," a middle-aged man says. He, too, is wearing a pumpkin vest with a tie that has the Cavern Palace art deco logo printed all over it. I wonder if that's mandated for the male employees, or if he bought it from the gift shop with his employee discount. "I'm Mr. Cavadini, the museum floor supervisor. Though all of you will be assigned team supervisors, those supervisors report to me. I'm the one who makes the schedules, and the person who approves your time cards. So you may think of me as the person you most want to impress for the next three months."

He says this with all the excitement of a funeral director and manages to frown the entire time he's speaking, but that might be because his dark blond hairline seems unnaturally low—like his forehead is half the size it should be.

"What a woeful twat," Grace says in her tiny voice near my shoulder.

Wow. Sweet little Grace has a filthy mouth. But she's not wrong. And as Mr. Cavadini begins lecturing us on the Cave's history and how it attracts half a million visitors every year, I find myself looking around the lobby and scoping out the places I could be assigned—information desk, guided tours, lost and found, gift shop . . . I wonder which position would allow me to deal with as few disgruntled guests as possible. On my application, I checked off the boxes for "behind-the-scenes" and "working alone" preferences.

Café tables sit around an open balcony on the second floor, and I'm seriously hoping I don't get stuck working in food service. Then again, if I worked in the café, I would get to stare at not only a life-size reproduction of a pirate ship suspended from the ceiling, but also a skeletal sea monster attacking said ship. File that in the "not genuine" part of the Davenports' collection of oddities.

Movement catches my eyes. On a set of floating slate-rock stairs that curve around the pirate ship, two museum security guards in generic black uniforms are descending. I squint, not believing my eyes. How small is this town, anyway? Because one of those guards is the dark-haired dude from yesterday who was pulling his drugged-up friend off the road. Yep, that's definitely him: the hot surfer boy with the Frankenstein scars on his arm.

My panic meter twitches.

"And now," Mr. Cavadini says, "you'll split up into two teams and tour the museum with a member of our security. This side, please follow our senior security officer, Jerry Pangborn, who has worked for Cavern Palace since it opened to the public forty years ago."

He points the left side of the group toward a frail wisp of an old man whose white hair sticks up like he just exploded a beaker of chemicals in a science lab. He's super friendly and sweet, and though he probably couldn't stop a ten-year-old ruffian from stealing a piece of candy out of the gift shop, he eagerly steers his team of recruits to the left side of the lobby, toward a large archway marked VIVIAN'S WING.

Mr. Cavadini motions the surfer boy forward toward our group. "And this is Porter Roth. He's worked with us for the last year or so. Some of you might have heard of his family," he says in a bone-dry, unimpressed voice that makes me think he doesn't think too highly of them. "His grandfather was surfing legend Bill 'Pennywise' Roth."

A little *o-oh* ripples through the crowd as Mr. Cavadini hushes us with one hand and grumpily tells us all to meet him back here in two hours for our scheduling assignments. One side of my brain is screaming, *Two hours?* And the other side is trying to remember if I've ever heard of this Pennywise Roth guy. Is he a real celebrity, or just some local who once got fifteen minutes of fame? Because the sign on that Pancake Shack down the road proclaims its almond pancakes to be world-famous, but come on.

Mr. Cavadini heads back to employee hall, leaving us alone with Porter, who takes his sweet time strolling around the group to look us over. He's got a stack of printouts that he's rolled up into a tube, which he whaps against his leg as he walks. And I didn't notice it yesterday, but he's got a little light brown facial scruff going on—the kind of scruff that pretends to be bad-boy and sexy and rebellious, but is too well groomed to be casual. Then he's got all these wild, loose curls of sun-streaked brown hair, which might be fine for Surfer Boy, but seem way too long and irreverent for Security Guard.

He's getting closer, and the evader in me is not happy about this situation. I try to be cool and hide behind Grace. But she's easily half a foot shorter than me—and I'm only five five—so I instead just find myself staring over her cropped hair directly into Porter's face.

He stops right in front of us and briefly holds the rolled-up papers to his eye like a telescope.

"Well, all right," he says with a lazy California drawl and grins slowly. "Guess I lucked out and got the good-looking group. Hello, Gracie."

"Hey, Porter," Grace answers with a coy smile.

Okay, so they know each other. I wonder if Porter's the person who told her this job was "boring but easy." I don't know why I even care. I guess I'm mostly concerned that he'll remember me from the car yesterday. Fingers crossed that he didn't hear that cowardly squeal I belted out.

"Who's ready for a private tour?" he asks.

No one answers.

"Don't everyone speak up at once." He peels one of the papers off his rolled-up tube—I see EMPLOYEE MAP at the top of the sheet—and hands it to me while glancing down at my legs. Is he checking me out? I'm not sure how I feel about that. Now I wish I'd worn pants.

When I try to accept the map, he hangs on to it, and I'm forced to snatch it out of his fingers. The corner rips off. *Juvenile, much?* I give him a dirty look, but he just smiles and leans closer. "Now, now," he says. "You aren't going to scream like you did yesterday, are you?"

LUMIÈRE FILM FANATICS COMMUNITY
PRIVATE MESSAGES>ALEX>ARCHIVED

@alex: Do you ever feel like a fraud?

@mink: What do you mean?

@alex: Like you're expected to act like one person at school, and another person in front of your family, and someone else around your friends. I get so tired of living up to other people's expectations, and sometimes I try to remember who the real me is, and I don't even know.

@mink: That happens to me every day. I don't deal with people very well.

@alex: You don't? That surprises me.

@mink: I'm not shy or anything. It's just that . . . okay, this is going to sound weird, but I don't like being put on the spot. Because if someone is talking to me, talk talk talk, it's all fine until they ask me my opinion, like "What do you think about chocolate chip cookies?" And I hate CCCs.

@alex: You do?

@mink: Not everyone likes them, you know. (I like sugar cookies, just in case you were wondering.) ANYWAY, if someone asks me, when I'm put on the spot, I blank out and try to read their face to see what they expect me to say, and I just say that. Which means I end up saying I like CCCs, when I really don't. And then I feel like a fraud, and I think, why did I just do that?

@alex: I DO THAT ALL THE TIME. But it's even worse, because after it's all over, I'm not even sure whether I like chocolate chip cookies or not.

@mink: Well, do you?

@alex: I love them. I'm a fan of all cookies except oatmeal.

@mink: See? That was easy. If you ever need to figure out who you really are, just ask me. I'll be your reality check. No pressure or expectations.

@alex: Deal. For you, I will be my 100 percent real, oatmeal-hating self.

"It's not my fault you're, like, in love with me, or something!"
—Lindsay Lohan, *Mean Girls* (2004)

3

Porter hands out the rest of his maps while the other group's voices fade away. We then obediently follow him to the opposite side of the lobby, through the arch marked JAY'S WING, where we trade in the crisp, too-cold lobby air for musty, too-warm mansion air.

I feel like this is the part of the orientation I should be enjoying, but I'm so rattled by Porter recognizing me that I'm not paying attention to my surroundings. I want to hang back and get away from him, but there's only like fifteen of us, and Grace merrily drags me by the arm to the front of the group. Now we're walking right behind him—so close, he probably thinks we're devotees of his ass, which is pretty nice, to be honest.

"There are forty-two rooms in Jay's Wing, a.k.a. the world's biggest man cave," Porter says as he stops in the middle of a drawing room filled with all things trains. Train signs. Train tracks. Victorian first-class passenger train seats with stuffed velvet cushions. At the back of the room, there's even an old-fashioned ticket booth from London that looks to have been converted into a bar. "Our beloved insane millionaire loved hunting, gambling, railroads, booze, and pirates," Porter said. "The pirates, especially. But who doesn't, really?"

Okay, so the boy's got a certain charm about him. I'm not immune to charm. And while he's talking, I realize he's got a low, gravelly voice that sounds like it belongs to a video game voice-over actor—easygoing and cocky at the same time. God, I bet he's so full of himself.

Why is he giving us this tour anyway? I thought security guards were supposed to stand around, waiting to yell at punks for putting their grimy hands on paintings.

When we head into the next area, I find out why.

"This is the slot-machine room," he says, walking backward as he talks. The room is filled with a maze of counters, at which you can sit and play one of a hundred different antique tabletop slot machines. Looks like the rarer ones are behind ropes.

Porter stops. "You might be asking yourself at this point, *Are all the rooms named after what's in them?* And the answer to that is yes. The museum owners are not creative—unless it comes to stretching out the workforce, in which case they are extremely creative. Take my job, for instance. Why pay a customer service manager to handle guest disputes when you can just send in your security team? You'll quickly find that the irrepressible Mr. Cadaver . . . sorry, Mr. Cavadini"—he gets a few snickers for that one—"likes everyone to be able to do every job, just in case you have to fill in for someone else. So don't get comfortable, because you, too, could be giving the next wave of new hires a tour in a couple of weeks. Better memorize that map I gave you, pronto."

Ugh. Great. I don't like the sound of this. Maybe it's not too late to apply for that cotton-candy-vomit-cleaner-upper job Grace was talking about earlier.

Over the next half hour or so, Porter breezily snarks us through the rooms in this wing. Rooms filled with: fake mummies (Mummy Room), weird Victorian medical equipment (Medical Equipment Room), and walls of aquariums (Aquarium Room). There's even a collection of sideshow oddities housed inside a gigantic circus tent. It's major sensory overload up in this place, and it's all blurring together, because there's no rhyme or reason to the mansion's lay-out, and it's all twisty turns and secret staircases and hidden rooms behind fireplaces. If I were a museum guest and had several hours to waste, I'd be thrilled. Total eye candy everywhere. But knowing I was supposed to memorize all this? Headache city.

At the end of the first floor, the maze opens up to a gigantic, dark room with a double-high ceiling. The walls are all fake rock, and a night sky rigged with LED stars twinkles above stuffed buf-falos and mountain lions, a glowing fake campfire, and a bunch of teepees—which several members of the male half of our group decide to explore, like they're five-year-old boys. It smells like musty leather and fur, so I opt to wait by the fake campfire with Grace.

Unfortunately, Porter joins us. And before I can slip away, he points to my name-tag sticker. "Were your parents obsessed with the circus when you were born, or did they have a thing for Irish cream whiskey?"

"Probably about as much as your parents liked wine."

He squints at me. "I think you mean beer."

"Whatever." Maybe I can duck into the teepee with the others. I pretend to be looking at something across the room in hopes that he'll ignore me and move on, a low-level evasive tactic, but one that usually works.

Not this time. Porter just continues talking. "And yes, my parents did name me after beer. It was between that and Ale, so . . ."

Grace playfully pushes Porter's arm and chastises him in her tiny, British voice. "Shut up, they did not. Don't listen to him, Bailey. And don't let him start with the name thing. He called me Grace 'Achoo' for half of junior high . . . until I tripped his ass in gym class."

"That's when I knew you were harboring a secret love for me, Gracie, so I felt sorry for you and gave you a break." He ducks away from her swat and grins, and I kind of hate that grin, because it's a really nice boyish smile, and I'd rather it wouldn't be.

Grace, however, is immune to its power. She just rolls her eyes. Then she volunteers more info about me. "Bailey's new. She'll be going to Brightsea with us in the fall."

"Oh?" Porter says, lifting a brow in my direction. "Where are you from?"

For a moment, I genuinely don't know how to answer. I'm not even sure why, but my brain is hung up on his question. I can't tell if he's asking what neighborhood my dad lives in. Maybe I should just say DC, because that's where I've been living with Mom and Nate—or even New Jersey, where I was born and raised. When I don't answer immediately, he doesn't seem to know what to do with me. He just stares expectantly, waiting for an answer, and that makes me choke up even worse.

"Probably Manhattan," he finally says, looking me over. "Just going by the way you're dressed, like you're headed to a *Mad Men* cocktail party. If you're going to stand there and make me guess, that's my guess."

Was that a slight? How was I supposed to know that the orientation dress code was going to be shorts and flip-flops? No one told me! "Um, no. Washington, DC. And I guess you're supposed to be part of some local famous family or something?"

"My granddad. Got a statue in town and everything," he says. "It's tough being legendary."

"I'll bet," I mumble, unable to keep the edge out of my voice.

He squints at me and sort of chuckles, as if he's not sure how to take that remark. We glare at each other for several long seconds, and suddenly I'm extremely uncomfortable. I'm also regretting I said anything to him. None of this is me. At all. I don't argue with strangers. Why is this guy getting under my skin and making me say this stuff? It's like he's provoking me on purpose. Maybe he does this with everyone. Well, not me, buddy. Find someone else to pick on. I will evade the crap out of you.

He starts to ask me something else, but Grace interrupts—

thank God. "So, which job here is the best?" she asks Porter. "And how do I get it?"

Snorting, he crosses his arms over his chest, and his jagged scars shine in the fake campfire light. Maybe Grace will tell me where Porter got the scars; I'm definitely not asking him. "The best job is mine, and you can't have it. The next best is café, because you're above the main floor. The worst is ticketing. Believe me, you do not want that shit."

"Why?" I ask, self-preservation trumping my desire to avoid interaction with him. Because if there's a position here I need to avoid, I want to know about it.

Porter flicks a glance at me and then watches the males in our group emerge from the big teepee, one by one, laughing at some joke we missed. "Pangborn says every summer they hire more seasonals than they can afford, because they know at least five of them will quit the first two weeks, and those are always the ones running the ticket booth."

"Seems like information desk would be worse," Grace says.

"It's not, believe me. I've worked them all. Even now, I spend half my day at ticketing, fixing problems that have nothing to do with security. It sucks, big-time. Hey, don't touch that," he calls out over my shoulder toward a guy who's sticking his finger in a buffalo's nose. Porter shakes his head and grumbles under his breath, "That one won't last a week."

Everyone is done exploring this room, so Porter leads us out of the Wild West and through the rest of the wing, taking a path that snakes back around to the lobby—which is empty, because we've beaten Pangborn's group. While we wait for them, Porter corrals us all next to a panel in the wall near the lost and found and flips it open. Inside is a small cubby where a black phone hangs.

"I know what you're all thinking," he says. "This might look like an antique, but it isn't a museum display—shocker! See, a long time ago, people used telephones with cords. And even though you might find a few rare examples of technological advances in this museum, like the 1990s security cameras, or the junked printers in the ticket booth, the museum phone system is not one of them."

He picks up the receiver and points to three buttons on the side. "You can make outgoing calls on these, but unless it's an emergency, you'll probably get fired. The only reason you should ever use this fine antique is for intercomming. This green button, marked 'SECURITY,' will allow you to call me if there is some emergency you can't handle alone. Like this—" He presses the button, and a little radio on his sleeve beeps. "See? It's magic. O-o-o."

Then he points to the red button. "This one marked 'ALL' pages the entiiiire museuuuum," he says like he's yodeling across a canyon. "The only reason you'd do that is if you work in information and are telling everyone the museum is closing or on fire. Don't use it."

"What does the yellow button do?" I ask. I mean, I guess it's stupid to think I can avoid talking to the guy about work stuff, right? He has information I need. Maybe if I act professional, he'll do the same.

He points at me. "Good question, Baileys Irish Cream. The yellow button is a lobby-only intercom—see? *L-O-B-B-Y.* And it's mainly used by the information desk to page lazy dum-dums who've lost their kids or wives." He hits the button and an unpleasant sound crackles from unseen speakers. He holds out the receiver to me. "Go on, say something, superstar."

I shake my head. Not happening. I don't like the spotlight. Now I'm regretting that I asked about the yellow button.

He tries to coax me into taking it with that laid-back voice of his, but his eyes are 100 percent challenge, like this is some sort of contest, and he's trying to see who'll break first. "Come on. Don't get shy on me now, glamour girl."

Again with the catty nicknames? What is his problem? Well, he can forget it. Now it's a matter of principle. I cross my arms over my chest. "No."

"It's just a little-bitty intercom," he says, wiggling the receiver in front of me.

I shove his hand away. Okay, maybe I kind of slap it away. But I've just about had it with him. I'm genuinely irritated.

And I'm not the only one. The easy-breezy manner leeches out of his face, and I can tell he's kind of pissed at me now too. I don't really care. He's not my boss, and I'm not doing it.

His jaw flexes to one side for a moment. Then he leans closer and says in a calm, condescending voice, "You sure you're cut out for this? Because speaking on the intercom is part of your job description."

"I . . ." I can't finish my thought. I'm angry and embarrassed, and I'm freezing up all over again like I did when he asked me where I was from. Part of me wants to cut and run, and another part of me wants to slug Porter in the stomach. But all I can do is stand there like a dying fish with my lips flopping open and closed.

It takes him all of five seconds to lose patience with me. I see the moment his eyes flick to the waiting crowd behind us—the moment he realizes he's supposed to be talking to them, not me—and something close to embarrassment crosses his face. Or maybe I imagined it, because it's gone a heartbeat later.

He holds the phone up to his mouth. "Testing," he says, and it echoes around the cavernous lobby. "My name is Bailey, and I'm from DC, where apparently mismatched shoes are the latest trend."

A few people chuckle as I glance down at my feet. And to my horror, he's right. I'm wearing the same style flats: one black, one navy. I have three pairs in three different colors, and because they're small and comfortable, I packed a pair in my carry-on. I was in such a frenzy to iron my dress this morning, I threw them on without looking before I walked out the door. WHAT IS WRONG WITH ME?

And, to top it all off, I now realize that Porter was never checking out my legs—he'd been staring at my shoes the entire time.

My cheeks catch fire. I want to melt into a puddle and slide under the tacky orange carpet. I can't look at him now, much less come up with a witty response. My mind has flipped on the auto-pilot switch and blanked out, and all I'm aware of is the sound of my own pulse throbbing in my ears. I'm so numb, I can't even manage to feel anything more than the smallest drop of relief when Pangborn shows up and swaps groups with Porter so we can tour the other wing.

I swear, if I never see that boy again, it'll be too soon. And if life is the least bit fair, I'll be assigned a job that's light-years away from him. I'll do anything. Clean toilets. Take out trash. I'll even make announcements on that stupid-ass phone. As long as it means I'll have little to no contact with Porter freaking Roth, I'll do it with a smile. Because one of his job requirements seems to be Getting a Laugh at Bailey's Expense, and I would rather get on a plane and fly back home to Mom and Nate if that's how things are going to be around here.

I think about Alex, and how much better I'd feel if I could go home and tell him about all this. He would definitely sympathize. And I need someone to vent to, because, really, could this day get any worse?

When the tour is over, and we get our schedule assignments from Mr. Cavadini, I find out the answer to that is: yes, oh hell yes, it sure enough can.

I stare at my printed schedule in disbelief. I've been assigned to ticketing.

LUMIÈRE FILM FANATICS COMMUNITY
PRIVATE MESSAGES>ALEX>NEW!

@mink: I started my summer job today. It was terrible. I hate it more than Dick Van Dyke's fake accent in Mary Poppins.

@alex: WHOA. That's a lot of hate, gov'ner! Are you still working with your mom like last summer? Or am I not supposed to ask? Is this a Forbidden Zone topic? I'm mentally checking the list and don't see it on there.

@mink: Not my mom. (It's on the list, but I'll give you a break this time. The list IS kinda long.)

@alex: You can shorten it any time you'd like. Say the word and I'll give you my e-mail. Or even my *gasp* real name!

@mink: o.O

@alex: All right, all right. Tell me about your terrible, no-good, really bad day. Does your boss suck?

@mink: Eh. Too soon to tell. I got stuck with the crap assignment and one of my coworkers is a colossal dickbag. He's going to make my life miserable. I can already tell.

@alex: Make him miserable right back. You are Mink! Hear you roar!

@mink: *cough* *sputter* *broken meow*

@alex: Chin up. You'll best this loser. Boys are dumb.

@mink: So true. How was your day, BTW?

@alex: Not bad. Now that summer's started, I'm back to the full-time, two-job routine. Usually I get all the dimwit coworkers at my main job, but maybe they sent them your way. Besides, I'm still holding out hope that my groovy friend Mink might get up the nerve to come visit her dad this summer and come see North by Northwest at the film festival with me. How can you resist Hitchcock? (And you call yourself a film snob. Prove it!)

"Whatever happened to chivalry? Does it only exist in '80s movies?"
—Emma Stone, *Easy A* (2010)

4

The rest of my training is a blur. I'm not even sure how I manage to find my way back to my dad's house. All I know is by the time Pete Rydell walks in from work, I'm armed and ready with a memorized list of calm, collected reasons as to why I can't work at the Cave . . . which quickly degenerates into me flat-out begging him to please-please-please let me quit. But he's not having it. Not even when I promise to apply to Pancake Shack and bring us home free pancakes every day for life. "It's just a ticket booth, Mink," he says, flabbergasted that I could be so bent out of shape about taking money from strangers. And when I try to justify my bitter dislike of Porter, one of his eyebrows is lifted by so much rising suspicion, it could inflate a hot air balloon. "The boy we almost hit on the crosswalk?"

"I know, right?" He remembers the drugged-out friend. He sees the light now.

Only, he doesn't. Things are now being said about how much

trouble he went through to pull strings to get this job, and how bad it would look for me to quit so early, and how living out here isn't cheap, especially on a single parent's salary—one that isn't a lawyer's salary, like Mom's—and that he'd like me to help pay for the insurance on the Vespa and my cell phone bill.

"This is good for you," he says in a softer voice, squeezing my shoulders. He's still in his CPA long sleeves and tie, not in one of his geeky 1980s sci-fi T-shirts, so he looks like more of a responsible adult at the moment. And I don't ever remember him being this decisive and firm. It's weird, and I'm not sure how I feel about it. It's making me a little emotional. "I know you don't believe me now, but you will. Sometimes you have to endure painful things to realize that you're a whole lot stronger than you think."

Ugh. He's so earnest. I know he's talking about what he went through in the divorce, and that makes me uncomfortable. I blow out the long, deep sigh of a girl defeated and duck out of his kind fatherly grip in one smooth movement, instantly feeling relief.

Once I have time to think things over rationally, I understand where he's coming from . . . in theory. If the point of me sticking it out at the Cave is because I need to be bringing in my own paycheck and showing him that I can be responsible, I'll just have to tough it out somehow. Figure out a way to see as little of Porter Roth as possible.

I might be an evader, but I suppose I'm no quitter. It's just a summer job anyway, right? That's what I tell myself.

Besides, I have other things to think about.

The next morning, I break out a map of Coronado Cove the second Dad's car has rumbled out of earshot. Time to do a little detective work. The Cave didn't schedule me for my first real shift until tomorrow, so at least I have one day of respite before I'm forced to start serving my jail term. I'd already messaged Alex, but he doesn't answer right away. I'm wondering if that's because he's at the day job. During the school year, he only works the day job after school, and every once in a while on the weekends. But now that it's summer, he said he's working there pretty much every morning, and clocking in at another job later.

My stomach goes haywire just thinking about it.

This is what I know about Alex's day job: I know that it's a family business, and that he hates it. I know that the business is on the beach, because he's said that he can see the waves from the window. I also know that there's a counter, so obviously it's a retail business. A retail shop on the boardwalk. That narrows it to. . . I dunno, about several hundred stores? But two details that may help me pin him down are ones that seemed unimportant when he first mentioned them. First: He complains that the scent of cinnamon constantly makes him hungry because a churro cart is nearby. Second: He feeds a stray beach cat that suns itself outside the shop and answers to the name Sam-I-Am.

Not a lot, but it's a start.

After studying the map, I strap on my scooter helmet and head down Gold Avenue toward the northern end of the boardwalk—opposite the Cavern Palace, a mile or so away. Sunshine's burning through the morning fog, the air smells like pancakes and ocean. The beach is already bustling with people. Locals and tourists, freaks and geeks. They throng the boardwalk like ants on a picnic. The water's too nippy for swimming, but that doesn't stop people from lining the sand with blankets and towels. Everyone's ready to worship the sun.

I've always disliked the beach, but as I find a place to park near the north end of the boardwalk and slather my vitamin-D-deficient legs and arms with mega-super-sensitive sunblock created for babies, the frail, and the elderly, I'm feeling slightly less hateful at the horde of bouncy string bikinis and tropical-patterned board shorts jostling past me, laughing and singing as they file toward the sand. There's not a soul here that I need to impress. No one to worry about accidentally bumping into. Coming out west is my do-over. A clean slate.

That was one reason I wanted to move out here. It wasn't just missing my dad, or Mom and Nate LLC fighting, or even the prospect of meeting Alex. In a strange way, the reason I don't know much about Alex, and vice versa, was one of my main incentives for moving.

Mom's a divorce lawyer. (Oh, the irony.) Four years ago, when I was fourteen, Mom took a case that ended up giving the wife full custody of the couple's daughter, a girl about my age. Turned out the jilted husband had a leak in the ol' brain pipe. Greg Grumbacher, hell-bent for revenge against my mother, found our address online. This was back when my folks were still together. There was . . . an incident.

He was put in prison for a very long time.

Anyway. It's a relief to have an entire country between me and old Greg.

So that's why our family doesn't do "public" online. No real names. No photos. No alma maters or job locations. No breezy status updates with geotags or posts with time stamps like, *Oh my gawd, Stacey! I'm sitting at my fav tea shop on 9th, and there's a girl wearing the cutest dress!* Because that's how messed-up people track you down and do bad things to you and people you care about.

I try not to be paranoid and let it ruin my life. And not everybody who wants to track somebody down is a sicko. Take, for instance, what I'm doing now, looking for Alex. I'm no Greg Grumbacher. The difference is intent. The difference is that Greg wanted to hurt us, and all I want to do is make sure that Alex is an actual human being my age, preferably of the male persuasion, and not some creep who's trying to harvest my eyeballs for weird, evil laboratory experiments. That's not stalking, it's scoping. It's protection for both of us, really—me and Alex. If we're meant to be, and he's the person I imagine him to be, then things will all work out fine. He'll be wonderful, and by the end of the summer, we'll be crazy in love, watching *North by Northwest* at the film festival on the beach, and I'll have my hands all over him. Which is what I spend a lot of my free time imagining myself doing to his virtual body, the lucky boy.

However, if my scoping turns up some bad intel and this relationship looks like it might have more fizzle than pop? Then I'll just disappear into the shadows, and nobody gets hurt.

See? I'm looking out for the two of us.

Shoulders loose, I slip on a pair of dark sunglasses and fall in step behind a herd of beach bunnies, using them as a shield until we hit the boardwalk, where they head straight to the beach and I go left.

The boardwalk area is just under half a mile long. A center promenade spills out onto a wide pedestrian pier, which is anchored by a Ferris wheel at its base and capped by a wire that ferries couples in aerial chairlifts to the cliffs above. And all of that is enveloped in midway games, looping roller coasters, hotels, restaurants, and bars. It's half this: laid-back California vibe, skaters, sidewalk art, comic book shops, organic tea, seagulls. And half this: bad 1980s music blasting through tinny speakers, schlocky Tilt-A-Whirls, bells dinging, kids crying, cheap T-shirt shops, overflowing trash cans.

Whatever my feelings about what this place is, I suspect it isn't going to be easy to find Alex. Those suspicions only grow stronger when I veer away from the Midway area and hit a stretch of retail shops near the promenade (maybe here?) and realize the scent that's been driving me crazy since yesterday isn't the Pancake Shack, it's freshly fried dough. And that's because there's an official Coronado Cove boardwalk churro cart every twenty or thirty feet down the promenade. Churros are like long Mexican doughnut sticks that have been fried and dipped in cinnamon or, as the sign tells me, strawberry sugar. They smell like God's footprints. I've never had a real churro, but halfway down the promenade, I make a decision to give up on everything: finding Alex, finding another job, the meaning of life. Just give me that sweet fried dough.

I plunk down some cash and take my booty to a shady bench. It is everything I hoped for and more. Where have you been all my life? It makes me feel better about my failed morning. As I'm licking the cinnamon sugar from my fingertips, I spy a fat orange tabby cat sunning on the sidewalk near the bench.

No. Could it be?

I glance across the promenade. Looks to be a vintage clothing store, a surf shop—Penny Boards, which may or may not be named after Porter's stupid grandfather—a medical marijuana dispensary, and a café of some sort. The cat stretches. I pull down my shades. Our eyes meet. Am I looking at Alex's stray cat?

"Here, kitty," I call sweetly. "Sam-I-Am? That wouldn't be your name, would it? Sweet boy?"

His listless gaze doesn't register my voice. For a moment, I wonder if he just died, then he rolls to one side, turning a cool shoulder to me with snotty feline aplomb.

"Was that your lunch?" a tiny English voice says.

My pulse jumps. I jerk my head up to find a friendly, familiar face staring down at me. Grace from work. She's dressed in shorts and a white spaghetti-strap top that says NOPE in sparkly gold rhinestones.

"It was the most delicious thing I've ever eaten in my life," I tell her. When she squints at me, I explain, "I'm from New Jersey. We only have boring old funnel cakes at the beach."

"I thought you were from DC."

I wave a hand, dismissive. "It's a long story. I only lived in DC for a few months. That's where my mom and her husband are. My dad went to college in California, at Cal Poly, and moved back west a year ago. A couple of months ago, I decided to move out here with him, and, well . . . here I am."

"My dad's a lab technician. He's from Nigeria," she says. "I've never been, but he left Nigeria and met my mum in London. We moved here when I was ten . . . so seven years ago? To tell you the truth, except for flying back and forth to England for Christmas, I've only ever been out of the state once, and that was just to Nevada."

"Eh. You aren't missing much," I joke.

She studies me for a moment, adjusting her purse higher on her shoulder. "You know, you don't really have a New Jersey accent, but you do sort of sound like you're from the East Coast."

"Well, you don't have a California accent, but you do sort of sound like a British Tinker Bell."

She snorts a little laugh.

I smile. "Anyway, this was my first churro, but it won't be my last. I'm planning to quit the museum and become a churro cart owner. So if you don't see me at ticketing tomorrow, give Mr. Cavadini my regards."

"No way," she squeaks, looking genuinely panicked. "Don't leave me in ticketing alone. Promise me you'll show up. Porter said three people already quit. We're the only people scheduled tomorrow afternoon."

Suddenly, my churro isn't sitting so well inside my stomach. "You and Porter sure are buddy-buddy." I don't mean to sound so grumbly about this, but I can't help it.

She shrugs. "We've been mates for years. He's not so bad. He'll tease you relentlessly until you push back. He's just testing your limits. Besides, he's been through a lot, so I guess I give him some slack."

"Like what? His world-famous grandfather won too many surfing trophies? It sure must be a drag, seeing statues of your family members around town."

Grace stares at me for a moment. "You don't know about what happened?"

I stare back. Obviously, I don't. "What?"

"You don't know about their family?" She's incredulous.

Now I'm feeling pretty stupid for not bothering to look up Porter's family on the Internet when I got home last night. Truth is, I was so mad at him, I didn't care. Still don't, really. "Kinda not into sports," I say apologetically, but honestly, I'm not even sure if surfing is considered a sport or a hobby or an art. People get on boards and ride waves, but is it an Olympic thing, or what? I'm clueless.

"His father was a pro surfer too," she tells me, sounding like she truly cannot believe I don't know this already. "The grandfather died, and then his father . . . It was all pretty horrible. You haven't noticed Porter's scars?"

I start to tell her that I did but was too busy being humiliated in front of my coworkers, but Grace is now distracted. Someone's calling her from a store down the promenade.

"Gotta go," she interrupts in her tiny voice. "Just please be there tomorrow."

"I will," I promise. Don't really have any other choice.

"By the way," she says, turning around and pointing at the orange tabby with a sly smile on her face. "That cat isn't answering you because he is a she."

My heart sinks. Wrong cat.

Well, it's only the beginning of summer, and I'm a patient girl. If I have to eat my way through every churro cart on the boardwalk, come hell or sunstroke, I will find Alex before *North by Northwest*.

LUMIÈRE FILM FANATICS COMMUNITY
PRIVATE MESSAGES>ALEX>NEW!

@mink: Guess what I got in the mail today? A brand-new copy of The Philadelphia Story.

@alex: Nice! Love that movie. We should watch that together sometime if I can find a copy.

@mink: Definitely. It's one of my favorite Cary Grant/Katharine Hepburn films!

@alex: Well, in other good news, since I know you LOVE gangster movies so much [insert sarcasm here], I just sent you a ton of Godfather screens with Alex-ified captions, changing things up for you.

@mink: I'm looking at them right now. You think you're pretty funny, don't you?

@alex: Only if you do.

@mink: You made orange juice go up my nose.

@alex: That's all I ever wanted, Mink.

@mink: Your dreams may be closer to reality than you can possibly imagine. . . .

"You won't find anything cheap around here!"
—Lana Turner, *The Postman Always Rings Twice* (1946)

5

My first real shift at the Cave begins the next day at noon, and when I see the jammed parking lot, I nearly turn the Vespa around and head back to Dad's house. But Grace spots me before I can. She's waiting at the employee door, waving her arms, and now there's nothing I can do but march off to my doom. We clock in, stow our stuff in our assigned lockers, and don our orange vests.

Shit just got real.

Mr. Cavadini and his pointy blond vampire hairline greet us in the break room, clipboard in hand. "You are . . . ?"

"Bailey Rydell," I supply. It's been one day; he's already forgotten.

"Grace Achebe."

"What's that?" he says, leaning closer to hear her.

The irritation in her eyes is supreme. "ACH-E-BE," she spells out.

"Yes, yes," he mumbles, like he knew it all along. He hands

us plastic name tags. The sticker printed with my first name is stuck on crooked. It feels like a bad omen. "All right, ladies. Your supervisor on duty is Carol. She's tied up with a problem in the café right now. The morning shift at ticketing is ending in three minutes, so we need to hurry. Are you ready to get out there and make some magic happen?"

Grace and I both stare at him.

"Terrific," he says with no feeling, and then urges us out the door and into the employee corridor. "First thing you usually do is go to security"—he points down the hall toward the opposite direction—"to count out a fresh cash drawer, like we showed you in training. But today there's no time. You'll just have to trust that the supervisor on duty didn't steal anything or foul up the drawer count, because it comes out of your paycheck if they did. . . ."

I freeze in place. Grace speaks first. "Wait, what's that?"

"Come on, now," Mr. Cavadini says, pushing me forward. "Two minutes. Shake a leg. Security will meet you at the ticketing booth to get you set up and answer any questions. If you last a week, we'll consider assigning you a key to the booth. Otherwise, you'll have to knock to get inside, because it locks automatically. Good luck and don't forget to smile."

And with that, he guides us into the lobby and promptly abandons us.

The museum was empty during orientation. It's not now. Hundreds of voices bounce around the rocky cavern walls as patrons shuffle through the massive space, heading into the two wings.

The café upstairs is packed. People are eating sandwiches on the slate stairs, talking on cell phones beneath the floating pirate ship. So. Many. People. But the only person I really see is standing against the ticket booths.

Porter Roth. Beautiful body. Head full of wild curls. Cocky smile.

My archnemesis.

His eyes meet mine. Then his gaze drops to my feet. He's checking to see if my shoes match. Even though I know they do, I check them again, and then want to take them off and bean them at his big, fat head.

But he doesn't say a word about it. He only says, "Ladies," and nods when we approach. Maybe this won't be as bad as last time. Balancing two covered cash tills in one hand, he raps on the ticketing booth's rear door four quick times before turning toward us. "Ready for the thrill of hot cash in your hands?"

The door to the booth swings open. For what seems like forever, Grace and I stand waiting while Porter enters the booth, swapping out the cash drawers, and two wide-eyed new hires spill out of ticketing, wiping away sweat like they've just been inside the devil's own boudoir and seen unspeakable, depraved acts that have scarred them for life.

Now I'm getting really nervous.

Porter's pissed. He's saying something obscene into the radio doohickey on his sleeve, and for a second, I wonder if he's telling off Mr. Cavadini, but then a shock of white hair comes bounding through the lobby and the other security guard—Mr. Pangborn—appears. He looks frazzled. And way too tired to be doing this job.

"Sorry, sorry," he says, completely breathless.

Porter heaves a long sigh and shakes his head, less angry now, more weary. "Just escort them back to cash-out and watch them count their tills until Carol gets down from the café." He turns back toward us and whistles, tugging a thumb toward the booth. "You two, inside."

"Balls," Grace mumbles. "I don't remember how to run the ticketing program!"

"You'll do it in your sleep, Gracie," he assures her. For a second, he almost seems nice, and not the same boy who humiliated me in front of the entire staff. A mirage, I tell myself.

The booth is small. Really small. The booth smells. Really bad. There are two swivel stools, a counter that holds the computer screen, and a shelf beneath, on which the tickets print from ancient printers. The rear door is centered behind us, and there's barely room for a third person—much less Porter—to stand behind us and give directions. In front of us, it's just Plexiglas covered in smudged fingerprints separating us from a line of people wrapped around stanchions. So many people. They are not happy about the delay.

The dude standing at my window is mouthing, *Four*, and he's holding up four fingers, saying something nasty about me being an idiot female. That churro cart is looking better and better.

"Green means on, red means off," Porter's voice says near my face, a little too close. An unwanted shiver chases down my arm where his wild hair brushes my shoulder. It smells briny, like ocean water; I wonder if he's been surfing today. I wonder why I care. His arm reaches around my body and taps the counter, startling me.

"Right, yes," I say.

Dumbly, I glance down at the two-way intercom controls, marked OUTSIDE (to hear the customers) and INSIDE (so they can hear me). Green. Red. Got it.

"You'll pretty much want to keep the outside mic on all the time, but if you want to hang on to your sanity, you'll only engage the inside microphone on a need-to basis. Finger on the trigger," he advises.

They told us that in training. It's coming back to me now. Grace is freaking the hell out, so Porter has shifted over to her area. The jerk in front of my window is pressing four impatient fingers against the glass. I can't hold on any longer. I hit both green buttons and smile.

"Welcome to the Cavern Palace. Four adult tickets?"

The computer does all the work. I take the man's credit card, the tickets print, Mr. Jerkface goes through the turnstile with his jerky family. Next. This one's cash. I fumble a little with the change, but it's not too bad.

And so on.

At some point, Porter slips out and we're on our own, but it's okay. We can handle it.

I remembered how cold the Cavern lobby was during orientation, so I wore another cardigan. Ten customers into the line, and I now realize why they nickname the ticket booth the Hotbox. No air-con inside. We're trapped in a box made of glass from the waist up, with the sun beaming down on our faces, lighting us up like we're orchids in a freaking greenhouse.

I strip off the cardigan through my vest's gaping sleeve holes, but every few minutes, I have to swivel around to let someone inside the door—Carol, the shift supervisor, the guy from the information booth telling us to retake a season pass photo because the customer "hates" it, sweet old Mr. Pangborn delivering change for all the big spenders who want to pay with hundred-dollar bills. Every time I swivel around to open the ticket booth door, (A) I bust my kneecaps on the metal till, and (B) a blast of freezing cave air races over my clammy skin.

Then the door shuts, and the Hotbox reheats all over again.

It's torture. Like, this is how the military must break enemy combatants when they want to get information out of them. Where are the Geneva Conventions when you need them?

It gets worse when we have to start juggling other things like pointing out where the restrooms are, and handling complaints about ticket prices going up every year. Is this museum scary? How come we don't give senior discounts to fifty-year-olds anymore? The wind just blew my ticket away; give me a replacement.

It's a circus. I'm barely exaggerating. No wonder people quit the first day.

ALEX, APPROXIMATELY • 59

Not us. Grace and I have this. We're champs, fist-bumping each other under the counter. I handle the job the best way I know how. Avoid eye contact. Play dumb. Shrug. Evade the hard questions. Point them toward the information desk or the gift shop.

If we don't sweat away all our bodily fluid, we'll make it.

A couple of hours into our shift, things slow down considerably—as in, no one in line.

"Did we scare them all away?" Grace asks, wiping sweat from the back of her neck.

"Is it over?" I say, peering over the intercom to see around the stanchions. "Can we go home now?"

"I'm asking someone to bring us water. They said we could. It's too hot. Screw this." Grace uses the phone to page Carol, and she says she'll send someone. We wait.

A couple of minutes later, I hear four quick raps on the door and open it to find Porter. It's the first time we've seen him since the beginning of our jail sentence. He hands us plastic bottles of water from the café and gives me that slow, lazy smile of his that's entirely too sexy for a boy our age, and that makes me nervous all over again.

"You've both got that sweet Hotbox sheen. Looks better on the two of you than the last pair. By the way, one of them is . . ." He swipes his thumb across his throat, indicating that the kid quit, and not that he actually offed himself. I hope.

"Another one?" Grace murmurs.

He leans back against the door, one foot propped up, scrolling through his phone. The propped-up foot puts his knee in my space, mere centimeters from mine. It's like he's purposely trying to crowd me. "This job weeds out the weak, Gracie. They should flash their photos over the teepees in the fake starry sky in Jay's Wing."

"What time is it?"

He consults a fat red watch on his wrist with a funny digital screen and tells us the time. When I stare too long, he catches me looking and explains, "Surf watch. Swell direction, wave height, water temperature. Completely waterproof, unlike this stupid phone, which I've had to replace twice already this year."

I was actually staring at his Frankenstein scars, thinking about how Grace had started to tell me something tragic about his family yesterday on the boardwalk, but I'm relieved he thought I was looking at the watch.

"How did you get to be security guard, anyway?" I ask, cracking open my bottled water.

He spares a moment's glance from the screen and winks at me. Actually winks. Who does that? "Eighteen opens up all sorts of doors. You can vote, legally engage in any and all imaginative sexual activities with the consenting person of your choice, and—best of all—you can work full-time as a security guard at the Cavern Palace."

"Only one of those things I want to do and don't need any law to give me permission," Grace says sweetly from the other side of the booth.

I don't look at him. If he's trying to make me uncomfortable with all of that "imaginative sexual activities" talk, he can give himself a pat on the back, because it's working. But he's not going to see me sweat. Except for the fact that I've been sweating for the last two hours in the Hotbox.

"Taran's gone overseas for one week and you're already turning to me to satisfy your womanly needs?" he says.

"You wish," she retorts.

"Every day. What about you, Rydell?"

"No thanks," I say.

He puffs out a breath, acting wounded. "You leave a boyfriend wailing for you back east?"

I grunt noncommittally. Grace's stool creaks. I can feel both of them looking in my direction, and when I don't reply, Porter says, "I know what will fix this. Quiz time."

Grace groans. "Oh, no."

"O-oh, yes."

I risk a glance at his face, and he's grinning to himself, scrolling madly on his phone. "A quiz is the best way to get to know yourself and others," he says, like he's reading a copy from a magazine.

"He's obsessed with stupid quizzes," Grace explains. "He inflicts them on everyone at school. *Cosmo* quizzes are the worst."

"I think you mean the best," he corrects. "Here's a good one. 'Why Don't You Have a Boyfriend, Girlfriend? Take this quiz to find out why a super girl like you is still sitting home alone on Saturday night instead of pairing up with the boy of your dreams.'"

"Nope," Grace says.

"I'll just take this back, then," Porter says, attempting to snatch the water from Grace's hand. They wrestle for a second, laughing, and when she shrieks, spilling cold water on her orange Cave vest, I almost get Porter's elbow in my face. He holds the water over her head, out of reach.

"All right, you win," Grace says. "Do your damn quiz, already. Better than just sitting here, I suppose."

Porter hands her water back, settles against the door, and reads from the quiz. "'Your older sister takes you to a campus party while you're visiting her at college. Do you: (A) dance with her and her friends; (B) skinny-dip in the backyard pool; (C) grab a hottie and go make out in an empty bedroom upstairs; (D) sit alone on the couch, people-watching?'"

I don't bother answering. A young couple comes to my window, so I flip on the mics long enough to greet them and sell two tickets. When I'm done, Grace has chosen answer A.

"What about you, Rydell?" Porter asks. "I'm thinking you're answer B—secret exhibitionist. If you don't quit today, who knows. I might just look up on the monitors tomorrow and find you stripping by the Cleopatra Pool in Vivian's Wing."

I snort. "Is that what you've been imagining back in the security booth?"

"All afternoon."

"You're an ass."

He holds my gaze. "Scratch that. I think you're actually answer

ALEX, APPROXIMATELY • 63

C. You'd grab a 'hottie'"—he makes one-handed air quotes—"and go make out in an empty bedroom. Am I right?"

I don't answer.

He's not dissuaded. "Next question." He swipes the screen of his phone, but he's not looking at it; he's staring at me. Trying to intimidate me. Trying to see who'll blink first. "Did you leave DC because (A) you couldn't find any hotties to make out with? Or (B) your East Coast boyfriend is an ankle buster and you'd heard about legendary West Coast D, so you had to find out for yourself if the rumors were true?" he says with a smirk.

"Idiot," Grace mumbles, shaking her head.

I may not understand some of his phrasing, but I get the gist. I feel myself blushing. But I manage to recover quickly and get a jab in. "Why are you so interested in my love life?"

"I'm not. Why are you evading the question? You do that a lot, by the way."

"Do what?"

"Evade questions."

"What business is that of yours?" I say, secretly irritated that he's figured me out. And who is he anyway, my therapist? Well, I've got news for him, I've been to two of the best therapists money can buy in New Jersey, once with my mom and once on my own, and neither one of those so-called experts was able to keep me in the chair for longer than two sessions. They said I bottled up my feelings, and I was uncommunicative, and that evasion was a "maladaptive coping mechanism" to avoid dealing with a stressor, and that it was an unhealthy way to avoid panic attacks.

Says the man who wanted to charge my parents more than a college education for his expert advice. I'm coping just fine, thankyouverymuch. If people like this will just leave me alone . . .

Porter scoffs. "Seeing how this is your first day on the job, and may very well be your last, considering the turnover rate for this position? And seeing how I have seniority over you? I'd say, yeah, it's pretty much my business."

"Are you threatening me?" I ask.

He clicks off his phone and raises a brow. "Huh?"

"That sounded like a threat," I say.

"Whoa, you need to chill. That was not . . ." He can't even say it. He's flustered now, tucking his hair behind his ear. "Grace . . ."

Grace holds up a hand. "Leave me out of this mess. I have no idea what I'm even witnessing here. Both of you have lost the plot."

He makes a soft growling noise and turns back to me. "Look, I was just giving you a hard time—lighten up. But the fact is, I've been working here forever. You've been working here a few hours."

"But don't you already have me pegged? You know all about me, Mr. Famous Surfer Boy?"

He mockingly strokes his chin in thought. "Hmm . . . well, Little Miss Vogue," he says in that low, gravelly voice of his. The one I thought was all sexy and charming when he was giving us the tour. "Let me hazard a guess. You're some stuck-up East Coast sophisticate whose daddy got her this job where she's forced to have normal conversations with surf trash like me." He crosses his arms and smiles defiantly at me. "How'd I do?"

My mouth falls open. I'm so stunned, I feel as though I've had the wind knocked out of my chest. I try to untangle his words, but there's just so much there. If he's really just giving me a hard time, then why do I sense . . . so much bitterness?

How did he know my dad helped get me this job? Did someone in the office tell him? I mean, it's not like I'm some spoiled, incompetent rich kid with zero work experience and mega connections. My dad's just a CPA! But I'm not going to bother explaining that or anything else. Because right now, I'm halfway convinced a hole in my skull has blown right off and my brains are flowing out like molten lava. I think I might well and truly hate Porter Roth.

"You know nothing about me or my family. And you're a goddamn dickbag, you know that?" I say, so enraged that I don't even care that a family of four is walking up to my window. I should have. And I should have noticed that I left the green switch turned on from the last pair of tickets I sold. But the family's wide-eyed faces clue me in now.

They've heard every nasty word.

For one terrible moment, the booth spins around me. I apologize profusely, but the parents aren't happy. At all. Why should they be? Oh God, is the wife wearing a crucifix pendant? What if these people are fundamentalists? Are these kids homeschooled?

Did I just ruin them for life? Jesus fu—I mean, fiddlesticks. Are they going to ask to speak to Mr. Cavadini? Am I going to be fired? On my first day? What is my dad going to say?

If I was hot before, I'm not now. Icy dread sends an army of goose bumps over my skin. I point the scarred family to Grace's window and bolt out of my stool, shoving past Porter as I race out of the booth.

I don't even know where I'm going. I end up in the break room and then outside in the employee parking lot. For a second, I consider driving away on Baby, until I remember that I don't even have my purse; it's back in my locker.

I sit on the sidewalk. Cool down, get myself together. I have a thirty-minute break, after all, don't I? Thirty whole minutes to wallow in embarrassment over saying what I said in front of that family . . . thirty minutes to wonder how in the world I allowed Porter to provoke me into yet another argument. Thirty minutes to freak out over being fired on my first day. Me! The Artful Dodger. How did this happen?

This is all Porter's fault. He provoked me. Something about him just brings out the worst in me and makes me want to . . . lock horns. He thinks I'm a snob? He's not the first. Just because I'm quiet doesn't mean I'm aloof. Maybe I just want to be alone. Maybe I'm not good at conversation. We all can't be cool and gregarious and *Hey, bro, what up?* like he apparently is. Some of us aren't wired for that. That doesn't make me snotty. And why does he keep talking about the way I dress, for the love of God? I'm more casual today than I was on orientation. So sue me if I have style. I'm not changing myself to please him.

I'm not sure how much time passes, but I eventually head back into the break room. A few employees are milling about. I wait a few minutes, but no one comes to get me. I expect to be called into Mr. Cavadini's office, or at least for the shift supervisor to want to speak to me. When no one comes, I don't know what to do. I've still got several hours left on my shift, so I head back to the lobby, scanning for signs of an inquisition on the march. I bump into someone. I look up and see Mr. Cavadini, clipboard smashed against his chest, and my pulse triples.

"So sorry," I say, apologizing for what must be a record-breaking number of times in the last half hour. This is it. I'm done for. He's come to ax me.

"Please watch where you're going, Miss . . ." He pauses while his eyes dart toward my name tag. "Bailey."

"I . . ." Can't apologize again. I just can't. "Yes, sir."

"How's ticketing working out for you? Are you on a break?" His nose wrinkles. "You aren't quitting, are you?"

"No, sir."

He relaxes. Straightens his Cavern Palace tie. "Terrific. Back to your post," he says absently, focus returned to the clipboard as he shuffles away. "Don't forget to smile."

Like I could do that right now. I head to the ticketing booth in a daze, still unsure what I'll find there. I take a deep breath and knock on the door. It swings open. Porter is gone. A small line is forming on the other side of the glass, and Grace is handling it alone. Her shoulders relax when she sees me. She quickly switches off her mic.

"Hey," she whispers. "Are you okay?"

"Yeah. I'm not going to be fired?"

She stares at me like I've gone nuts then shakes her head. "Porter just apologized and let them in free of charge. People will forgive anything if you give them stuff for free. Don't quit! It's all good. And I need your help now, yeah?"

"Okay."

I close the door behind me and sit on my stool, waving the next person in line over to my window. I'm not sure how I feel. Relieved? Wiped out? Still humiliated and angry at Porter? I don't even know anymore.

Before I click on my mic, I look down and see a fresh bottle of water and three cookies sitting on a printed Cavern Palace napkin. One chocolate chip, one sugar, one oatmeal. A note in scraggly, boyish handwriting is inked on the napkin's corner, along with a drawing of a sad face. It says: *Sorry.*

LUMIÈRE FILM FANATICS COMMUNITY
PRIVATE MESSAGES>ALEX>NEW!

@alex: I need cheering up.

@mink: Me too. Want to watch Gold Diggers of 1933?

@alex: Blues Brothers?

@mink: Dr. Strangelove?

@alex: Young Frankenstein?

@mink: Young Frankenstein.

@alex: You're the best.

@mink: You're not so bad yourself. Tell me when you're ready to hit play.

"Sometimes you're better off not knowing."
—Jack Nicholson, *Chinatown* (1974)

6

I spend the next morning on the boardwalk. It's going much the same as my first morning on the boardwalk, which is to say that it's a bust. Despite zero signs of Alex, I've run into that stupid orange tabby again hanging around my favorite churro cart. I've now dubbed her Señor Don Gato (from my dad's and my favorite children's song, "Meow-meow-meow"). After all, she fooled me into thinking she was a "he" the first time around.

After pigging out and feeding churro crumbs to some bossy seagulls, I still have some time before I have to head over to the Cave for my afternoon shift. I'm not looking forward to facing Porter again. We didn't see each other after the cookies. Yeah, that was a nice attempt at making up for his dickery, but whatever. Maybe don't say anything you need to atone for in the first place.

Ugh. Just thinking about him makes me want to kick something. It also reminds me that I wanted to find a scarf to tie up my hair, so that it doesn't stick to the back of my neck when the sweating starts in the Hotbox. I throw away my crumpled churro paper in the trash can, say good-bye to sleepy Señor Don Gato, and head to a shop I spied during my previous Alex sleuthing—Déjà Vu. It's a small vintage clothing store with old mannequins in the window that have been pieced together from several different mannequin bodies—male, female, brown, pink, tall, small. When I go inside, a small bell over the door dings, a sound that's barely audible over the congo drums of the 1950s exotica music thumping over the speakers. The shop is dark, and it smells of a mix of musty old clothes and cheap detergent. Everything is jammed in tight, a browser's dream. There's only one other shopper in the store, and a bored college-aged girl with purple dreadlocks is running the register in the back.

I spot a rotating rack of old scarves near the counter. Bingo. Some of them smell funky, and a few are way too psychedelic for my taste, but there're dozens to choose from. Halfway through the rack, I find a gray-and-black striped one that won't clash too badly with my pumpkin vest at work. I pay the girl at the register. When she's ringing me up, the bell over the door rings. I glance over my shoulder to see two boys walking through the store. One is a burly Latino guy in a sleeveless T-shirt. The other is lanky and white blond, wearing shorts and no shirt at all. He walks with a limp, as if he's got an injured leg.

Crap. I know him. It's Porter's friend. The other guy from the crosswalk—the drugged-up one who slammed his fists on my dad's car. They both approach us.

"What up, *mamacita?*" he says in a lazy, raspy voice to the girl at the register as he sidles up to the counter next to me while she's getting my change out of the register. I glance up at his face. He's got high cheekbones and deep hollows beneath them, pock-marked by acne scars. His white-blond hair is a mess. Despite this, he might be more classically handsome than Porter. Almost model pretty. But he has a scarier vibe. Something's off-kilter.

"I told you not to bother me at work, Davy."

"Yeah, well, it's an emergency. I'm driving down to La Salva this afternoon. Need you to help a brother out."

"Not now."

He puts his hands on the counter and leans closer, blocking my view of their faces. I can still see her purple dreads draped over one bare shoulder. "Please," he begs.

"I thought you were chipping," she says in a hushed voice.

"I am, but you know how it goes. I just need a little." His soft tone matches hers, but I can still hear every word they're saying. I mean, hello. This conversation isn't private. Do they know that? "It's just for today."

"That's what you said last week," she argues.

"Julie, come on." He runs a hand down her arm, stroking a dreadlock with the tips of his fingers. "Julie, Julie, Julie."

She sighs. "I'll make a call and text you. Might be a couple of hours."

Satisfied, he turns back around and seems to notice me for the first time. "Hi there."

I don't reply, but I can feel him looking me over while I accept my change. I quickly shove it into my wallet, and then grab the bag with my scarf and head down the narrow aisle toward the door. I just want to get out of here, like, yesterday.

But I'm not fast enough. Footfalls dog my heels.

"Whatcha buyin'?" I feel a tug on my bag and turn around to see Davy pulling the scarf out. "Are you a cowgirl or a gang-banger?"

I snatch the scarf out of his hand. "Neither."

His companion snickers behind him.

"Whoa, now. Just curious," Davy says. "Haven't seen you around. What's your name?"

"I don't think so."

"O-oh, burn," the burly guy murmurs.

"Come on, cowgirl," Davy says. "Don't be that way."

I can't get through the door fast enough. Too fast. For the second time in twenty-four hours, I slam straight into another human being. The real Artful Dodger would be so disappointed in my slipshod getaway skills. My cheek smacks against a breastbone made of steel. I jerk back, overcorrecting, and nearly lose my balance. Hands grip my forearms.

I'm staring at a Quiksilver Surfboards logo. I crack my jaw and raise my line of sight. Now I'm staring at the angry face of Porter Roth.

"For the love of rocks," I mumble.

The hard lines around his eyes soften when he sees me. Just

slightly. Then he looks above my head and gets pissed again. "What the hell do you think you're doing here?" He's not talking to me. That's when I realize he's not angry at me either; he's angry at the person standing behind me.

"Who are you, my mom?" Davy's raspy voice answers. "Relax, man. Ray and I were just grabbing something to eat then heading to Capo's place."

Porter's hands are still gripping my arms. I can't tell if he's holding me up or trying to keep me away from Davy. But standing so close, he smells strongly of coconut oil and wax—which smells pretty freaking good, frankly. And while I'm busy being intoxicated, he's still drilling Davy. "You mean to tell me that I didn't just see you walking out of Déjà Vu?"

I turn my head to see Davy backpedaling. "Julie asked us to come inside. It was nothing. We were just chatting about Capo's new dog. Get your panties unbunched."

Umm, he's lying. But there's enough testosterone flying through the air to start a war, no way am I tattling on Davy. And what do I care? Not my business. I just want to get out of here and go to work. And why is Porter still holding on to me? He seems to finally notice this too, and at the same time I shake him loose, he lets go of me and holds his hands back like I'm radioactive.

"And what are you doing here?" he asks me.

"Buying a scarf," I say, moving away from him. Why is he always in my personal space?

"You two know each other?" Davy asks, absently rubbing his

right leg. Looks like that's the injured one—the cause of the limp.

"We work together." Porter eyes Davy, and then my bag, like he doesn't believe either one of us. I'm insulted to be lumped in with this loser.

"Small world," Davy says, grinning. "You gonna tell me your name now, cowgirl?"

"Seems to me you're going to call me whatever you want, so what's the point?"

"Damn, girl." He hikes up his shorts. "Is she this mean to you at work?" he asks Porter.

Porter slides a glance down at me. I dare him with my eyes to say something smart. Go on, buddy. Show off. Tell him how you riled me up, acting like a pig, called me a snob, and I almost got myself fired. Make yourself look tough in front of your dirtbag friend.

But all he says is, "She's cool."

Huh.

Davy gives me another slow once-over and then snaps his fingers. "You should come to a bonfire. Saturday night at sunset, the Bone Garden."

I have no idea where that is, nor do I really care. Especially not after that dubious exchange I heard inside the shop.

Porter snorts. "Don't think I don't know that's where you first hooked up with Chloe."

"So?" Davy challenges. "Chloe's in LA now. Why you gotta bring up the past?"

"Why are you inviting her to the bonfire?" Porter jerks his thumb toward me.

Davy shrugs as his friend Ray urges him down the boardwalk, away from the vintage clothing shop. "It's a free country."

I'm not sure what that was all about, but I'm feeling pretty awkward being left alone with Porter. "I gotta get to work."

Midday sun lights up golden streaks on top of Porter's dark curls, and when he turns his head toward the ocean, the scruff on his face almost looks red. "Yeah, me too."

Crap. We're both working together again today? I forgot to check the schedule in my rush to get out of there after everything that happened yesterday. I'm not sure how much more of this strained togetherness I can handle. But he's looking at me sort of funny, scratching the back of his neck, like he wants to say something else. And now I remember the cookies he left me, and I'm wondering if he's remembering them too. Sure, as far as gestures go, it was okay. But for all I know, he could've stolen them from the café. I should have just thrown them in the trash, but I gave the chocolate chip one to Grace and ate the others.

Feeling uncomfortable, I mumble a good-bye and turn to leave. That chick from the shop, Julie, is standing outside, both arms and purple dreadlocks crossed over her chest, warily watching us. I avoid eye contact and keep walking.

"See you later, cowgirl," Davy calls in the distance somewhere behind me.

Let's hope not. As I pass the churro cart, I notice Porter heading in the same general direction, but his muscular legs carry him faster. Someone whistles, flagging him down. It's a middle-aged man, maybe my dad's age, with wavy, gray-brown hair, closely cropped. He's dressed in board shorts and a sleeveless T-shirt and looks like he could have been handsome when he was younger, but he's had some hard knocks. One of his arms is covered with faded tattoos; the other arm is missing—as in, completely gone.

I'm surprised to recognize Porter's eyes in the man's when I pass, then I glance at the puckering pink scars where the arm once was. Porter catches me staring. I quickly look away and keep going, face flaming.

I think this is probably Porter's dad and the "horrible" thing that Grace was talking about.

What in the world happened to that family?

LUMIÈRE FILM FANATICS COMMUNITY
PRIVATE MESSAGES>ALEX>ARCHIVED

@mink: What do you want to do after high school?

@alex: You mean, with my life?

@mink: I mean college. When I was younger, I used to think I wanted to go to film school. Be a director. But now I don't think I'd be so good at being in charge. I don't want that kind of pressure. Now I think I'd rather be behind the scenes, cataloging something.

@alex: Professional film hobbyist?

@mink: *blink* Is that a real job? Hopefully, it pays huge sums of cash.

@alex: Right there with you. My dad expects me to take over the family business, and I don't want to. Don't get me wrong: I like the family business. I enjoy it as a hobby. But I don't want the pressure of doing it full-time for money. What if I want to do other things, you know?

@mink: I hear ya. And I guess we have to start applying for colleges in the fall. Sort of scary. Too many schools. West Coast? East Coast? I don't know.

@alex: Enjoy your multitude of choices. Meanwhile, I'll be stuck at the local community college, working two jobs. My future is already mapped out for me.

@mink: That can't be true.

@alex: Some of us aren't so lucky, Mink.

"I used to hate the water."
—Roy Scheider, *Jaws* (1975)

7

My dad says the second day of something is always better than the first because you know what to expect, and he's right. The Hotbox is slightly more tolerable today. I sacrifice my long waves for an updo and tie the scarf pinup-style, which keeps the sweat from rolling down the back of my neck. Grace has taken preventative measures too, bringing in a battery-powered oscillating fan from home that she's mounted between our stations. Our biggest obstacle is juggling bathroom breaks, because we're drinking more water than horses after the Kentucky Derby.

Halfway through my shift, I get my thirty-minute break. Shucking my orange vest, I head upstairs to the café, where I find a lull in the line. The sugar cookie Porter gave me yesterday was pretty scrumptious, so I buy two and find an empty table in a private alcove under the pirate ship. I pull out my phone and look up what's been hounding me since I clocked in today.

Bill "Pennywise" Roth was a professional surfer who won a bunch of World Surf League championship titles and Triple Crowns in the 1980s. According to his online biography, he's continually ranked as one of the top surfers of all time. It looks like he died eight years ago. There's a photo of a life-size memorial statue out by the surfer's crosswalk, taken at sunset, with a bunch of flowers and surfboards propped up against it.

I start to read about how he grew up in a poor Jewish family and started surfing at the age of six, and how he fostered this entire multigenerational family of professional surfers: his son, Xander Roth, and his grandchildren—

Hold on. Porter has a younger sister, Lana, sixteen, and she's a state and nationally ranked surfer who'll be competing professionally for the first time this fall and predicted to join a yearlong world tour starting next January. But Porter won't? And what happened to his dad?

A shadow falls over my phone. I hit the power button, but not fast enough.

"Reading up on me?"

I grimace, squeezing my eyes shut for a moment. How did he find me up here? "Are you stalking me on the security cameras?"

"Every move," Porter says. Metal legs squeak against the slate floor as he spins another chair around backward and straddles it, legs spread, like he's riding a horse. He crosses his arms on the chair's back. "If you wanted to know something about my family, all you had to do was ask."

"I'm good, thanks." I start to gather up my stuff, but I'm only halfway through the first cookie, so it's pretty obvious that I just sat down.

"I saw you staring at my dad today." An accusation.

"I wasn't—"

"You were."

A tiny groan escapes my mouth. My shoulders fall. "I didn't know . . . I mean, Grace kind of mentioned something happened, but I didn't know what, exactly, so I was just . . ." *Just what? Digging my grave a little deeper?* "Curious," I finally finish.

"Okay," he says, nodding his head slowly. "So what do you already know?"

I turn my phone back on. "I got to here," I say, and point to the article.

He leans over the back of the chair and squints at the screen. "Ah. That's it? So you know who my grandfather was and how he died?"

"Didn't get to the death part," I say, hoping that doesn't sound as bad as I think it does.

He doesn't seem to take offense. "He was a big wave surfer. That means he had steel balls. Took stupid risks, even when he got too old to be doing it. In the winter, after big storms, the waves will crest really high north of the cove, up at Bone Garden. He took a big risk one morning after a storm when I was ten. I watched him from the cliffs. The wave ate him whole and spit him out onto the rocks. That's why they call it Bone Garden, by the way. He wasn't the first idiot to die there. Just the most famous one."

I don't even know what to say. A large family stops near our table to pose for a photo in front of the sea monster. We lean to get out of their shot, once, twice, three times. They're finally finished, and we're left alone again.

Uninterested in dredging up his grandfather again, I try to think of something else to talk about. My mind turns to what I thought I witnessed in the vintage clothing shop. "Was that your buddy or something? That Davy guy?"

Porter grunts. "We grew up together." He squints at me and says, "Was he bothering you?"

"Not successfully."

Porter's mouth twists at the corners. He chuckles softly. "Now, *that* I believe. He's not very bright. But he's pernicious. I do my best to keep my eye on him, but . . ." Porter trails off, like he was going to say more but thinks better about it and clams up. I notice his gaze flick over me, head to bare legs—not really in a lurid way. His eyes are tight, wary, and troubled, and there's something behind that dark emotion connected to Davy that I don't understand. I wonder if it has to do with that Chloe girl they were talking about.

Whatever it is, I decide not to pursue this any further. Another evasion tactic I've learned: Change the subject as many times as you need in order to avoid uncomfortable conversation.

"I see you have a sister who surfs."

"Yeah," he says, and he looks happy that I changed the subject too. "Lana's killing it. She's got crazy potential. People say she'll be way bigger than my pops—maybe even bigger than my granddad."

I wonder if this is a point of contention between them, if it hurts his boy pride. But he's digging his phone out from his pocket to show me photos. A girl on a board inside the tunnel of a giant, curling wave. I can't really make out much about her face, only that she's wearing a yellow-and-black wet suit like a second skin and looking like she's about to be swallowed by the ocean. Porter shows me others, some closer, some in which she looks impossibly upside down in the middle of the wave. The last one he shows me is the two of them together on the beach, both of them with curly hair drying in the sun, wet suits peeled down to their waists, brown skin gleaming. He's behind her, arms around her shoulders, and they're both grinning.

And right now, sitting across from me, there's nothing but pride on his face. He doesn't even try to hide it. His eyes are practically sparkling.

"She's pretty," I say.

"Looks like my mom. It's our Hapa genes." He glances up at me and explains, "Half Hawaiian. My grandparents were Polynesian and Chinese. My dad met my mom when he was my age, surfing the Pipeline on the North Shore. Here." He pulls up another photo of his mother. She's gorgeous. And she's standing on the boardwalk near my favorite churro cart, in front of a familiar shop: Penny Boards. Well. Guess that answers that; it was his family's shop, after all. Note to self: Pick another churro cart, already!

Feeling strangely shy, I glance at his face and then quickly look away.

"Is it weird having a younger sister who's going pro?" I ask, more out of nervousness than anything else.

Porter shrugs. "Not really. She'll be heading out on the Women's Championship Tour for the first time next year. It's kind of a big deal. She gets to travel all over the world."

"What about school?"

"My dad's going with her. He'll homeschool her during the tour. I'll stay and help my mom run the shop." Porter must see the look of doubt on my face because he blinks a few times and shakes his head. "Yeah, it's not ideal, but Lana doesn't want to wait until she's eighteen. Anything could happen, and she's on top of her game now. On the tour, she gets a small salary and a chance to win prize money. But the big thing is the exposure, because the real money is in the product endorsements. That's pretty much what we used to live off of until Dad lost his arm."

Sounds a little pageant mom–y, making the kid perform on stage for money, but I keep this opinion to myself. "You guys don't own the shop?" I say, nodding toward his phone.

"Sure, but what people don't understand is that the shop barely breaks even. The overhead is ridiculous; rent keeps going up. And now that my dad isn't surfing anymore . . . well, no one wants a one-armed man pimping hats."

Yikes. This conversation is heading into awkward waters. I turn away to find the sea monster's big eye judging me—*You had to be on your phone, looking this up at work, didn't you? Couldn't wait until you got home?*—so I turn back toward the table and pick at my half-eaten cookie.

"I knew one out of three had to be right."

"Mmm?" I swallow cookie while trying to look cool and nearly choke.

"You like sugar cookies. I didn't know which one. I was just hoping you weren't vegan or gluten-free or something."

I shake my head.

He breaks off a piece of my cookie and eats it, and I'm not sure how I feel about that. I don't know where his hands have been. We aren't friends. And just because his dad's missing an arm, doesn't mean I've forgiven him for being a grade-A assbag.

"You aren't going to ask me?" he says. "Or do you already know?"

"Know what?"

"How my dad lost his arm?"

I shake my head. "No, I don't already know. Are you going to tell me?" *Or should I just wait until you leave and look it up? That works for me, thanks, see you later,* hasta luego.

"Three years ago, I was fifteen, a year younger than Lana. I went down to Sweetheart Point to watch my dad surf for this charity thing. It wasn't a competition or anything. Mostly older surfers, a few big names. Out of nowhere . . ." He pauses for a second, lost in thought, eyes glazed. Then he blinks it away. "I see this big shape cut through the water, a few yards away. At first, I didn't know what it was. It heads straight for my dad and knocks him right off his board. Then I saw the white collar around its neck and the mouth open. Great white."

My mouth falls open. I shut it. "Shark?"

"A small male. They say it's like getting struck by lightning, but damned if it didn't happen. And let me just tell you—it wasn't like *Jaws*. Hundreds of people around me on the beach and no one screamed or ran. They all just stood there staring while this thousand-pound monster was dragging my dad through the water, and he was still leashed to his board by the ankle."

"Oh, my dear God," I murmur, stuffing half of the second cookie in my mouth. "Whaa haaappened next?" I say around a mouthful of sugar.

Porter takes the rest of the cookie, biting off a corner and chewing while shaking his head, still looking a little dazed. "It was like a dream. I didn't think. I just raced into the water. I didn't even know if my dad was still alive or whether I would be if I bumped into the shark. I swam as hard as I could. I found the board first and followed the leash to the body."

He pauses, swallowing. "I tasted blood in the water before I got to him."

"Jesus."

"The arm was already gone," Porter says quietly. "Skin flapping. Muscles hanging. It was a mess. And I was so scared I was going to make it worse, carrying him back to shore. He was heavy and unconscious, and nobody was coming to help. And then the shark doubled back and tried to get my arm too. I managed to hit him and scare him off. Took sixty-nine stiches to sew me back together."

He unfolds his left arm until it's extended in front of me, and rucks up the short sleeve of his security guard uniform. There, above the bright red surf watch, are his zigzagging pink scars, bared for my perusal. Looking at them feels pornographic. Like I'm doing something I shouldn't be doing, and any moment, someone will catch me . . . but at the same time, I can't make myself look away. All this golden skin, all these eggshell-glossy scars, a railroad track, crisscrossing miles of sculpted lean muscle. It's horrifying . . . and the most beautiful thing I've ever seen.

Seeing the scars reminds me of something else about myself. Something I can't tell him. But it tugs on a dark memory inside me that I don't want to think about, and a fluttering of unstable emotions threatens to break the surface.

I breathe deep to push those feelings back down, and when I do, there's that scent again, Porter's scent, the wax and the clean coconut. Not the suntan-lotion fake kind. What is this stuff? It's driving me nuts. I don't know if it's the lure of this wonderful smell, or his story about the shark, or my urge to contain my own unwanted memories, but before I know what I'm doing, my fingertips are reaching out to trace the jagged edge of one of the scars by his elbow.

His skin is warm. The scar is raised, a tough, unyielding line. I follow it around his elbow, into the soft, sensitive hollow where his arm bends.

All the golden hairs on his forearm are standing up.

He sucks in a quick breath. I don't think he meant to, but I heard it. And it's then that I know I crossed some kind of line. I snatch my hand back and try to think of something to say, to erase what I just did, but it just comes out as a garbled grunt. And that makes things even weirder between us.

"Break," I finally manage. "Gotta get back."

I'm so embarrassed, I stumble over my chair as I leave. The ensuing metallic grate of metal on slate echoes through the café, causing several museum guests to look up from their afternoon coffee. Who's artful now, Rydell? That never happens to me. I'm not clumsy. Ever, ever, ever. He's messing with my game. I can't even look at him anymore, because my face is on fire.

What is happening to me? I swear, every time I have any interaction whatsoever with Porter Roth, something always goes screwy. He's an electrical outlet, and I'm the stupid toddler, always trying to poke around and stick my finger inside.

Someone needs to slap a big DANGER! sign on that boy's back before I electrocute myself.

LUMIÈRE FILM FANATICS COMMUNITY
PRIVATE MESSAGES>ALEX>NEW!

@mink: Have you ever had a serious girlfriend?

@alex: Yes. I think. Sort of. What do you qualify as serious?

@mink: Hey, you're the one who said yes. I was just curious. How long and why did you break up?

@alex: Three months and the short story is she said I didn't want to have fun anymore.

@mink: Ouch. The long story?

@alex: Her idea of fun included hooking up with my best friend when I was out of town.

@mink: I don't know what to say. I'm sorry.

@alex: Don't be. I'd checked out. It wasn't all her fault. If you don't pay attention to things, they wander off. I learned my lesson. I'm vigilant now.

@mink: Vigilant with who?

@alex: I think you mean with WHOM.

@mink: :P

@alex: No one in particular. I'm just saying, I'm not the same person I used to be. I confessed; now your turn. Anyone you've been vigilant about in the past?

@mink: A couple of guys for a couple of weeks, nothing major. Now I pretty much look out for myself. It's a full-time job. You'd be surprised.

@alex: One day you might need some help.

"You see how picky I am about my shoes, and they only go on my feet."
—Alicia Silverstone, *Clueless* (1995)

8

I don't work with Porter for the next few shifts. Grace, either, which bums me out. The museum sticks me with some older lady, Michelle, who's in her twenties and has problems counting her cash fast enough. She's slowing down the line and it's driving me crazy. Crazy enough to march up to Mr. Cavadini's office, peer around the corner . . . and then just change my mind and clock out for the day instead of saying anything.

That's how I roll.

One morning, instead of roaming the boardwalk, Sherlocking my way from shop to shop, stuffing my face with churros, I spend it pummeling Dad in two rounds of miniature golf. He took a half day off from work to hang with me, which was pretty nice. He gave me the choice of either the golf or paddleboarding—and no way in heaven or hell was I dipping my toe in the ocean after hearing Porter's tale of terror on the high seas. Nuh-uh. I told Dad the whole story, and he was a little freaked himself. He said he'd seen Porter's dad outside the surf shop and knew the family were surfers, but just assumed the missing-arm incident had happened a long time ago. He had no idea how it went down, or that Porter had rescued him.

See. Only ten days in town, and I was already filling Dad in on choice gossip he hadn't heard, living here for an entire year. The man needs me, clearly.

My reward for spanking Dad's behind in putt-putt is that I get to pick our lunch location. Since we grabbed a light breakfast before our golf excursion, I call a breakfast do-over at the Pancake Shack. It's got a 1950s Americana diner vibe inside, and we grab stools at the counter, where a waitress in a pink uniform brings us glasses of iced tea while we wait for our pancake orders. My dreams have finally come true! Only, they haven't, because the Pancake Shack doesn't exactly live up to my expectations, not even their "world-famous" almond pancakes, which I give one thumb down.

When I voice my lukewarm grade, Dad sticks a fork in my order and samples a corner. "Tastes like Christmas."

"Like those almond cookies grandma used to make."

"The gross, crumbly ones," he agrees. "You should have ordered a Dutch Baby. Taste mine. It's terrific."

His is way better, but it's no churro.

"Still haven't found him, huh?" he asks, and I know he's talking about Alex. I told him the basic deal, that I'm gun-shy about confessing to Alex that I've moved out here, and that I'm trying to find him on my own. Dad and I are a lot alike in many (unfortunate) ways. He gets it. Mom wouldn't. Mom would have freaked her pants off if she knew Alex even existed in the first place, so there's that. But Mom didn't really pay much attention to anything going on in my life back in DC, so it wasn't like I went to any trouble to hide him. And now that I'm here, I notice that she still isn't all that concerned, as I have yet to receive any communication from her since the initial *Did Bailey arrive okay?* phone calls. Whatever. I try not to think about her lack of concern too much.

From my purse, I retrieve a tourist map of the boardwalk. It's just a cartoony one I picked up for free one morning. I'm using a marker to X out the shops that I've either surveyed or that don't fall into the parameters that Alex has unwittingly provided me— can't see the ocean from the window, not a shop with a counter, et cetera. "This is what's left to cover," I tell Dad, pointing the sections of the map I haven't hit yet.

Dad grins and chuckles, shaking his head. I try to snatch the map away, but he holds it against the diner counter, moving aside the cast-iron skillet that holds his half-eaten Dutch Baby. "No, no. Let me see this marvelous thing. You're thorough and precise, a chip off the ol' block."

"Ugh," I complain. "Weirdo."

"What? This is quality CPA blood running in your veins, right here," he says proudly, thumping the map like a dork. "Wait, how do you know he just wasn't working in one of these places on the day you went by? Or unloading a truck out in the alley?"

"I don't, but I figure I'll hit every shop twice." I show him my homemade legend on the corner of the map. Dots for even-day visits, squares for odd. Male symbol for a boy my age working there—but ruled out as a possibility for Alex upon initial assessment. Triangles for churro cart locations. And wavy lines for all three stray boardwalk cats I've found so far, including Señor Don Gato.

He puts his arm around my shoulder and kisses the side of my head. "With superior deductive skills like this, how could you not find him? And if he's not worth the hunt, you have nothing to be ashamed of."

"I knew I liked you."

"You kind of have to," he says with a grin.

I grin back.

Someone walks over to the counter, and Dad leans forward to look past me. His face goes all funny. He clears his throat. "Good morning, Sergeant Mendoza."

Waiting for a waitress to take her order is a tall, curvy Latina cop in a navy uniform. Wavy hair, brown woven through with strands of gray, is pulled tight into a thick ponytail at the base of her neck. A pair of dark purple sunglasses sits on her face. I recognize those: She's the cop who flashed her lights at Davy and Porter at the crosswalk, the first day I got into town.

"Morning, Pete," she says in a husky voice. One corner of her mouth curls at the corner. Just slightly. Then her face turns unreadable. I think she's peering down at me, but it's hard to tell, especially with the sunglasses on. "Dutch Baby?" she says.

"You know it," my dad answers, and laughs in an odd way.

I look between them. My dad clears his throat again. "Wanda, this is my daughter, Bailey. Bailey, this is Sergeant Wanda Mendoza of the Coronado Cove Police Department."

Like I couldn't figure that out. She smiles and sticks out her arm to offer me a firm handshake. Wow. Knuckle-cracking firm. I'm awake now. And I'm not sure, but I think she might be uncomfortable. Do cops get nervous? I didn't think that was possible.

"Heard a great deal about you, Bailey." She has? Who the heck is this and why hasn't Dad mentioned her? Are they friends?

"I do the sergeant's taxes," Dad explains, but it sounds like a lie, and both of them are looking in different places—him at the counter and her at the ceiling. When her head tilts back down, she taps her fingernails on the counter. I glance at the gun holstered to her hip. I don't like guns; they make me uncomfortable, so I guess we're even.

"I like your brows," she finally says. "Glamorous."

I'm caught off guard for a second. Then I'm pleased. "I do them myself," I tell her. Finally someone who appreciates the importance of a good arch. Plucking is painful.

"Impressive," she confirms. "So, how're you liking California?"

"It's a different planet." I realize that might not sound positive, so I add, "I like the redwoods and the churros."

That makes her smile. Almost. She lifts her chin toward my dad. "Have you taken her to the posole truck?"

"Not yet," he says. "She's never had posole. Have you?" he asks, giving me a questioning look.

"No clue what you're talking about."

She blows out a breath and shakes her head like Dad has let down his entire country. "I've got a messed-up schedule right now, but sometime in the next couple of weeks, we should take her."

We? Take her? They are a *we*?

"It will knock your socks off," Dad assures me while the cop places a to-go order with the waitress. He stands and fumbles with his wallet. "That reminds me . . . Bailey, give me a second. I need to talk to the sergeant about something." He hands me a wad of cash to pay for our check and then he walks with the cop down the counter, where they lean a little closer, but don't seem to be talking about anything all that important. That's when it all comes into focus.

Jeezy creezy. My dad's dating a cop.

She seems nice. Has a great handshake. Pretty hot. The same height as him. Hope she likes him as much as he likes her, because he's smiling like a doofus. Then I hear her quietly laughing at something he says, and see her push her purple glasses up to rest atop her head and that makes me feel better.

As I wait for the CPA–cop macking session to come to an end, I pack up my boardwalk map and look around the diner.

Without my dad's body blocking the view, I now notice the person who's been sitting on the stool adjacent to his. It's a boy about my age with sandy-blond hair. He's eating eggs and drinking coffee. When he moves his arm, I see two things: (A) He's wearing a red T-shirt screen-printed in black with Cary Grant's face, and (B) he's reading a guide to the summer film festival.

My heart picks up speed as my gaze flicks over him. He's eating slowly, engrossed in his reading, taking small bites of scrambled eggs. His well-fitting shorts reveal toned, tan legs. Worn sandals slap against the counter's metal footrest as his knee bounces. The orange-and-blue key chain sitting next to his plate is printed with a familiar logo that I've seen on the boardwalk: Killian's Whale Tours. That's not by definition a retail shop, but it is a storefront along the boardwalk that has a view of the ocean. One with a counter, and possibly a family-owned business. I mentally call up my map and place the shop about three stores away from a churro cart. No resident cat, but then again, cats are mobile.

Could it be . . . ?

My brain is telling me to slow down, but my heart is thinking, *Pennies from heaven!*

He's cute. But he's no Porter.

God, what's wrong with me? Who cares about stupid old Porter, anyway? I push him out of my mind and focus on what's in front of me, try to match it to the Alex I have in my mind. Could this guy be witty? Sensitive? He looks well-groomed. Are serial killers well-groomed?

This is harder than I thought it would be.

I pull myself together and remember that if it is Alex, he doesn't know who I am. To him, I'm just a girl sitting in a diner. I'm not Mink. Deep breath.

"Grant," I say.

He looks up from the brochure. "Excuse me?"

"Your shirt," I explain. "Cary Grant. *Only Angels Have Wings*, if I'm not mistaken." I'm not. I'm totally showing off. What a total geek I am, but I can't help myself.

His head drops. He smiles now, and he's got great teeth, a big, white smile. "Yes. You're the second person ever to recognize that, and I've been wearing this for almost a year." His voice isn't what I imagined. Sharper, somehow. But still good.

"I'm a huge Grant buff," I say. "*Bringing Up Baby, The Philadelphia Story, The Awful Truth, His Girl Friday.*" I tick them off on my fingers, getting a little carried away and flushed in the cheeks. *Reel it back in, Rydell.* I clear my throat. "And *North by Northwest,* of course," I add, dangling that like the bait that it is.

"Everyone loves that," he agrees.

Huh. Can't tell if he's being droll or sarcastic. Then again, Alex has a superior sense of humor. Hard to tell.

He thinks for a moment, then says, "If I had to pick one, it would be *My Favorite Wife.*"

"Seriously? I love that movie," I say. "Irene Dunne and Randolph Scott are brilliant."

"Adam and Eve," he agrees, smiling.

"I've seen it a hundred times."

"You know, Randolph Scott and Cary Grant were lovers."

I nod. "Probably. No one's ever proven it, but I don't doubt it. I think he probably liked men *and* women." I shrug. Who cares anyway? Cary Grant was sex on a stick. More important, he was charm on a stick. At least on the big screen. I don't really care what he did off the screen.

"Patrick, by the way," he says, and it takes me a second to realize he's introducing himself.

Patrick. Huh. Not Alex, but Patrick? Of course, we aren't using our real names online, so that means nothing. More important, does this feel right? I honestly can't tell, but my pulse is racing, so if that's any indication, maybe that's a yes? And he still doesn't know to connect the Me sitting here with the Online Me, so I guess it's okay to give out my real name now. Besides, my dad's a few feet away, not to mention a cop with a badass handshake.

"I'm Bailey," I say, then decide to add, "I'm new in town."

"Cool. Nice to meet another movie aficionado." He slides the film festival brochure toward me. "We have a summer film festival every year. This year's lineup is so-so. A few good things, like the Georges Méliès shorts and *North by Northwest*."

Heart. Pounding. So. Fast.

"I would love to see all of those," I squeak out in a voice higher than Grace's.

"Right?" he says, grabbing his keys and gesturing toward the festival brochure. "Keep that. It's hot off the presses. Anyway, gotta get back to work. I'm at the whale tours up on the board-walk—Killian's. Orange and blue, down by the big gold Ferris wheel. Can't miss it. If you ever want to have coffee and talk about Cary Grant, come by and see me."

"I might take you up on that offer." I hate coffee, but whatever. It sounds so adult, so romantic. This is not a boy who'd get me fired or embarrass me in front of dozens of people. This boy is sophisticated. Whale watching! That sounds so much nicer than surfing.

He raises a hand, a triangle of toast clamped in his mouth, and jogs out the front door.

I'm reeling. Seriously, truly reeling.

"Who was that?" my dad murmurs over my shoulder, watching Patrick get into what appears to be some sort of red Jeep.

"I'm not one hundred percent sure," I say. "But I think I'm getting warmer."

LUMIÈRE FILM FANATICS COMMUNITY
PRIVATE MESSAGES>ALEX>NEW!

@mink: Anything new in your life?

@alex: Like . . . ?

@mink: I don't know. Something happened recently that made me have a little more hope about the future.

@alex: Me too, actually, now that you mention it. Maybe. For your future hope . . . how far ahead are we talking? Tomorrow? Next week? (Next month?)

@mink: I'm a one-step-at-a-time kinda gal. So I guess I'll try tomorrow and see where that leads.

@alex: You definitely don't dive into anything, do you? (I was hinting.)

@mink: I really don't. (I know you were.)

@alex: Maybe sometimes you should. Take a chance. Do something crazy. (Are you going to ask your dad about the film festival?)

@mink: Is that what you would do? (Maybe I already have.)

@alex: With the right person? Yes. (When will you let me know?)

@mink: Interesting. (He's thinking about it. And so am I.)

"You're a good man, sister."
—Humphrey Bogart, *The Maltese Falcon* (1941)

9

I'm standing behind the Hotbox with Grace and Mr. Pangborn. He lost his key. We're holding our register tills, waiting for Porter to come back from the cash-out room and unlock the door. I'm not even sure if Porter's made it through the lobby yet, escorting the other ticketing agents we're supposed to be replacing. Heck, I don't even know if Porter knows we're locked out. I do know that it's a few minutes past noon and the line is pretty long. Freddy, the guy in charge of taking tickets at the turnstile, keeps peeping around the corner at us, the look on his face progressing from Antsy to Dismayed.

Mr. Pangborn sniffles and rubs his nose. "We'll give him another minute to make it to cash-out before I buzz him. No sense in making him panic. He's got to get the tills to the room first."

Grace and I look at each other, shrug, and both make *he's got a point* faces. What are we going to do? There's no one at the information desk right now. The lady who's supposed to be stationed there, who also has a key to ticketing, is outside in the parking lot, schmoozing with a tour party. Mr. Cavadini is on an extended lunch break with the shift supervisor. Besides, Mr. Pangborn doesn't like to bother him, and who am I to argue?

He leans back against the booth's door, a little breathless, and crosses one ankle over the other, revealing a pair of white-and-black striped socks. I sort of love them. And I sort of love Pangborn, even though his eyes are slits and he reeks of weed. Grace says she caught him vaping up in his car before work yesterday. He's got to be in his seventies. Let the guy have a few bad habits, I say.

"Next month will be my fortieth anniversary working at the museum," he muses in a soft voice. He's got a gentle way about him that makes you want to listen to what he has to say. I'm not sure why Porter gets so frustrated with him. He's just an old man. Have a heart.

Grace's lips pucker. "That's nuts."

"You must like it if you've stuck with it this long," I say.

"Eh, I like talking to people. And I don't have any college or training, so what else am I supposed to do? This is all I know." He scratches his head and his crazy white hair sticks up in different directions. "They tried to make me retire about ten years ago, but I didn't really have anything to do at home. I never married. I've got a dog, Daisy, but she gets tired of seeing me all day. So even though they didn't pay me, I just kept showing up for work."

"What?" Grace says, unable to hide her disbelief. "For how long?"

"Oh, about three months or so. Mr. Cavadini finally got sick of telling me to go home, so he officially rehired me and put me back on the schedule." He smiles, big and wide, lifting his shoulders. "And here I stand. It hasn't killed me yet. I think Porter should be in the cash-out room by now. Cover your ears, ladies. He's not going to be happy."

Grace knocks shoulders with me while Pangborn radios Porter. "Glad we're finally scheduled together again."

"Me too," I say, genuinely meaning it. "Team Grailey, taking care of business."

"Team Baice, dropping the hammer."

We both laugh until Freddy peeps around the turnstiles again and Grace makes a hissing sound at him. He leaves us alone now. "Got plans this weekend?" she asks me.

"I don't know. Why?"

"There's a bonfire on Saturday after work. Party on the beach."

I grip my till harder, thinking of Porter's friend Davy. "Is this the one at the Bone Garden?"

"Yeah. You've heard about it?"

"Only in passing."

"The core of it is a surfer crowd, but other people show up, too. They're usually every Saturday night in the summer. Sometimes they're boring, sometimes they're fun, but I thought it might be a good place to meet people from Brightsea, since you're new. I can introduce you."

The evader in me cowers, readying an excuse to turn her down, but the weird thing is, I think I want to go. Especially with Grace. So I say, "Sure, why not?" And before I know it, I'm telling her where my dad lives, and we're making plans for her to pick me up in her car. What do you know? I guess I'm a social butterfly. Must be all this fresh air and sunshine.

Or maybe it's just that I'm feeling more hopeful about life in general after finding out my dad has a new girlfriend. A kickass cop girlfriend. "We're just friends. Taking things slow," he assured me on the ride home yesterday. That was all he offered, so that's where we left it. As long as he's happy and there's no weirdness, I'm fine with it.

And speaking of fine, there's the other more important thing buzzing around in my brain: bumping into Patrick at the Pancake Shack. Patrick, and only Patrick, I remind myself for the millionth time, who may or may not be Alex. But I decided last night that I'm going to muster up the gumption to go talk to him again. I've been daydreaming about it off and on for hours. Epic sigh.

A rush of cool museum air blows across my arm, and my daydreaming is cut short when I have to step to the side to avoid the buffalo that is Porter, charging the ticketing booth.

"I'm going to rip out your large intestines, sew this key to the end of them, and then stuff them back inside your body."

Porter opens Pangborn's hand, shoves down a key, and closes the man's fingers on top of it. "Don't. Lose it. Again."

The older security guard smiles. "You're a good boy, Porter.

Thank you." Pangborn pats him on the shoulder, completely unfazed by Porter's bad attitude. He's a better man than most. "Come along, ladies. Freddy's got ants in his pants. Let's bust up this line and sell some tickets."

Team Grailey—I win the name game—kicks butt, per usual, and we do bust up that line, because we are the best. Our shift supervisor remarks on the good work we do, and when Mr. Cavadini drops by to check on us, for once, he even gets our names right. It's a good day, right up until about four p.m.

Museum foot traffic has slowed. My break's almost over and I'm nearly ready to power through my last couple of hours, but I've still got a few minutes, so I'm strolling through Vivian's Wing. I'm in the San Francisco Room, which has a Golden Gate Bridge that visitors walk beneath and a fake Chinatown street, where you can peer inside staged storefront windows that look like they did in the late 1800s. As I'm gazing at a Chinese tea shop, I notice two kids, maybe thirteen, fourteen years old, acting a little weird. They're standing a few yards from me, in the nearby 1940s San Francisco film noir display, eyeing a replica of the Maltese falcon, which is sitting on the desk of famous fictional detective Sam Spade—played by Humphrey Bogart on the big screen. One of them, a blond boy in a white polo shirt and Top-Siders, is experimentally touching the statue, while his friend, a drowsy kid with a backpack, keeps a lethargic lookout.

I can guess what they're planning. Morons. Don't they notice the security cameras? The backpack kid does see them, though, and he's inching around, blocking his Richie Rich friend with his body, looking up at the camera and judging the angle. I don't know what they hope to accomplish. Everything in the museum is glued, nailed, screwed, or locked down.

Only it's not.

Polo shirt touches the falcon, and it jiggles. Just a little. But enough.

They're going to rock it off its mounting. The jerks are planning a heist.

I glance around. Only a few museum guests in this room. I keep my head low and casually walk to the other end of the room, where I know from memorizing the stupid employee map that a call box is hidden in a wall panel. Making sure I'm not seen, I duck behind a potted palm, pop open the panel, and hit the button for security. Porter's voice booms over the old line.

"Talk to me." He's on his radio doohickey. I can tell by the click and static.

"It's Bailey," I whisper. "I'm in the San Francisco Room."

"That's a long way from ticketing, Rydell. And speak up. I can't hear you. Or are you trying to come on to me? Is this your sexy voice? I like it."

I groan and seriously consider hanging up. "Shut up and listen to me. I think some kids are trying to steal."

"I think you have the wrong number, sir."

"Porter!" I grind out. "They're stealing the Maltese falcon."

"Keep your pants on. I'm two rooms away. I'll be right there.

Don't take your eyes off them, but don't approach. They might be dangerous or something. I'm being serious right now, in case you can't tell."

The phone goes dead. After closing the panel, I casually step from behind the palm and pretend to be looking at some paintings while keeping an eye on the kids. They're still rocking the falcon statue. A couple is passing under the Golden Gate Bridge, and the two boys see them, so that halts their thieving for a moment. I disappear behind the potted palm again.

Come on, Porter. I know the falcon's not actual movie memorabilia, much like most of the rest of the stuff in this place; only two statues were used in the original film, and one was auctioned off for several million dollars. But it's the principle of the thing, and it makes me mad.

"Where are they now?" Porter's warm breath grazes the hair around my ear. My neck and shoulder involuntarily clamp together, and for some reason, he finds this amusing. "Ticklish, Rydell?" he whispers.

I ignore that comment and lower a palm branch to show him the boys, who are now rocking the statue again. "There. White polo shirt and backpack."

"Dirty little pigs," he mutters incredulously. "The falcon?"

I won't lie. A little thrill goes through me that Porter's as mad as I am. I like that we're on the same page about this. "What are we going to do?" I whisper.

"Rule number one in apprehending thieves and shoplifters

according to the Cavern Palace guidelines is that we absolutely do not make a scene. No chasing. No nasty blowups. Nothing that causes the other guests to feel uncomfortable, so that means we've got to smoke them out, nice and easy."

"I don't follow," I whisper.

Porter drops his head to speak in a lower voice. "We let them steal it."

"What?" My face is near his face, so close I can see all the golden flecks in his brown eyes. Did I know they were brown? I never noticed until now. "We can't do that."

"We can and we will. Then we'll follow them to the exit and bust their asses in the parking lot."

"Oh," I say, more than a little intrigued by this prospect.

"Now, they might split up. I've had this happen once before with a pair of Jay's cuff links last summer. Bastards got away with a thousand bucks' worth of gold while my ass got chewed out by Cadaver. So I might need some help. Will you?"

"Me? I don't know . . . My break's over."

"Bawk, bawk," he whispers back, cawing like a chicken. The tip of his nose touches mine, and we're so close, I can now see his chest lifting up and down . . . and the jumping pulse of a vein on his neck. Were his shoulders always this broad? Mother of Mary, he seems bigger up close. And instead of wanting to punch him in the stomach, which should be my normal Porter response, I'm starting to want something else that makes my breath come faster. My clothes suddenly feel too tight.

Oh.

God.

So what? He's attractive and has a certain damaged charm about him. It's just chemical attraction. Perfectly natural. Means nothing.

And because I'm on my break and it's cold in the museum, I'm wearing the cardigan, and that covers up the majority of the headlight problem that is now happening in my breast locale. Disaster averted. And the thought of it being a near miss is enough to throw a proverbial bucket of cold water onto the situation. God, this is ridiculous. It's just dumb old Porter. What am I afraid of? Nothing.

To prove it to myself, I move back and lift my head, meeting his gaze and his challenge. "Radio Grace and tell her I'll be late."

His smile could power a lighthouse. He quickly radios Pangborn and briefs him on the situation, giving the older guard a description of the boys and instructions to track them on the security monitors. But before he can notify Grace, our thieving boys are on the move.

The falcon is gone. I didn't see them take it. But the boys are huddled and the backpack's being swung from the shorter kid's shoulder. They're stashing the bird.

"Porter!" I whisper heatedly, tugging his sleeve.

"I see it," he says, keeping the palm frond bent to peer into the room. He radios Pangborn again, who saw it too.

"Got it all on tape," the old stoner confirms, his words coming from the tiny black box on Porter's shoulder. Apart from losing keys, this is probably more excitement than the two of them have had in months. "Go smoke 'em out, Porter. I'm watching from heaven."

Heaven. The security room. I wonder if Porter really does watch me from there, or if that's just him talking big.

The dopey-eyed kid zips up the backpack and slings it over his right shoulder, looks around, and then the two little robbers make their way beneath the bridge, strolling like it's Sunday and they didn't just commit a crime. The nerve!

"Time to follow," Porter says, nudging me out of our hiding place with a tap on my wrist. "We'll hang back at a safe distance, but not too far. There are a lot of exits, and they likely know that. Main entrance and gift shop are the fastest escape routes, but the easiest for us to track. Fire exits will set off alarms, but they could run and lose us—that's how the cuff-link bandits beat me last summer. And then there's the delivery door and the employee entrance."

"They're turning right," I say. "Heading toward the lobby."

"That kills three of the fire exits. Don't stare too hard. Just act like we're having a friendly chat. It's good that you're not wearing your vest. You look like you're asking me for help. Maybe you're just my girlfriend, visiting me for lunch."

I nearly choke. "Dream on."

"What? I'm not good enough for your champagne tastes?"

"Don't be ridiculous."

He snorts. "You prance around here, trying to look like a movie star in your expensive clothes, driving a Vespa, lawyer mom back in Washington, DC—"

His tone is light, almost teasing—not like our usual arguments—but it's what he's saying that surprises me. I stop in my tracks, but he pushes me forward. "Do you want to catch these guys? They're turning into the Egyptian Room. Might have just seen me too. We need to be careful."

We hang back for a second while Porter glances into the room. As he does, I say, "How did you know my mom's a lawyer?"

"Gracie told me."

Oh. "My clothes aren't expensive, they're vintage. I can't help it if your sense of style doesn't register anything higher than stoner chic and beach bum."

"Ooaf," he says, feigning offense. "You wound my tender sensibilities, Rydell."

"And my dad bought me the Vespa. It's restored. It's not like it's new or anything."

"That model's worth more than a new ride. Anyone who knows wheels knows that. The Cove's a collector's paradise for scooters. You need to keep that thing locked up at all times."

"I'm not an idiot," I tell him.

"Crap!"

"What?" I angle to see around him.

"Polo Shirt definitely spotted me. They're circling around to the main hallway." He radios Pangborn again. "You still see them?"

"Yeah, I got 'em on the overheads in the main corridor," Pangborn's voice says over the radio. "Looks like they're heading for the lobby."

The museum closes at six, and it's past four, so at this time of day, the main hallways on both wings begin to fill up with guests making their way back out to warm sun and fresh air. Our miscreant boys duck into the crowd and for a few seconds, we lose them in the flow. My pulse speeds as I bounce on the balls of my feet, trying to see over the heads of the slow-moving herd.

"Stop that," Porter says. "You're going to blow our cover. I can see them. They're hugging the south wall, so I don't think they'll break for the main gate or the gift shop."

"Employee hall?"

"Maybe. Or they could head straight to Jay's wing and try to use a fire exit there."

Porter's legs are longer than mine, and it's hard for me to keep up with him without doubling my pace. "I don't have champagne tastes. Just because I have style doesn't mean I'm a snob. And in case you haven't noticed, I'm not living with my mom anymore; I'm living with my dad. And I'm working this job, probably making a whole heck of a lot less money than you, Mr. I'm Eighteen; I Can Work Full-Time and All My Sexual Activity Is Legal.'"

"Unless it's with someone like you, then it would be illegal, because you're underage."

"Right." Before I can think of a wittier comeback, we're at the end of the corridor, and our suspects have taken a sharp right.

Porter was right: They aren't headed to the main gate or the gift shop. But they aren't going to Jay's wing or the employee hall either.

"What the . . . ," Porter murmurs. "The brats are going spelunking?"

Sure enough, the two boys stride through the back of the lobby, making a beeline to the gaping mouth of the cave. Why they'd head there, I don't understand. There's no exit inside, just a dark, looping path that ends up right back at the mouth of the cave. . . .

"Any cameras in there?" I ask.

"A few. The image quality isn't great," Porter admits.

"They're trying to lose us."

He thinks about this for a second and swears under his breath. We race to the mouth of the cave, where the boys have jogged down the stone steps and disappeared under the stalactites lit by creepy orange spotlights. Only problem is, the steps go two ways: left and right. The main route snakes through the cliffs, crisscrossing in the center like a pretzel where they open up into the center cavern. And the boys have split up.

"You go left," Porter tells me. "I'll go right. Whichever one of them you find, don't take your eyes off him."

"Meet you in the center." I take off down the stairs, cool air drafting up as I jog. It's dark and creepy down here, and the metal handrail that's been here since the museum opened has a clammy feel to it that gives me the heebie-jeebies, so I can't touch it. This makes running difficult, because caves are dark and damp, and the low lights around the walkway might be great for setting a mood, but they don't provide much in the way of illumination when you're chasing someone. Luckily, there aren't too many people lingering in the cave—and even fewer racing through it. I spot White Polo Shirt a few yards ahead, on another landing.

There isn't much to see in the cave, especially compared to the rest of the jam-packed museum, just a few info plaques with facts about caves in California and animals that live there, and the occasional bench for hot-blooded people to rest and enjoy the dark and gloomy view. I sail past a woman leaning against one of these benches and head around the pretzel turn toward the red-and-green glow of the main cavern.

Rocky walls lined with organically formed crevices and holes separate the cave into multiple chambers. It's a great place for hiding, and those little bastards know it. Several people mingle around the main plaque, marking the spot where Jay and Vivian found their pirate gold. A cheesy chest overflowing with carnival doubloons sits atop a flat rock. It's ridiculous. I'm embarrassed for everyone who has to gaze upon it, including myself.

But more than that, I'm embarrassed that I've lost the stupid kid I'm supposed to be trailing. I finally spot Porter, and he acknowledges me with a chin nod, but I can tell by the angle of his brow that he can't find the backpack kid either. How could this be? I glance around one more time, and out of the corner of my eye, I spot something: two white sneakers slipping through one of the larger hole formations in the rocky cave walls. Not Polo, but the backpack kid. Sneaky little monkey is doubling back up the stairs.

Porter's attention is elsewhere, and I'm not losing this kid again, so I take off after him. Up I go, back the way I came, twice as fast, pounding the stone steps.

The backpack kid tosses me a glance over his shoulder. He knows I'm chasing him, and he's not stopping. Too bad. Neither am I.

When he reaches the mouth of the cave, he hesitates long enough to spot his cohort, slamming up the steps on the other side. Then they're off, racing together through the lobby.

Porter said not to make a scene, but what about now? Do I just let these jerks get away? I quickly decide: No, I don't.

I book it as fast as I can go, giving chase. They nearly bowl over an entire family, who startle like ducks on a pond, jumping out of their way.

"Someone stop them!" I yell.

No one does.

I think about Porter surrounded by people that horrible day on the beach years ago, when no one would help him save his dad from the shark. If strangers won't help when someone is dying, they're definitely not going to stop two kids from running out of a museum.

Pulse swishing in my temples, I race around the information booth, pumping my arms, and watch them split up again. Polo is heading for the easy way out: the main exit, where there's (1) only a set of doors to go through, and (2) Hector, the laziest employee on staff.

But Backpack is headed for the ticketing booth and the connecting turnstiles. Freddy should be there, but no one's entering the museum, so he's instead chatting it up with Hector. The turnstiles are unmanned.

Like a pro hustler who's never paid a subway fare, Backpack hurdles over the turnstiles in one leap. Impressive. Or it would have been, had his backpack not slipped off his shoulder and the strap not caught on one of the turnstile arms. While he struggles to free it, I take the easier route and make for the wheelchair access gate.

I unhitch the latch.

He frees the strap.

I slip through the gate, and just as he's turning to run, I lurch forward and—

I jump on his back.

We hit the ground together. The air whooshes out of my lungs and my knee slams into tile. He cries out. I don't.

I freaking got him.

"Get off me, you crazy bitch!" He squirms below me, elbowing me in the ribs. I clamp my hand over his arm to hold it down. A breathless, evil laugh comes out of me in fits. I can't even say anything; I'm too winded.

"Oh no you don't," a triumphant male voice says nearby.

I twist to the side and spit hair out of my mouth. Porter is dragging Polo by the arm. He doesn't look half as winded as I feel. Stupid surfer genes. But now Freddy and Hector are coming—to gawk, I guess. And here's Grace, too; finally, someone with sense.

"What in the world is going on?" she asks.

"Watch him," Porter tells the three of them as he parks Polo on the ground. Then he pulls me off Backpack.

"She's crazy," the boy repeats. "I think she broke my leg."

"Whatever. She's got the strength of a tater tot," Porter says, pulling the boy to his feet, who protests and hobbles, but manages okay.

"Oww," he whines.

"Shut the hell up, you thieving-ass rat." Porter grabs the boy by his shirt, wrenches the backpack off his arm, tosses it to me. "Check it."

I unzip the pack. Nested in a wadded-up hoodie is the statue. I hold it up like a trophy.

The boy groans and tries to wriggle out of Porter's grip. "Nuh-uh," Porter says, urging him down next to Polo and pressing the button on his sleeve. "You and your punk-ass friend aren't going anywhere right now. We're going to sit tight while my buddy Mr. Pangborn makes a little phone call to our friends at the CCPD. Got that, Pangborn?" he asks into his radio.

"Got it," Pangborn's voice answers.

While the boys exchange panicked looks, a small crowd is forming. I brush off my skirt and notice that a small trail of blood runs from a nasty scrape on my knee. I don't even care. I'm still on an oh-so-sweet adrenaline high.

Porter grins, eyebrows high. "Damn, Bailey. You took him downtown. Full-on atomic drop body slam. I had no idea you had it in you."

Me neither, to be honest. "No one steals from Sam Spade and gets away with it," I say.

He holds his hand up, and I slap it, but instead of it being a simple high five, he laces his fingers between mine, squeezing. It's probably only for a second, but it feels longer. When he releases my hand, I'm a ball of chaos: fingers tingling from where his just were, mind trying to make sense of it. Is he just being friendly, or is this maybe some sort of surfer handshake?

Now he's crouching in front of me, inspecting my knee. "Ouch," he says. Gentle fingers prod the skin around my wound. "You busted that up pretty good."

"Yeah, stop poking it," I say, but I'm not mad.

"You okay?" he asks in a softer voice.

"It's fine."

He nods and stands, then gestures for the falcon, *gimme-gimme*. When I hand it over, he turns to the two punks.

"You know this thing is worthless, right? If you ding-dongs would've just hustled a little faster, I suspect all you'd get for it on eBay would be ten lousy dollars, and we'd just order a new one online the next day. But now you're going to start your teenage lives with criminal records."

"Screw you," Polo Shirt says. "My dad's a lawyer. A hundred bucks says he'll get you and the bitch fired."

Porter laughs and tugs a thumb in my direction as Mr. Cavadini rushes toward us through the gift-shop exit. "Nice try. Her mom's a lawyer too."

Uh, divorce lawyer living all the way across the country, but who cares? We both share a secret smile. Who knew that my archnemesis could make such a good partner? A crime-solving partner—that's all. No other kind of partner. I really need to wipe all those other thoughts out of my head, especially the confusing lusty thing that happened before we chased down these two kids. And the hand-holding. And the secret smiling.

Ugh.

Must rectify this tangled mess quickly, and I think I know how.

LUMIÈRE FILM FANATICS COMMUNITY
PRIVATE MESSAGES>ALEX>NEW!

@mink: I have a horoscope for you.

@alex: Do you? Lay it on me, because I've had a REALLY confusing day, and I need some guidance.

@mink: Okay, here it is: If life suddenly gives you a choice to say yes to a new experience, you should accept.

@alex: What if that experience might be a pain in the ass?

@mink: Why would you assume that?

@alex: Instinct. I've been burned before, remember?

@mink: Instinct is no match for reason.

@alex: At this point, I'm not even sure I've got either one of them on my side.

"Story of my life. I always get the fuzzy end of the lollipop."
—Marilyn Monroe, *Some Like It Hot* (1959)

10

I'm doing this. I've got the day off, and I'm heading toward the Killian's Whale Tours booth. It's eerily gray and foggy this morning. So foggy, it's nearly noon and I still can't see much of the ocean. This is okay by me. Fewer tourists running around. It's like I have the boardwalk to myself.

So what if I've changed my mind twice? I'm really doing it this time. I mean, come on. It's Alex. At least, I *hope* it's Alex. And if it is, I'll know, because I know him. I should, shouldn't I? I've been talking to him online for months. We're practically soul mates. Okay, maybe that's a little much, but we're at least friends of some sort or another. We have a bond that stretches beyond our common interest.

Then there's the whole Porter situation. After the cops came and picked up the thieving kids yesterday—two run-of-the-mill officers, not my dad's Sergeant Mendoza—Porter was involved in paperwork to do with all that, so I didn't really see him again.

Which is good, because all these crazy feelings I was feeling about him . . . they were just a byproduct of adrenaline and elation over capturing those two boys.

Anyway, I'm not thinking about Porter Roth right now. I'm especially not thinking about his fingers twined through mine after the victory high five. That's banned from my brain. As if to underscore the matter, a low foghorn bellows offshore, making me jump. *Here be dragons, Rydell. Keep away, if you know what's good for you.*

I clear Porter from my head and continue walking. The orange and blue of the Killian logo appears. *We'll show you a whale of a good time!* Gee, if this really is Alex's family, I already see why he hates working here. Lame-o. The business is situated between two others, Shoreline Bicycle Rentals, and the booth that sells tickets to the Ferris wheel. I hover by the bike rental place until I spot Patrick's blond hair.

He's working. And it looks like he's alone.

I wait while he points someone down the boardwalk, giving them directions through the fog somewhere, then before I can lose my nerve again, I take three long strides and slow near the carved whale bench outside the ticketing window. A couple of seagulls scatter when I approach.

"Hi," I say. "Remember me?"

"From the Shack," he says. He's wearing an orange Windbreaker and white shorts. His sideburns are cropped shorter than they were in the diner, and the morning breeze is blowing blond hair across his eyes. "I never forget a film buff. But I do forget names. Remind me . . . ?"

I'm sort of crushed. "Bailey."

He snaps his fingers. "Bailey, that's right. Patrick," he says, extending his hand, and I pretend that I didn't remember his name either as I shake it.

Now I've got to play it cooler than I planned, so I say, "I was just taking a walk, seeing if there were any used-DVD stores on the boardwalk." I know there's one. I've already been inside it three times. "And then I saw you, and I thought, *Hey, maybe that guy would know.*" Ugh. So awkward, but he doesn't seem to notice.

"Yeah, there's a little place called Video Ray-Gun, right in the middle of the promenade. Giant sci-fi ray gun outside. Hard to miss."

Crap. This is going to be harder than I thought. Didn't I give him a hint online last night? Unless this really isn't Alex . . .

"So, do you get a break here any time soon? Maybe you'd want to go browse some DVDs with me?" I hear myself saying. "You mentioned getting coffee sometime, but, you know . . ." My voice is getting smaller and smaller.

Come on. If this is really Alex, surely he'll remember me dropping the horoscope hint last night . . . won't he? I mean, he's always so attentive online. He remembers everything I say. Always gets my jokes, even remembers punch lines to gags from months back. But now he can't even remember my actual name? Maybe it really was a good idea that I didn't tell him I was moving out here, after all.

Hesitating, he leans over the counter and looks one way, then the other, peering into the fog. "All right. Yeah, sure. Why not. Business is slow. The current tour won't be back for a bit, so I guess I can take thirty. Hold on, let me close the gate and put up the sign."

I let out a long breath.

He jumps off his stool and reaches above his head to pull down a rolling metal shutter over the window, disappearing for a few seconds. When he reappears through a door on the side of the booth, he's got a GONE WHALING! BE BACK IN A FEW MINUTES sign, which he hangs on the shuttered window.

"Okay, Bailey. Let's go," he says with an inviting smile.

Feeling better, I fall into step with him, and we make our way to the promenade. He asks me polite questions—how long have I been in town? Where am I from? Oh, DC. Have I seen the president or toured the White House? Have I been to Dupont Circle?

By the time we get to the giant ray-gun sign, the only thing I've been able to ask him is how long he's lived in Coronado Cove (all his life), and where he goes to school—Berkshire Academy. The private school. This throws me for a loop. I never pegged Alex as a private-school kind of guy. I'm trying to figure this out as we step inside the shop.

Video Ray-Gun has one of those great dusty-musty smells that come with old stores, though most of their inventory doesn't date back more than a few years. They specialize in campy sci-fi movies, and because that's my dad's catnip, he's in love with this place. A few movie-related collectible posters and and toys grace the walls around the register, behind which hangs a TV where a *Godzilla* movie is playing. Two middle-aged long-haired men are paying more attention to the movie than to us when we walk past. Thank God, because I was just in here with Dad a couple of days ago, and I don't want them to recognize me.

The store is busier than I expected—not exactly the best place for a quiet, romantic get-to-know-you date, but what can I do now? It's all I have to work with. We stroll past oversize boxes of candy in retro theater packaging and a rack of upcoming Blu-ray DVDs available for preorder, and I try to pretend like I don't know where I'm going as Patrick leads me to the Film Classics section.

"They don't have a lot of stuff right now," he tells me, turning the corner around a bay of shelves. "I was just in here yesterday. But check this out." He grabs something off a shelf and hands it to me. "Boxed set of classic gangster films from the 1930s. It's a steal."

I accept the box and look at the back. "I'm not a huge fan of gangster movies."

"Are you kidding? *White Heat?* The 1932 version of *Scarface?* That was insanely violent for its time, really pushed the envelope."

"Yeaaah," I drawl, handing him the box back. "Not a big gun fan."

"Oh," he says, reshelving it. "One of those, huh?"

"Excuse me?"

He holds up both hands. "Hey, whatever you're into is fine. No argument from me. I just think film is film, and that you shouldn't paste your political views onto a piece of art."

Jeez. This isn't going well. I take a deep breath and pause for a moment. Maybe this is my fault? I don't really think so, but I strive to be the bigger person. "It's not that. I had a bad personal experience, so it's just . . . kind of a thing for me. Just not my cup of tea."

"Oh, God," he says, resting a sympathetic hand on my shoulder—just the tips of his fingers, actually. "I'm so sorry. I assumed. I'm being an ass. Forgive?"

"Forgotten," I say with a smile.

"Oh! What about *Breakfast at Tiffany's*? Everyone loves that."

Is he being serious? I mean, I love Audrey Hepburn, but I just can't watch Mickey Rooney playing a broadly caricatured Japanese man for goofs and giggles. No thanks. I tell him so. His argument isn't as strong for this one, but he's still disbelieving that I'm not singing its praises.

This is so weird. Our film mojo is off. Sure, we disagree online (all the time), but it's all good-natured. In person, it feels so . . . personal. We go through the classics section, shelf by shelf, but nothing seems to click with either one of us. It's like we're two completely different people, and the longer we're testing each other's tastes, the less we're liking each other. I'm starting to sweat in weird places and make awkward flirty jokes that don't land.

This is not going well.

The worst part is that he notices too.

"Sometimes they have more stuff in the back," he finally says after we haven't spoken in several long, excruciating seconds. "Let me go ask Henry if they've gotten anything new in. Be right back."

Great. Now I'm worried that he's giving me the slip. The first time I get up the nerve to ask a guy out on a date—a guy I've been fantasizing about for months—and it goes hellishly wrong. If he doesn't come back in one minute, I'm seriously considering sneaking out myself.

"*Breakfast at Tiffany's* is an overrated piece of fluff."

I freeze. No one's around. I glance down the aisle in both directions. Did I just imagine that? Or did someone overhear Patrick and me talking from before, and now I'm overhearing another conversation?

"It's not supposed to be a love story, you know. Which is the ironic thing in this particular situation, actually."

"Hello?" I whisper.

A DVD moves aside. I'm now staring at a pair of eyes. Someone's in the other aisle. I move another DVD and reveal more of the face through the wire shelving: scruffy jaw, slow grin, wild, sun-kissed curls. Porter. My hand clenches. "What the hell are you doing here?"

"It's my day off."

"And you're following me around?" I say, exasperated.

"No, you're following me around. I was in here when you paraded in with Patrick Killian on your arm."

I stand on tiptoes to peer over the top of the shelves. He raises his head to meet me and cocks both brows, a smug look on his face. My heart starts pounding, big-time. Why does he have this effect on me? Can't my body just be normal around him?

"How do you know him?" I whisper hotly, glancing around to make sure Patrick isn't listening. I don't spot him, so I guess he's either in back or has flown the coop.

Porter casually rests an arm on the top of the video rack. "I've known him since we were kids. He thinks he's a movie snob because his family is one of the local companies that sponsors the annual film festival. Big whoop."

Wait one stinking minute. Big warning bells ding in my head. I definitely think Alex would have mentioned if his family sponsored the festival. That's something you'd brag about to your film-geek friend, Forbidden Zone personal-detail restrictions aside. No way would he keep that from me. This is all wrong. But I don't think Porter is lying, because now I'm remembering when Patrick gave me the film festival brochure: "hot off the presses," he said. He got an early copy of it because his dad's a festival sponsor? It's still in my purse, and I'm fighting everything not to pull it out and scan the sponsor page for the Killian name.

Inside, I'm quietly panicking that Patrick isn't Alex, but all I can say to Porter is, "Oh, and you know better." It's a weak taunt, but my heart isn't into it.

"I know that you were right about *Breakfast at Tiffany's*," he responds. "Truman Capote's novella is about a gay man and a prostitute. Hollywood turned it into a romance. And don't get me started on Mickey Rooney. That was an embarrassing shambles. But..."

"But what?"

"I still think it's worth watching for Hepburn's performance. What? Don't look so shocked. It was my grandma's favorite movie. You don't know everything about me."

Apparently, I know nothing. *Who are you, Porter Roth?*

"And I'm not sure if you know everything about your date—"

"Jesus, do you have to talk so loud?" I whisper. "He's not my date." Not at this rate, anyway.

"Whatever he is, I'm telling you this because I hate to see you wasting all that primo flirt material on someone who doesn't appreciate it." He leans across the rack, beckoning me closer. "Patrick has a boyfriend in Guatemala."

My eye twitches. I blink. Stare at Porter.

Holy shitcakes . . . I think back to when I first met Patrick in the Pancake Shack, and him talking about Cary Grant and Randolph Scott being lovers. Patrick hesitating when I asked him to come here today. No wonder he was asking me about Dupont Circle; if I'd let him talk instead of running my nervous mouth, he'd probably have been seconds away from asking if I'd attended the annual Capital Pride festival there.

I don't say a word. I just slowly sink back down onto the flats of my feet, the top of Porter's face disappearing from my view. I straighten my skirt and turn, resigned, adding up my tally of humiliations for the morning. (1) My so-called date is a bust. (2) I'm a loser who can't tell straight from gay. (3) I'm no closer to finding Alex than I was weeks ago when I first came to town. (4) Porter witnessed the whole thing.

Patrick is striding toward me. "Nothing new in the storeroom," he says. His gaze darts to the second aisle, where Porter emerges from a section marked BLAXPLOITATION AND KUNG FU FLICKS. He's dressed in long gray board shorts and an unzipped army-green jacket with the words HOT STUFF embroidered next to a cartoon baby devil on a tattered breast pocket. His curly mop seems longer today; the bottom of his hair kisses the tops of his shoulders. His gaze connects with mine and sticks for a second, which does something funny to my pulse.

"Oh hey, Porter," Patrick says cheerfully. "How's Lana? Heard she was hitting the pro circuit."

"Indeed she is," Porter says, all lazy and casual. Still looking at me.

Patrick's eyes flit back and forth from Porter to me, like he's suspicious we've been talking behind his back. Great. Now I feel guilty on top of being humiliated. "Hey, Bailey, it's been fun, but my dad texted from the boat, so I probably should get back to work. Coffee sometime?"

He seems to mean it, surprisingly, and it hits me for the first time that, unlike me, he never thought this was a date. He just assumed we were two like-minded people hanging out. Does that make me an even bigger jerk if I walk away from this never wanting to see him again because he prefers another man's ham sandwich instead of my lady bits? I decide that yeah, it does. Add that to my never-ending list of major malfunctions.

"Coffee would be great. Or tea," I amend. "You want my phone number? Maybe we can catch some of the film festival together, or something."

"Sure," he says, smiling, and we head to the front of the store together, exchanging digits, before he waves good-bye, heads off into the fog, and leaves me standing outside with a tiny scrap of my dignity intact.

I should probably message Alex—just to feel things out, make sure he knows nothing about this fiasco. But at the same time, maybe I need to clear my head first. I wanted to find Alex so badly that I'd jumped to conclusions about Patrick and ignored good sense. That was a stupid mistake, but I don't want to beat myself up about it too much. I just . . .

I don't know what I want anymore, honestly.

"You okay?"

Porter stands next to me. The door to Video Ray-Gun swings shut behind us.

I let out a long sigh. "Yeah, I'm . . . just having a really bad day. It must be the fog."

"Can't be that," he says. "Foggy days are the best."

I wait for the punch line, but it never comes. He glances down at my knee; it's scabbed over from yesterday's takedown of the Maltese falcon thieves, but I was too vain to wear a Band-Aid today.

"I thought California was supposed to be sunny all the time," I tell him. "Foggy days are depressing."

"Naaa. They're kind of magical."

"Magical," I repeat dismally, not believing him.

"What, is magic too lowbrow for you?"

"Don't start with me today," I say, more weary than frustrated, but if he goes much further, I can't promise that won't change. "Do you enjoy picking fights with people?"

"Just you."

I search his face, unsure if he's teasing. "You fight with Pangborn all the time."

"Not true. He never fights back."

"So that's what you like?" I ask. "Someone who fights back?"

"Everyone enjoys a little witty repartee now and then."

Is that a compliment? I can't tell.

He shrugs one shoulder. "Maybe I do like someone who fights back. It's a mystery, even to me. I'm just a beach bum, remember? Who knows what goes on inside this simple brain of mine?"

Yikes. Awkward. Some part of me wonders if I should apologize for that, but then I remember all the craptastic things he's said to me.

A long moment stretches.

"Ever ridden a Ferris wheel in the fog?" he suddenly asks. "Oh! What about the aerial lifts?"

"Um, I don't do amusement park rides."

"Why?"

"They always break down and the seats are sticky."

Porter laughs. "Jesus, Bailey. What kind of busted rides do they have back in our nation's capital?" He shakes his head in mock disapproval and sighs. "Well, just because I feel sorry for your pitiful amusement park ride education, I suppose I'll take you on the Bees."

"What are the Bees?"

"The Bees. Buzzz." He tug-tug-tugs on my shirtsleeve, urging me toward him as he walks backward, smiling that lazy, sexy smile of his. "Those wires with the chairlifts that are painted like bumblebees? The ones that take people up to the redwoods on the cliffs above the beach? You board them next to the big golden wheel on the boardwalk with the shiny, shiny lights? Get to know your new town, Rydell. Come on."

"I just want somebody I can have a decent conversation with over dinner."
—Tom Hanks, *Sleepless in Seattle* (1993)

II

"What's the matter?" Porter asks as we head down the boardwalk. Then it hits me: like the Ferris wheel, the ticket booth for the Bumblebee Lifts is next to the stupid whale tours window. I didn't think this through.

"Crap. I really don't want him to see me again," I say.

Porter is confused for a second. "Patrick? Why would he care?"

My answer is a long, sad sigh.

"All right, all right," he grumbles, but I don't think he's genuinely irritated. I'm more convinced he feels sorry for me, and that might be worse. "Go stand at the gate over there. I'll be right back."

I don't have the energy to argue. I drag my feet to the chairlift entrance and wait while a stooped, Filipino man—name tag: Reyes—with a raspy voice helps a few stragglers off one of the lifts. Other than one other touchy-feely college-aged couple, it doesn't look like anyone else is waiting to get on. I don't blame them.

Tendrils of fog cling to the swinging seats, which look much like ski lifts, painted yellow and black. The fat wires that carry the lifts over the boardwalk to the rocky cliffs rest on a series of T-shaped poles; one wire carries the ascending lifts, one wire holds the descenders. Big white lights sit atop each pole, but halfway up the line the fog is so thick that the lights just . . . disappear. I can't even see the cliffs today.

"Mornin'," the Bumblebees' operator says when I greet him.

"What do you do if something happens to one of the lifts?" I ask. "How can you see it?"

He follows my eyes, cranes his neck, and looks up into the fog. "I can't."

Not reassuring.

After what seems like an extraordinarily long time, Porter returns, breathless, with our tickets and a small, waxed bag. "Yo, how's it hanging, Mr. Reyes?" he says merrily to the operator.

"No food allowed on the Bees, Porter," the elderly man rasps.

Porter stuffs the bag inside his jacket and zips it halfway up. "We won't touch it until we get to the cliffs."

"All right," the man relents, smiling, and he extends an arm to escort us onto the next lift.

Before I can change my mind, we're boarding a swaying chair behind the groping college-aged couple. Each seat accommodates two people, snugly, and though we're covered by a plastic yellow-and-black striped bonnet above, it leaves our torsos exposed. This means (A) the coastal wind whips through the chairlift against our backs, and (B) we have a perfect view of the lovey-dovey couple ahead of us and their roaming hands. Terrific.

The operator pulls a handlebar down that locks us in around the waist. I sneak a glance at Porter. I didn't expect to be sitting so close to him. Our legs are almost touching, and I'm wearing a short skirt. I make myself smaller.

"Fifteen minutes up," the operator says as he walks alongside our slow-moving chair, "fifteen minutes back down, whenever you're ready to return. Enjoy yourselves."

And we're off. My stomach lurches a little, which is stupid, because we're not even off the ground yet; these Bees need more zippity-do-dah.

"You all right, there, Rydell?" Porter asks. "Not afraid of heights, are you?"

"Guess we'll find out," I say as my dragging toes leave the ground and we begin to take flight, ever-so-slowly.

"You'll love it," Porter assures me. "It'll be great when we hit the fog in a few minutes."

Once the lift operator ambles away to the gate, out of sight, Porter unzips his jacket a few inches and sticks his hand inside. A second later, he's pulling something out. It's cream colored and about half the size of a golf ball. I smell vanilla for one glorious second before he shoves the whole thing in his mouth.

His eyes close in pleasure as he chews. "Mmm. So good."

"What is that?" I ask.

"Illegal to eat on the Bees," he reminds me, slipping his phone out of his shorts pocket. "You sure you want to break the rules?"

I skipped breakfast. I was too nervous about meeting Patrick. What a dork. I still can't believe that all happened. It's like a bad dream that I can't shake. And now Porter's got warm vanilla wafting up from his jacket, right in my face.

"What the hell, Porter?" I whine. "It smells really good."

"Gracie did mention that you've got a mean sweet tooth when it comes to pastries." He's flipping through his phone, digging out another ball of whatever it is he's got. I think it's a vanilla mini muffin. I smell coconut, too. That might just be him, though.

"See if I tell her anything again," I complain, kicking my feet as we lift a little higher off the ground.

"Here we go," he says, finding something on his phone. "New quiz. Let's make a deal."

"NO QUIZZES."

"I'll be nice this time," he says. "Promise."

"Why should I believe you?"

"Because I've got a pocketful of moon muffins," he says with a slow smile.

I don't know the hell that is, but I really want one. My stomach growls.

"Wow, Rydell. You have a dragon living inside there, or what?"

My head lolls forward as I make little weepy noises. I finally give in. "Okay, but if you piss me off while we're stuck on this stupid flying bumblebee, just know that my nails are sharp, and

I will go for your eyes." I flash him my freshly painted ruby reds, filed to a vintage almond shape.

He whistles. "Pointy. That's one glam manicure. And here I was, thinking you were aloof. Sugar brings out the demon in you. Porter likey."

I get a little flustered, but not enough to stop wanting the muffins.

"So here's how this works. First"—he pulls out one of his prizes—"this is a moon muffin. Local Coronado Cove specialty. Fresh out of the oven over at Tony's Bakery right there." He points backward. "You think you like those sugar cookies at work? Well, you're going to love this."

He holds it in the tips of his fingers. I snatch it up, give the sniff test, and then tear it in two, ignoring him when he acts like this is a mistake. I taste it. Totally lovely. Spongy. Light. Dusted in vanilla sugar. "Yum," I tell him.

Porter makes a victory face. "Told you. Okay, quiz time. This one is for both of us. It's a . . . friendship quiz. We both have to give answers and see how we match up. To see if we'll make compatible friends or bitter enemies."

"Pfft," I say around a mouthful of moon muffin, brushing crumbs off my boobs. "Enemies. Quiz over; give me another muffin." I wiggle my fingers in his face.

He laughs and bats away my fingers. "No muffin until we answer the first question. Ready? Question one." He starts reading. "'When we fight, (A) it's like World War Three, and takes days for us to speak again; (B) we fight hard but make up fast; (C) we never fight.' What do you think? A, B, or C?"

God, what is it with him and quizzes? Grace wasn't wrong; he's obsessed. "Not C, that's for sure," I say. "But not A, either. I guess we're B. We fight hard, but we make up fast. But that's mainly because you bribe me with food. Keep that up, and we'll be okay."

"B it is." He holds out another muffin without looking up from his phone. I take it while he reads the next question. "'Our favorite way to spend our downtime is: (A) surrounded by friends at parties, the more the merrier; (B) always on the go, never staying still; (C) chilling alone.'"

"I'm guessing you'll say one of the first two things, but I'm more of a C kind of girl. Does that ruin our score?"

"Nope. I'm C too, actually."

Umm, okay. I'm not sure I believe that. Then again, it's his day off, and he's hanging out in a video store by himself, which isn't how I pictured him. "Oh, look!" I say, gazing down my side of the chairlift. "We're almost above the Ferris wheel now."

The boardwalk looks weird from here, just small bursts of color, and the tops of buildings. Cars rush by on my left, but who wants to look at the town? Unfortunately, I can't help but glance forward and catch the couple in front of us with their hands all over each other. I think there's more than kissing happening— wow. I quickly look away.

"These lifts sure are slow, aren't they?" I complain.

"I've taken naps on here," Porter says. "No lie. Next question.

'If one of us has a problem, we will: (A) keep it to ourselves; (B) immediately come to the other for advice; (C) drop hints and hope the other figures it out eventually.'"

"Put me down for selection A." Delicately, I dip my hand into Porter's gaping jacket until my fingertips hit the waxed-paper bag and find another muffin. It isn't until I'm pulling it out that I look at Porter's face and hesitate.

"No, please, go on," he says. "Do help yourself."

I give him a self-conscious grin. "Oops."

"You always go around sticking your hands down boys' clothes?" he asks.

"When they're full of baked goods."

"Tomorrow I'm coming to work with ten pounds of pastries in my pants," he mumbles to himself, making an *ooaff!* noise when I punch him lightly in the arm.

"Next question, for the love of vanilla," I beg. "How long is this quiz, anyway?"

"Back up—you chose A for the last one? I chose B," he says, and I struggle to remember what the question was. "That probably screws up our compatibility factor. Last one. 'The most important quality in a . . . uh, friendship is: (A) that we share the same interests; (B) that we like each other; (C) that we're always there for each other, no matter what.'"

I swallow the last of my muffin. "What kind of question is that? Shouldn't there be another option, like, (D) All of the above?"

"Well, there isn't. So you have to pick one."

"I refuse."

"You can't refuse."

"Think I just did, Hot Stuff."

He snorts at that. "But how will we know if we're compatible?" he moans. I can't tell if he's only teasing me, or if there's something more beneath the silliness.

"Gee, I don't know. Guess we'll have to actually be friends and find out for ourselves instead of taking a quiz."

He shuts his phone off dramatically and shoves it in his pocket. "No one appreciates the fine art of a good quiz anymore. Oh, here we go. Buckle your seat belt; it's about to get weird. Hope you're not scared of the dark, or anything. Feel free to stick your hand inside my jacket again if you need to."

Just in time, I turn my head forward as the lift enters the thick bank of fog that's rolling off the ocean. Porter was exaggerating. It's not pea-soup fog. We can still see each other. But the couple in front of us is a little hazier, and except for the occasional truck or tall building, the ground below, too. And it doesn't really have a scent, exactly, and it's not wet, either. But it feels different in my lungs.

"Why is it so foggy here in the summer?"

"You really want to know?"

I'm not sure how to answer that. "Uh, yes, I guess?"

"Well, you see . . . fog forms over the water because it's cold. And the Pacific stays cold here for two reasons. First, cold air from Alaska comes down along the California Current, and second, cold water comes up deep from the bottom ocean by something called upwelling, which has to do with wind blowing parallel with the coast and pushing the ocean surface southward. This stirs up the Pacific and brings up icy brine from the bottom of the ocean, which is so cold, it refrigerates the ocean air, condenses, and creates fog. Summer sun heats the air and makes it rise, and the fog gets sucked up."

I stare at him. I think my mouth is hanging open, I'm not sure.

He scratches his forehead and makes a growling noise, dismissing the whole speech. "I'm a weather nerd. It's because of surfing. In order to find the best waves, you have to know about tides, swells, storms . . . I guess I just picked up an interest in that stuff."

I glance at his fancy red surf watch peeking out from his jacket cuff with all its tide and weather calculations. Who knew he was such a smarty-pants? "I'm seriously impressed," I say, meaning it. "Guess you're the guy to sit next to if I need to cheat in biology."

"I aced AP Biology last year. I'm taking AP Environmental Science and AP Chem 2 this year."

"Yuck. I hate all the sciences. History and English, yes. No sciences."

"No sciences? Bailey, Bailey, Bailey. It appears we are opposite in every conceivable way."

"Yeah," I agree, smiling. I'm not sure why, but this makes me sort of giddy.

He laughs like I told a great joke, and then leans over the bar.

"So what do you think of our California fog now? Cool, right?" He cups his hand as if he can capture some of it.

Testing, I stretch my hands out too. "Yeah, it is. I like our fog. You were right."

We sit like that together, trying to catch the ocean in our hands, for the rest of the ascent.

At the end of the line, a waiting chairlift operator releases our bar and frees us. We made it to the top of the cliffs. Along with a tiny gift shop called the Honeypot—I really hate to break it to them, but bumblebees don't make honey—there's a small platform here lined by a railing and a few of those coin-operated telescopes that look out over the ocean. If it were a clear day, we'd be looking out over the Cavern Palace, but there's not much to see now, so only a few people are milling about. It's also breezy and chilly, especially for June.

I never knew California had such crazy weather. I ask Porter to tell me more about it. At first he thinks I'm making fun of him, but after not much prodding, we lean against the split-fence cedar railing, and while we polish off the last of the muffins, he tells me more about ocean currents and tides, redwood forests and ferns and ecosystems, and how the fog has been declining over the last few decades and scientists are trying to figure out why and how to stop it.

It's weird to hear him talk about all this, and like the scars on his arm, I'm trying to fit all his ragged pieces together: the security guard at work with the lewd mouth who made fun of my mismatched shoes; the surfer boy, struggling to pull his drugged-up friend Davy off the crosswalk; the brother whose eyes shine with pride when he talks about his sister's achievements; the guy who high-fived me when I took down the kid who stole the Maltese falcon statue . . . and the science geek standing in front of me now. Maybe Walt Whitman was right. We all really do contradict ourselves and contain multitudes. How do we even figure out who we really are?

Porter finally seems to notice how much he's talking and his golden face gets ruddy. It's pretty adorable. "Okay, enough," he finally says. "What are you nerdy about?"

I hesitate, wanting to talk about classic film as passionately as he told me about ocean rain, but then I remember the incident with Patrick and my stomach feels a little queasy. I don't relish rehashing all that again. Maybe some other time.

"History," I tell him, which, though a compromise, is also true. "Confession time. I've been thinking lately that I sort of want to be a museum archivist."

He brightens, as if I've just reminded him of something. "Like, cataloging things?"

"Yeah, or I might want to be a curator. I'm not totally sure." Admitting it aloud makes me uncomfortable. I get a little squirmy and feel the need to flee the scene, but we're standing on a cliff, and there's nowhere to run. "Anyway, working at the Cave may not be a dream come true, but it's a start. You know, for my résumé. Eventually."

He squints at me, and I tell him a little more about my museum dream—which fits in with my Artful Dodger lifestyle: behind the scenes, low stress, geeking out over old things, preserving historically valuable pieces that most people find boring. As much as I love film, there's no way I'd ever want to be a director. I'm realizing that more and more. Put me in the shadows, baby. I'll happily plow through boxes of old files. "I like uncovering things that people have forgotten. Plus, I'm really good at organizing things."

Porter smiles softly. "I've noticed."

"You have?"

"Your cash drawer. Bills all facing the same way, creased corners straightened. Everything stacked and clipped together for the drop bag all perfect. Most people's drawers are a wreck, money turned every which way."

My cheeks warm. I'm surprised he's paid attention to details like that. "I like things neat and orderly." Stupid CPA blood.

"Orderly is good. Maybe you've got some science in you after all."

"Pah!" I exclaim. "Nice try, but no."

His eyes crease in the corners when he chuckles. "Guess you don't want to work in the Hotbox forever, though, huh?"

"God no," I say, pulling a sour face. "Not the Hotbox."

Just mentioning it by name makes us both thirsty, so we head inside the Honeypot and grab some drinks. By the time we're done with those, the sun's breaking through the fog—sucking it up, now that I learned that tidbit of science—and the warming midday air smells like my dad's backyard, of pine and redwood, clean and fresh. I breathe it in deeply. Definitely doesn't smell like this out east.

When we finally get back on the chairlifts, we're sitting closer. A lot closer. I feel Porter's arm and leg, warm against mine. His board shorts are longer than my skirt, his legs longer than my legs, but when the lift sways forward, our calves press together. I stare where our bodies are joined. For the tiniest of moments, I consider pulling away, making myself small again, like I did on the ride up. But—

I don't.

And he doesn't.

The bar comes down, trapping us together. Arm against arm. Leg against leg, flesh against flesh. My heart beats against my rib cage as if it's excitedly keeping time with a song. Every once in a while, I feel his eyes on my face, but I don't dare look back. We ride in silence the entire way down, watching the town get bigger and bigger.

A couple of yards before we hit the ground, he speaks up in a voice so quiet, I can barely hear him. "What I said the other day about you having champagne tastes?" He pauses for a moment. Mr. Reyes is smiling, waiting to unhitch our bar. "I just wanted you to know that I like the way you dress. I like your style. . . . I think it's sexy as hell."

LUMIÈRE FILM FANATICS COMMUNITY
PRIVATE MESSAGES>ALEX

NO NEW MESSAGES

"If what I think is happening is happening, it better not be."
—Meryl Streep, *Fantastic Mr. Fox* (2009)

12

I'm a mess. It's been eight hours since Porter and I parted at the Bees and I haven't been able to get his words out of my head. Sexy as hell.

Me!

He!

What?

He didn't say anything else, barely even looked at me when he told me he had to "skedaddle" because he promised to help his mom unload something at the surf shop that afternoon. I think I thanked him for the muffins and the chairlift ticket. I'm not even sure. I was so flustered. I might have told him I'd see him at work. Mr. Reyes asked me if I was okay, so I know I stood there too long, looking like a complete lunatic. Then I walked a half mile in the sand to the wrong parking lot and had to backtrack to get to Baby.

"That's all you're eating?" Dad asks from my left elbow.

I look down at my bowl. It's mostly full, but not because it's bad. It's really, really good, in fact. I'm sitting at a pink picnic table on the northern end of the cove, far from the madding crowd of the boardwalk. Wanda—sorry, Sergeant Mendoza—sits across the table. It's hard to think of her as a cop now, because she's dressed in jeans, and we're eating dinner with her on the beach in front of a pop-up food truck, the infamous posole truck. Also because Dad keeps calling her Wanda, and every time he says it, he smiles a little, only I don't think he knows he's doing it. I think they might be playing footsie under the table in the sand, but I'm too distracted to check.

Posole, it turns out, is this amazing Mexican slow-cooked stew made from dried corn, broth, chilies, and meat. They have red, green, and white posole for sale at the truck, and I'm having white, which is the pork kind, and the mildest. It's topped with sliced fresh radishes and cabbage, and there're plates of lime wedges at the tables. The sun is setting over the Pacific, so the sky is this crazy gold-and-orchid color, and the posole truck has these multicolored lights strung up over the tables, so it's all festive and fun. At least, it should be. But we can see a few surfers silhouetted in the dusky waves, and that's making me think of Porter, which freaks me out.

So no, I can't eat.

But I have to. I'm starving, and this is silly. I'm not going to be one of those girls who goes all woobly-woo over a boy and picks at her food. It's Porter Roth, for Pete's sake. We're practically archenemies. Look at our stupid compatibility quiz—didn't we fail that? Or did we? I can't remember now. All I remember is how cute and earnest he looked, talking about phytoplankton and ocean currents, and how the tiny hairs on his leg tickled when the chairlift rocked.

I feel feverish, just thinking about it again now, God help me.

But then, maybe he didn't even mean it. He might have only been teasing me. Was he only teasing me? A fresh wave of panic washes over my chest.

No, no, no. *This cannot be happening* is all I can think, my mind gleaming with terror.

I cannot like Porter Roth.

"Bailey?"

"Huh? No, I love it. Seriously. It's delicious," I answer my dad, trying to sound normal as I pick up my spoon. "I had a weird day, is all."

I push Porter out of my mind. Eat my soup. Concentrate on watching seagulls soaring around the shore. Then I hear my dad tell Wanda in a salacious voice, "She had a date today."

"O-oh," Wanda says, mouth curving into a smile.

"Dad, jeez."

"Well, you didn't tell me how it went. What was his name? Patrick?"

"If you must know, it went like this," I say, giving a thumbs-down sign and blowing a big, fat raspberry. "Turns out your daughter gets a failing grade in relationship chemistry, because, funny thing, but Patrick is gay."

Wanda makes a pained face. "And he didn't tell you before?"

"Not his fault," I say. "I guess I just made some wrong assumptions."

Dad grits his teeth and looks several shades of uncomfortable. He has no idea what to tell me. "Oh, honey. I'm . . . sorry?"

I shake my head. "Like you always say, never assume."

"Makes an ass out of 'me' and 'u,'" he finishes, quoting one of his favorite goofy word games. After a moment, he loosens up and drapes an arm around my back. "I'm truly sorry, kiddo. It wasn't meant to be, but don't let it get you down. This town is lousy with cute boys."

Wanda smiles to herself.

"Gee, Dad. I can't believe you just said that in front of your girlfriend," I say in a stage whisper, letting my head fall on his shoulder.

"Me either," he admits, rubbing my back. "Being a parent is weird."

Wanda wipes her mouth with a napkin, nodding her head. "So true. My baby is two years older than you, Bailey. And he's just gone through a crazy breakup."

"Wait, you have a son?"

She nods. "Been divorced for five years. He's nineteen. Went to a year of community college, and now he's taking summer classes at your dad's alma mater, Cal Poly. Electrical engineering. He's a smart kid."

As she's telling me more about her son, I dig into my stew,

wondering if I'll ever meet this guy. What if my dad remarries? Will I have a stepbrother? That's bizarre to think about. Then again, Wanda seems pretty cool, and the way she's talking about Anthony—that's her son—you'd think he was the most awesome guy on the planet. Besides, my dad's like me: He doesn't make rash decisions. I can't picture him rushing headlong into another marriage, not like Mom—who still hasn't called, just for the record. Not that I'm counting the days or anything, crying my eyes out for her like a ten-year-old kid who's been shipped off to summer camp and misses Mommy.

But still. One call? One e-mail?

If she thinks I'm calling first, she can think again. I'm not supposed to be the adult here.

When I'm done eating, I get up from the table and grab my phone out of my purse, which is stashed in the seat of Baby; I drove and met Dad and Wanda here. On my way back to the table, I notice that some of the distant surfers have stripped out of their wet suits. They've stuck their boards in the sand, propped them up like gravestones, and are trudging to the posole truck. My pulse leaps as I scan the three boys for Porter's face. I don't find it, but I do spot someone else limping across the beach: Davy.

Crud.

I don't really want to see him again, especially not while I'm with my dad. Unfortunately, no matter how low I duck as I sit back down next to my father, it's not low enough to escape his hazy gaze.

"Look who it is, little miss thing," he says in a rough voice. "Cowgirl. You work with Porter at the Cave."

I raise my hand a couple of inches off the table in a weak wave and lift my chin.

"Davy," he says, pointing at his chest, which is, as always, naked—even when the other two surfers are clothed. He's shivering. *Put a damn shirt on, dude.* "Porter's friend, remember?"

"Hey," I say, because it would be weird not to. But why did he have to mention Porter?

"Is that your Vespa?" he asks. "Sweet ride. Looks legit. Has it been restored?"

Wanda sits up straighter and speaks up before I can answer. "What are you doing out here, Mr. Truand?"

"Oh, hello, Officer Mendoza," Davy says, seemingly unfazed by her presence. "Didn't recognize you out of uniform."

"It's *Sergeant* Mendoza, and I can still arrest your ass, no matter what I'm wearing."

"I'll keep that in mind," he says, smiling like an insurance salesman.

Two older girls in bikini bottoms and T-shirts get up from a nearby table to throw away their trash, and Davy's friends start hitting on them in the worst way possible. All I hear is "ass for days" and "bury my face down there" and I want to either die or punch them all in the junk. The girls flip them off and after a short but brutal exchange, his friends give up and head to the posole truck like it's no big deal. Just another few minutes in their day.

Now that the circus is over, Davy seems to remember he was talking to me.

"So anyways, cowgirl, you're still invited. Remember?" He holds up a finger to his lips and winks at me. It takes me a second to realize that he's talking about the bonfire. I guess. Who really can tell when it comes to this idiot. I don't respond, and he doesn't notice. He and his buds are already distracted by the next thing—another car, this time full of more dudes. They race to go meet them. Thank God. I'm totally embarrassed to be on the same beach as these morons. They're bringing society down by several pegs, just breathing the same air as us.

"Go far, far away, please," I mutter.

"You know him?" Wanda asks, suddenly very concerned in a cop sort of way.

Now my dad's concerned too—in a father sort of way.

"No, no," I say, waving my hand. "He knows someone I work with."

"Porter Roth?" Dad says. "I thought he was a security guard, not a beach bum."

Guess that's where I picked up that phrase. "He is. I mean, he's not," I say. *Oh, crap.* I don't want my dad associating the two of them together. "Porter's not like Davy. I don't even know if they're really friends anymore. I ran into Davy on the boardwalk and he started calling me cowgirl because I was buying a scarf, and then he invited me to hang out, but that didn't mean I was going or anything—"

"Whoa," Dad says. "Slow down."

"Davy seems like such a dirtbag, ugh."

Wanda seems satisfied by my answer. "Stay away from him, Bailey. I mean that. He's trouble. Every time I bust him, he gets off on a technicality. But he's barely keeping his head above water. I'm talking serious narcotics—not weed or alcohol. He needs help, but his parents don't care enough to give it to him."

Jesus. I think about the vintage clothing store and that weird conversation I witnessed—how mad Porter was catching Davy coming out of the shop.

"But Porter isn't . . . ," I say, and wish I hadn't mentioned his name before I can even finish.

"Porter's okay," she says, and I hope she doesn't notice how relieved I am. "At least, I think he is. The Roth family's been through a lot, but they're good people. Still, you'd be better off staying away from that crowd. If Porter's hanging around with Davy, I'd advise you to steer clear and save yourself some grief." She says this last part more to Dad than me, and he gives her a little nod, like yeah, he understands. Message received.

Death by association. Porter Roth has now got a big red mark against him in my dad's book. I'm not sure what that means for me, because I don't even know what's going on between me and Porter. But if I did want something to be going on, hypothetically, does that mean it's impossible now?

I do know one thing: telling my dad about the bonfire is out of the question. Because chances that Wanda knows about this little

Saturday night hootenanny are pretty good, and he might ask her about it. Problem is, I really want to go now. Grace asked me, and I don't want to back out. Besides, Porter might be there . . .

But. (Why is there always a but?)

There's one person I haven't considered in any of this mess. Alex. Maybe I should ask his opinion. Or at least make an attempt to tell him what's going on. After all, he's probably just been carrying on, being his usual awesome self, while I've been spending the day wronging him left and right all over town, because I'm a horrible, horrible person. Doesn't he deserve a say-so in any of this?

LUMIÈRE FILM FANATICS COMMUNITY
PRIVATE MESSAGES>ALEX>NEW!

@alex: That horoscope prediction you gave me kind of came true in a weird way.

@mink: It did?

@alex: I followed your advice and it worked out. I took a risk and had one of the best days I've had in a long time. You were right. It's good to open yourself up to new things.

@mink: It's funny you say that, because I was going to ask your advice about whether or not I should do something. (This isn't about flying out there, by the way. Just so we're clear. Not saying it won't happen, but it's on hold for the moment.)

@alex: My advice is YES. Do it.

@mink: You don't even know what it is yet.

@alex: And I didn't know what your horoscope meant, but it worked out. Take a chance, Mink. You helped me; now I'm helping you. Whatever it is you're thinking about doing, my advice is to just do it. What's the worst that can happen?

"Nobody ever lies about being lonely."
—Montgomery Clift, *From Here to Eternity* (1953)

13

I don't work with Porter on my next shift. In fact, I'm not scheduled to work with him again until Saturday—not that I've obsessively checked the schedule. But the level of disappointment that hits me when I pick up my till and see Mr. Pangborn's white hair instead of Porter's tangle of curls is so crushing, I have to give myself a mental shake. Why am I getting so worked up over a boy? This isn't like me. At all.

"We're still on for tonight?" Grace says when Pangborn is escorting us to the Hotbox, merrily whistling what I think is a Paul Simon song. When I hesitate too long, she grabs my orange vest. "Don't you bail on me, Bailey Rydell."

"I'm not," I say, laughing as I push her away. "It's just complicated. I might need to fib a little to my dad about who we're hanging out with, so when you pick me up, don't mention any surfers."

She wrinkles up her face, and then gives me a *whatever* look. "Eight o'clock."

"Eight. I'll be ready, promise."

Pangborn does a little shuffling dance outside the ticketing booth door, one hand on his stomach, singing about some guy named Julio down by the school yard. "Yaa da-da-da-da!"

Grace grins. "That must be some fine chronic you got your hands on this morning."

"Nature's medicine, my dear," he corrects, making a quieting signal with his hand as he glances around—probably looking for Cavadini. "Never know who's listening around here."

A terrible thought crosses my mind. "You guys don't have sound on the security cameras, do you?" All the things Porter claims Grace tells him about me . . . what if he's been listening in on our conversations inside the Hotbox?

"Sound?" Pangborn chuckles. "We barely have sight. No, there's no sound."

Sweet baby Jesus. I sigh in relief.

"Why?" he asks.

"Uh . . . I just wondered if you guys were listening in while we gossiped in the Hotbox," I say, trying to cover up as best I can—and doing a crap job of it.

He chuckles. "No, nothing like that. We can't hear unless you call us, so gossip away. The system's old. Hasn't been upgraded in a decade, in fact. They're going to have to spend money soon. The offsite company that monitors the alarm system went out of business two weeks ago. Now if anything goes wrong in the middle of the night, all we can do is call the local police."

"Just call Bailey," Grace says. "She'll chase down criminals and jump them."

I bump her shoulder. "Shut it, Grace Achebe, or I'll start counting change as slow as Michelle."

"Noooo!" She waves her hand at Pangborn. "Hey, you gonna let us in any time soon? Not all of us have the luxury of your natural medication to make the day pass by faster."

The old security guard smiles goofily and knocks on the door, announcing, "Team Grailey reporting for duty, boys. Open up. I seem to have misplaced my key again. . . ."

After we're situated and on a roll, Grace turns off her mic and says, "Why were you asking Pangborn all that stuff about listening in on our gossip?"

"It's nothing, really," I say, but she's not letting it go. "I was just worried that Porter might be hearing our conversations."

"Why?"

"Because of some things he said a couple of days ago. It's nothing. Stupid, really. He knows I have a sweet tooth—"

"I told him that."

"Yeah, that's what he said."

"He's been asking about you lately. Quite a bit, in fact."

"He has?"

"Uh-huh." She glances at me from the corner of her eye.

"Like what about?"

She shrugs. "Just things. He's curious. That's his personality."

"Like a cat, huh?" So this is nothing out of the ordinary. She doesn't offer anything more, so I say, "Well, anyway. That's all there is. He was just teasing me with these muffin things on the Bees, and—"

I feel rather than see Grace's head swing in my direction. "WHAT DID YOU JUST SAY?"

"Oh my God, Grace. My ear holes. I didn't know you could be so loud." We still have a line, so I plaster a fake smile on my face and pass tickets through the tiny hole in the window. "That actually hurt my eardrums."

"But that's what you said, right? You said you were on the lifts with Porter? Why were you on the lifts with Porter?"

"It's a long story."

"We've got six hours."

I sigh. Between customers, I give her the short version of the story. I don't tell her about my ongoing hunt for Alex, because that seems too personal—I just tell her that I met Patrick and didn't realize I was barking up the wrong tree.

"Patrick Killian?"

I sigh. *How small is this town, anyway?*

"He should have told you," she says.

"I should have picked up on it."

Grace shakes her head. "I still say he should have made it clearer. No way both of you got signals crossed. Shame on him."

"I don't know about that," I say, but I appreciate her show of support.

She gives me the hurry-up signal.

I keep going with my story, leaving out most of the details, especially any details with secret feelings and legs touching. "He was just trying to cheer me up," I say, when I tell her about Porter and the Bees. "It was no big deal."

"Hmm," is all she says.

"What does that mean?"

"It means, that's all very interesting."

"Why?"

Four quick raps on the Hotbox door. I startle. Grace squeals. Four knocks only means one person. My nerves go crazy as Grace opens the door.

"Ladies," Porter says.

"Why, speak of the bloody devil," Grace says, giving me a smile that is so wicked, I can hardly believe it's on her sweet little face. I immediately regret I told her anything and try to signal back with my eyes: *IF YOU GIVE AWAY ANYTHING, I WILL STRANGLE YOU IN YOUR SLEEP.*

Porter glances at her, then me. I catch his gaze and try to look away, but it's like honey. I'm stuck. I can feel my insides melting and my heart trying to outrun a horde of zombies. I can't seem to inhale enough air. Stupid Hotbox. It's sweltering. I feel physically ill and fear I'm going to pass out.

"Hey," he says in a soft voice.

"Hey," I say back.

Somewhere in the distance, I hear a light tap-tap-tapping.

"Bailey." I really like it when he says my name. God, how silly is that?

"Yep," I answer.

"Customers."

Dammit. I manage not to say that aloud, but I do, however, spin around on my stool too fast and bang my skinned-up knee— which still hasn't completely healed—and yelp. The pain helps to break whatever crazy hoodoo spell Porter's got over me. Until something warm touches my hand.

I glance down. Porter's trying to hand me a folded-up tissue. My knee's bleeding again. I mutter, "Thanks," and press it against the newly opened scab while juggling the ticket window one-handed.

"You going to the bonfire tonight?" Porter says. He's talking to Grace, not me.

"Yep. I'm taking Bailey, if she doesn't lose her leg before the end of our shift. You never know in the Hotbox. It's a war zone in here. Better get out while you can."

"I'm getting, I'm getting," he says, pretending to be grumpy. Do I detect a jovial tone in his voice? Is he happy I'm going to the bonfire, or is that just my imagination? "Guess I'll see you both tonight, unless someone needs an ambulance first."

Grace shows up at my house promptly at eight. I've barely had enough time to change out of my work clothes into what I'm assuming is appropriate for a bonfire party on the beach, which for me means I'm dressed like Annette Funicello in one of the *Beach Party* movies from the 1960s: ruched red-and-white polka-dot top that fits me like a glove, scalloped white shorts, wedge espadrilles. When Grace sees what I'm wearing, she looks me over and says, "Cutest thing I've ever seen, truly, but you're going to freeze to death and then fall and break your neck. Ditch the shoes and find a proper jacket."

Crud. I trade the espadrilles for red sneakers. Meanwhile, my dad has fallen hard for Grace's charm and is trying to convince her to stay awhile and order pizza, play a game of The Settlers of Catan. She has no idea what that is, and he's doing a terrible job explaining. He's a long-winded talker when he's excited about stuff he likes, and I need to get us out the door, but now he's breaking out the ancient board game box. God help us all.

"Dad," I finally say. "We're meeting Grace's friends. No time for sheep trading."

He raises both hands in surrender. "Understood. You girls have fun. But, Grace, please bring her home at midnight. That's her curfew."

"It is?" I ask. We've never discussed such a thing.

"Does that work for you?" he asks. Now he's unsure too.

"Well, it doesn't work for me, Mr. Rydell," Grace says, "because that's my curfew too. So I'll have her home by a quarter of, because it takes me fifteen minutes to drive to my house from here. How's that, yeah?"

"Perfect!" Dad says, beaming. He's made the right parenting choice that syncs up with the choices of other normal parents. Life is good. And it's good for me, too, because now I can sneak out of here like some horrible juvenile delinquent daughter and go do something he wouldn't want me to do, while I've lied and told him we're going to the boardwalk. Before I lose my nerve, I grab a hoodie, tell him good-bye, and rush Grace out the door.

Grace drives a cute two-seater with a sunroof. All the way to the beach, she tries to give me the lowdown on who will be there and what the party could be like, but I'm still unprepared. The setting sun is turning the sky magenta as we pull off the road, well north of the cove, and park with a hundred other cars every which way alongside the highway, half in the scrabbly sand. Rocky cliffs rise up from the ocean, turning into mountainous coastal foothills in the distance. And the surf slams so hard here, it almost sounds like ominous music—only, there's that, too, pumped in from someone's car speakers. It echoes around a crescent-shaped bowl of jagged rock, a couple hundred yards or so below the road. And inside this crescent is a hollow sandy pit, where several dozen teens are congregated around a massive bonfire that throws wildly flickering light around the craggy walls.

The Bone Garden.

Grace and I make the downhill trek on a well-worn path through coastal grass. As we do, we're greeted by a motley array of scent and sound. Roasted marshmallows and skunky beer. Laughing and shouting and roughhousing. A boy crying in the shadows and another boy telling him he's sorry and please don't leave. *Me too, dude*, I think, because I'm having the same panic attack.

"Too late now," Grace says, sensing my need to flee. "It's a long walk back to civilization, anyway."

Like this calms me down?

Before I know it, we're leveling out, and she's seeing people she knows. And Grace knows everyone. She's hugging necks and waving at people. If there were any babies out here, she'd probably be kissing them. She's a natural-born politician, this girl. And she's introducing me to so many people, I can't keep up. Casey is a cheerleader. Sharonda is president of drama club. Ezgar was in juvie, but it wasn't his fault (I'm not sure what, but it wasn't). Anya is dating Casey, but no one's supposed to know that. And in the middle of all this, here's a surfer, there's a surfer, everywhere there's a surfer. Oh, a few skaters and bikers. One paddleboarder, because "that's where it's at," apparently.

There are just so many people. Most of them don't seem to be doing anything wrong, so as we wind through the crowd, I feel a smidge less guilty about lying to my dad tonight. Sure, I see a few people drinking beer and smoking, and I smell the same sweet scent that clings to Pangborn's clothes, so someone's passing around weed. But for such a big group, nothing crazy is going down. I mean, no sign of Davy and his bunch so far, fingers crossed. No sign of anyone else, either . . .

At some point during all this meeting and greeting, I lose Grace. I don't even know when it happens. One minute I'm listening to a confusing story about a fender bender involving an ice cream truck and an electrical pole, and the next thing I know,

I'm surrounded by people whose names I only half remember. I try not to panic. I just quietly slip away and pretend like I know where I'm going while I search for Grace's cropped hair, turning on my dazzling Artful Dodger charm: look casual and bored, but not too bored. Keep moving. That's the key to no one taking pity on you, the strange new girl. Because there are certain gregarious types who always will try to take you under their wing—the drama kids, for sure—and I can spot them circling like vultures. Must avoid.

But there's only so much pretend mingling you can do before people realize that you're just walking around doing nothing—not talking to anyone, not lining up at the keg that's sticking out from a pit in the sand, from which people are constantly pumping red plastic cups of nasty-smelling beer. So I finally make myself scarce and find an empty spot on a piece of driftwood in the shadows. The seating situation is a mishmash of rusting lawn chairs, wooden crates, flat rocks, and a couple of ratty blankets. It looks more haphazard than organized, like maybe some of this stuff just washed up on the beach earlier in the day, and I'm regretting I wore white shorts. It's probably cleaner sitting in the sand.

"Are you: (A) mad, (B) sad, or (C) lost?"

My stomach flips several times in quick succession.

Porter, or the silhouette of Porter, because he's standing in front of the bonfire, hands in the pockets of his jeans.

"C, lost," I tell him. "I had no idea Grace was so popular. She's also compact, so it's possible she's in the middle of one of these groups and I just don't see her. I was going to give her five more minutes to surface before I texted." I wasn't really, but I didn't want him to think I was going to sit here for hours alone.

"I think she was a fairy in a previous life. Everyone believes she's going to grant their wishes or something." He gestures at the empty space on my driftwood log. I gesture back, *Please, be my guest.* The fragile wood creaks with his weight. He mimics my pose, digging his heels into the sand, folded arms on bent knees. Firelight dances over the patchwork of his scars, etching shadowy patterns over his shirt. Our elbows are close but not touching.

I'm relieved he's not partaking in one of the various vices floating around. At least, he seems his normal sober self. No plastic cup in hand, no reek of smoke. Actually, he smells nice tonight, like soap. No coconut, though. I'm almost disappointed.

His head dips closer. "Are you sniffing me, Rydell?"

I rear back. "No."

"Yes, you were." He grins that slow grin of his.

"If you must know, I was just curious if you'd been drinking."

"Nah, I don't drink anymore." He stares into the bonfire, watching some idiots roasting marshmallows whose sticks catch on fire. "I remember being a kid and my parents hauling Lana and me over to my grandpa's house, and he'd have these wild parties on the patio. Surfers from everywhere came. I'm talking crazy stuff went down there. Drugs everywhere. Free-flowing booze. People getting naked in the pool. Famous musicians dropping by and playing in the living room."

"I can't imagine growing up like that." It seems weird. Foreign.

"Don't get me wrong. It wasn't like that in my house, or any-thing. My parents are the exact opposite. My pops, especially. I guess because he saw his dad partying all the time, he got sick of it. He's insanely competitive and everything is about surfing, so that means staying at the top of your game. No drugs, no drink-ing, staying in shape. Imagine an army drill sergeant and multiply that by fifty."

His dad and my dad couldn't be more different. I'm com-pletely thankful for that and once again feel a pang of guilt for lying to him about being out here.

"As for my mom," he continues, "she's just trying to keep the shop afloat, because after everything that's happened, she'd rather have us all at home than on the water."

I can understand why. "Do you . . . plan on surfing profession-ally, like your sister?"

"That's a sore question, Rydell."

"Sorry, never mind."

He shakes his head. "No, it's cool. It's not that I can't do it, physically. I'm pretty good." He smiles a little, giving me a sideways glace, and then shrugs. "It's just that for a while, after the shark, I had The Fear. And you can't have The Fear. The ocean will eat you alive." He blows out a hard breath, lips vibrating, and cuts his hand through the air as if to say, *The end.* "But I eventually powered through that. Funny thing was, once I did, I wasn't sure if I cared about it anymore. I mean, I still like surfing. I hit the waves almost every morning. But I'm not sure if I want to compete anymore. I want to surf because I enjoy it—not because I have to, you know?"

"I know exactly what you mean." And I do, because he doesn't light up about surfing like he does when he's talking about ocean currents and weather patterns.

Someone hollers Porter's last name. He glances up and curses under his breath. A towheaded figure strides around the bonfire.

"Hey, cow patty."

Oh, terrific. It's Davy. I think he's loaded. Not like he was that time in the crosswalk, but he's definitely been drinking, because he stinks, and he's got that stuttering laugh that stoners have when they're high. He's also not limping, which makes me think he's not feeling much pain right now.

"What's going on over here? You two look awfully cozy."

"We're just sitting here, talking, man," Porter says, highly irritated. "Why don't you go see Amy and we'll catch up with you."

"Oh, you'd like that, wouldn't you?"

"What are you talking about, Davy?"

"Trying to get me back for my past sins? Because I invited her here"—he nods lazily toward me—"but looks like you're making a play for her, which isn't cool."

Um, what? Grace invited me, but no way am I getting in the middle of this.

"You're wasted," Porter says carefully, pointing an unwavering finger in Davy's direction, "so I'm going to give you five seconds to get out of my face."

I'm getting worried now. Porter is more than intimidating: He looks scary as hell. I've never really known many guys like this, more on the man side of the sliding masculinity scale. Not up close and personal, anyway.

Davy does something with his face that might be classified as a smile. "Hey, relax, man. It's cool. Forget it. Brotherhood over Bettys."

Gross. Am I the "Betty"? Porter's knuckles press against the side of my thigh—a warning. I guess he's got this.

"Besides, I've been planning something special for you. You know what today is, right? Anniversary of Pennywise's death, man. I'm giving him a salute. Check it out."

Davy marches off around the bonfire, calling out for somebody to bring him the "salute," whatever that means.

"Idiot," Porter mumbles. "It's next month, not today. He's such a waste of space."

I'm just relieved he's gone and that no one's punching anyone, but when I see Porter's brow lowering, I know it's not over. There's a loud noise, and sparks shoot in our direction. We sway backward as the crowd o-o-ohs! Someone's hauling more wood onto the bonfire on the other side. Several someones. Wooden crates, pieces of chairs, driftwood—all of it's being tossed into the sandy pit. The fire roars up like a beast. The partygoers gasp in delight. In no time, it's twice as tall as it once was.

Loud cheers fill the beach. Fire big. Fire strong. The horde is pleased.

Well, not everyone. Porter, for one. He's pulling me to my feet and cursing a string of obscenities near the top of my head. "Do they ever learn?"

"What's the matter?" I say, and it's then that I notice the fringes of the crowd beginning to unravel: here and there, several people are starting to pull away and head up the trail to the parked cars.

"It's the bonfire," Porter says. "When it's too high, everyone can see it from the road. People who live around here tolerate it until they can see it. Then they call the cops. It's like a goddamn Bat Signal. Morons!"

But it's not just that. Something else is happening across the bonfire from us. I get Porter's attention and point to where two boys are lifting Davy onto a large, flat rock on the edge of the beach. The surf crashes into the rock, spraying his legs with foam. He doesn't seem to care or notice. He's too busy holding something up in his hand that looks like a big stick, and when he shouts for everyone to shut up, the crowd quiets and listens.

"In honor of all our fallen brothers who've bashed their bones against these rocks in the garden of good and evil, tonight, on the anniverseary-rey," he stumbles, and then gets it right, "anniversary of Pennywise's death, I'm doing a military-style three-volley salute. Ready?"

What the hell is he talking about?

"Oh, God," Porter says.

Davy turns to face the wall of rocks, perches the stick on his shoulder, and then—

My world changes.

I'm . . .

Not on the beach.

I'm fourteen years old, and I'm standing in the living room of our old house in New Jersey. I just walked home from school. And there's broken glass and blood dripping on the expensive carpet. And my mom is screaming, but I can't hear anything at all.

Then the carpet turns back to sand and the crowd's roaring gleefully and everything's back to being okay. Only, it's not.

"Bailey!" Porter is shouting in my face, shaking me.

I swallow, but my throat is too dry.

"Bailey?"

I really am all right now. I am. It's okay. I'm mainly afraid I'm going to cry in front of him, and that would be humiliating. But it's too late, because I check my face and a few tears have already leaked out. I swipe them away and take a few breaths.

Boom!

The terrible memory flashes again, but I don't disappear this time. It just rattles me, hard. Maybe it wasn't Porter shaking me before. Maybe I'm just shaking.

"Jesus, what's the matter?" Porter says. He's pushed hair away from my forehead, trying to check if I'm running a fever.

"I'm okay," I finally say, moving his hand away. Not because I don't want his help, but I need to see what Davy's doing. He's reloading. Three-volley salute, he said, so there's still one more. I think he's got a shotgun. It's hard to tell from here.

I hate this. Hate being like this. It hasn't happened in a long time. And I wasn't prepared. If I know it's coming, I can brace myself. But this . . .

Davy puts the gun against his shoulder. Final one. I cover my ears with both hands. For a brief moment, I see Porter looking anguished and confused, then he pulls my head against his chest and wraps his arms around me. *Boom!* I jump against him, but he doesn't let go. And it helps. The explosion is muffled. I have a solid anchor, and I don't want to let go. It's embarrassing how hard I'm clinging to him now, but I don't even care, because he's safe and warm. It's just that he's prying me off him, trying to tell me something, and I really should be listening.

"We have to go, Bailey," he's telling me. "Now."

I see why.

Red and blue lights. The police are here.

"To repress one's feelings only makes them stronger."
—Michelle Yeoh, *Crouching Tiger, Hidden Dragon* (2000)

14

"I have to find Grace," I shout at him as we're racing across the sand.

It's total chaos, everyone scattering, half of them clogging the upward trail to the parked cars—but that's where the police lights are.

"Gracie knows how to take care of herself," Porter yells back. He's got my hand locked in his, and he's shouldering his way across the main path, heading toward the dark area of the beach, away from the bonfire. Away from the people. "She's been in this situation before, and she's got a million friends who can get her home."

That doesn't feel right to me. I try to tell him that, but it's so loud, I can't even hear my own voice. Now it's two cop cars—not one. And it strikes me just now: What if it's Wanda? Would she arrest me, even if I haven't been drinking? I picture Dad having to come pick me up from the police station and my stomach twists.

"CCPD," a booming male voice says over the squad car speaker. "Hands up where I can see them."

Holy crap. They're arresting someone. Hopefully it's Davy and his rock-blasting shotgun.

Porter gets us past the main herd of fleeing cattle. We jog around a boulder and he spots a secondary path through dry coastal brush that a couple of other partygoers are climbing. It's dark but serviceable. "Stay low," Porter tells me, and we head that way, sneaking through the dry grass. Just before we crest the hill, we have to stop and wait for a cop car with a high-beam spotlight to finish sweeping the area. When I'm half a second away from having a stroke, I get a text from Grace: *Where are you?* To which I reply: *Escaping with Porter. Are you safe?* She answers: *Yes, okay. Was worried I lost you. Tell P to go N on Gold to Cuangua Farm. Text me when you get home.*

I show Porter the texts. He nods, and when the coast is clear, we jog past a million parked cars until we get to what appears to be a sky-blue Volkswagen camper van—the kind from the 1960s and '70s that are long and surrounded with a ring of windows. Surfer vans, my dad calls them, because they're big enough to haul longboards on top. This one is covered with peeling surfing stickers on the back windows and has painted white fenders. Porter opens the passenger side and slips into the driver's seat from there, then beckons me in after him.

"Shit!" He's shoving the keys in the ignition as flashing lights head in our direction again. The engine protests and doesn't want to catch, and it's like a bad horror movie. "Come on, come on." And then—finally!—it rumbles to life, loud as you please. Wheels spin, kicking up sand, and then we're off, turning away from this nightmare, trundling as fast as a fifty-year-old bus can go, which isn't very fast at all, but who cares? The whole nasty scene is in Porter's rearview mirror.

I click on my seat belt and immediately melt into the seat. "Jesus."

"Are you okay?"

"I don't know."

"Do you want to talk about what happened back there?"

"No."

His brow furrows. "I'm sorry about all that . . . about Davy."

"Yeah. He's a complete dirtbag. No offense, but why are you friends with him?"

Fingers lift and fall on the steering wheel.

"We grew up surfing together. He used to be my best friend. His family life has gone down the toilet, so my dad took him under his wing for a while, trained him. My mom felt sorry for him. He practically lived at our house for a while. Then he got hurt surfing a few years ago. Has a leg full of metal and pins."

The limp.

"He's in a lot of pain, and it screwed up any chance he had of surfing seriously. Made him bitter and angry . . . changed him." Porter sighs heavily and scratches his neck. "Anyway, he started screwing up, and I told you about how my dad is. He wouldn't tolerate Davy's BS, so he stopped training him until he gets his act cleaned up. And on top of all that, Davy basically thinks I'm an idiot for not wanting to go pro, because he says I'm privileged and throwing it away. Also . . ."

Whatever he was going to say, he seems to think better of it and clams up. I wonder if it had to do with all the drunken smack talk Davy was spewing at the bonfire. About that girl they mentioned outside the vintage clothing shop, Chloe.

"Anyway, I'm sorry about all that," he says. "I'll go talk to him tomorrow when he's sobered up. No use seeing him tonight. It'll just turn into a fistfight. Always does. And who knows, maybe he got arrested this time. Might do him some good."

I don't know what to say to that. I can't imagine having a best friend you hate. That's messed up.

"It smells like you in here," I say after a long moment.

"It does?" The steering wheel on this van is enormous. I just noticed. Also, the seat is one giant thing that goes across the whole front of the van. And there're tiny rubber monsters stuck to the dash: an alien and a hydra and a Loch Ness Monster and a Godzilla. Wait, not an alien: a green shark. Huh. They're all sea creatures—all famous water monsters. What doesn't kill you . . .

"Coconut," I say. "You always smell coconut-y." Then, because it's dark in the van, and because I'm wiped out from all the panic and my guard is down, I add, "You always smell good."

"Sex Wax."

"What?" I sit up a little straighter.

He reaches down to the floorboard and tosses me what looks like a plastic-wrapped bar of soap. I hold it up to the window to see the label in the streetlight. "Mr. Zog's Sex Wax," I read.

"You rub it on the deck of your board," he explains. "For traction. You know, so you don't slip off while you're surfing." I sniff it. That's the stuff, all right.

"I bet your feet smell heavenly."

"You don't have a foot fetish thing, do you?" he asks, voice playful.

"I didn't before, but now? Who knows."

The tires of the van veer off the road onto the gravelly shoulder, and he cuts the wheel sharply to steer back onto the pavement. "Oops."

We chuckle, both embarrassed.

I toss the wax onto the floorboard. "Well, another mystery solved."

"Not a big one. Let's get back to yours." He turns down a small road on the edge of town. This must be the way Grace suggested. "I remember you mentioning something about not liking movies with guns in them when you were with Patrick in the video store."

Ugh. This again. I hug my stomach and look out the passenger window, but there's nothing but residential houses and it's dark outside. "God, you really did hear everything that morning, didn't you?"

"Pretty much. What happened? I mean, I did tell you about the whole shark incident, and I barely knew you then."

"Yeah, but you're all open and talkative. You probably tell everyone that story."

"I actually don't." His head turns toward me, and I see his eyes flick in my direction. "People at school know better than to ask me."

And I didn't.

"Look, I'm not going to force you to talk about something," he says. "I'm not a shrink. But if you want to, I'm a good listener. No judgment. Sometimes it's better to get it out. It festers and gets weird when you bottle it up. I don't know why, but it does. Just speaking from personal experience."

I don't say anything for a long while. We just ride in silence together through the dark streets, silhouettes of mountains rising on one side of the town, the ocean spreading out on the other. Then I tell him some of it. About my mom taking the Grumbacher divorce case when I was fourteen. About her winning it for the wife, about the custody she got for the wife's daughter.

And about Greg Grumbacher.

"He started harassing my mom online," I say. "That's how it started. He'd post nasty comments on her social media. When she didn't respond, he started stalking my dad, and then me. I didn't even know who he was. He just started showing up after school a lot, hanging outside where the parents carpool. I thought he was one of my friends' fathers, or something.

"We only lived two blocks from school," I continue, "so I usually walked home with a friend. One day when I walked home alone, he walked with me. Said he was my mom's coworker. And because he'd done all this detailed research online, he rattled off all this stuff about her, so it seemed like, yeah, he did know her. And I was too trusting. A stupid kid."

"I did stupid things when I was younger too," Porter says softly. "What happened?"

"I knew something was wrong by the time we'd gotten to the door, and I wasn't going to let him into the house, but it was too late. I was small and he was big. He overpowered me and pushed his way inside. . . ."

"Shit," Porter murmurs.

"My mom was home," I continue. "She'd forgotten some paperwork she'd needed for a case. It was just a lucky coincidence. If she hadn't have been there . . . I don't know. Everyone's still alive today, so that's a good thing. Still, when there's a crazy man waving a gun around in your house, threatening your mom—"

"Jesus Christ."

Deep breath. I check myself, making sure I'm not heading into shaky territory again, but I'm okay this time. "It was the sound that caught me by surprise at the bonfire. That's what does it to me in movies, too. Cars backfiring sometimes have the same effect. I don't like loud explosions. Sounds stupid to say it like that."

"Umm, not stupid. If that happened to me, I'd probably be the same way. Trust me, I've got hang-ups." He makes a broad sweeping gesture toward the collection of sharks and hydras on the van's dash.

I chuckle a little at that, touching one of the bouncy sharks' heads, and relax. "Yeah. So anyway. I guess a gunshot wound isn't the worst possible outcome. And the guy went to prison, obviously."

"God, Bailey. I don't know what to say."

I shrug. "Me either. But there you go."

"Is that why your parents divorced?"

I start to say no, then think about this for a minute. "The divorce happened over a year ago, but now that you mention it, things never were the same after the shooting. It put a strain on our family."

He nods thoughtfully. "Mom says misfortune either breaks people apart or brings them closer. God knows our family has seen enough of it to know."

"But your parents are still okay." I try not to make this a question, but I don't really know.

He smiles. "My parents will be one of those couples you see on the news who are ninety years old and have been together forever."

Must be nice. I want to say I thought that about my parents too, but now I wonder if I ever really did.

He asks me for directions to my dad's place and knows the neighborhood; he's lived here all his life, so that's no surprise. As the van climbs the last few winding redwood-lined streets, we're both quiet, and now I feel awkward about what I just told him. And there's something else, too: a nagging sense that in the midst of all this, I've forgotten something. A block away from home, I remember. Alarm floods my chest.

"Stop the van!"

"What?" he slams on the brakes. "What's wrong?"

I unclick my seat belt. "I . . . I'll just get out here. Thanks for the ride."

"What? I thought you said it's the next street?"

"It is, but—"

"But what?"

I shake my head. "I can walk the rest of the way."

The confusion behind Porter's eyes sparks and catches fire. Now he's insulted. "Are you kidding? You don't want your dad to see me, do you?"

"It's not personal."

"Like hell it's not. What, my camper van is too busted for Redwood Glen? Are all the BMWs and Mercedes going to chase me back down to the shore?"

"Don't be an idiot. There are no BMWs here."

He points to the driveway in front of us.

Okay, one BMW. But it's not like my dad drives a brand-new luxury vehicle, or that we live in one of these fancy houses—his place used to be a vacation rental. He's dating a cop, not a doctor; he watches sci-fi movies, not opera. Come to think of it, Grace's family is way better off than we are. But Porter is being stubborn, and it's closing in on midnight. I don't have time to argue with him about petty stuff like this.

"I have a curfew," I tell him impatiently.

"Fine." He leans across my lap and pops open the door handle. "Get out, then. I don't want to embarrass you."

Okay, now I'm mad. How did we go from me spilling my guts to fighting? I'm totally confused as to why his feelings are so hurt. Is he really this sensitive? So much for the stereotype that girls are the only ones who wear their feelings on their sleeves. I think about something Alex told me online once: Boys are dumb.

Irritated and a little hurt myself, I push open the heavy door and swing my legs outside. But before I jump out, all my tumbling feelings stick in my throat and I hesitate. This isn't how I wanted things to end tonight.

Maybe he's not the only one being dumb.

"The problem is," I say, half inside the van, half out, "that my dad is dating a cop, and the three of us were eating at the posole truck the other day, and Davy was there, and he made an ass out of himself in front of them . . ."

I rush to get the rest of it out before I lose my nerve. "And she told my dad that he's bad news, and that he's involved with a bunch of serious narcotic stuff—and after tonight, I really don't ever want to see him again, no offense. But during all of this, Davy brought up your name in front of them, so when he left, I was trying to defend you to my dad and Wanda, and she said your family is okay, but by then the damage was already done. Because my dad has blacklisted Davy, and I basically lied to go to the bonfire tonight, so he thinks I'm at the boardwalk with Grace."

Porter makes a low noise.

"Anyway, that's why," I say. "Thank you for rescuing me. And for listening."

188 • JENN BENNETT

I get out of the van and shut the door. It's old and ornery, so I have to do it again. Then I slog up the hill toward my dad's house. I don't get far before the van's headlights go out and the engine cuts off. Then I hear change and car keys jingling as Porter jogs to catch up.

Wary, I glance up at his face as he falls in step next to me.

"You shouldn't walk alone at night," he says. "I won't let your dad see me."

"Thanks," I say.

Three slow steps in tandem. "You could have just said that in the first place, you know."

"Sorry."

"Forgiven," he says, giving me a little smile. "Next time tell me the truth *before* I mouth off and say stupid stuff, not after. Saves me from looking like a jerk."

"I kind of like you being all hotheaded," I joke.

"Hot Stuff, remember?"

"I remember," I say, giving him a smile. "That's my house, there."

"Oh, the old McAffee place. That's got the tree going through the sunroom in the back."

"Yeah," I say, amazed.

"My parents know everyone in town," he explains.

Maybe now he believes me about not being fancy. I whisper for him to follow me to the far side of the house near the mailbox, where my dad won't see or hear us approaching if he's in the living room or his bedroom. His muscle car is parked in the driveway, so I know he's home, but I can't see a light on. I wonder if he's waiting up. It's the first night I've stayed out this late, so chances are good that he's still awake—especially since we made such a big deal out of the curfew. Now I'm feeling guilty again. Or maybe that's just all my nerves jingle-jangling because it's almost midnight and I'm standing in damp grass with a boy I'm not supposed to be seeing.

"So," Porter says, facing me.

"So . . . ," I repeat, swallowing hard as I glance around the dark street. A few golden lights glow in the windows of nearby houses, but there's no sound but the occasional passing of distant cars and a frog singing along with some crickets in the redwoods.

Porter shifts closer. I back up. *He's always in my personal space,* I think weakly.

"Why did you come to the bonfire tonight?" he asks in a low voice.

I fiddle with the zipper on my hoodie. "Grace invited me."

"You snuck out of the house because Grace invited you?"

He steps closer.

I step back—and my butt hits cedar. *Crap.* I've run into the mailbox post. I start to shimmy around it, but Porter's arm shoots out and blocks me. *Damn!* Ten points for surfer agility.

"Not this time," he says, trapping me with his hand on the mailbox. His head dips low. He speaks close to my ear. "Answer the question. Why did you come to the bonfire? Why sneak out at all? Why risk it?"

"Is this a quiz?" I ask, trying to sound mad, but I'm really just insanely nervous. I'm cornered—which I hate. And he's so close, his hair is tickling my cheek, and his breath is warm on my ear. I'm scared and intoxicated at the same time, worried that if either of us says another word, I might push him away.

That I might not.

I'm trying-trying-trying not to breathe so fast. But Porter shifts, and the hand that isn't trapping me falls to the side. His fingers dance over my hand, a gossamer touch, and he traces soft patterns on my open palm, Morse code taps, gently urging, send a thousand electric currents of signals up my nerves.

"Why?" he whispers against my cheek.

I whimper.

He knows he's won. But he asks one more time, this time against my ear. "Why?"

"Because I wanted to see you."

I can't even hear my own voice, but I know he does when a sigh gusts out of him, long and hard. His head drops to the crook of my neck and rests there. The fingers that were teasing me with their little tap-tap-tapping messages now curl around my fingers, loosely clasping. And the arm pinning me to the mailbox is now lifting away, and I feel his hand smooth down the length of my hair.

A tremor runs through me.

"Shh," he says softly against my neck. I nearly fall to pieces.

I don't know what we're doing. What he's planning to do. What I want him to do. But we're swaying and clinging to each other like the earth might crack open beneath our feet at any given moment, and I'm a little bit afraid that I really might be having a stroke, because I can hear the blood swishing around in my temples and my knees suddenly feel like they've gone rubbery and I might collapse.

Then he freezes against me.

"Whatwasthat?" he slurs, pulling all his wonderful warmth away.

Now I hear it. Windowpanes shaking. "Oh, God," I whisper. I'm going to have a heart attack. "It's the surround sound on the TV. My dad's probably watching some stupid sci-fi movie. It shakes the windows during the battle scenes." *Now come back here.*

Then we hear a slam. That was no TV. That's the door to the—

"Carport!" I whisper. "Other side of the house!"

"Crap!"

"That way!" I say, shoving him toward a bush.

Two quick strides, and he's hidden. I hear the squeal of the trash bin in the carport and exhale a sigh of relief; Dad can't see us from there. But that was close. Too close.

"Bailey?" Dad calls out. "Is that you?"

"Yeah, Dad," I call back. *Stupid curfew.* "I'm home. Coming around."

Movement catches my eye. I turn in time to see Porter sneaking across the street. He's pretty good, I must admit. No Artful Dodger, but still. When he gets to the other side, he turns to look at me one last time, and I swear I can see him smiling in the dark.

"Never trust a junkie."
—Chloe Webb, *Sid and Nancy* (1986)

15

Tiny arms hug me from behind. I'm engulfed by the scent of baby lotion. "I'm so, so sorry," Grace's elfin voice says into the middle of my back as she squeezes me. "Will you ever forgive me?"

It's the following day, and I'm standing in front of my locker in the break room at work. We texted last night after Porter sneaked away—and after my dad got over being amazed that he never heard Grace's car drive up, and why didn't she come inside? Ugh. Once you tell one lie, plan on telling about twenty more, because they pile up like yesterday's garbage.

"There's nothing to forgive," I tell her. I'm just relieved she didn't think I ditched her for Porter—or ask why I was with him. "But for Halloween, I'm dressing up like a tree and you're going as a sloth. I'll carry you around while you eat my leaves."

"You probably could," she says, releasing me and flopping back against the lockers, arms crossed. "You've got all that secret strength for taking down adolescent boys. Were you on the varsity wrestling team back in DC? Coronado Cove's got a Roller Derby team, you know. The Cavegirls."

I snort a laugh. "No, I didn't know that, but I'll keep it in mind for this fall."

"Look, I really am sorry for losing you at the bonfire. I didn't mean to. I don't even know how it happened. Freddy started talking to me and you just disappeared. Someone said you were talking to the twins—"

"I was. They introduced me to someone else. I don't know. I'm not great at being social," I admit. "Anyway, it all worked out."

She glances around the break room. Only a few people are there, and no one's paying attention to us. "So, yeah. Do tell. Porter took you home? And . . . ?"

"And what?" *Crap. So much for avoiding that subject.* I can feel my face getting hot, so I busy myself feeling around inside my locker for some nonexistent thing.

"I'm just saying, the two of you are spending an awful lot of time together and asking an awful lot of questions about each other—"

"I haven't asked any questions." *Have I?*

"And you're giving him an awful lot of looks that say *I'd like to jump on you with my mighty roller-derby strength.* And he's giving you looks that say *I'd like to surf your waves.*"

"You are nutty."

"Mmm-hmm. Let's see about that," she murmurs, and then calls out past my face in a chipper voice, "Afternoon, Porter baby."

"Hello, ladies."

My heart rate jumps to a five on the Richter scale. I attempt to look casual, stay cool as I turn to my right. But there he is, hand braced on my locker door, and whatever self-control I tried to muster just blows away like paper napkins on a windy day.

"You're still alive, so I guess everything went okay with your dad," he says.

"No problems whatsoever," I confirm.

"Good, good. Glad to hear it."

"Yeah." Is it just my imagination, or does he smell extra Sex Wax–y today? Did he do that on purpose? Is he trying to seduce me? Or am I just being sensitive? And—what the hell?—is the air-conditioning broken in the break room, because it suddenly feels like the Hotbox up in here. Note to self: Do not think the words "sex" and "wax" while he's standing in front of you. Ever, ever, ever.

"So, yeah," he says, sort of smiling to himself while he taps on the top of my locker. "I was just going to tell you, uh, both—tell you both," he clarifies, looking over at Grace. "We got this new lock system . . . long story, but I have to help install it. So Pangborn and Madison will be dealing with all your Hotbox needs today. You know, in case you wondered where I was."

"Because we're always thinking about you," Grace says sarcastically.

"I know you are, Gracie," he replies, giving her a wink. He leans a little closer, hanging on my locker, and speaks to me in a lower voice. "So anyway, I was wondering what you're doing after work."

Heart. Exploding.

"What's that?" Grace says.

Porter playfully shoves her head away. "I think I hear someone calling you, Gracie. Is that Cadaver? He said you're fired for listening in on other people's private conversations."

"This is private?" she says. "It looks like a public break room to me, and we were talking before you sauntered up, if you do recall."

He ignores her and give me an expectant look. "Well?"

"I'm not busy," I tell him.

"Oh, good. Maybe want to get something to eat later?"

Be cool, Rydell. This sounds like it could be a date. "Yeah, why not?"

"Excellent. Umm, so . . . maybe we should swap numbers. We can leave from here, but, you know, just in case we need to call each other."

"Yeah, that makes sense." I notice Grace when I'm digging out my phone. She's standing next to me with eyes like two full moons. I think she might be temporarily stunned into silence. Which only makes me more nervous. And that's no good, because I can barely handle the basic exchange of a few single numbers, and I still almost mess that up.

"Okay, well . . . ," Porter says, tucking a curly lock of hair behind one ear. How can he be adorable and sexy at the same time? If he doesn't vacate the break room soon, I might swoon to death. "Go sell some tickets."

"Go lock some locks," I tell him.

He flashes me a smile and after he leaves the break room, I

quietly bang my head against the lockers. Lock some locks. *Who says that? What a dork. He's broken my brain.*

I look up and see Grace. She's still staring at me, all wide-eyed.

"Mmm—" she starts.

"Argh! Don't you say it," I warn her.

She keeps quiet until we get to cash-out. "I knew that lad was asking too many questions about you."

The only good thing about our shift is that it's insanely busy, so it passes quickly. I don't even see Porter once. Mr. Cavadini, either. Guess that lock business is time-consuming. So is being nervous, and by the time six o'clock rolls around, I'm wired and ready to get out of there. I count down my cash drawer, inform Grace that if she follows me out to the parking lot, I will slash her tires, and that, yes, I will tell her everything tomorrow, duh, and then I look around for Porter. Nada. No surfer boy in sight. But I do get a text from him: *Almost done. Meet you outside in five?*

Okay, cool. That gives me time to head out to Baby and swap my work shoes for some slinkier sandals, which I've got stashed under the helmet in my seat. I grab my purse from my locker and dash outside. The sky's looking dark. Overcast and grumpy. It hasn't rained since I've moved here, but it looks like that might change today. Driving Baby in the rain isn't my idea of a fun time, so I'm actually relieved Porter invited me out.

I . . .

Look around. To the left. To the right.

Where's Baby?

I parked her right here. I always do.

I double-check. I must be confused. Third aisle from the back door . . .

I spin around, looking for her turquoise frame and leopard-print seat. There's got to be an explanation. Maybe someone moved her for some reason, though. . . . I don't know how they would. . . . She was locked up. I always lock her up. Always. I go through exactly what I did when I arrived that afternoon, making sure I did—and yes, I know I did. I'm positive.

"Anything the matter, dear?"

It's Pangborn, strolling out from the employee entrance.

"My scooter's gone," I say.

"What? Gone?"

"I parked it right here at the start of my shift."

"You're absolutely certain? What color is it? Let me help you look," he says, putting a calming hand on my shoulder. "Don't panic just yet, now. Let's be sure first, okay?"

I blow out a breath and describe it. There are several scooters back here, but none of them are Vespas, none are vintage, none are turquoise, and, really, the employee lot isn't that big. I'm starting to feel dizzy. I think it's finally time to face facts.

Baby's been stolen.

"Aren't there cameras back here?" I say.

"Just over the building exits and the delivery door." Pangborn tells me. "Not on the lots and roads."

"That's the dumbest thing I've ever heard," I say. What kind of hick place is this? Don't they care if a truck pulls up and tries to rob the place?

I'm panicking now. What am I going to do? Should I call the police? Dad and Wanda drove to San Jose today to go dancing, or something. It's her only day off work this week. Now I've got to ruin their day? And how am I going to get to work for the rest of my scheduled shifts? And who's got my bike? Are they taking it around town for a joyride, with all my personal stuff in the seat? I think I'm going to be sick.

"What's going on?" Porter says, out of breath as he runs up to meet us.

"Her scooter's missing," Pangborn tells him in a quiet voice. He's still squeezing my shoulder. God, the old man's so nice, and that makes me want to cry.

"Missing, as in stolen?"

"Looks like it. Didn't notice anything unusual on the door cams, but you know how hard it is to spot anything coming and going way out here."

"It's impossible," Porter agrees, and he starts asking me the same questions all over again—when did I get there, where did I park, did I lock it? I snap at him a little and then apologize. I'm on edge and trying not to bawl my eyes out like a two-year-old kid in front of everyone, because—of course—now there are several other employees out here. And everyone's looking around the lots, making sure they don't see it abandoned in the regular parking area.

Just when I'm about to give up and call my dad, Pangborn says to Porter, "By the way, did your friend catch up with you?"

"Who?"

"The one with the bum leg."

Porter stills. "Davy?"

"That's the one. He was looking for you."

"Here?" Porter's confused.

Pangborn nods. "He was skulking around by the employee entrance when I was coming back from my . . . uh, afternoon medicine break." Pangborn's eyes dart to some nearby employees. "Anyway, he didn't recognize me at first, but I remembered him from when he worked here last summer for a few days. I asked him if he wanted me to page you, but he said he'd just text you."

"No, he didn't," Porter says. "What time was this?"

"Couple of hours ago?"

Porter's face goes as dark as the overcast sky. "Listen to me, Bailey. Does Davy know what your scooter looks like?"

"I . . ." It takes me a second to remember. "Yeah, at the posole truck. He saw me with it when I was with my dad and Wanda. Asked me if it had been restored."

Porter's head drops back. He squeezes his eyes shut. "I think I know who stole your bike. Get in my van. He's a couple of hours ahead of us, but I know where we can start looking."

I'm too stunned to talk until we're speeding away from the museum and headed south on Gold Avenue. I've never been this far on this side of town, and everything looks strange. That's when it hits me that I should probably ask where we're going.

"Is this the way to Davy's house?"

"No." Porter's angry. Really angry. The muscles in his arms are flexing as he holds the steering wheel in a death grip. "He'll try to sell it. He wants cash for drugs."

"Oh my God. Why me? Why my scooter?"

He doesn't answer right away. "Because he's pissed at me. Because he's mad about the party going to shit last night. Because he knows it was his fault. Because deep down he knows he's a screwup, but he hasn't hit rock bottom yet, so he's going to keep going until he's either dead or in jail."

I wait for several seconds, trying to figure exactly how to ask this, and then I just give up and come right out and say it. "What does any of that have to do with me and my bike?"

"Aghhh," Porter says, almost a sigh, somewhere between exasperated and guilty. "Because I went over to see him before work today, and we got into a huge fight. Somehow he's gotten it into his thick, stupid skull that you are . . ." He sighs now—a real sigh, low and long. "Okay, think of it like this. He's got the mind of a toddler, and because he thinks that I have a shiny new toy, you being that toy—not that you are a toy! God, I knew this was a bad analogy."

"Whoa, you are digging yourself in real deep, buddy."

"Look, he thinks I like you, therefore he wants you. And today I told him if he harasses you again or brings a gun anywhere near you, I will burn his goddamn house down."

Well. That's not something you hear every day. A foreign, uneasy feeling ping-pongs inside my gut.

"And because he's a brat, what he's doing right now is retaliation. If he can't have you, he's going to do dumbass, destructive things—like steal your shit and sell it for money, so he can get wasted and forget he's a total screwup. Because he's a maniac, and that's what he does."

"Jesus."

"Yeah," he says in a softer voice, one that's suddenly all out of rage. "So, basically, this is my fault, and I'm sorry, Bailey."

I glance down at my feet and line up the toes of my flats with the floor mat. "Davy *thinks* you like me, or you really do like me?" Last night in the yard seems like a million years ago.

Porter gives me a sideways glance. There's a wariness behind his eyes; he's not sure if I'm teasing. But the corner of his mouth lifts, just a little. "Both?"

"Both," I repeat softly, more than satisfied with that answer. "I think I understand now."

"So . . . ," he says, "I guess the real question is, how badly do you want to choke me right now for what's happened? (A) A little, or (B) a lot?"

I shake my head, both dismissing his question and unable to answer. I'm not mad at him. How could I be? It's not his fault that he's got crappy friends.

"Hey, Bailey? I'm going to get your bike back," he says, face turning stony and serious. "I meant what I said before. Davy will pay for this."

God help me, but at this moment, there is nothing I want more.

After another mile, the van slows, and I see where we're headed. On the left-hand side of the highway, just off the beach, a giant paved lot is banded by a sign that reads: MOTO PARADISE. There must be a hundred used scooters for sale here. Porter pulls up next to a fenced-in trailer that sits on the back of the lot and tells me to wait in the van. "This is the long shot, but it's the closest to the museum, so let's rule it out first. Just sit here and text if you see Davy. He drives a bright yellow pickup truck with blue lightning bolts airbrushed on the side."

Of course he does.

Porter's not even inside the trailer five minutes. My heart sinks. And it sinks again twice more, because we drive to other lots that look similar to this one, just farther out of town and smaller. Now I'm getting worried. What if it wasn't Davy? What if it was one of those two Richie Rich punk kids who tried to steal the Maltese falcon statue? Maybe they stalked me at work and were trying to get revenge. But Porter doesn't buy this. He says Davy has stolen stuff before, and that he never comes by the museum. It's too coincidental. I guess he's probably right, but I'm starting to freak out again, and I'm having a hard time thinking straight.

Porter is tapping the van's steering wheel. He snaps his fingers, and then tugs his phone out of his pocket and looks something up. A couple of minutes later, he's calling someone. That's a bust, but he calls someone else, dropping his family name—I hear him say "Pennywise"—and then a third person. That's the call that sticks, because he's suddenly all relaxed and loose-limbed, one hand atop the wheel, as he tells the person he's looking for Davy. After several grunts, he hangs up, and then five minutes later, someone calls him back.

"I think I may have a lead," is all he says after it's over.

So why doesn't he sound more hopeful?

A soft rain begins to fall. Porter turns on his windshield wipers as we pass a sign telling us that we're exiting Coronado Cove and another identifying some tiny township that has four thousand residents. Everything here seems to be about state parks and camping and hiking. Oh, and car repair—lots and lots of car repair. Auto body, auto detailing . . . auto restoration. There's a small industry built up out here, people who are into muscle cars and racing, and I wonder if this is where my dad bought his car.

But Porter's headed past the nicer places. He's going down a dirt road into the woods, to a cinder-block garage with a number six spray-painted on a door to the left of three closed bays. Carcasses of rusted motorcycles lay in heaps near the building, discarded with other metal scraps. This is some kind of motorcycle chop shop, a place good bikes come to die. I'm suddenly very scared for Baby. A little scared for us, too.

Porter parks the van several yards away, under the fanning branches of some pines. "Stay in the van."

"You must be kidding," I say.

"If he's inside, I don't want you to see what might go down."

He's scaring me a little, but I don't want him to know this. "No way. This area reminds me of *Deliverance* territory. We stick together."

He snorts, hand on his door. "That takes place in the backwoods of Georgia, but I'm not even going to ask how you know about that movie, because we don't have time. So just . . . come on."

Rain dots the dirt road in front of our steps as we make our way to the door with the red six. It's eerily quiet, no one leaving or coming, no signs that the place is even in business. But as we get closer, I hear the faint sounds of a radio and voices, and I get nervous.

As Porter lifts his hand to knock, the door cracks open. A goateed African-American man in a tight-fitting red T-shirt pokes his head out. He looks Porter over, eyes zeroing in on Porter's scars. "Roth?"

"Yeah. You Fast Mike?"

The man's face softens. "You look like your mama."

"Thank God. Everyone usually says that about my sister."

"Never seen her, but my cousin painted that old Thunderbird your mama had."

"Yeah? She sold that a couple of years ago," Porter says. "Hated to. She loved that bike."

Fast Mike looks past Porter and notices me.

"This is Bailey," Porter says. "The Vespa we're looking for belongs to her."

The man blows out a hard breath through his nostrils. He opens the door wider. "Better come inside, then. Got a feeling this isn't gonna be pretty."

We follow him through a small office with two tidy desks, a counter, and an old register. No one's there. Past an old couch and a coffeemaker, another door leads into the garage. Burnt engine oil and old paint fumes hit me as we step onto stained concrete. Seventies rock music plays on a radio on a work bench. Rows of fluorescent lights hum over three drive-in bays, the closest of which is occupied by two motorcycles. The middle bay is empty but for three people, sitting around in folding chairs, talking. But it's what's in the far bay that snatches 100 percent of my attention.

One mustard-yellow pickup truck, blue lightning on the side, passenger window covered in a black garbage bag.

And behind the truck: one turquoise Vespa with a leopard-print seat.

I feel like I might pass out. And maybe that's why it takes my brain a couple of extra seconds to realize that one of the people lounging around in the chairs is Davy. In a way that's good, because I suddenly feel like committing a wild and vicious attack on him. But in another way, it's really, really bad, because Porter isn't dazed like me. Just the opposite, in fact. He's a laser beam, and he's headed straight for his former best friend.

The two other seated people scatter. Davy now sees Porter coming and the look on his face is absolute panic. He rushes to leap up, but his foot slips, and he can't quite stand. Porter lunges with both arms, shoving him with so much unhinged violence that Davy flies backward. Boy and metal both slam against a concrete pylon and slide across the floor.

"You piece of shit," Porter says, stalking Davy to where he's now crumpled in a heap by the tire of his truck. "Too much of a coward to steal from me, so you jacked her stuff?"

Davy's groaning and holding his head in his hand. I'm worried he's got a concussion, but when he opens his eyes and looks up at Porter, there's nothing but rage. "I hate you."

"That makes two of us, junkie."

Davy cries out, a horrible battle cry that tears through the air and bounces around the garage. In quick succession, he leverages onto his good leg, grabs the folding chair, and swings upward. I scream. The chair bashes into Porter's face. His head jerks sideways. Blood spatters. The chair leg slips out of Davy's hands and sails through the air, clanging into his truck.

Porter's doubled over.

I try to run to him, but strong hands clamp around my arms. "Whoa," Fast Mike says in my ear. "He's okay. Let those boys work it out themselves."

But he's wrong. Porter's not okay. When he pulls his hand away from his face, there's blood all over it. A big gash crosses his cheek. Dumb boy that he is, he just shakes his head like a wet dog and refocuses.

"That's it," he growls and slams his fist into Davy's face. Hard.

After that, the whole thing is a mess. They're on top of each other, both throwing punches that land God knows where. It's not like a well-staged boxing match or a movie, it's just chaotic and weird, and more grappling than anything else. They're shouting and grunting and slugging each other in the ribs so hard, something's going to break or get punctured.

This is a nightmare.

I'm terrified they're actually going to kill each other. These aren't wimpy kids on the playground, giving each other bloody noses. They're rabid wolves, straining with muscle, teeth bared. And someone's going down.

"Let me go," I tell Fast Mike. I can't let Porter do this. If he gets seriously hurt, I don't know what I'll do. But I can help somehow . . . can't I? I look around for something to break up the fight. Maybe I can hit Davy on the head with something—

I can hardly believe what I'm seeing. Davy's grabbing Porter's hair—his hair! He has a fistful of Porter's dark curls, and he's wrenching his head back . . . is he going to bite his face? WHAT THE HELL IS HAPPENING?

Porter's lower body twists. He gives a powerful back kick to Davy's bad knee.

A sickening *crunch!* echoes around the garage.

Davy drops to the floor.

He doesn't get up. He's clutching his knee, mouth open. Silent tears begin falling.

Porter's chest heaves. All the veins stand out on his arms. A thick line of blood flows down his cheek and neck, disappearing into the black of his security guard uniform. "I'm calling your grandma, and I'm gonna tell her what you did today," Porter says as he stands over his friend, looking down at him. "I'm also telling my folks. I've given you so many chances, and you've thrown them all in my face. I can't ever trust you again. We're done."

"Love is the only thing that can save this poor creature."
—Gene Wilder, *Young Frankenstein* (1974)

16

We load Baby in the back of Porter's van. Except for the seat lock being popped, she seems to be in one piece. We found my helmet and all my stuff scattered behind the seat of Davy's truck. We also found my scooter lock hanging off his tailgate; he'd removed it with industrial bolt cutters.

Turns out that one of the two people sitting with Davy when we first walked into the garage was a friend of Davy's. Seeing how he was planning on helping Davy sell my scooter, I didn't say anything to the guy, but Porter told him to drive Davy to the hospital. When they left, Davy could walk—barely—but he was going to need X-rays. And probably some pain medication, which was just lovely, considering what I now know about Davy's history with drugs.

But after all that, Davy didn't say one word to me. He wouldn't even look me in the eye or acknowledge I was in the same room. Truth was, I couldn't really face him, either. It was humiliating for both of us, I guess. And I'm pretty much in such a state of shock over the whole fight that I can barely speak.

When we're ready to leave, Porter thanks Fast Mike, who advises me on a better-quality scooter lock. Turns out that his motorcycle garage isn't a chop shop at all; he was seconds away from kicking Davy out before he got the phone call about Porter looking for my Vespa. So once again, my assumptions and I are completely off the mark. He says to Porter, "Tell your mama next time she wants to sell a bike like that, to come to me first. I'll give her a good deal."

"You got it," Porter says, "We owe you big-time. You know anyone that needs a board, come by the shop."

Fast Mike gives us a wave. We race through the rain and hop inside the van, and then we drive away. The windows are all fogging up, and I'm trying to help, looking for the switch to turn on the defrost, but my hands are shaking. I'm still freaked out. I can't calm down. "The black button," Porter says, and I finally find it. I turn the fan all the way up and try to concentrate on making the windshield clear instead of the fact that he's still bleeding. It works until we come to the end of the dirt road.

"I think we should go see a doctor."

"It's fine."

"You're being ridiculous. Pull over at the first store you see and I'll get something to clean your wound."

He cranes his neck and appraises the damage in the rearview mirror. Yep. Listen to the smart person in the vehicle. Instead of turning right on the paved road to head back home, he turns left. Should he even be driving? Davy did punch him in the head a few times. *Or maybe he knows something I don't.* Now the road is going uphill. We're winding up some coastal cliffs, and the rain's coming down. And I see a sign that says SCENIC OVERLOOK. He slows the van and turns into one of those pull-over areas for tourists to park. It's got a couple of Monterey cypress trees and a redwood sign with a carving of the central coast of California and all the points of interest marked. It's also got a jaw-dropping view of the Pacific, which we might enjoy if it weren't overcast and drizzling, and he weren't bleeding all over the seat.

"This doesn't look like a store to me," I say anxiously when he opens up his door.

"We don't need no stinking store," he says in a way that almost reminds me of a line from a Mel Brooks movie, *Blazing Saddles.* I never liked that one as much as Brooks's other comedy classic *Young Frankenstein,* which I've watched online with Alex a couple of times. But it makes me a little guilty to think about that when I'm here with Porter.

Porter the animal. I'm still rattled over the insane amount of raw violence I just witnessed. And I'm not sure how I feel about it.

He jumps out, groaning, and heads around the van to a sliding side door, where he retrieves a small box. Then he comes back and slips back into the front seat and opens the treasure he's collected: a plastic first-aid kit covered in stickers.

"Surfers always carry supplies," he explains, rooting around the box with one finger. "We get banged up all the time."

After several seconds of watching him struggle, I realize his other hand is too busted up to use, and pity overrides whatever lingering shock I'm still experiencing. I snatch the kit away from him. "Let me see that. You can't nurse yourself, dummy."

"Oh, good. I did all this as an excuse for you to put your hands on me."

"Not funny."

"A little funny."

I find some alcohol swabs and a bunch of butterfly bandages, along with a couple of condoms, which I try not to think about too hard. "You scared the bejesus out of me. Look, here's a packet of Tylenol. It's been expired for a few months, but better than nothing. You have something to drink it with?"

"You need to work on your bedside manner, Nurse Bailey," he says, groaning as he leans to pick up a half-empty bottle of water wedged in the seat. He pretends to be irritated with me when I pretend to be mad at him as I hand him the pills. He swallows them and grunts.

I kneel on the seat and tear open a swab. The sharp scent of alcohol fills the van. We both make faces. He swings his door open, and the fresh air feels good. The sound of waves crashing against the rocks below is calming. Sort of.

Too chicken to start on his face, I tentatively pull back the collar of his shirt and swipe the cool swab over the dried blood on his neck. He shudders. "Cold."

"Sorry," I murmur. I make quick work of the trail of blood, but it's harder when I get to all his scruff. I unfold the swab, rearrange the first-aid kit in my lap, and get serious about cleaning him up. If I focus on this, then my mind will stop jumping back to frightening images of him ripping Davy apart like a wild beast. He leans his head back against the seat and closes his eyes.

"Porter?"

"Mmm?"

"Remember that time you saw Davy talking to me outside the vintage clothing store on the boardwalk?"

"Yeah."

"He didn't know I was listening, but I saw him come in the store and ask the girl at the counter, Julie, to help him out because he was going down to Monterey and needed something."

Porter's eyes fly open. "What? That's not what he told me."

"He was lying. And when he was talking to her inside the store, she said, 'I thought you were chipping.' And he told her that he was, but he just needed something for today, and that he promised it was only once, and she said she'd try to help him."

"I knew it." Porter hits the steering wheel.

I put a hand on his arm. He's going to reopen the gash on his cheek if he's not careful, and I haven't even gotten to clean it yet. "What's chipping?"

"He's such an embarrassment."

"Yeah, get that. Just tell me. Girl with the alcohol, remember? If you don't tell me, I will make you burn."

A sigh gusts out of his chest as he sinks into the seat, lazily propping one knee against the dash between us, making my knees press against his leg. I absently wonder if he did that on purpose—he's always closer than I'm comfortable being—but he's baring his cheek for me now, so I get back to work while he talks.

"Davy jacked up his leg surfing somewhere he shouldn't have been surfing three years ago. He wasn't watching the weather, and he took a risk. He had two surgeries. When the oxycodone prescriptions ran out, he started buying it from a kid at school. And when that ran out, he started looking for anything else—vodka, coke . . . but nothing kills the pain quite like opiates. And what's a better opiate than heroin?"

My hand stills. "Please tell me you're joking."

"It's surfing's dirty little secret."

"Like, shooting up?"

"As far as I know, he smokes it, but I'm not really around when he's doing it. I'm just going by what I've heard, and I've never seen any needle marks. That really, really stings, Bailey."

"I'm sorry. You probably need stitches. It's bleeding a little again." I push his hair back and see a nasty bump on his temple. He's lucky that chair didn't smash any bones in his face. I'm not entirely convinced it didn't, actually.

He winces. "Keep cleaning it, just be kind. Anyway, 'chipping' is something people do when they think they can outsmart heroin. They do just enough to get high for a weekend, or whatever, but don't allow themselves to have any more until the next weekend—cold turkey all week, so they don't go through with-drawals. If they aren't addicted, they're in charge, right?"

"That doesn't sound like it would work so well," I say.

"It doesn't. Because there's always that one holiday weekend that turns into three days, or they're having a bad week and need to blow off steam on a Wednesday. And before they know it, they're backsliding, and their conservative plan is busted. They're lying to themselves, thinking that they've got it under control. Like Philip Seymour Hoffman. People say that's what killed him."

I'm stunned. I know Wanda said Davy was into serious nar-cotics, but heroin? That sounds like something out of a movie. It doesn't happen in real life. Not to people my age, anyway. "Does this hurt?" I ask, lightly dabbing antibiotic ointment on his wound. It looks like a crevice in a dry desert, red and angry, cracked open.

"Nothing hurts when you're touching me," he says in a far-away voice.

I have to stop myself from smiling because I'm afraid he might open his eyes and catch me. And I don't want his eyes open, because I can look at him up close now. The sharp lift of his cheekbones. The way his wild curls, damp with misty rain, are honey where the sun has burnished them, darker beneath. The gentle upturn of the outer corners of his eyes, and the prominent jut of his nose.

"Is he going to be okay?" I ask.

"Davy? I really don't know," Porter says, sucking in a hard

breath as I fix a butterfly bandage to his cut. Three should do it, and that's all we have, so I guess it will have to. "I'm less worried about him right now, and more worried that you're sorry you ever gave me your number and will never go out on a date with me, because now you're thinking all my friends are trash and we really have nothing in common."

"Is that so?" I peel off the paper backing for the second butterfly bandage. "And why do you even like me if we have nothing in common?"

"Well, you're a knockout, obviously."

No one's ever called me this. I feel my chest getting fluttery and warm.

"And you laugh at my jokes."

A laugh bursts out—I can't help it. That's . . . so very Porter. It's self-absorbed and kind of endearing at the same time.

"Don't get me wrong, you're pretty witty yourself," he adds, cracking one eye open.

"Oh, am I? That's awfully generous of you."

He gives me a sheepish smile, chuckling, and shoves at my hands, because I'm playfully slapping him on the shoulder. "You're welcome. And, and—listen, now! Oww! I'm injured. Stop laughing, damn you, and listen to me. You have to admit, if you think about it, we get along really, really well when we're not fighting."

Is he right? Do we?

I think we just might.

Porter makes a growling noise. "See, but that's the other thing.

I talk too much when I'm around you. You make me feel way too comfortable, and that drives me bananas."

I laugh one final time and blow my hair out of my eyes. "You drive me bananas too."

There it is, that stupid, sexy smile of his. He reaches for my hand and stops halfway, groaning. "That is not a good way to move my arm."

Now I'm concerned again. I ball up the bandage papers and close the first-aid kit. "Davy didn't injure any anything serious, did he? Ribs?"

"If you want me to take my shirt off, all you have to do is ask, Rydell."

"I'm serious."

He sighs. "I don't think so, but I'm not gonna lie—starting to feel a little achy-breaky in the riblet region. Think I'd better take a peek, so you might want to look away if you're sensitive to dynamite male bodies. I don't want you swooning at the sight of raw surfer."

"Lord knows I've been forced to stare at Davy's naked chest a hundred times, so I'm pretty sure I can handle yours. Come on, let's see the damage."

But as he unbuttons his Cave guard shirt, it's the least sexy thing in the world, because all I'm preoccupied with is how I'm going to drive this van if he's got a broken rib. And it only gets worse when his shirttails flap open.

If I thought Davy was built, I was wrong. Davy is a twig. Porter is a cliff. He's what happens when people use all their muscles at once to balance on a tiny plank of wet wood on massive, monster waves every day for years. All at once, I'm amazed at the beauty of the human body, ashamed at myself for using mine to do nothing but walk around the block and watch movies on Dad's couch, and, most of all, I'm completely and wholeheartedly shocked by what Davy has done to him.

When people say black and blue, they mean later, after the bruises have had time to settle. But right now, his torso is mottled with big red welts, some of them slightly bloodied, some of them radiating jagged, crystalline lines of dark pink. It's a hideous map of bruises to come. The welt across his ribs looks like South America, it's so big.

His chin is tucked to his sternum as he holds his shirt open and inspects the damage, and I can tell by his groan that even he's startled. It hits me all at once. I'm freaked out that he's so hurt and didn't say anything, and I'm frustrated that he had to resort to testosterone-fueled rage to solve all this. I'm disturbed by all the violence I witnessed. I'm mad that he has a friend like Davy, and I'm still enraged beyond understanding that Davy stole my scooter.

But despite all that . . . look what he did. Look what he did. For me? And he's sitting here, in pain, falling apart, and all he's worried about is that I'm sorry I gave him my number and don't want to go out on a date with him?

It's just too much. I fall to pieces.

"Hey, hey," he says, alarmed, sitting up quickly, and then groaning a little. And that only makes me sob harder. He buttons his shirt halfway, covering up some of the evidence. "It's okay. I've had broken bones before. I'm not broken today, promise. I'm just sore."

"It's just awful," I say, choking back tears. "I'm so sorry you had to do that."

"He had it coming. You don't know everything he's done to me. This is just the last straw. Hey, whoa, shush." His hands stroke over my upper arms.

I calm down. Turn my head and wipe my nose on my shoulder. Brush away tears.

"There." He swipes a thumb over my cheek, going back over what I've missed. Traces the arch of my eyebrows. Chases a flyaway tendril of hair at my temple. "And you know what?" he says in a low, intense voice. "I'd do it again in a heartbeat, because you didn't deserve what he did to you. I will be your revenge."

My breath catches, and I am overcome. Before I even know what I'm doing, I lean forward and kiss him.

Not a polite kiss.

Not a gracious kiss.

And he definitely doesn't kiss me. O-oh, no. I'm the kisser, which is the first time in my life that's happened—not the kissing, I mean, the initiating. I mean, hello. Evader! Initiating is not my style. But here I am, mouth firmly pressed against his. I'm not ashamed to say that I'm desperate about it and more than a little insistent, and if he doesn't kiss me back soon . . .

But he does. Je-sus, he does. It's as if a switch flipped in his brain—by Jove, I think he's got it! And I nearly start crying again, I'm so relieved, so happy. But then his mouth opens over mine, and a switch flips on in my brain (ding!), and then his tongue rolls against mine, and a switch flips on in my body (ding! ding!), and holymotherofgod that feels good. We're kissing, and it's amazing, and his hand is stroking down my back, and chills are racing everywhere, and DEAR GOD HE'S GOOD AT THIS.

A massive shudder goes through me and I freak out a little. My head's suddenly filled with all the things he's said about being eighteen and sexual freedom, and there is no doubt in my mind that he's exercised his rights with other girls—which is fine, whatever. No judgment. It's just that I have . . . not, and all this super-filthy kissing makes me more than aware of the experience gap between us. Which worries me. And thrills me. And worries me.

(And thrills me.)

Dear God: Save me from myself.

He breaks the kiss—probably because he can sense all the internal freaking out I'm doing. And yeah, sure enough, he says, "Bailey?"

"Yeah?" I say, but now I'm done with the freak-out. Now that I see his face, I can't stop smiling. Because his eyes are like slits and he looks all dazed and confused, and that's how I feel: as if my body is a toy top, spinning so fast that I can't see anything outside the van. All I can see is beautiful banged-up Porter, and all I can feel is this delicious whirling, twirling, buzzing, and I don't want it to ever stop.

Now Porter's grinning too, and I'm sure we both look like raving lunatics. Thank goodness we're sitting in the rain in the middle of nowhere. "Hey," he says, all raspy and deep. "Am I crazy, or was that the best kiss you've ever had?" His smile is acres wide and miles deep.

He knows it is.

"Surprising thing is, it's the best you've ever had too," I shoot back.

Both brows raise, and then he laughs, eyes closed. "You win. Want to do it again? Maybe it was just a fluke. We should test it out."

We do. It was no fluke. I'm going to melt right through the car seat. It's ridiculous. This is how teen pregnancies happen, I'm fairly certain. I finally push him away, and we're both breathing heavy. "See, told you," I say. "Best you've ever had."

"Wanna know a secret? I knew if we ever would shut up and stop arguing, it would be. Come here. Don't get all shy now. I just want to hold you."

"You're injured."

"And you're soft. No more kissing, I promise. Please, Bailey. Let me hold you, no manhandling. Just for a little while. Until it stops raining. I like the rain."

He beckons me into the shelter of his arm, and since I'm on the side that didn't get too beat up, I gently curl against him.

He's warm and solid, and I try to be as weightless and small as possible, try not to cause more pain, but he pulls me against him more firmly, and I give in. He sighs deeply, and we sit like that together, watching the rain fall over the ocean. Not talking. Just us. Just quiet.

But in that quiet, images of his bloody fight with Davy race back. This body that's holding me right now so protectively . . . it was violently tearing another human being apart. How can he be both things—tender and brutal? Is this what boys are? Or is this what Porter is? He's so complicated. I swear, the more I learn about him, the less I understand who he really is.

His ferocity unnerved me today, so why did I kiss him?

And why do I trust someone who can shake me up like that?

I think of our heated arguments. If I'm being honest with myself, I'm not exactly an innocent bystander. He provokes me, but do I allow myself to be provoked? Do I want it? And what about my ruthless takedown of that kid who stole the Maltese falcon? Grace keeps teasing me that I've got secret strength, and it's starting to make me think more and more about my stupid therapist back in New Jersey and all his talk about me paying the price for my avoidance techniques. Shake up a bottle of soda long enough, when you take off the top, it's going to explode.

Am I more afraid of Porter . . . or the person he's unleashing inside me?

LUMIÈRE FILM FANATICS COMMUNITY
PRIVATE MESSAGES>ALEX>NEW!

@mink: Hey, sorry we haven't talked much recently.

@alex: MINK. I'm so glad you messaged me. I've been meaning to talk to you. You haven't made a firm decision about flying out here yet, have you?

@mink: No, why would you ask that?

@alex: God, it took you so long to reply, for a second I thought I'd lost you there. Anyway, that's actually a good thing. Things are crazy at work for me right now. So before you get your dad to buy a plane ticket, just check with me beforehand, okay? Since it's so busy here.

@mink: Yeah, okay. I've been busy too, actually.

@alex: Then you understand. So just let me know? In case my situation changes?

@mink: Okay. Sure. You know I never rush into anything.

"Fight back, you coward! Fight back!"
—Daniel Radcliffe, *Harry Potter and the Half-Blood Prince* (2009)

17

A couple of hours before my shift the next morning, sunlight is already breaking through the gray sky as I pull Baby into a narrow alley behind Penny Boards Surf Shop. Porter's supposed to meet me here. He says his dad can fix the wonky lock on my seat, since it appears that Davy took a crowbar to it and screwed up the lock. I'm nervous about meeting his dad. Really nervous.

This is a mistake. That's all I can think. I'm not sure how he talked me into coming here right now, but I didn't really know what else to do about my bike.

My own dad was none too happy when he got home last night from San Jose and I told him the story of the stolen scooter. If he only knew the entire story, he'd have a heart attack—so really, he's lucky to have a daughter who cares enough about the state of his ticker to make sure that he only got the bare details he actually needed. And those details were as follows: The bike was stolen from the Cave's parking lot, but one heroic security guard,

a Mr. Porter Roth, chased the unruly teens off the museum property, sustaining injuries in the process, and got my bike back. A
shame that Porter couldn't identify the boys who took it, otherwise he would have filed a police report.

"It all happened so fast," I told him. "I'm glad he was there."

"He didn't see the thieves' faces?"

Err . . . "It was raining. They hit him and took off running."

"I still think we should tell Wanda."

"The museum security is taking care of it, Dad. Let them do
their jobs, okay?"

My dad raised his hands. "All right, Mink. I'm just glad you're
okay. And Grace knows someone in town who's going to help you
get the seat fixed?"

Another lie. But it's necessary, because as great as my dad is in
a lot of ways, he's not handy. So he's fine with letting this mystery
person handle it; he's even happy to lend me money for a new
wheel lock. I don't deserve him.

So that's what started the stress train. What kept the train
chugging along the track was knowing I had to face Xander Roth,
son of Pennywise, survivor of the great white shark, father to the
boy I made out with . . . and then went home last night and
before I went to sleep did unspeakable things to myself under the
covers while thinking about all that making out with said boy.
Which is how teen pregnancies *don't* happen, I'm fairly certain.

Then, what sped the stress train up to full speed was getting those stupid messages from Alex this morning. Because it

sounded like he doesn't want me to fly out here. I mean, of course I'm already out here, but he doesn't know that. What if I'd already bought a plane ticket? And why did he suddenly get so freaking busy, anyway? Did he meet another girl? Because it sure sounds that way to me.

I don't know why this bothers me so much. It's not like I'm not doing the same thing (hello, double standard). And we never promised to save ourselves for each other. We might not even get along in real life. Isn't that why I was being so cautious in the first place, drawing out my elaborate map legend of the boardwalk and carefully tracking him down, just in case we weren't compatible?

It's just that nothing is working out like I'd planned. Alex and I have a connection—at least, we're simpatico on paper, but who knows about reality? On the other hand, Porter and I are simpatico in reality, yet we're also opposites. His life is pretty messy, and I don't like messy. Been there, done that. It's why I left my mom and Nate LLC in the first place. And then there's the small, eensie-meensie detail that I'm not even supposed to be anywhere near him, thanks to Wanda's police warnings, ugh. But that's part of the whole appeal, isn't it? Because being with Porter is crazy and exciting. And much like a great thriller film, I'm not sure who's going to end up dead by the closing credits.

A dark blue van pulls up behind me and parks in a space marked for the surf shop. But it's not Porter's van. And it's not Porter driving—or riding, for that matter. Two people jump out, both eying me with great curiosity. The first is Mr. Roth, wearing a lightweight yellow Windbreaker, one sleeve sewed up, and the second is someone I recognize from photographs as Porter's sister, Lana. They are both slightly damp, and, I assume from the droplets of water on the boards strapped to the van, have just come from the beach.

"Hi," Lana says, chewing gum, super friendly and open. "You're Porter's girl."

Am I? This makes my chest feel funny. "I work with Porter," I say as she saunters around the van. God, she moves just like him, slinky, like a cat. And she's wearing skintight long sleeves and shorts—whatever she's put on after getting out of her wet suit, I guess, but she's built like Porter too. Not model-thin, but muscular. Solid and shapely.

"Lana," she says, joyfully chew-chewing her gum.

"Bailey," I answer.

"Bai-ley. Yeah, I remember now," she says, slowly grinning. She's young and pretty, no makeup, long curly hair. Very laid-back. Open, like Porter. "He's yapped and yapped about you. Hey, Pops, this is the scooter Davy jacked."

Mr. Roth, who has completely ignored me up to this point, already has his hand on the back door to the shop. He looks at the scooter, then gives me a critical once-over. "You messing around with Davy?" he says brusquely. Not Porter. Davy.

Shock washes over me. "N-no. God no."

"Because the last one was, and why did Davy steal this if there isn't something going on?" He gives me a look like I think he's an idiot. "You expect me to believe my son comes home with his face banged up for no reason? Like he's just some hoodlum, fighting in the streets? I raised him better than that."

"Dad," Lana says, sounding almost as humiliated as I feel. "He was defending her honor."

"Why did it need defending?" Now Mr. Roth is waving his arm at me, angry. "Why did Davy steal this?"

"I don't know," I bark back at him, surprised at myself. "Maybe because he's a scumbag who thought he could make some quick cash. But I didn't encourage it. I don't even know him."

The door to the shop swings open. Porter rushes out, breathless. He looks . . . awful. The cut on his cheek is dark red and swollen. The bump on his temple is now an ugly shade of blue and brown. His usually perfectly groomed scruff is darker and thicker.

"Pops," he says. "This is Bailey Rydell. Remember, I told you about fixing the scooter seat last night? Like that one you fixed before, Mr. Stanley's."

Right now I'm wondering how a one-armed man is going to fix anything—and frankly, with his crummy attitude, I don't think I want him to bother.

His father doesn't say anything for several seconds. Then he looks at me. "I don't know any Rydells. Who're your parents?"

Before I can answer, Porter says, "I told you already. Her dad lives in the old McAffee place. He's an accountant. He's seeing Wanda Mendoza. Bailey moved here in May, from the East Coast."

"Oh, yeah. Sergeant Mendoza. She's all right," his dad says, still gruff, but a little softer, like he only half believes Porter, but maybe he's thinking about considering believing him one day soon. And—poof!—just like that, the interrogation is over. "Get inside and help your mom," he tells Lana before turning to Porter. "Go get the green toolbox out of the van. I'll also need the keys to her seat."

Mr. Roth isn't addressing me. I am dismissed. I'm not sure how I feel about this. Pretty lousy, I think. Porter used to think I was too fancy for him, but now his dad thinks I'm not good enough to date his son? And what was all that business about him assuming I was seeing Davy because "the last one" did? Is this the Chloe girl Porter and Davy were arguing about outside the vintage clothing shop on the boardwalk? Man. This guy is a piece of work. When Porter described him as a drill sergeant, he wasn't kidding. I think Porter dropping Wanda's name was the only thing that gave me a pass.

Coming here was definitely a huge mistake. I'm regretting it so hard and wishing I could leave somehow, but I can't see a way out of it.

When I give Porter my scooter keys, he mouths, *Sorry*, to me and squeezes my hand, and just this tiny bit of skin-on-skin contact feels like when you wake up on the weekend and smell breakfast cooking: completely unexpected and delightful. One crummy kiss (okay, two—okay, AMAZING KISSES), and my body doesn't even care that Porter's dad hates my guts and I'm seconds away from a panic attack; it's too busy enjoying all the actual, real, live tingles being generated by surfer-boy touch. Not good. I'm so terrified his dad will see me react, all I do is drop his hand like a hot potato.

Coward that I am, I'm about five seconds away from turning heel and running down the alley, never to return again, so when Lana nods her head toward the shop, I'm already in such a state of confusion, I just follow her inside. Better than staying outside with the drill sergeant. Or Porter—who I might swoon over in front of his dad. I can't trust myself anymore. WHAT IS HAPPENING TO ME?

"Pops doesn't mean to come off like that," Lana says as we head through a storeroom filled with shelves of boxes. "He's just grumpy. I think he's in pain twenty-four-seven, but he'll die before he admits it. You ever hear about the whole phantom-limb thing?"

"Yeah," I say. Vaguely. Amputees come back from war and still feel their missing limbs.

"I've heard him tell Mom that he still feels pain in the arm, even though it's not there. He has a lot of nightmares and stuff. He won't take pills or go see a doctor because he's scared of getting addicted. Our grandpa was an alcoholic. Pops doesn't want to turn into him."

I don't have time to process any of this before she pushes open another door and we're blinking into the sunlit windows of the surf shop. Redwood and brightly colored boards surround the walls; music plays from speakers hanging from the ceiling. It's not busy, but a few people mingle, looking at boards and wet suits, chatting around displays of gear.

Funny, but this is one of the places that was closed for lunch every time I came by to mark it off my Alex map; either that or I got distracted, because my favorite churro cart is outside—I can see it from here, along with the waves slamming against the pier—and it's that churro cinnamon scent I smell now, mixed with Porter's coconut wax. It's a heavenly combination, almost erotic. Definitely not something I want to think about when I'm meeting his family.

Lana serpentines around the displays, cheerfully greeting customers, and heads to the back of the store. She leans over the counter and tugs on the arm of a bronze-skinned middle-aged woman with generous curves and a massive cloud of frizzy ebony hair. Lana pulls her away from a conversation, whispering in her ear. The woman is definitely Polynesian, and definitely their mother. Like, whoa, crazy familial resemblance. Mother and daughter look in my direction. Both of them smile.

"Hello," the mother calls out, coming around the counter to meet me. She's dressed in jeans and a loose top. Unlike the rest of the family, she's not muscular and fit, but more on the soft and plump side. Her big cloud of hair is pulled behind one ear and hangs to her hips. "I'm Porter and Lana's mom. You can call me Mrs. Roth or just Meli. Everyone does."

God, she's so pretty . . . so nice. Smiling so wide. It feels like a trap.

"Bailey," I tell her.

"Bailey Rydell," she says, surprising me. "Porter tells me you work with him at the Cave."

"Yes, ma'am."

"Pops was super mean to her," Lana reports.

Mrs. Roth scrunches up her face. "I'm so sorry. He gets like that sometimes. The trick is to either play his junkyard dog game and show your teeth"—she imitates a snapping dog, which is kind of adorable—"or you do what I do and just ignore him."

"And don't let his big talk fool you," Lana says. "My mom totally wears the pants in this family."

"That's right, baby." Mrs. Roth wraps her arms around her daughter. "How'd you do this morning? Find anything good to surf?"

"Nah, just paddled. Porter was right, as usual. Onshore winds were crumbling the waves." Lana looks at me and brightens. "You should come out with us one morning, watch us surf. Porter likes it when someone's there to cheer him on instead of Pops yelling at him."

Mrs. Roth nods, smiling. "And boy oh boy, would he show off for you, my dear. You tell him you want to come see him surf one morning when the waves are fine. He'd love that. Just say the word, and he'll be texting you weather reports at the butt crack of dawn."

"He's obsessed with weather," Lana tells me.

"I know," I say too quickly, unable to stop myself.

They both grin back at me like I've solved some big family secret code.

Mrs. Roth glances over Lana's head and raises a hand to a customer. "Hey, baby?" she says to Lana. "Can you do me a favor and help Mr. Dennis?"

Lana makes a gagging noise. "Maybe when you start paying me an actual salary."

Mrs. Roth gives me a sheepish look. "Don't spread that around, okay? We're not forcing them into child labor; it's—"

"Technically, you sort of are," Lana mutters, giggling when her mom pinches her waist.

"—just that times are tight right now," Mrs. Roth finishes explaining.

"And Porter and I are the only suckers in town who'll work for free," Lana adds. "I'll go help Mr. Dennis, but only if you let me stay out an extra hour tonight."

"Half an hour, and go, go, go. He's got that pissy look on his face." Mrs. Roth swivels toward the front door and makes an exasperated noise; someone's unloading a stack of boxes by the front door. "Deliveries go through the back. How many times do I have to tell that guy? Oh, Bailey, I have to take care of this, I'm sorry. I wanted to do girl talk with you. Stay here."

As she races away to redirect the delivery man, I watch Lana struggling to pull down a surfboard from a high-up rack, where it's stacked in the middle of several others. She's all muscle—no eyelash-batting doll—but it's hard work, and she's breathing heavy, shaking out her arm and joking that she nearly smashed her hand getting the board out. It strikes me that there's no one else working here. It's just the four of them, running this place? And with Mr. Roth's limitations, that leaves all the physical stuff dumped on the mom and two kids, neither of whom are getting paid. And then Porter has to turn around and work full-time at the Cave.

This really, really sucks.

And what about when school starts in the fall, and when Lana and her dad go on the surfing tour? Is Mrs. Roth going to run the store by herself? How will Porter keep his grades up and help her and hold down his job at the Cave?

My phone buzzes with a text. Surprisingly, it's from Patrick, as in, Patrick of Killian's Whale Tours and my broken gaydar: *Hey. You free? Wanna get coffee at the Shack? I've got new stuff from the film festival.*

Well, what do you know? He doesn't think I'm a total loser after our "date" fail in the video store. Before I can text back, the back door swings open and Porter breezes in, a huge smile on his face. Delight rushes through me until I see his father behind him . . . then I freeze up. "Pops fixed the seat. You're good to go."

Mr. Roth hands me my keys without looking me in the eyes. I think. I'm not looking him in the eyes either. This might work if we both keep avoiding each other. "Still dented," he mumbles, "and it might stick when you unlock it, but there's nothing I can do about that."

"You'll just have to wiggle the key some and knock it with your palm," Porter volunteers cheerily.

"Or take it somewhere to get it fixed professionally," Mr. Roth says. "But the worst problem you'll have is locking yourself out, so you might want to carry your helmet inside with you until you're more sure about it. And get a better wheel lock."

"I'm headed to buy one right now," I tell him. I scratch my hand, uncomfortable. "Thank you for doing this."

Looking away, he grunts and shrugs the shoulder that doesn't have an arm. After a few seconds of awkward silence, just when I think he might turn and leave without another word, he pins me with a hard stare and points a finger in my face. "You really want to thank me? Next time you see Davy Truand, you call me day or night and I'll finish what Porter started. That boy is stupid and dangerous, and he's obviously got you in his sights, so I'll tell you what I tell my own daughter: You stay away from him as best you can, but if he comes anywhere near you, get your phone out and start dialing my number—hear me?"

Um . . . ?

I feel the rattle of the weird, low note that escapes the back of my throat. He's sort of yelling at me again, but it's in a concerned-parent way, and I'm not sure, but I think he's offering to kick Davy's ass for me now. I look at Porter for confirmation and he's grinning.

So very confused.

All I can do is nod. So I do, several times. This seems to meet

Mr. Roth's approval. He nods back at me, also several times. And then he tells Porter to quit standing around like a lump and help his mom with the delivery that's now coming around to the back door. I watch him head toward Mrs. Roth, and I'm stunned.

"He likes you," Porter whispers near my ear, sending a small cascade of shivers over my scalp. It freaks me out that he has that effect on me in public, especially when his family is halfway across the store.

I find my voice and ask, "How can you tell?"

"For my dad, that was practically hugging and welcoming you into the family. He said you have grit."

Artful Dodgers don't have grit. Is this because I snapped at him outside? It's hard for me to think too hard about it, because Porter is linking his index finger with mine.

"Hey, Porter," a voice calls out.

I drop his finger and look up to see Mrs. Roth smiling sweetly from the door to the back room, her dark storm cloud of hair haloed around her shoulders. "Aw, I'm sorry, kids," she says.

"You ladies met?" Porter asks.

"We did," she answers, "And Bailey's going to come watch you do your thing one morning."

Porter raises both brows and has a look on his face that's hard to decipher, like maybe he's embarrassed, but kind of happy, too. "Yeah?"

"If you want," I say.

"Yeah, maybe," he says. "You should come see Lana, for sure. If you can get up that early."

"Yeah, maybe," I say, mimicking him. "I mean, I know nothing about tides and waves, and all that, so you'll have to alert me when and where it's going down."

Mrs. Roth gives me an enthusiastic thumbs-up sign from the door and then quickly lowers her arm before Porter can see it. "Sounds like a plan to me," she says. "And I'm sorry to break this up, but I really need some help back here—Porter?"

"Sorry, duty calls," he tells me.

I shake my head, dismissive. I've got to buy that new wheel lock before work. There's plenty of time for that, but he's clearly got stuff to do here, so I don't say that. I just tell him I'm busy too, thank him again, and ask him to thank his dad again, who has disappeared with Lana. Mrs. Roth waves good-bye over the top of a stack of boxes when I leave through the back door.

I still have a couple of hours to kill before work, plenty of time to buy my new wheel lock, so I text Patrick back and make plans to meet up with him at the Pancake Shack as I test out my newly repaired seat lock. As I'm doing this, high up on the gutter of the roof, I catch a glimpse of white fur: a cat. Two cats, actually. It's my tabby from the churro cart, Señor Don Gato, and she's stalking a big, fluffy white feline. I laugh out loud—I can't help it—because it's just like that children's song. My Don Gato has found her true love.

"Don't jump," I call out to Don Gato. Both cats look down at me quizzically. "Trust me on this one, you'll only break your leg and die. That stupid white cat is not worth it. But if you do jump, remember that during your funeral, the scent of fish will bring you back to life—or probably, in your case, the smell of churros."

Don Gato plops down inside the gutter and starts licking his paw. She couldn't care less about my warning. Well, I tried. Somewhere on this boardwalk, I silently hope that Sam-I-Am is living a smarter life than these two love cats, risking bodily harm on the roof . . . and then I remember Alex blowing me off.

"You know what? Screw it. You've both got nine freaking lives," I call back up to the cats as I strap on my leopard-print helmet. "Live them a little."

LUMIÈRE FILM FANATICS COMMUNITY
PRIVATE MESSAGES>ALEX>NEW!

@alex: Hey, Mink? You're not mad at me, are you?

@mink: And what would make you think that?

@alex: I don't know. I was just worried that you might be mad when I asked you to check with me before buying a plane ticket to come out here. You haven't messaged since then.

@mink: I'm not mad. I would have thought you knew me better than that.

@alex: Err . . . Is that a joke? I can't tell.

@mink: Sometimes it's hard to tell someone's tone online. Anyway, too busy to talk now. Catch you later.

"Please let me keep this memory, just this one."
—Jim Carrey, *Eternal Sunshine of the Spotless Mind* (2004)

18

You'd think that two people who maybe, just might like each other (sometimes) and who definitely, usually (almost always) work together would find some time—or any time, really—to be alone. If not for kissing, then at least for talking. But an entire week passed, and all I got from Porter after the visit to his family's surf shop was a daily greeting, a lot of smiling, and enough desperate across-the-lobby stares to fill up the entire cavern.

Every day, I watched the bruises on his face lighten and his wound heal, but as they disappear, so does the memory of what happened between us, and I am feeling something akin to physical withdrawals. Sure, I received some texts from him during work hours. They included the following:

On a scale from 1 to Hades, how humid is the Hotbox today?

You should wear sandals to work more often. Your feet are sexy.

Maybe I'm the one with the foot fetish.

I thought about sneaking out to your house last night, but I didn't want to risk getting you in trouble with your dad if I got caught.

I'm tired. Let's go take a nap together in the big teepee.

And when he texted me, *I think I need medical care. Will you come nurse me again?* I nearly fell off my stool in the ticket booth. But when I texted him back that I would be right there, his reply was: *Sigh. I wish. Pangborn is sitting next to me. Awkward.*

The boy is killing me. K-i-l-l-i-n-g.

Things were much simpler when we were archenemies.

"Sometime I feel like Porter is Pangborn's nurse," I mutter under my breath.

Grace hands tickets through the window and mutes the microphone. "Know what I heard? That all that weed Pangborn vapes might actually really be medicinal. The old goat might have the big *C*."

I frown. "What? Cancer? Who told you that?"

"It's just a rumor going around. Don't know if it's true. You know how people talk. That girl Renee up in the café says she heard that he's been in remission for years, and that he just uses it as an excuse to get high. So who knows? He doesn't look sick to me."

Me either, but can you really tell? And it's not like I'm going to walk up and flat-out ask him. I hate rumors. It makes me sad that people are talking about Pangborn behind his back.

"What the hell is going on between you two, anyway?" Grace asks me as she adjusts the portable fan.

"Pangborn and me?"

She gives me a classic Grace eyeroll that clearly communicates: *You know what I'm asking about; don't play dumb.* "Porter and you."

"Beats me," I say, thoroughly grumpy. I'd already told her about the kissing. No details. Well . . . some details. Grace has a way of dragging things out of me. "Maybe he's dating someone else, and he's trying to juggle two girls at once."

Grace shakes her head. "No other girlfriend. He works at the surf shop after he leaves here every day. It's open until nine. Then he turns back around and works there every morning—and that's if he hasn't been surfing. When has he got time for another girl?"

Good point. I feel guilty for even joking about it.

"I saw him arguing with Mr. Cavadini about the schedule that just got posted," she notes as her phone buzzes. She checks the message, texts something back, and smiles to herself.

"And?"

She shrugs as she passes tickets through the window.

Now my phone buzzes with a text. It's Porter. *We both have tomorrow off. If you're not busy, would you like to go on a date? Time: tomorrow afternoon until? Chance of being caught by your dad: very low. (Please say yes.)*

I look up at Grace. "Did you know about this?"

"About what?" she says, the picture of innocence. "And, yes, I'll cover for you. You can tell your dad you're spending the day with me. But my parents want to actually meet you, so you're coming round for dinner on Tuesday. We don't play nerdy board games, but my dad cooks and will force you to help in the kitchen while he tells stupid jokes, so fair warning there."

"I owe you big-time, Grace." I can't type *Yes* fast enough.

The next day at noon, I park Baby in the alley behind the surf shop, neatly wedging her into a small nook between the building and Mr. Roth's van. Mrs. Roth says she'll keep an eye on it but assures me that no one in their right mind would steal anything from them. One look at Porter's scary-ass dad and I believe her. But I'm not really all that concerned about Davy rejacking Baby, I'm just relieved to stow the scooter back here, where my dad won't be likely to see it if he's out and about.

I slide into the passenger side of Porter's van and smooth the hem of my vintage-patterned skirt as he speeds out of the alley, making all the rubber sea monsters on his dash bobble comically. It's sunny and clear, a beautiful summer day, and we haven't said all that much to each other. We're both nervous. At least, I know I am, and I'm pretty sure he is too, because he's exhaling deeply an awful lot and not his usual chatty self. He hasn't told me where we're going yet, only that I should be prepared to do some strolling. "It's air-conditioned, don't worry. I wouldn't subject you to Hotbox temperatures on your day off," he told me yesterday in the parking lot after work. I've been in the dark about everything else.

"You really aren't going to ask where we're going?" he finally says when we're headed south on Pacific Coast Highway, following the ocean past the boardwalk and the Cave.

"I like a good mystery." I have a couple of flashbacks of our last trip this way, when we were looking for my lost scooter, but I'm not going to bring that up. Instead, I've been trying to solve the puzzle on my own, deducing things from the direction we're headed and the time we're leaving—not exactly primo romantic date time—and what he's wearing, which is a pair of jeans with an untucked wine-colored shirt that fits obscenely well across his chest. I can't stop sneaking glances at his arms. Because, let's face it, they are great arms. Great arms that lead to great hands . . . and I wish those hands were touching me right now.

Once you've had an amazing kiss, can you die if you don't get another one? Because I feel like that's what's happening to me. Maybe I like him way more than he likes me. God, that thought makes me feel off balance and a little queasy. Or maybe I don't like him at all. Maybe our relationship is being held together by the thrill of a good quarrel and raw sexual attraction, and my initial instincts about him were right. I hope this date wasn't a mistake.

"I'm glad you trust me," he says, relaxing for the first time today and showing me a hint of that beautiful smile of his. "Since we've got some miles ahead of us, let's test your musical tastes."

"Oh, brother." We both break out our phones, and he lets me scroll through his music library, finding we have little in common there—big surprise. But, and I'm not sure why this is, I'm almost glad about it. Because we spend the next half hour debating the

244 • JENN BENNETT

merits of the last few eras of music history—disagreeing about almost everything—and it's . . . fun.

Really fun.

"This is going to sound weird," I say after some thought, "but I think we're compatible arguers."

He considers this for a moment. "You enjoy hating me."

"I don't hate you. If I hated you, things would be much simpler, believe me. I just think we're good at arguing with each other. Maybe it's because we respect each other's point of view, even if we don't agree."

"Maybe it's because we like the other person so much, we're trying our best to convince them to come around to our way of thinking."

I snort. "You think I like you that much, huh?"

He holds his palms upward on the steering wheel, gesturing toward the open road in front of us. "I've planned this for an entire week like a complete loser. Who's the one who's whipped here?"

Warmth spreads up my neck and cheeks. I quickly stare out the passenger window and hope my hair shields the rest as I listen to him exhale heavily again. I'm happy and embarrassed at the same time when I think about how much trouble he went to arranging this. He argued with Cavadini for both of us to get the day off. And I wonder who's covering for him at the surf shop—his sister?

"I was beginning to worry you'd changed your mind about me this week," I say to the window.

I feel a tug on my sleeve. Porter pulls my hand across the seat and offers me a tentative, unsteady smile that I return. It feels so good to finally touch him again, and now I'm the one exhaling deeply. I'm still nervous, but it's a different kind of jitters. Before, my anxiety was singing solo. Now all this weird anticipation and jumbled excitement has added some strange harmonies into the mix. I'm a barbershop quartet basket case.

It takes us almost an hour to get to our destination, which is the closest nearby city, Monterey. It's about the same size as Coronado Cove, but it has a different feel. Fewer surfers, more boats and bicycles. Porter points out a few things, shows me Cannery Row, which was made famous by local legend John Steinbeck, in the book of the same name. We didn't read that in school—it was *The Grapes of Wrath*—but Porter's read everything by Steinbeck, which surprises me, until he starts talking about tidal pools and a marine biologist named Ed Ricketts who was immortalized in Steinbeck's book as a character named Doc. Then it starts to make sense.

We park a few blocks from the beach near a Spanish-style building with a terra-cotta roof and a stone whale sculpture out front. The sign on the wall reads: PACIFIC GROVE MUSEUM OF NATURAL HISTORY.

Porter clips his keys onto a leather strap that dangles from his belt against his hip as we stand across the street. He's examining the blank look on my face, which I quickly try to disguise. "I know this may seem strange. You're thinking, *Hey, we work in a museum all day long. Why would we want to come here?*"

"I wasn't thinking that." Maybe just a tiny bit. "I like museums."

And I really, really do.

"That morning on the Lifts you told me you wanted to work in a real museum one day," he says softly, shoving his hands in his pockets.

I nod, suddenly more than a little embarrassed and wishing I hadn't shared so much of myself with him—yet, at the same time, touched that he remembered.

"Anyway, this isn't really part of the date. We have an appointment."

"An appointment," I repeat, confused.

"Just . . . come on."

The building doesn't look all that big from the outside, and when we head past Sandy the Whale through the front doors and Porter pays the optional meager entrance fee, it doesn't pull a Doctor Who trick and look any bigger on the inside, either. But it's two stories and brightly lit. And it's packed full of natural specimens collected in glass cases—stuffed birds and animals, artifacts, dried plants, rocks—all from central California. And even though natural history really isn't my thing, it has an old-school museum vibe that immediately makes me fall in love with it.

Yeah, totally digging this.

"My parents used to take Lana and me here when we were kids," Porter tells me as we stroll into the main room and pause in front of an eight-foot-tall brown bear that stands into the second story.

"It's fantastic," I say, craning my neck to glance at the bear's face. And before I realize how geeky I sound, I add, "The lighting is excellent."

He's pleased. "Unlike the Cave, all this stuff is the real deal. And the docents are cool. They know their stuff." He glances at his surf watch. "We're a little early. We've got half an hour, which is almost enough time to do a quickie tour of the whole museum, if you're interested, that is."

"Half an hour until our appointment with . . . ?" I ask.

"You'll see." He tucks his wild curls behinds his ears, looking devious and excited, and for a brief moment I panic, wondering if I'm being led into some kind of *Carrie* situation—any second now, prom will be ruined by a big bucket of pig's blood being dumped on my head. I start to ask him about this, just to double-check, but he interrupts my horror-movie thoughts.

"No sense sitting around while we wait when there's so much cool stuff in here. There's a jumbo squid that Ed 'Doc' Ricketts donated and a preserved baleen whale eyeball," he says with the enthusiasm of someone who just scored two tickets to a red-carpet premier of the next Marvel blockbuster movie.

"Okay, I'm game." I'm still nervous about this appointment thing, but eager to see the museum at the same time, so I follow him.

Case by case, he guides me through the galleries of butterflies, mollusks, abalone, fossils. There's a garden out back, and a million taxidermied birds—California condors, ahoy! And when he finally points out the preserved baleen whale eye, I think it might haunt me forever. Especially when, as I'm leaning over to inspect it, Porter gooses my sides. I squeal so loud, a group of small children are startled. He can't stop laughing. I think we're in danger of getting kicked out, so I pretend to slug him in the shoulder a few times, and that alarms the children even more.

"It's always the quiet ones who are the most violent," he tells one of the wide-eyed toddlers as I drag him away.

"You're a menace to society," I whisper.

"And you've got terrible taste in boys. It's time for our appointment."

I follow him back through the galleries to a small gift shop, where we meet a jolly, brown-haired security guard named Ms. Tish. "You look just like your dad," she says, shaking his hand heartily. For the love of surfing, does everyone in California know the Roths? And do they all have an opinion on which parent Porter favors the most? It's ridiculous. Then it hits me that Ms. Tish is a museum security guard . . . and Porter's a museum security guard. Is there some secret guard network I don't know about?

Porter introduces me and says, "So, yeah, like I said on the phone, Bailey maybe wants to be future curator in an actual real museum—not a schlocky tourist attraction like the Cavern Palace—so I was hoping maybe you could give us a peek behind the curtain."

"Not a problem," she says, nodding toward a door marked STAFF. "Follow me."

I'm in a daze as she leads us through the back hallways. First she gives us a tour of the archives and storerooms, where a guy and girl are quietly tagging fossil samples at a big table, listening to music. They are nice enough when we're introduced, but you can tell that they're relieved we're heading back out. I don't blame them one bit; the solidarity I'm feeling is total and complete. Swap out those fossils with old movie stills, and this would be my dream job: peace and quiet, nothing to do but concentrate on what you love. Absolute bliss.

Then we're on to the museum offices, which look a lot different than the Cave's. It's smaller, sure. But people are actually working on stuff that matters back here. Real museum things—not making sales quotas and driving more customers. There are desks and clutter and flurry, and people are discussing exhibits and education programs and outreach.

Ms. Tish stops in front of an office marked with a sign that says EXHIBIT CURATOR. She knocks on the doorjamb and a handsomely dressed woman looks up from her desk.

"Mrs. Watts?" the guard says. "These kids are from Coronado Cove. They work at Cavern Palace. This one here says she wants to steal your job one day, so I thought you might to see what she looks like and prepare yourself."

I'm momentarily appalled until Mrs. Watts grins and stands behind her desk, gesturing for us to come inside. "A future curator? I'm delighted. Have a seat, why don't you?"

Everything's a big blur after that. She's friendly and asks a lot of questions that I'm not prepared to answer. When she realizes that I'm not really all that into natural history, I think she's disappointed, but Porter picks up my slack and starts talking about kelp forests and limpets and she's back on board. Then it gets better because she's doing all the talking, telling us what she does, and it's actually really interesting. And she's super laid-back and cool, and I do want her job—I mean, in a theoretical kind of way.

While she's talking, I sneak a look at Porter, and I'm overwhelmed. This is not technically a romantic date, but it's the most romantic thing anyone's ever done for me. All he had to do was take me to the movies. Heck, I would have been content to park at the end of the alley. Who does this kind of thing? No boy I've ever known, that's for sure.

I'm not certain how long we're in there—a minute or two?—but she gives me her business card, and before we leave she shakes my hand and tells me, "We'd never turn down a good intern. If you'd ever want to put in some time on the weekends, I'm sure something could be arranged. Shoot me an e-mail."

"Thank you," I manage to say.

Ms. Tish and Porter make small talk about surfing as we leave the museum, and I think he gives her someone's phone number to get free tickets to some sort of surfing competition event, I'm not sure. She seems happy. We both thank her and jog down the stairs in tandem, passing Sandy the Whale on our way back to the van.

"Porter."

"Bailey." Lazy smile.

"Porter."

"Bailey." Lazier smile.

"That was so . . . Ugh. I don't know what to say."

"You didn't think it was stupid?"

I bump his arm with my shoulder as we cross the street. "Shut up." I'm full-on lost for words now, completely thunderstruck. Could he be any nicer? Doing this today was beyond thoughtful. . . . It's almost too much.

I exhale hard several times. I'm unable to express how I feel. My words come out fast and crude. "Jesus, Porter. I mean, what the hell?"

He grins. "So I did good?"

It takes me several strides to answer. I swallow hard and finally say, "Today was great—thank you."

"Don't make it sound like it's over—it's not even two o'clock yet. Strap yourself in, Rydell; we're headed to stop number two."

I don't mean to laugh. I sound like a demented person. I think I'm nervous again. I also feel a little drugged. Porter Roth has that effect on me. "Where to now?" I somehow manage to get out of my mouth.

"If this place was a slice of my childhood, then I'm about to give you a front-row seat to my nightmares."

Porter's family has an annual membership to the Monterey Bay Aquarium, and it comes with a guest pass, so he gets us both in for free. This is no Podunk attraction. Porter tells me it draws two million visitors a year, and I believe that. It's huge and beautiful and more professional than anything in Coronado Cove.

Today the crowds are sporadic, and Porter weaves around them. He's clearly been here a hundred times, and at first I think it might be a repeat of the museum: He's going to be giving me a tour, pointing out all manner of marine life. But after we stop to watch a little kid nearly fall headfirst into the stingray pool, things . . . get so much better.

We start holding hands in the middle of the darkened kelp forest exhibit. Unlike the natural history museum, this place is completely romantic, and I hope Porter doesn't hear the little happy sigh that escapes my lips when his fingers slip through mine. I don't even care that his knuckles are making my fingers ache a little, I'm not willing to let go.

The next dark place is the jellyfish room. They are gorgeous, all lacy and ethereal, shockingly red and orange floating up and down in tubes of bright blue water. Porter's thumb follows their fanciful movements, skimming my palm in dreamy circles. A hundred shivers scatter over the surface of my skin. Who can concentrate on jellyfish when I'm getting all this hand action? (Who knew this kind of hand action could be so exciting?)

I would've been perfectly content to stay with the jellies, but a tour group is making things much too crowded, so we seek another place where it's less populated. We didn't exactly verbalize this to each other, but I'm almost positive we're on the same page.

"Where?" I ask.

He weighs our options. We try a few places, but the only thing that seems to be empty right now is the place he doesn't really want to go. Or the place that he does.

The open sea room.

And I think I know why.

"This is what I wanted to show you," he says in a gravel-rough voice, and I'm both excited and a little worried as we step inside.

It's almost like a theater. The room is vast and dark, and the focus is an enormous single-pane window into blue water and a single shaft of light beaming through. There's no coral, no rocks, no fancy staged fish environment. The point is to see what's like to look into the deep ocean, where there's nothing but dark water. It's effective, because it certainly doesn't look like a tank. It's endless, no perception of depth or height. I'm a little awestruck.

A few people mingle in front of the enormous viewing window, their black shapes silhouetted against the glass as they point at schools of bluefin tuna and silvery sardines gliding around giant sea turtles. We step up to the glass, finding a spot away from everyone else. At first, all I can see are the bubbles rising and the hundreds of tiny fish—they're busy, busy, always on the move—and then I see something bigger and brighter moving in the dark water behind the smaller fish.

Porter's hand tightens around mine.

My pulse quickens.

I squint, trying to watch the bigger, brighter thing, but it slips away, into the black deep. I think I catch sight of it again and move closer to the window, so close that I feel the cool glass against my nose. With no warning, bright silver fills up my vision, blocking out the dark water. I jerk my head away from the glass and find myself inches away from a ginormous shark gliding past.

"Shit!" I start to chuckle at myself for jumping, and then realize that my hand is being squeezed to mincemeat and that Porter hasn't moved. He's locked in place, frozen as if by Medusa's stare, forehead pressed against the glass.

"Porter?"

He doesn't respond.

"You're hurting my hand," I whisper.

It's like he doesn't even know I'm there. Now I'm getting freaked out. I forcibly pry my fingers out of his, and it's beyond difficult: It's impossible. He's got me in a deadlock, and he's crazy strong.

For a brief moment, I panic, looking around, wondering what I should do. Wondering if anyone else notices what's going on. But it's dark, and there's barely anyone in here. He's suffering in silence.

What do I do? Should I slap him? Shout at him? That would only draw attention to us. I can't imagine that helping.

"Hey," I say urgently, still working on loosening his fingers. "Hey, hey. Uh, what kind of shark is that? Is that the same shark that bit you?" I know it wasn't, but I'm not sure what else to do.

"What?" he asks, sounding bewildered.

"Is that your shark?"

"No," he says, blinking. "No, mine's a great white. That's a

Galapagos. They rarely attack humans." I finally break our hands apart. He looks down between us for the first time and seems to notice something's wrong. "Oh, Jesus."

"It's fine," I assure him, resisting the urge to shake out my throbbing fingers.

"Fuck." His face goes cloudy. He turns away from me and faces the tank.

Now I'm worried our beautiful, perfect date is ruined.

I have to summon all my willpower to push back the wave of chaotic emotion that threatens to take me under, because the truth is this: I've never been on a date before. Not a real one. Not one that someone planned. I've been on a couple of double dates, I guess you'd call them, and some spur-of-the-moment things, like, *Hey, do you want to go study at Starbucks after class?* But no real dates. This is all new territory. I need this to be okay. I need this to be normal.

Do not panic, Bailey Rydell.

I keep my voice light and tug on the leather key strap that dangles at his hip until he turns to face me again. "Hey, remember how freaked I got at the bonfire? Please. You aren't half as screwed up as me."

"You don't know that."

"Sorry, I do. This time you're going to have to trust me."

"Bailey . . ."

The shark swims by again, a little higher. I jiggle his keys in my palm. "I will admit, though, despite what I've been through,

Greg Grumbacher looks like a dandelion compared to that beast. Now tell me how big your shark was compared to the Galapagos."

His shoulders drop, his Adam's apple rises and falls, and the way he's looking at me now, suddenly clear-eyed and sharp, satisfied—as if he's just made an important decision—makes me feel all funny inside. But I'm not worried anymore—not about him, and not that our date is ruined. The danger has passed.

We both face the window, and he begins to tell me in a low, steady voice about the Galapagos and another impressive shark that swims by, a hammerhead, telling me sizes and shapes and diets and endangered status. And as he talks, he moves behind me and wraps his arms around my waist—questioningly at first, but when I pull him in tighter, he relaxes and rests his chin on my shoulder, nestling into the crook of my neck.

He knows all about these sharks. This place is therapy for him. And sure, he got stuck there for a second, but look at these things. Who wouldn't? Not for the first time, I'm amazed at what he went through. I'm amazed by him.

"In Hawaiian mythology," he says into my hair, his voice vibrating through me, "people believe spirits of their ancestors continue to live inside animals and rocks and plants. They call an ancestral spirit an *aumakua*—like a guardian spirit, you know? My mom says the shark that attacked us is our *aumakua*. That if it had wanted to kill us, it would have. But it was just warning us to take a good, hard look at our lives and reassess things. So we're supposed to honor that."

"How do you honor it?" I ask.

"Pops says he's honoring it by admitting that he's too old to be on a board and that he's better off serving his family by staying on dry land. Lana says she's honoring it by being the best surfer she can be and not fearing the water."

I trace the scars on his arm with my index finger. "And what about you?"

"When I figure that out, I'll let you know."

As the silver of the hammerhead shark glides past, Porter slowly turns me around in his arms. I'm vaguely aware of the silhouettes of the people who stand farther along the viewing window, but I don't care. In our little corner of peaceful darkness, it feels like we're alone. With my arms circling him, I dare to dip my fingers under the loose hem of his untucked shirt, reaching upward until I touch the solid, bare skin of his back. Right over the same place on me where one of my own scars is, though I'm not sure if I subconsciously mean to do that or if it's an accident.

He shivers violently, and it's the sweetest victory.

A pleasant warmth spreads through my chest. The water's reflection shimmers on the sharp lines of his cheekbones as he holds my face in both hands and bends his head to kiss me, softly, delicately, like I'm something special that deserves to be honored.

But the thing he doesn't know, the thing that shocks even me, is that I'm not the gentle guardian spirit; I'm the hungry shark. And I fear his arm won't be enough. I want all of him.

"You're sweet, and sexy, and completely hot for me."
—Heath Ledger, *10 Things I Hate About You* (1999)

19

If I was worried about dying from not kissing before, now the pendulum has swung in the opposite direction. We definitely overdid it. I got home well before curfew, at eleven, but by then, Porter and I had time to eat dinner in Monterey at a cool restaurant that served a raw ahi tuna salad from Hawaii called *poke*—so good—and lots more time to park at Lovers Point Park and watch the sunset behind the cypress trees as the waves crashed over the beach.

Or, in our case, not watch the sunset. Which is what we ended up doing. A lot.

And now my dress is covered in grass stains, and because of Porter's stupid sexy scruff, my face looks red and swollen, as if I got attacked by a swarm of angry bees. And did he really give me three hickeys on my neck? THREE? He swore it was an accident, and that I'm "too white" and bruise too easily. At first I got a little offended by this, but maybe it could be true, because I don't remember any Hoover-like suction happening during the proceedings. And he did apologize a million times. . . .

Then again, I was pretty distracted, because we were lying in the grass on an elevated area above the beach, and he was pressed against me and it was delightful. I mean, nothing serious happened, really. Mostly just a lot of touching that didn't stray to any untoward areas, unless my hips and side boobs count. (They don't, in my opinion, but it was nice. Very nice.) But there was a lot of heavy breathing, and we both agreed once again that we are compatible arguers and kissers. And when he dropped me off at the surf shop, he tapped his temple and told me, "Today is moving up in the brain bank as best day in recent memory."

In my own brain bank, my Artful Dodger eyes turned into cartoon hearts that pinwheeled.

But things got a little tricky after that.

"What in the name of planet Earth happened to you?" my dad said when I walked in the door, looking at my unholy, bedraggled state.

"Grace and I were goofing around outside in the grass," I said. "Just wrestling and stuff with some other people from work. No big deal."

He made a face. "Wrestling?"

Yeah. That sounded like me, all right. I mentally cringed.

"What happened to your mouth?" he asked. He looked appalled and concerned, like I was contagious, and held the sides of my head while he inspected me, lest he catch it too. "Did you get into poison oak or something?"

"Uh, maybe?"

"Should I get some oatmeal? I don't have any calamine lotion. Should I go to the twenty-four-hour drugstore?"

I was pretty much horrified at this point. "I'm sure I'll be fine. Just a mild burn or something."

My dad narrowed his eyes at me. His gaze wandered lower. Don't look at my neck, don't look at my neck, don't—

Uh-oh.

Now we were both horrified. He released my head. "Okay. If you're sure."

"Yep-yep-yep, so sure," I said.

"Did you find your film-fanatic guy? What's his name, Alex?"

I made a face, because just the mention of his name stings. "I'm not speaking to him at the moment. I think he's got a girlfriend now, because he blew me off. And no, I haven't found him yet."

"Bailey—"

"Dad, just . . . please don't."

"Let me say this, okay?" he said, suddenly irritated, which is really unlike him, so it took me aback. And it took him a moment to calm down enough to finish. But when he spoke again, he was serious and eerily fatherly. "You have grown into a beautiful young lady, and people are going to take notice of that, which I don't particularly relish."

Oh, brother.

He raised a hand. "But I accept it. However, what I want to

talk about is you. Because the thing is, Mink, sometimes when traumatic things happen to people, they retreat until they feel comfortable. Which is okay. But when they're finally ready to step back into the world, they can be overconfident and make mistakes. Which is not okay. Do you understand what I'm saying?"

"Not exactly."

"Do you remember when your mom had just won that big divorce case for that state senator and was driving too fast on that icy road in Newark on the way to Mr. Katter's party and the car slid, and then, instead of easing us back on the road, she yanked the wheel and oversteered in the other direction, and we overturned into the ditch?"

"Yeah," I said. We all nearly died. It was a nightmare. Hard to forget.

"Think about that."

Cryptic, but I got what he was saying. He thought I was whoring myself out with some stranger just for kicks. For a brief moment, I wanted to break down and tell him everything about Porter, that I wasn't oversteering and throwing caution to the wind. And for the love of guns, it had been four years! How long did I have to be in "trauma" mode? Wasn't I allowed to make some decisions for myself and enjoy life? I appreciated his heartfelt concern, but I knew what I was doing . . .

Mostly.

Anyway, that's all he said about it. Still, my dad may be the nicest guy in the world, but he's no dummy. The day before I was scheduled to eat dinner at Grace's house, he suggested driving me over there so he could personally meet Grace's parents. What could possibly go wrong? When I told her, she laughed so hard and long, I worried she was having a stroke.

In the meantime, though my kiss-stung face has returned to normal, my heart and all working body parts are absolutely not normal. Because every time Porter so much as even walks within ten feet of me at work, I have the same reaction. Four knocks on Hotbox door? I flush. Scent of coconut in the break room? I flush. Sound of Porter cracking jokes with Pangborn in the hallway? I flush.

And every time this happens, Grace is there like some taunting Greek chorus, making a little *mmm-hmm* noise of confirmation.

Even Pangborn notices. "Are you ill, Miss Rydell?"

"Yes," I tell him in the break room one day before work. "I'm apparently very ill in the worst way. And I want you to know that I didn't plan for this to happen. This was not part of my plan at all. If you want to know the truth, I had other plans for the summer!" I think of my boardwalk map, lying folded and abandoned in my purse.

Pangborn nods slowly. "I have no idea what you mean, but I support it completely."

"Thank you," I tell him as he walks away, whistling.

Half a minute later, Porter pulls me into a dark corner of the hallway, checks around the corner, and kisses the bejesus out of me. "That's me, destroying all your other plans," he says wickedly.

And if I didn't know any better, I'd think he sounds jealous. Then he walks away, leaving me all hot and bothered.

I'm going to have a nervous breakdown.

Tuesday night at the Achebe house comes. Grace's family lives in a swank part of town, in an adobe-style house with a perfectly manicured lawn. When my dad and I ring the doorbell, my pulse rockets. Why oh why have I been using Grace as a cover for my time with Porter? That was so stupid, and now that everyone is meeting, I feel like we're going to get caught—which is the last thing I want to happen, for obvious reasons. And because I don't want to mess up what I have going with Grace. She's the first decent friend I've had in a while.

Footfalls sound on the other side of the door. I think I might vomit.

The door swings open to reveal a willowy woman with long ebony curls and dark skin. Her smile is warm and inviting. "You must be Bailey." Not Grace's tiny voice, but definitely her British accent.

I say hello and start to introduce my dad when a broad-shouldered man appears behind her, wiping his hands on a dish towel. "This is her?" he says in a big, booming voice full of cheer. He smiles big and wide. "Hello, Bailey girl. Look at that hair of yours. It's like an old-fashioned Hollywood star. Which one? Not Marilyn Monroe."

"Lana Turner," I provide.

He makes an impressed face. "Lana Turner," he says slowly,

with a cool African sway to his words. "Well, well, Miss Turner. I am Hakeem Achebe. And this is my wife, Rita."

"Pete Rydell," my dad says, shaking his hand. "We're both fond of Grace."

I see Grace poke her head down the stairs in the distance, smiling but gritting her teeth at the same time. She's nervous we're going to get caught in a lie too. *Crap!*

"We're fond of Grace as well," Mr. Achebe says jovially. "We think we'll keep her."

My dad laughs. I can already see him planning to hit up Mr. Achebe for board game night—but I really want this conversation to be as short as possible, so I hope he doesn't.

"She's gone on a lot about working with Bailey in that dreadful Hotbox," her mom says with a smile.

"I hear complaints about that too," my dad says. "But I'm glad they've been spending more time together outside work."

Double crap! Please don't bring up the fake story I concocted about Grace and me "wrestling" in the grass, Dad. Would he do that? Surely not. I glance at Grace. She backs up one step on the stairs. *Don't you dare abandon me!* Just in case, I prepare to flee the scene. Where I'll run, I don't know. Maybe I could pretend to faint.

"Well, tonight, it's work before play," Grace's father says, pointing the dish towel in my direction. "We have much preparation to do in the kitchen before dinner. Miss Turner, are you up for the task?"

Oh, thank God. Mr. Achebe: my new hero.

Grace's mom asks my dad to stay for dinner, but he declines, and when he tells me to have a good time, I cannot get inside the Achebe house fast enough.

Grace's dad makes a Nigerian rice dish called Jollof for dinner—it's pretty delicious—along with steak and grilled vegetables. He puts me and Grace in charge of skewering the vegetables. She was totally right: He tells the worst jokes. But he tells them with so much glee, it's hard not to laugh a little. She gives me a look like *I told you so*.

We spend the rest of the night listening to music out by their backyard pool. It's mostly 1970s and '80s bands, I think, her parents' music collection. Grace takes off her shoes and tries to get me to dance. When I refuse, her dad won't take no for an answer. So we dance to a ska song by The Specials, "A Message to You Rudy." And it's silly and fun, and I'm a terrible dancer. Grace laughs at me and then joins in with her mom.

When everyone's exhausted, her parents go back inside to clean up, and Grace and I end the night cooling our heels in the shallow end of the pool, trading stories about growing up on opposite sides of the country and her childhood in England. She then tells me about Taran, her boyfriend, who is in Mumbai visiting his aunt and uncle for the summer. Grace and Taran have been seeing each other for an entire year and are already planning to apply to the same colleges in the fall. I'm a little surprised, because she doesn't really talk about him all that much at work. I want to ask her more about their relationship, but I'm afraid.

Maybe things aren't as good as she claims they are. I wish I could see this Taran guy in person and judge for myself.

"When is Taran supposed to come back to California?" I ask, lying next to her by the edge of the pool with my legs dangling from the knees down in the chlorine-laced water.

Her tiny voice answers, "I'm not sure."

That doesn't sound good. I don't want to have to figure out a way to inflict deadly force against a boy on another continent, but if push comes to shove, for Grace, I will. I scooch a little closer and we lean our heads together, staring up at the stars, until my dad comes to pick me up.

I underestimated just how much wrangling had to go into my one true date with Porter, because over a week goes by and we can't manage another. Turns out that when you combine my sneaking-out requirement with our job schedules, Porter's surf shop obligations, and any other time spent on family duties, you get very little to work with.

And sometimes when you least expect it, you're just walking along, minding your own business, and the universe leaves you a winning lottery ticket right in the middle of the sidewalk. . . .

Friday and Saturday nights in the middle of the summer, the Cave closes at its usual time, six p.m., and then reopens from eight until ten p.m. for people to purchase tickets to the ghost tour. It's basically three groups of people who pay twice the normal ticket price to tour the museum afterhours with cheap flashlights while listening to fake ghost stories. It's a total rip-off. And I know this because the ghost tour guides are Pangborn and Porter, and they're the ones who wrote most of the ghost tour script last summer.

It was mostly Pangborn, Porter admits. He was extremely stoned when he wrote it. He's also extremely stoned when he's giving the tours, and everyone loves him camping it up, especially with his shocking white hair that practically glows in the dark. I work the Hotbox alone, since it's a limited ticket engagement. Once we sell out, I get to put up the AT SPOOK CAPACITY sign in the window and go inside the break room to read magazines until ten, waiting for the tours to finish.

Last night was my first ghost tour, and Porter had to rush home afterward, which sucked, because we never got to spend any time alone.

Tonight's a different story.

It's Saturday, and my dad and Wanda are spending the night in San Francisco. They're coming back first thing in the morning, Dad informed me a hundred times, like I was worried he was going to hop a train and never be seen again. But I think now that he's met Grace's parents, he feels better about those stupid hickeys that neither of us has ever, ever acknowledged again. So after the ghost tour winds up, Porter and I plan to do the unthinkable: We might go on a—wait for it—second date, and on that date, we may be going out to catch a movie.

A MOVIE.

268 • JENN BENNETT

Sure, it will probably be whatever current blockbuster is playing at the local Cineplex, and that's fine. I don't expect him to appreciate my supreme good taste in film. At least, not right away. He can be educated, and I'm happy to oblige. But all I'm thinking about now is that it's a movie and it's Porter—together.

I'm trying not to get too giddy. After all, he's got to get up early and work in the surf shop, so we can't stay out all night, but a couple of hours sounds like heaven. Heaven that might even still get me home by curfew, or thereabouts. See? I'm not even really cheating. Good daughter, right here.

Sometime around ten fifteen p.m., I stop checking for updates from Alex on my phone in the break room (there are none, as usual, and I'm not sure why I even bother caring) and stretch my legs. We're supposed to get to leave around ten thirty. Even though we close at ten, it takes Porter and Pangborn that long to shoo the last tour group out, lock up, put away the flashlights, and make a final sweep of the place to ensure there aren't any dopey kids hiding out or people having heart attacks in the restrooms. After the guests are gone, I'm supposed to help with the flashlights—there are a hundred of them—so when the only other two employees who were working tonight clock out and leave through the employee exit, I head out to the lobby to take care of that. On my way there, I bump into Pangborn.

"How did it go?"

"Excellent," he tells me. He's wearing bright orange socks with little black ghosts on them, which are easy to see because his pants are riding so high, thanks to the matching suspenders. He changed just for the ghost tour. God, I love him. "One woman gave me a twenty-dollar tip."

"How about that," I say, actually impressed.

"I didn't keep it, of course. But it was still a nice gesture." He smiles and pats me on the shoulder in that comforting way he always does. "Your boyfriend is making the final sweep on Jay's corridor. The doors are locked and the system's backed up. Except for the flashlights, we're done for the night."

I know he just said a bunch of words, but all I heard was "your boyfriend." Did Porter tell Pangborn we went out? Or has he noticed anything going on between us at work? I'm too chicken to ask, especially when Pangborn's eyes crinkle up sweetly in the corners.

"I'll get the flashlights," I offer.

"I was hoping you'd say that," he says. "I'm feeling more exhausted than usual tonight, and I've got to open in the morning, so I'm going to head home a few minutes early. Don't want to nod off on the road."

"Hey, not funny." Now that I'm looking at him, he really does look tired. Like, insanely tired. For the first time since Grace told me, I suddenly remember the rumors about him being sick. They may not be true, who knows, but I know one thing for sure: He's too old to be working this late. And Cavadini is an asshole to schedule him opening tomorrow morning.

"I'll stay alert, don't worry," he assures me. "But your concern is much appreciated. I just need a good night's rest. Daisy Dog and I need our beauty sleep. Tell Porter I'm locking the two of you in with the new master code. He'll have to punch in the override to get out. He'll know what I'm talking about."

"Got it." At least he has a dog to go home to. I tell him to be careful driving and when he's gone, I head out to find Porter. It's weird being alone in the museum. It's dark and eerily quiet: Only the after-hours lights are on—just enough to illuminate the hallways and stop you from tripping over your own feet—and the background music that normally plays all the time is shut off.

I quickly organize the flashlights and check their batteries, and when I don't hear Porter walking around, I stare at the phone sitting at the information desk. How many chances come along like this? I pick up the receiver, press the little red button next to the word ALL, and speak into the phone in a low voice. "Paging Porter Roth to the information desk," I say formally, my voice crackling through the entire lobby and echoing down the corridors. Then I press the button again and add, "While you're at it, check your shoes to make sure they're a match, you bastard. By the way, I still haven't quite forgiven you for humiliating me. It's going to take a lot more than a kiss and a cookie to make me forget both that and the time you provoked me in the Hotbox."

I'm only teasing, which I hope he knows. I feel a little drunk on all my megaphone power, so I page one more thing:

"PS—You look totally hot in those tight-fitting security guard pants tonight, and I plan to get very handsy with you at the movies, so we better sit in the back row."

I hang up the phone and cover my mouth, silently laughing at myself. Two seconds later, Porter's footfalls pound down Jay's corridor—*Boom! Boom! Boom! Boom!* He sounds like a T. rex running from Godzilla. He races into the lobby and slides in front of the information desk, grabbing onto the edge to stop himself, wild curls flying everywhere. His grin is enormous.

"Whadidya say 'bout where you want to be puttin' your hands on me?" he asks breathlessly.

"I think you have me confused with someone else," I tease.

His head sags against the desk. I push his hair away from one of his eyes. He looks up at me and asks, "You really still haven't forgiven me?"

"Maybe if you put your hands on *me*, I might."

"Don't go getting my hopes up like that."

"Oh, your hopes should be up. Way up."

"Dear God, woman," he murmurs. "And here I was, thinking you were a classy dame."

"Pfft. You don't know me at all."

"I aim to find out. What are we still doing here? Let's blow this place and get to the theater, fast."

We race each other through the lobby and grab our stuff out of our lockers. When we get to the back door, Porter pauses by the security system panel and tilts his head quizzically.

"Oh," I say, snapping my fingers. "Pangborn said to tell you that he was using the new master code to lock us in, and that you'll have to punch in the override code to get out."

Porter sort of shakes his head, mumbling to himself, and then appears to dismiss it. He unhooks his leather key fob thingy from his belt. I recognize his van keys on it, because there's a tiny shark on the key ring. But when he swings it into his palm he pauses again.

"O-o-oh, s-h-h-i-i-i-t," he drawls. His head drops. He's silently swearing to the floor, eyes squeezed shut.

"What?" I say.

"Pangborn took my key earlier," he says in a small voice. "Right before the tour. He left his at home during the break between the regular shift and the ghost tours, and he had to open the back door. I was about to start a tour, and I forgot to get it back from him. That son of a bitch."

"But you can just use the master code to let us out, right?"

Porter snorts and throws up his hand toward the panel. "If he'd used the master code, yes. But he didn't. See this here, this number? That code indicates that the system is on lockdown."

"And that means . . . ?"

"It means," Porter says, "that you and I are now locked up alone together inside the museum for the rest of the night."

"All night long I've had the most terrible impulse to do something."
—Audrey Hepburn, *Sabrina* (1954)

20

That can't be true. I mean, not really. There's always a way out of a place this big, right?

"Remember that day when I had to reinstall all the locks on the doors?" Porter asks.

I do.

"And you know I had to do that because we lost live off-site monitoring of our security system, and that instead of switching to one of a hundred other companies, management just decided to buy this cheap-ass system you see before you now?"

"Uh-huh?" I say, but I'm not totally following, and he's getting really angry. Steam is practically pouring out of his nostrils.

He takes a deep breath and calms down. "What this means is that Pangborn vaped too much weed again, left his manual keys at home, took mine, punched in a code that locks all the doors for eight hours, and drove off."

I stare at Porter.

He stares back.

"But you can deactivate this code, right?"

He shakes his head. "Pangborn is the lead security officer. I don't have clearance for a lockdown code." Oh, the irony. "He lives fifteen minutes from here. So we will have to wait until he gets home, and then—and this is where it gets really funny—we will try to call him."

"Why is that funny?"

"He usually turns his home phone off at night. He doesn't like to be woken up. 'Bad news can wait until morning' is his policy. And if we can't get him on the phone . . . well, I'm not really sure what to do. I guess we could try to call one of the other guards at home, but it's ten thirty on a Saturday night. And not only will they be pissed, but Pangborn could get fired for this. And pretty much everyone is looking for a reason for that to happen. In case you haven't noticed, he's kind of a mess."

That makes my heart twist.

"Mr. Cavadini? One of the shift managers?" I suggest and immediately realize the fault in that plan. Pangborn could get fired, and maybe Porter, too, for letting him go home early.

We both shake our heads.

I sniffle and scratch my nose with the side of my hand. "So basically what you're telling me is that unless we can get Pangborn on the phone, we're stuck here?"

"Let's take one thing at a time," Porter says, but I can tell by his grim expression that he doesn't have much hope. He leads me back to the security room, and I'm so panicked, I barely have time to register that I'm finally inside the inner sanctum: "Heaven." It's weird to be back here. Dozens of tiny black-and-white monitors cross two walls, all numbered, and an L-shaped desk with four computers, two of which appear to be a decade or more old.

We plop down at the desk in two rolling chairs. A swing-arm lamp casts a light over an old phone, where Porter proceeds to speed dial Pangborn's home number a zillion times. Of course the old man doesn't have a cell. Or he used to, Porter says, but he never charged it, and it sat in the glove box of his car for several years; it may still be there.

"Porter?"

"Yeah," he says, completely miserable, head in his hands.

"Is Pangborn sick?"

He doesn't answer right away. "You've heard rumors?"

"Yeah."

"He had colon cancer two years ago. He's in remission. But he went to the doctor last week, and he won't tell me what happened, and that worries me. He's always bragging about his appointments, because he's got a crush on his doctor. So I'm kind of thinking maybe it's back and he's going to have to go through chemo or something. I don't know."

"Oh, no." Grace's intel was right.

"Yeah, it sucks. And that's why he can't get fired, because the last thing he needs is to be screwing around with changing up his doctors and health benefits right now."

My chest aches. Why do bad things happen to good people? And if he does have cancer, and he's still showing up here for these stupid ghost tours, dressing up in his little suspenders and ghost socks, turning down tips from guests . . . it shatters my heart into a million pieces.

After half an hour of calling, we give up. It's not happening.

Deep breath. Time to evaluate the situation: (1) A cancer-stricken, nice old man has accidently locked us inside the Cave overnight. It's hard for me to get too mad at him about that. (2) It's not like we're going to run out of air or food or water. (3) We're not going to freeze or die of heat stroke. (4) We're not in danger of being eaten by bears or tigers. (5) This isn't our fault.

"Look on the bright side," Porter says, obviously having similar thoughts. "The lockdown will release at six thirty in the morning, so you'll still be able to beat your dad home from San Francisco. And if I call my parents and explain what happened, they'll totally understand. They both know Pangborn. And I spent the night on the couch here once before when we were resetting the security system last summer."

I glance over at the beat-up couch in the corner and my heart speeds up. "But what about me? I mean, will you tell them I'm here too? My dad would freak the hell out if he knew we were locked in here together alone all night."

The tension falls out of Porter's face, and the corners of his mouth slowly curl upward.

Oh, boy.

"Well, well, well," he says, leaning back in his chair in front of a bank of security monitors. He temples his fingers together over his chest. "This is an interesting situation, isn't it? Here we were, ready to run off to some crowded theater, but now we have the entire museum to ourselves. For the whole night. A boy prays and prays and prays, and is on his very best behavior, but he never dreams that something like this will just fall into his lap—so to speak."

"So to speak," I say weakly.

"Lots of room to spread out in this big place." The side of his knee bumps mine. A question.

All my earlier boldness has fled the building along with my courage. Now I just feel trapped. I withdraw both my legs and hide them under the desk. "What about all the cameras? I mean, won't this show up on the video footage? If someone reviews it later, or whatever?"

He chuckles. "You think the Cave pays for data storage? Think again. If we want to record something, we have to do it manually. Nothing is automatically recorded."

I glance up at the monitors and search for the Hotbox. There it is. It's empty now, of course, and dark, so I can't see much, but it's surreal to imagine Porter watching me from here. I make a mental note not to wear gaping tops to work, because that is a primo cleavage camera angle.

"However," Porter says, "if you're still worried, I know all the spots that the cameras miss. You know, if that would make you more comfortable."

I give him a dirty look. "Who says I want to get comfortable? We went on one date."

"Whoa." He holds up both hands in surrender. "Now you're making me feel like some sort of criminal sex pervert. Jesus, Bailey. An hour ago, you were talking about putting your hands on me in the back of a theater. I was just teasing you."

I blow out a hard breath. "I'm sorry. I'm just nervous and weirded out. I've just . . ."

"Just what?"

"I've just never . . . spent the night in a museum with anyone before."

Porter's brows lift. "Oh?"

I grimace. "Can you turn around or something? I can't look at you and talk about this."

"What?"

I make twisting movements with my hand. "Face the wall."

He looks at me like I'm nuts, and then gives in and slowly swivels around in his chair, keeping his head facing me, squinting, until the last possible moment. When he's facing the wall, I sigh and start talking to his back.

"Like I said before, we just went on one date." I'm a coward, yes, but having this conversation is so much easier when I don't have to look in his eyes. "And it was a great date. I mean, wow. I don't have much to compare it to, but I think it had to be up there in the history books. And even though you gave me those hickeys and ruined my favorite skirt, I would do it all over again."

"I'm still sorry about the hickeys, but for the record, I got grass stains on my clothes too. And every time I leave the house now, my mom teases me about going out for a roll in the hay and Pops has started calling me Grasshopper."

"Oh, God," I whisper.

"Totally worth it," he says. "But please continue."

"Anyway," I say, trying to gather my thoughts. "We went from enemies to a first date to now having the possibility of spending the night together in a museum, and not that I haven't thought about spending the night in a museum with you, because believe me, I've thought about that a lot."

His head turns sideways, but he still doesn't look at me. "A lot?"

"You have no idea."

"O-oh, that's where you're very wrong, my friend." His knee starts bouncing a nervous rhythm.

I smile to myself as a little thrill zips through me. "Well, what I'm saying is that I'm not opposed to such a thing. But I'm guessing you've spent many a night in many a museum, and you know, whatever. Good for you. But that intimidates me. And when it comes to this, I need you to let me give the green signal."

"First," he says, holding up a finger over his shoulder, "I want to say that I'm insulted that you'd think that I wouldn't. So thanks for making me feel like a sex criminal, again."

"Oh, God," I mumble.

"Second"—another finger joins the first—"I've been with two

girls, and one of those was a long-term girlfriend who, I might add, cheated on me with Davy, so it's not like I spend all my weekends in museums, to use your terminology. So there's no need for all the slut shaming."

I'm glad he can't see my face right now, because I'm pretty sure it's the exact shade of a broiled lobster. Is he mad? I can't tell by the tone of his voice. Ugh. Why did I make him face the wall? I scoot my chair closer and lay my cheek on his head, burrowing my face into his curls.

"I'm an idiot," I mumble into the back of his neck. "I don't know what I'm doing, and I'm so, so sorry."

His hand reaches around the chair, grasping blindly, patting around until he grabs my shirt and hangs on. "I accept your apology, but only because I'm trapped in here with you all night, and it would be awkward if we spent the entire time fighting."

"We're not fighting."

"We're always fighting. That's part of our charm," he says.

"Porter?"

"Yes?"

"Is the girlfriend you were just mentioning . . . Is that the girl you were arguing about with Davy outside the vintage clothing shop? Chloe?"

"Yeah. Chloe Carter. Her dad makes custom surfboards. They were really close with my family. She's friends with my sister, so the whole thing was kind of a big mess."

"Were you in love with her?"

who, from the sound of things, is completely sympathetic about the situation. But then he waits for her to tell his dad, and suddenly he's gesturing for me to duck under the desk because his dad is making him switch to a video call—like he doesn't believe his story. I hear Mr. Roth's sullen voice demanding that Porter repeat everything all over again, and Porter is showing him the computer screen, which clearly says LOCKDOWN and has a timer showing the remaining time left until the doors unlock and, thankfully, even shows the first few letters of Pangborn's last name as being the person who initiated the command. By now, it's eleven forty-five, and even grumpy-puss Mr. Roth admits that Porter's options are few and getting Pangborn fired isn't one of them.

"I could drive down the beach to his house and wake him up," Mr. Roth suggests.

Mrs. Roth's voice interrupts. "It's a quarter till midnight, and the man may be sick for all we know. Let him be. Porter, baby, is there a blanket there? Can you sleep okay on that sofa?"

He assures her that he'll find something, and she says that Lana will cover for him in the surf shop tomorrow morning if he can't get any sleep. And while they're winding things up, I text my dad and tell him I'm safe—that's not a lie, right?—and that I hope they're having fun in San Francisco. His reply is immediate and includes a geeky Settlers of Catan joke, so I assume he's in a genuinely good mood: *Having a blast. We bought you a surprise today. Love you more than sheep.*

I text him an equally geeky reply: *Love you more than wheat.*

He pauses a little too long for my comfort. "No, but it stil[l] when she cheated on me. We were friends for a long time bef[ore] started dating, so that should have meant something, you kn[ow].

Plus, it was with Davy, someone who was supposed to [be my] best friend, so it was a double betrayal, but I don't say this.

Several seconds tick by. I sigh.

"Porter?"

"Yes?"

"This sofa is kind of small, but we have to sleep some[where.] And I do like the idea of sleeping next to you."

"Me too."

After a long pause, I add, "In addition to sleeping, wha[t if I] want to see some of the places in the museum that the [others] don't go . . . just from a distance? Maybe. Possibly. Theo[retically.] I mean, does everything have to be all or nothing?"

Heavy sigh. "You're driving me crazy, you know that, [right?"]

"I know."

"Bailey, I spend most of my days looking at you thro[ugh a] tiny square screen up there. I'm just grateful to be in t[he same] room. And the fact that you'll even let me touch you at [all is a] freaking miracle of the century. So whatever you want [or don't] want from me, all you have to do is ask. Okay?"

"Okay," I whisper, mentally floating away on fluffy whi[te clouds.]

"Okay," he repeats firmly, like that's all decided, an[d pushes] away from the wall. "Now let me call my folks."

He makes the call on his cell, explaining everything to [them]

• • •

I have no idea where Porter's taking me that is off camera.

First he digs up a weird old-fashioned key out of a desk drawer in the security room. Then we gather up our stuff and head to the lost and found, where we score a baby blanket. Sure, it's gross to think about using some stranger's blanket, but whatever. It smells fine. Then he takes me all the way down to the end of Vivian's wing. There's a door here that's been painted the same dark green color as the wall, and because of the lighting, it's hard to see. I also know from memorizing the employee map that it's not supposed to be there—as in, it shouldn't exist.

"What is this?" I ask.

"Room one-zero-zero-one," he says, showing me the old key, which has a tag attached to it. "Like, *One Thousand and One Nights*, *Arabian Nights*, Ali Baba, and all that."

"There's another room? Why isn't this open to the public?"

He hoists his backpack higher on his shoulder and flattens his palm against the door. "Now, look. This is a huge Cavern Palace secret. You have to solemnly swear that you'll never tell anyone what I'm about to show you on the other side of this door. Not even Gracie. *Especially* Gracie, because I love her, but she knows everyone, and it will fly around faster than the chicken pox virus. Swear to me, Bailey. Hold up your hand and swear."

I hold up my hand. "I swear."

"Okay, this is the Cave's dirtiest secret." He unlocks the door, flips on the lights, which take a second to flicker on, and we step inside a perfectly round room lit in soft oranges and golds. It smells a little musty, like a library that hasn't seen a lot of action. And as Porter closes the door behind us, I look around in amazement.

Thick, star-scattered indigo curtains cover the walls. A cluster of arabesque pendant lamps hang in various lengths from the domed ceiling over a low, velvet cushion about the size of a large bed. It's tufted and comes up to my knees, and crowning one side of it, like a half-moon, it's surrounded by hundreds of small pillows with geometric designs that look like they came straight out of a palace in Istanbul.

"It's beautiful," I say. "Like a dream. I don't understand why it's not open. Are these pillows from the 1930s? They should be preserved."

Porter dumps his stuff on the floor next to the velvet cushion. "Don't you remember your Cave history? Vivian hated Jay. When their marriage fell apart, he wouldn't give her a divorce, so she had this room constructed as big middle finger to him. Come feast your eyes on her revenge. But don't say I didn't warn you."

He steps up to one of the starry blue curtains on the wall and lifts a golden cord to reveal a mural on the wall beneath. It's a life-size art deco painting of Vivian Davenport dressed up as a Middle Eastern princess, with bells on her fingers and flowers in her long hair, a sheer gown flowing over her buxom, naked body. Throngs of men in suits bow down at her feet.

"Oh . . . my . . . God," I murmur.

There are several big-eyed smiling cartoon animals looking on, like even they can't look away from the glory that is naked Vivian.

"Is that . . . Groucho Marx?" I say, squinting to look at one of the kneeling men.

"Vivian made history come alive," Porter answers, grinning.

"Make it stop," I say, laughing, and he closes the curtain.

I'm scarred for life, but it was worth it. We fall on the velvet cushion together, and a small cloud of dust motes flies up. I guess the janitorial service doesn't come back here much. Porter fake coughs and brushes off the rest of the cushion.

That's when it hits me that this is a bed we're sitting on. "You don't think Vivian had crazy sex parties right here, do you?" I ask, moving my hand off the velvet. "More revenge against her husband?"

"Doubtful. But if she did, it was a hundred years ago," he says, squinting his eyes merrily at me. "And it all ended so tragically for the both of them, what with her shooting him and killing herself, you almost hope she had some fun before it all went sideways, you know? Like maybe she actually modeled for that portrait."

"Yeah."

After a few moments of silence, a heavy awkwardness blooms in the space between us. Porter finally sighs, sits up, and begins stripping the radio equipment from his shoulder. My heart hammers.

He slides a sideways glance in my direction. "Look, I'm not getting naked or anything—cool your jets. How could I compete with all that wackiness on the walls, anyway? I just can't sleep with a bunch of wires and crap attached to me. Or shoes. I'm leaving the shirt and pants on. You can leave on whatever you want. Ladies' choice." He winks.

His good humor puts me somewhat at ease, and I slip off my shoes next to his. He shuts off his radio and sets a timer on his phone for six thirty a.m. But when he takes off his belt, all the blood in my brain swooshes so loud, I worry I might be having an aneurism.

The belt buckle hits the Turkish-patterned rug with a dull *thump*. "You're a great mystery to me, Bailey Rydell."

"I am?"

"I can never tell if you're scared of me, or if you're about to jump me."

I chuckle nervously. "I'm not sure of that myself."

He pulls me closer and we lie down, facing each other, hands clasped between us. I can feel his heart racing against my fist. I wonder if he can feel mine.

"I'm scared," I tell him, "of what I feel when I'm around you. I'm scared of what I want from you, and I don't know how to ask for it." I'm also scared that if I do, it might be terrible or not live up to my expectations, but I don't say this, because I'm afraid it will hurt his feelings.

He kisses my forehead. "Know what I'm scared of?"

"What?"

"That I like you way too much, and I'm afraid once you get to know me, you're going to realize that you can do lots better, and you're going to break my heart and leave me for someone classier."

I breathe him in deeply. "When I first came to town, there was someone else. Not Patrick," I say, as if either of us needs that reminder.

"Your so-called other plans?" he asks.

"Yeah," I say. "I guess you could say he's classy, I don't know. But just when you think you understand someone, it turns out that you didn't really know them at all. Or maybe the real problem was that you didn't understand something about yourself."

"I don't follow."

I blow out a long breath. "It doesn't matter. What I'm trying to say is that before I moved out here, I didn't know I liked churros and moon muffins and Hawaiian *poke* and Jollof rice, and I didn't know I would fall for you. But I did. And who wants classy when you can eat posole out of a food truck on the beach? I had no idea what I was missing."

He slowly traces a wavy tendril near my temple with one finger. "You've fallen for me, huh?"

"Maybe." I hold up my fingers and measure a small amount. "This much."

"That's it? Guess I'm going to have to try harder, then," he says in a low voice against my lips, almost kissing me, but not quite. Then again. Little almost-kisses. Teasing me.

My breath quickens.

"Let's take a quick quiz, why don't we?" he murmurs. "If I put my hand here—"

His fingers slide under my shirt over my belly. It's delicious . . . for all of two seconds. Then he's too close to the off-limits area of my scar. And—no! He's actually touching my scar. No way am I stopping this to explain that. I just . . . can't. No.

He feels me tense up and immediately withdraws. "Hey. I—"

"No, no, no," I quickly whisper. "It's not you. It's something else. Don't take it personally, I . . . just, um." I move his hand to the middle of my bare thigh, under my skirt. Talk about dangerous waters.

"Bailey," he says. A warning.

"Quiz me," I challenge.

He mumbles a filthy little curse, but his hand begins to climb upward, oh-so-slowly. "Okay, Rydell. If you're locked in a museum all night with a guy you're falling for, and he's cool enough to show you the Cave's dirtiest secret—God, your skin is so soft."

"Mmphrm?" I murmur, moving around to give him better access.

"Oh," he murmurs back cheerfully.

Hand firmly gripping my upper thigh, he kisses me, and I kiss him back, and it's desperate and wonderful.

"Okay," he says, sounding drugged. "Now, where was I? Oh yes, here." Much to my delight, his hand continues its roaming ascent. Only, there's not much farther it can go. He hesitates, chuckling to himself, and switches legs, repeating the same pattern on the other thigh.

Then stops.

I whimper. I'm genuinely frustrated.

Until he shifts a little, and I feel him pressed against my hip. No mistaking that.

"I'm having some trouble concentrating on this quiz," he admits, smiling against my neck.

"Whatever you do, don't you dare give me another hickey."

He pretends to bite me, and then he shows me other things besides moon muffins and posole that I didn't know I was missing, things two people locked in a museum overnight can do with their hands and fingers and a whole lot of ingenuity. The boy has every right to be wearing that HOT STUFF cartoon devil patch on his jacket.

Unlike our previous roll in the grass, this touching definitely is not rated PG, and when Porter offers to do the thing to me that I normally do for myself, who am I to look a gift horse in the mouth? It's possibly the most amazing thing that's ever, ever happened to me. I even return the favor—still pretty amazing, though much more so for him, for obvious reasons.

But wow.

All of that touching wears me out, and it's two in the morning, which is too late for my blood. I'm wound up in him, arms and legs, and he's the big spoon to my little spoon, and as I'm dozing off, in and out of consciousness, lights flicker. I hear voices. Not alarming voices. No one's in the museum; we're still alone. But he's reached over me and wedged his laptop out of his backpack, and it's sitting on the velvet cushion above our heads. There's something playing on the screen.

"What's going on?" I say, my voice sounding thick to my own ears as I tilt my head upward. I can't quite open my eyes all the way, but I can make out shapes and moving light through my eyelids.

"Sorry, sorry," he says in a bone-weary voice. "Is it bothering you? I can't get to sleep without a movie or TV on."

"S'fine," I slur, snuggling back against him. A few seconds later, I say. "Is that *Roman Holiday*?"

His deep voice vibrates through my back. "It's an indie film. They're quoting it. Wait, you know *Roman Holiday*?"

"Pfft," I say sloppily, too tired to explain my love of film. "Question is, how do *you* know *Roman Holiday*?"

"My grandma—my mom's mother—lived with us before she died. She'd stay up late watching movies in the den, and when I was a kid, I'd fall asleep in her lap on the couch."

How funny. That's how he knew about *Breakfast at Tiffany's*, too. "Maybe you and I have more in common than you think," I say before I drift into dreams.

"Life does not stop and start at your convenience."
—John Goodman, *The Big Lebowski* (1998)

21

Porter was right. I get out of the museum in plenty of time to beat
dad home from his trip. I'm so tired, I even go back to sleep for
a few more hours. When I wake a second time, it's almost time
for me to get ready for another shift at the Cave, which is crazy. I
might as well just move in there. But it's hard to be too sour about
it, because I spent the night with a boy.

SPENT.

NIGHT.

BOY.

That's right. I did that. I did some other things too, and they
were all excellent. It's a beautiful day, the sun is shining, and I
don't even care that I have to spend four hours in the Hotbox. At
least I don't have to work a full shift today.

I shower and dress before bounding downstairs just in time
to run into Dad and Wanda returning from San Francisco. Talk
about two exhausted people. They look happy, though. I don't

292 • JENN BENNETT

really want to know what they did all night, so I don't pry. But they dig around in the trunk of my dad's muscle car until they find the gifts they bought for me: a leopard-print scarf and a pair of matching sunglasses.

"To go with Baby," my dad says, looking hopeful but unsure.

"The scarf is to cover up any future hickeys," Wanda adds, one side of her mouth tilting up.

Oh, God. Her, too? Does everyone know? My dad tries to repress a smile. "I'm sorry, kiddo. It's sort of funny, you have to admit."

Wanda crosses her arms over her chest. "Own it, I say. If your dad gave me a hickey and anyone at the station gave me grief, I'd tell them where they could go. I picked out the sunglasses, by the way."

I sigh deeply and slide them on. The lenses are dark and huge, brand-new, but very Italian retro cool. "They're fantastic, thank you. And I hate both of you for the scarf, but it's still awesome. Stop looking at my neck, Dad. There are no new hickeys." I checked just to be sure.

After they give me a briefing of their day in the Bay Area, I race out the door and drive back to the Cave. I know Porter's working, and I'm zipping and floating, high as a kite, eager to see him again. I want to know if he feels as good as I feel after last night. I also want to see Grace and tell her how crazy things were. Though this time, I don't think I'll be sharing so many details. Some things are meant to be private. What happens in Room 1001 stays in Room 1001.

But when I park Baby in my normal spot, I see Porter standing outside his van, which is weird. He's typically inside the building long before I get there. It's not just that. Something's wrong: He's holding his head in his hands.

I slam on the brakes and jump off the scooter, race over to him. He doesn't acknowledge me. When I pull his hands away from his face, tears are streaming down his cheeks.

"What's wrong?" I ask.

His voice is hoarse and barely there. "Pangborn."

"What?" I demand, my stomach dropping.

"He didn't show up for work this morning," he says. "It happened sometime last night in his home. There wasn't anything we could've done. He lied to me about where the cancer was. It was pancreatic this time, not colon."

"I don't understand what you're saying." I'm starting to shake all over.

"He's dead, Bailey. Pangborn's dead."

He gasps for a single shaky breath, and curls up against me, sobbing for a second along with me, and then goes quiet and limp in my arms.

The funeral is four days later. I think half of Coronado Cove shows up, and it doesn't surprise me. He was probably the nicest man in town.

I sort of fell apart the first couple of days. The thought of Porter and me doing what we were doing while Pangborn was dying was a pretty heavy burden. Porter was right: There was nothing we could have done. Pangborn's cancer was advanced. His younger sister tells Grace and me at the funeral that the doctor had given him anywhere from a few days to a few weeks. She says when it's at that stage, some people get diagnosed and die that week. He didn't know when it would happen, so he kept living his life normally.

"He was stubborn that way," she says in a feminine voice that sounds strangely familiar to his. She lives a couple of hours down the coast with her husband, in a small town near Big Sur. I'm relieved to learn that she's adopting Daisy, Pangborn's dog.

We leave the church and drive to the cemetery. I can't find Grace at the graveside service, so I stand with my dad and Wanda. It's really crowded. They've just played "Me and Julio Down by the School Yard" to end the service, which, it turns out, was Pangborn's favorite song. This makes me fall apart all over again, so I'm in a weakened state, sniffling on my dad's shoulder, when the Roths walk up: all four of them.

Well.

I'm too tired to keep this charade up, and it seems like a shame to dishonor Pangborn's memory. So I throw caution to the wind and my arms around Porter's torso.

Not in a casual *we're friends* way either.

He hesitates for a second, and then wraps me in a tight embrace, holding me for an amount of time that's longer than appropriate, but I just don't care. Before he lets me go, he whispers in my ear, "You sure about this?"

I whisper back, "It's time."

When we pull apart, Mrs. Roth hugs my neck briefly—she's wearing a fragrant, fresh flower tucked over one ear that tickles my cheek—and Mr. Roth surprises me by squeezing the back of my neck, which almost makes me cry again, and then I finally face my dad. I can tell by the funny look on his face that he's tallying things up and wondering how in the hell I know this family. His gaze darts to Mr. Roth's arm and a moment of clarity dawns.

"Dad, this is Mr. and Mrs. Roth, and Porter and his sister, Lana."

My dad extends his hand and greets the Roths, and Wanda already knows them, so they're saying hello to her, too. And then Porter steps forward and faces my dad. I'm suddenly nervous. My dad's never really met any boys who were interested in me, and he's definitely never met any boys whom he specifically forbid me to see . . . and I specifically went behind his back and saw anyway. And though, in my eyes, Porter has never looked more handsome, dressed up in a black suit and tie, he's still sporting that mane of unruly curls that kisses the tops of his shoulders and all that scruff on his jaw. On Mr. Roth, tattoos peek out around the collar of his shirt on his neck. So no, the Roths aren't exactly prim and proper. If my mom were standing here doing the judging, she would be looking down her nose. I mentally cross my fingers and hope my dad won't be that way.

After an uncomfortable pause, Dad says, "You're the boy from work who recovered my daughter's scooter when it was stolen."

My heart stops.

"Yes, sir," Porter answers after a long moment, not blinking. Defensive. Bullish.

My dad sticks his hand out. "Thank you for that," he says, pumping Porter's arm heartily, using his other hand to cover Porter's in one of those extra-good handshakes—making it seem as if Porter saved my life and not a measly bike.

My heart starts again.

"Yes, sir," Porter says, this time visibly relieved. "Not a problem."

That was it? No snotty comments about the hickeys? No accusations? No fifty questions or awkwardness? God, I couldn't love my dad more than I do right now. I don't deserve him.

"You really didn't get a look at who stole it, huh?" Wanda says, narrowing her eyes at Porter. "Because I'd really like to know if you have any information."

Crap.

"Uh . . ." Porter scratches the back of his head.

Lana smacks her gum. "What do you mean? It was—"

"Shut it, Lana," Porter mumbles.

Wanda turns her narrowed eyes on me now. "I remember someone eyeing your scooter at the posole truck a few days before it got jacked."

Oh, crud. She really doesn't miss anything, does she? Guess that's why she's a cop.

Mr. Roth puts a hand up. "Sergeant Mendoza, Porter and I

have had a long talk about this, and I think we all want the same thing. Hell, we probably want it even more than you do." Mr. Roth suspiciously eyes my dad, who is probably the only person here who hasn't put two and two together that Davy is the one who stole my scooter—or maybe he has. I can't tell. Regardless, Mr. Roth clears his throat and says, "What with my kid getting pummeled that day, driving out to Timbuktu to get her bike back."

Too much information in front of my dad, ugh.

"I wouldn't say 'pummeled,'" Porter argues good-humoredly. "You should've seen the other guy."

Mr. Roth ignores him and continues. "What I'm trying to say is that no one wants to punish that joker more than I do. But Porter handled things the best way he knew how at the time, and I support that."

"Hey, I got a kid," Wanda says. "And off the record, I don't disagree with you. But that 'joker' is still out there, and mark my words, he's going to strike again. Next time, you may not be so lucky. He may hurt himself or someone else."

Mr. Roth nods. "I hear you loud and clear. I worry about it all the time. In fact, I saw him hobbling around on the boardwalk last week and it was all I could do not to put him in the hospital again."

A knot in my gut tightens. Last I'd heard, Porter had found out through the rumor mill that Davy had been laid up at home for the last couple of weeks due to Porter reinjuring his knee during the fight at Fast Mike's garage. Guess he's back on his feet again.

Wanda points a finger around our group. "Make me a promise, all of you. Next time Davy Truand does anything, or even starts to do anything, you call nine-one-one and tell them to send me. Let's not meet again at another funeral, okay?"

After the service, my dad doesn't give me any grief about Porter. He doesn't even give me any grief about Davy being the one who stole my scooter. So when we're alone, I just tell him that I'm sorry I kept it all from him, and I explain why I did, and that I won't do it again. Ever, ever, ever.

"It hurts me that you felt the need to lie, Mink," he says.

And that makes me cry all over again.

And because he's the nicest guy in the world, he just holds me until I'm all dried out. And when I'm no longer in danger of drowning the entire cemetery in my misery, à la Alice in Wonderland, he straightens me up and lets me go home with Porter for the rest of the afternoon.

The Roths live in an old house a block away from the beach on the outskirts of town in a neighborhood that probably was halfway nice ten years ago. Now it's starting to get a little rundown, and half the homes have FOR SALE signs in the sandy yards. Their clapboard fence is sagging, the cedar paneling is starting to buckle, and the brutal ocean wind has beaten up the wind chimes that line the gutters. But when I walk inside, it smells like surf wax and wood, and it's stuffed from ceiling to floor with trophies and driftwood and dried starfish and family photos and a bright red Hawaiian hibiscus tablecloth on the kitchen table.

"I'm starving," Lana says. "Funerals make me hungry."

"Me too," Mrs. Roth says. "We need comfort food. P&P?"

"What's P&P?" I ask.

"Popcorn and peanuts," Porter informs me.

She looks around for approval, and everyone nods. I guess this is a Roth family tradition. Sounds a little strange, but I'm on a winning streak with food around this town, so who am I to argue? And when she pops the popcorn in a giant pan on the stove with real kernels, it smells so good, I actually salivate.

While she's salting the popcorn, Porter goes to his room and changes out of his suit, and I help Mrs. Roth dig out bowls in the kitchen. It's weird being alone with her, and I secretly wish Porter would hurry up. Now that he's not here as a buffer, I feel like an actor shooting a scene who's blanking on all her lines. What am I supposed to be saying? Maybe I need cue cards.

"How's your mom feel about you being out here in California?" she asks out of the blue.

"I don't know," I say. "I haven't heard from her."

"Are you not close?"

I shrug. "I thought so. This is the first time I've been away from h-home." *Man. Seriously? I can't cry again. Funerals are the worst.* I swipe away tears before they have a chance to fall, and shake it off.

"I'm sorry, sweetie," Mrs. Roth says in a kind voice. "I didn't mean to dredge up bad stuff."

"It's just that she hasn't even e-mailed or texted. I've been gone for weeks. You'd think she'd want to know if I'm okay. I could be dead, and she wouldn't even know."

"Have you tried calling her?"

I shake my head.

"Does your dad talk to her?"

"I don't know."

"Maybe you should ask him. At least talk to him about it. She could be going through something in her marriage or at work—you never know. She might need to hear from you first. Sometimes parents aren't very good at being grown-ups."

She pats my shoulder, and it reminds me of Pangborn.

We head to a sofa in the den under a giant wooden surfboard suspended from exposed rafters; the board is engraved in pretty cursive with the word PENNYWISE. I sit in the middle of Porter and Lana, holding a big plastic bowl of popcorn with just the right amount of salt and roasted peanuts. The peanuts are heavy and fall to the bottom of the bowl, so we're forced to constantly shake it up and hunt for them, making the popcorn spill all over our laps, which they argue is half the fun. The Roths sit nearby in a pair of recliners, though Mr. Roth's recliner looks like it was manufactured in 1979.

"It's his favorite chair, Bailey, and he won't give it up," Mrs. Roth says, stretching her arm out to touch Mr. Roth's face. "Don't look at it too long or it will grow legs and walk out of here."

Lana giggles. Mr. Roth just grunts and almost smiles. Out of the corner of my eye, I see him kiss his wife's hand before she takes it away.

While eating our feast, we watch *The Big Lebowski*, which is sort of bizarre, because Alex was trying to get me to watch this a couple of months ago. And the Roths have it on DVD, so they are all amazed I've never seen it. Turns out, it's really good. And what's even better, in addition to Porter preparing me for the sound of gunshots in the movie—so I won't be caught off guard—and quoting lines along with the actors, which makes me smile despite the dreary events of the day, is when he leans close and whispers into my ear, "You belong here with me."

And for that moment, I believe that I do.

22

I don't really know how long it takes for people to start feeling normal again after someone dies. But I think I expected Porter to bounce back faster because he's so confident. I have to remind myself that he's already emotionally scarred, and that some of his cockiness is just for show. So when I see him sinking into what I fear is depression after Pangborn's funeral, I wonder if I should say or do something to help him. I just don't know what, exactly.

He tells me he'll be okay, that he just needs time to get over it. When I ask if he wants to grab something to eat after work, he says he might be too tired. He does look tired. He apologizes a lot. That doesn't seem like him—at all, frankly.

Dad tells me not to push him too hard. I'm not exactly a pushy kind of person. But after what seems like an endless stretch of Porter's melancholy, I'm starting to wonder if I need to start nudging. But Grace echoes my dad's advice, telling me to give Porter some space. And what's even weirder is that for once, I'm the one who doesn't want to be alone. I guess Grace can sense this, or something, because she's been asking me to hang out a lot. Our prework breakfast dates at the Pancake Shack are now becoming routine. A definite bright spot of my day. It's helped to get my mind off Pangborn—and stopped me from worrying so much about Porter. Sort of. It doesn't soothe the funny ache in my heart when I think about him dealing with all of this on his own. I wish he'd let me help. I wish he'd talk to me. At this point, I'd give my right pinky toe for one of our good, old-fashioned arguments. Can you miss someone you see almost every day?

A couple of weeks after Pangborn's funeral, at six forty-five a.m., I'm awakened by a series of buzzes. It's my phone. Who's texting me this early? My first reaction is panic, because, let's face it, life has been a shit sandwich lately.

Porter: *Wake up.*

Porter: *Waaaake uuuuup.*

Porter: *How late do you sleep, anyway? You need an alarm clock. (I'd like to be that alarm clock, actually.) (God, please don't let your dad pick up your phone.)*

Porter: *Come on, sleepyhead. If you don't wake up soon, I'm leaving without you.*

I type a quick reply: *What's going on?*

Porter: *Good surfing, that's what.*

Me: *You mean, surfing for you?*

Porter: *That was the idea. So, are you coming to watch me surf?*

Me: *Try and stop me.*

I'm so excited, I throw off the covers and leap out of bed. Okay, so maybe this isn't a romantic invitation, because a few more texts tell me where I'll be meeting his family, but I don't care. I'm just relieved that he sounds cheerful. My only problem is Grace, my breakfast date this morning. She's already up, and when I text her to ask for a rain check, she asks if she can tag along. When I don't answer right away, two more texts follow—

Grace: *Pretty please?*

Grace: *I really need a chin-wag.*

Me: *???*

Grace: *A chat. Girl talk. Yeah?*

Normally, I'd say sure, but I haven't spent time with Porter since the *Big Lebowski* viewing after the funeral. What if he doesn't want a big audience? I consider the best way to handle it as I get dressed, but my mind keeps wandering to Porter.

When I head out, the fog hasn't cleared. The place I'm meeting the Roths is a spot a couple of miles north of town, just up the beach from the Bone Garden. It's pretty out here, all wild and pebble-strewn. And though it's not crowded like the beach at the boardwalk, I'm surprised to see anyone at all this early in the morning. Apparently, it's a popular surf spot, because a dozen other vans are parked along the road and several other onlookers gather, including a couple of people walking along the beach with their dogs as the waves roll and crash.

Clearly, this wasn't a private affair. I even see Sharonda, the president of Brightsea's drama club, who Grace introduced me to at the bonfire party. For a moment, I remember Grace, and tell myself I need to text her back, but Mrs. Roth waves me down, and she's brought doughnuts. I don't want to be rude, and she's in a great mood, so I put Grace out of my mind for the time being and silence my phone.

While I make small talk with Mrs. Roth, I catch sight of the rest of the family. Mr. Roth is in training mode, unloading a board with Lana, and barking commands. But I'm having trouble paying attention to anything but Porter. If there are any traces of melancholy left on him, he's packed them away. It's a new day, and I can see the change in the way he walks across the sand, the way he holds his head high. He's ready to move on.

He's donned a sleeveless black-and-aqua wet suit, and it's clinging in all the right places. Standing next to Mrs. Roth, I'm afraid to look too closely all at once, but hot damn. I catch his eyes once when his mom's busy chatting with Sharonda, who is apparently friends with Lana. I can't wink, so I just look him up and down and mouth, *Wow*. He gives me a spectacular grin in return. He's so cocky; the boy knows how good he looks. I roll my eyes, but I can't stop smiling, and he loves the attention. He could build sand castles on the beach and never even surf one wave for all I care. Mission accomplished.

After that exchange, his focus shifts. I notice the moment it happens. He's stretching, both him and Lana, legs and arms, normal stretches and some weird jumping. They're both super limber. And the entire time, his eyes are on the water. He's calculating the big waves. Timing them, or something. He checks his watch occasionally, but mostly he's watching the water and checking the sky. He's very intense. I like him this way.

There's some sort of surfing etiquette I don't understand, but I can tell Porter and Lana are waiting their turn. And I can also tell that the other surfers aren't very good, and some of them are giving up and clearing out. After a minute, Mr. Roth gives his wife a head signal.

"Okay, girls," she says to me and Sharonda. "We're going up there."

"Up there" is a short hike up a massive sand dune that gives us a great view of the ocean. From here, we can see the waves rolling in much more clearly and all the other surfers who are either surfing on the smaller waves closer to shore (not impressive), or trying to ride the bigger waves farther out and not lasting very long. The ocean is eating them alive. Now I'm a little worried.

"They're not surfing those, are they?" I ask. The big waves looked smaller and flatter from the beach.

"You bet your sweet patootie they are," she says, all fierce mom pride. And from the looks of the crowd gathering behind us to watch, she isn't the only one interested in the show.

I hope this is a shark-free zone.

Lana's in yellow and black, and she goes first. She lies flat on her board and paddles out, and that takes longer than you'd think. Porter gives her some distance, but he's paddling now too. The farther out they go, the scarier it gets. They sometimes disappear under the smaller rolling waves, like speed bumps in a road, then reappear on the other side.

"Have you seen them surf before?" I ask Sharonda, taking a bite of doughnut. I hate to break it to Mrs. Roth, but this is no churro or vanilla moon muffin.

"Yeah, I live down the road, so I see Lana surf a couple of times a week. Sometimes I go watch events, if they aren't too far. I once rode down to Huntington Beach with the Roths. Remember that?"

"Sure do, honey," Mrs. Roth says, watching the water.

"What about Porter?" I ask.

Sharonda nods. "I've been watching Porter compete locally since he was, like, thirteen. He used to have hair down to here," she says, putting her hand halfway down her back. "Nothing but curls. All the girls in our class had a crush on him."

Mrs. Roth sticks out her bottom lip, looking sentimental. "He was such a sweet boy. My little grommet."

"Oh, and we'll be watching all of Lana's surfing heats together on TV," Sharonda says excitedly, reaching around me to tap Mrs. Roth's arm. "Maybe we can have viewing parties?"

This surprises me. It hadn't even crossed my mind that Lana will be that professional. Now that I know her, she just seems like a good-natured kid who chews a lot of gum and drools when she falls asleep on the couch, which is what happened that afternoon at their house.

Lana and Porter are both floating on their boards, bobbing in the

308 • JENN BENNETT

rolling waves. I'm not sure what they're waiting for, but everyone is tense. Before I can ask what's happening, Lana's yellow-and-black suit pops onto her board. She's standing, crouched on her board, and cutting through a massive wave I didn't even realize was there.

There she goes!

She's like a beautiful black-and-yellow bee, zipping through the water, making tight zigzag motions that seem to go on forever. I can't believe she can ride the wave for so long. It's crazy. How is this possible? Seems like it goes against nature.

"Yeah, Lana," Mrs. Roth calls out to the ocean, clapping in time with all of Lana's zigzagging. "Go, baby, go!"

By the time Lana finishes, she's so far on the other side of the dune, it's going to take her five minutes to walk back to us. No wonder these kids are in shape. This surfing gig is exhausting.

The crowd on the sand dune explodes into applause and whistles, and I clap along, too. Mrs. Roth rotates her hand in the air, egging them on. "That little peanut is going to win it all," she tells everyone around us, and some of them high-five her.

She's so proud. Everyone's smiling. It's all exciting, but now I'm watching Porter, because he's paddled out just a little farther, and that makes my stomach drop.

Mr. Roth comes bounding up the sand dune, eyes on the water. How long has it been since Porter's surfed like this? I'm suddenly nervous. If he crashes, or whatever it's called, I don't want him to do it in front of me and be embarrassed later. I can't handle that. I want to look away, maybe make some excuse, like

I got sick from the doughnut and had to leave. I can hear about it later.

Then he pops up on his board.

Too late. Can't look away now.

His wave is bigger than Lana's. His stance is different from Lana's. He rides the board up the curling water, up, up, up . . . (please don't fall!) and at the top, he's— Holy Mother of Sheep, he's flying up in the air, board and body! Impossibly, on a dime, he turns the board one hundred and eighty degrees, sharply. Then he rides the wave right back down, smooth as glass, white foam kicking out from the tail of his board like the train of a wedding dress.

"YES!" Mr. Roth bellows, holding up his arm.

The crowd behind me shouts along with Mrs. Roth.

It's happening so fast. That was just one move, and though Porter doesn't take the board up in the air again, he's already made turn number two (crouching low at base of wave, wait, wait . . . rides up again), and whoosh! Turn three! Now he's riding back down, still going, arms out for balance, like fins.

Lana's style was fast and quick, full of spunk; Porter is slower and his moves are grander. Poetic. Beautiful. He's cutting through the water as if he's painting a picture with his body.

I didn't know surfing looked like this.

I didn't know Porter could do this.

He makes the last turn at the end of the wave, a baby turn, because there isn't much wave left to ride, and then neatly comes to a stop where the sand rises toward the beach, the wave washing all around him, as if the ocean found him shipwrecked and is delivering him safely to shore.

The crowd roars.

I crush my doughnut in my hand. "Holy shit," I say in amazement, then apologize, then say it again several times, but no one is listening or cares.

Mr. Roth turns around, grins at the crowd—grins!—and kisses his wife before running down the other side of the dune to greet his son. Mrs. Roth picks me up in a bear hug. For a woman who isn't an athlete, she sure is strong. When she puts me back down, she cups my face in her hands and, shockingly, kisses me straight on the lips. "Thank you, thank you, thank you. I knew you could get him out here."

"I didn't do anything," I say, flushing with excitement and a little embarrassment.

"Oh baby, yes you did," she says, her eyes shining. "He hasn't surfed like that since the shark."

Porter surfs nearly a dozen more big waves. He screws up once, falling off his board pretty hard trying to pull an aerial "alley-oop." Mrs. Roth blames the wipeout on the wind. But otherwise, he's pretty much a demon. He and Lana engage in a friendly sibling competition, and it's awesome. After a couple of hours, word has spread, and a hundred people or so line the beach. My throat goes hoarse from cheering.

When it seems as though they're slowing down—both the waves and the surfers—Mrs. Roth tells her husband to call her "babies" back to shore soon. She doesn't want Porter overdoing it and injuring himself. Mr. Roth grunts and seems dismissive, but he slowly makes his way back down the dune. I guess Lana was right when she said her mom wears the pants in their family.

Someone taps me on the shoulder. "How are they doing?"

I turn around to find Grace, dressed in a magenta jacket and oversize gold sunglasses. Her mouth is arrow-straight, matching the tense line of her shoulders. She is not a happy camper.

"Grace," Mrs. Roth says cheerfully. "You should have come earlier. Porter was on fire."

Grace smiles at her, and it's almost genuine. "Is that so? I'm sorry I missed it. Took me a bit to find out where they were surfing."

"You could have called me," Mrs. Roth says absently, only halfway paying attention.

Grace aims two bladelike eyes on me. "It's fine. I texted Porter and he was more than happy to let me know."

Oh, God. "Grace," I whisper. "I totally forgot to text you back."

"No big deal. I'm not exciting enough, I suppose," she says, and walks away.

My heart sinks. The Artful Dodger in me whispers to let Grace go, but another part of my brain is panicking. I get Mrs. Roth's attention. "Sorry, but I need to talk to Grace."

Mrs. Roth makes a shooing motion. "Go on, baby. They're just about done. I'll send Porter to find you after he's back to shore."

Quickly, I follow Grace away from the small crowd on the beach, down the sand dune, calling her name. She stops near a rock with a clump of yellow lupine scrub growing out of it. My throat is tight, and I can't look her in the eyes. She's so agitated, I can almost feel the emotion radiating off her like heat from a furnace. And she's never been upset at me. Ever.

"Why do you want to talk to me now?" Grace says. "You didn't bother to answer my texts this morning."

"I'm sorry!" I blurt out. "I was going to text you back, but—"

"I called two times"—she angrily claps along with her words to drive her point home—"after the texts. It went straight to voice mail."

I wince. My fingers itch to dive into my pocket and check my abandoned phone, but I resist. "It's just—"

"Easy to forget about your friend when your boyfriend is suddenly back in the picture. When he was moping, you had all the time in the world for me. But the second he calls, you throw me away faster than yesterday's news."

Shame and regret roll through me. "That's not true. I just got distracted. I didn't throw you away."

"Well, that's what it feels like. Don't think I haven't been here before with other friends. The second they fall for someone, they forget all about me. Well, I'll tell you what, Bailey Rydell. I'm tired of being the placeholder. If you don't want a real friendship with me, then find someone else who doesn't mind being disposable."

I don't know what to say. Don't know how to make this better.

I'm a surfer, wiping out and drowning under one of those monster waves. Only, I don't think I'm skilled enough to get back up again.

After a long, awkward silence I say, "I'm not good at this."

"At what?"

"Being close to people." I gesture at her, then me. "I screw it up. A lot. It's easier for me to avoid things than deal with confrontation."

"That's your excuse?" she says.

"It's not an excuse. It's the truth."

Why did I do this? If I could wind the clock back to this morning, I'd text her back and everything would be fine. Whether I actively or passively avoided Grace's texts, forgot them on purpose or unintentionally, none of it matters. I failed her. And maybe in doing so, I failed myself a little too.

I don't want to lose Grace. Somehow, while Porter barged in my front door, she sneaked in the back. I try the only thing I have left: the truth.

"You're right," I tell her, words tumbling out. "I took you for granted. I forgot about you this morning because I assumed that you'd always be there, because you always are. I can count on you, because you're dependable. And I'm not. I wish . . . I wish you could count on me like I can count on you. I want to be more like you. You're not a placeholder for me, Grace."

She doesn't say anything, but I can hear her breathing pick up.

"I guess I told myself you wouldn't miss me," I say, picking at the yellow lupine shrub. "That's how I justified it."

"Well, I did miss you. You picked a fine day not to show.

Because I really could have used a shoulder today," she says, still somewhat upset, but now moving into another emotion I can't quite put my finger on. It's hard to decode people when they're wearing big sunglasses and their arms are crossed over their chest.

A wind whips through my hair. I wait until it passes, then ask, "Did something happen?"

"Yes, something happened," she complains. But now I can hear the distress in her voice, and when she lifts her sunglasses to rest them atop her head, I see it mirrored in her eyes. "Taran's not coming back. He's staying in India for the rest of the summer. Maybe for good."

"Oh, God. Grace." My chest constricts painfully.

Slow, silent tears roll down her cheeks. "We've been together for a year. We were going to attend the same college. This isn't how life is supposed to work."

Tentatively, I reach for her, not sure if she'll accept me. But there's not even a heartbeat of hesitation, and she's throwing her arms around me, crying softly as she clings. Her sunglasses fall off her head and land in the sand.

"I'm sorry," I choke out, surprised to find that I'm crying along with her. "For everything."

My old therapist warned me that avoidance is a dysfunctional way to interact with people you care about, but now I'm starting to understand what he meant when he said it could hurt them, too. Maybe it's time I figure out a better way to deal with my problems. Maybe Artful Dodger isn't working so well for me anymore.

23

In the middle of July, Porter and I have another day off together. He tells me we can do whatever I want with it, that he's my genie and will grant me one wish. I tell him that I don't want to see another soul for an entire afternoon. I have something I'm ready to share.

He picks me up in the camper van at noon, two hours after my standing breakfast date with Grace.

"Where are we going?" I say, folding down the visor to block the sun as I hop into the passenger side. I'm wearing my white vintage Annette Funicello shorts and the leopard sunglasses Wanda and Dad brought me back from San Francisco. My Lana Turner 'do looks especially perfect.

Porter glances at my sandals (they're the ones he likes), and then my shorts (which he continues to stare at while he talks to me). "You have two choices, beach or woods. The woods have a stream, which is cool, but the beach has an arch made of rock, which is likewise cool. God, those shorts are hot."

"Thank you. No people at either location?"

"If we see anyone, I will act crazy and chase them off with a stick. But no, these places are both usually deserted."

After some thought, which included taking deep-woods insects into consideration, there's really no choice for the purpose I have in mind, so I gather my gumption and say, "Take me to the beach."

The drive is about fifteen minutes. He has to squeeze through a narrow, rocky road through the woods to get to the beach, pine branches brushing against the top of the van. But when we emerge from the trees, it's glorious: sand, gray pebbles, tide pools, and rising up from the edge of the shore, an arch of mudstone rock. It's covered with birds and barnacles and the waves crash through it.

The beach is small.

The beach isn't sexy.

The beach is ours.

Porter parks the van near the woods. He slides open the side door, and we take off our shoes and toss them in the back. I see he's got his board and wet suit neatly stowed; he's been surfing almost every day.

We splash around in the tide pools for a while. They're teeming with starfish, which I've only ever seen dried on a shelf in a souvenir store. He points out some other critters, but I have more than coastal California wonders on my mind. "Hey, where's the nude beach?"

"What?"

"There's supposed to be a nude beach in Coronado Cove."

Porter laughs. "It's up by the Beacon Resort. It's not even fifty feet wide. There's privacy fencing on both sides. You can't see inside, nor would you want to, I promise."

"Why?"

"It's a swingers' club for retirees. Our parents are too young to get in."

"No way."

"Yes way. Ask Wanda. They get busted for violating after-hours noise ordinances with all their swingers' drinking parties. That's why they had to put up the fencing. People complained."

"Gross."

"You say that now, but when you're eighty and just want to get nude and be served a fruity umbrella drink on the beach by another eighty-year-old nude person, you'll be thankful it's here."

"I suppose you're right."

He squints at me. "Why are you asking me about this?"

I shrug. "Just curious."

"About getting naked on a beach?"

I don't say anything.

His eyes go big. "Holy shit, that's what you're thinking, isn't it?" He points at me and shakes his head. "Something's not adding up here. This isn't you. Now, me, I'm a fan of all things naked. And if you asked me to strip right now, I will. I'm not ashamed. I spent the first few years of my life on this planet naked in the ocean."

I believe that. I really do.

"But you?" He squints at me. "What's this all about?"

Hesitating, I chew the inside of my mouth. "You remember when we were making out that night in the museum?"

"Like every waking minute of my day," he says with a slow smile.

I chuckle. "Me too," I admit before refocusing. "You remember when you started to touch my stomach, and I stopped you?"

His smile fades. "Yeah. I've been wondering when you were going to tell me about that."

"I think I'm ready now."

He nods several times. "Cool. I'm glad."

Of course, now that I've said this, fear overtakes me. I hesitate, gritting my teeth. "Thing is, I need to show you, not tell you. I think this is one of the reasons I've hated beaches for so long . . . the bikini issue. So I think I should just do this, you know?" I'm not sure if I'm talking to him or myself, but it doesn't matter. "Yeah. I'm going to do it."

He looks confused.

"I'm about to get naked on this beach," I tell him.

"Oh, shit," he says, looking truly stunned. "Okay. Um, all right. Yeah, okay."

"But I've never been naked on a beach with anyone, so this is weird for me."

He points at me and grins. "Not a problem. Would you like some company? I'm fond of being naked. It's easier when the playing field's even."

I consider his proposition. "Yeah, okay. That actually would make it easier."

"I just want you to know that there are so many jokes I could make right now," he says.

We both laugh, me a little nervously, and then decide upon a strip-poker method to the clothing removal. Porter volunteers to go first. He scans the beach to make sure we're still alone, and without further ado, peels off his T-shirt. Nice, but it's not really fair, because (A) I've seen it before, and (B) he's not really exposing anything he can't expose in public. He signals for me to go next.

Carefully considering all my options (I'm smartly wearing good matching undergarments), I take off my shorts. He's surprised. He also can't take his eyes off me. I like that . . . I think. I haven't decided yet. I just tell myself that it's the same amount of fabric as wearing a bathing suit, so what's the difference?

"You play dirty, Rydell," he says, unbuttoning his shorts. Before I can open my mouth to argue, he's in nothing but a pair of olive-colored boxer shorts.

Whew. He's got great legs.

Okay, my turn again, as he helpfully reminds me with *get on with it* hand gestures. *Guess it's the shirt,* I think as I pull it over my head and toss it to the sand. A bra is the same amount of fabric as a bathing suit, and it's a good bra. I hear him suck in a quick breath, so I think that's good? My boobs aren't great, but they aren't bad, either, and—

His fingers trace the bottom of my scar. "Is this it? This is what I felt?"

I look down at my ribs and cover his hand, pressing it against my stomach. Then I uncover them and we look together. It's bright and sunny, and we're both halfway naked. And if there's anyone I feel safe with . . . if there's anyone I trust, oddly enough, it's Porter.

"Yes, this is it," I say.

He looks at it. Glances at my face. Waits.

"That's where the bullet went in," I tell him, fingering the puckered ridge of scarring that's never completely healed right. I turn to the side and show him my back. "Here's where it exited."

"I don't understand."

"Greg Grumbacher. That's where he shot me."

"You told me . . . I mean, I thought he shot your mom?"

I shake my head slowly. "My mom wasn't supposed to be home. He followed me home that day because his plan was to kill me. He had a note to leave with my body. His reasoning was that my mom took away his kid in the divorce, so he was taking away hers."

Porter stares at me.

"Mom lunged for the gun, so he missed most of my vital organs. I bled a lot. They had to sew up some stuff. My lung collapsed. I was in the hospital for a couple of weeks."

His shoulders sag. "I'm so sorry. I didn't know."

"You're the first person I've told. My classmates heard, but my mom put me in another school after it happened. Anyway, there you go. Told you I was screwed up," I say, giving him a small smile.

He curls his hand around my waist, rubbing from the front scar to the back. "Thank you for telling me. For showing me."

"Thanks for not making it weird. I don't want it to be a big deal anymore, you know? That's why I wanted to show you. Out here in the sun."

"I get it," he says. "I totally get it."

I lean forward and press my lips against the sweet dip where his collarbones meet. He pushes back my hair with his palm and kisses me in the middle of my forehead, both eyelids, on the tip of my nose. Then he pulls me tight against him and folds me up in his arms. I breathe him into my lungs as deeply as I can, all his sun-burnished, warm goodness. *Thank you, thank you, thank you*, I try to tell him with my body. And from the way he's holding me— like I'm a whole person, not a broken toy—I think he understands.

"Does this mean you want to stop our game now?" he murmurs after a time.

I tilt my head back to see his face. "Are you chickening out on me?"

He grins that slow and cocky grin of his and pushes me back until I'm an arm's length away. "Both at the same time, on the count of three."

"Not fair! I've got two pieces of clothing left."

"I'll close my eyes until you say I can open them. One, two . . ."

With a euphoric cry, I fumble with my bra strap and strip off my underwear. I did it!

"Holy shit, you're beautiful," he murmurs.

"Cheater." I'm 100 percent naked. On a public beach. And more important, I don't care, because Porter's taken off his clothes too, and that's far more interesting than any fleeting sense of modesty I have. Because he's naked. And he's gorgeous.

And he's very excited about our mutual sans-clothing situation.

"Oh," I say, looking down between us.

"I'm pretty proud of that," he admits with a smile, urging my hand forward. When I touch him, he stands on tiptoes for a moment and looks like he might pass out, which makes *me* very excited about our mutual sans-clothing situation.

"Now I'm thinking about the back of the camper van," I say.

He blows out a hard breath and pushes my hand away. "I think that's a dicey idea. Maybe we should get dressed first. God, you're so beautiful."

"You mentioned that."

"Let me look at you some more first. I need to memorize all of you for later. In case I never get to see this again. Shit. I can't believe you talked me into . . ." His eyes are heavy-lidded. "This is either the best or worst idea I've ever agreed to. You're killing me, Bailey Rydell."

"I know you've got condoms in that first-aid kit."

A wave crashes again the rock bridge.

"Bailey . . ."

"Porter."

"It might be terrible. Trust me, I have experience in these matters."

"It might not, though, right?"

Seagulls circle overhead, squawking.

"Are you sure?"

"I'm sure," I say. I've been thinking about it a lot over the last few weeks. And I've made up my mind. "If you want to, with me, that is. I'm not trying to pressure you."

He swears softly. "It'll be a miracle if I can make it all the way back to the van. But if you change your mind, you can, you know? At any point. Even in the middle of it."

But I don't change my mind.

Not on the way to the van, or when we're dumping his surfboard out to make room. And not when he's asking me a dozen times if I'm sure, and trying to convince me otherwise by doing the fabulous thing he did to me in the museum with his fingers, which only makes me want him more. Not when we start, and he's being careful and slow and deliberate, and I can't bear to look at his face, but I don't know where to look, so I'm looking between us, because I'm worried it will be messy, and that it's going to hurt, and it does, but the pain is over fast, and then it's just . . . so much more intense than I expected. But he's going so slow, and then he says—

"Are you still okay?" in a husky, breathless voice.

Yes, I still am.

And I don't change my mind in the middle of it, when it's

overwhelming, and he stops, because he's afraid I want him to stop, but I'm okay—I'm so okay—and convince him to keep going.

And not after, when we're clinging to each other like the world just fell apart and is slowly clicking back together, piece by piece, breath by breath . . . heartbeat by beautiful heartbeat.

I do not regret a single moment.

"What is this?" I ask some time later, tugging on something white that's wedged in a crevice as we lie tangled together on an old blanket in the back of the van. In the back of my mind, I'm thinking that I know for sure I saw another condom in the first-aid kit, and I'm wondering how long I have to wait to bring this up without looking too eager. But I'm propped up on my elbows and Porter's lazily running his fingers across my back, meandering down my butt and the back of my leg, and this feels pretty freaking good, so I guess I'm in no hurry.

The jagged object I shimmy out of the crevice is about an inch long and triangular, and it's got a piece of silver fitted on one side, through which a silver jump ring is attached.

"Huh. I thought I lost that," he says, pausing my sensual back scratch to take it from me. "That came out of my arm. Genuine great white tooth. It's a lucky charm. Or a curse, whichever way you want to look at it. I had it on my key chain, but I was switching keys out and set it down. Must have rolled off the seat or something."

"It's huge," I say.

"No way, that's just a baby tooth. You saw the sharks at the aquarium. Great white was twice their size. And he was a teenager."

I try to imagine the tooth implanted in Porter's arm. "I know it's a bad memory, but the tooth itself should be survivor's pride, or something. A badge of honor."

"You want to borrow it?"

"Me?"

"For your scooter keys. Might match your whole animal-print vibe." He pauses. "I mean, if it's too much, no big deal. I'm not trying to brand you, like you're my girl or anything."

Because if people see this, they'll definitely know we're dating each other. "Am I? Your girl, I mean."

"I don't know. Are you?" He offers the shark tooth in his open palm, hesitates, and closes his fingers around it. "If you are, you have to promise me something first."

"What's that?"

"You've got to start opening up to me." He glances toward my back. "Look, I totally understand why you didn't tell me the whole story about the gunshot wound until now, but you can't be that way around me anymore. I already had a girlfriend who kept things from me, and I spent weeks walking around oblivious while she was screwing Davy behind my back."

"First, ew, I have better taste than that, and second, I would never do that to you."

He kisses my ear. "I believe you."

"So, yeah, speaking of Chloe . . . Were you and Davy having sex with Chloe at the same time?"

"Together?" He sounds appalled.

I smile. "You know what I mean."

"No," he says, sounding sheepish. "Chloe and I were going through a dry spell at the time. There was no cross-contamination, if that's what you're worried about."

I sort of was.

"And we always used condoms. Every time."

"Good to know," I mumble. *Very good.*

"Anyway, back to you," he says. "What I'm trying to say is that you're sort of bad about bottling things up. And I'm not saying you've got to turn into Grace. I like you just the way you are. But in order for this to work, you've got to tell me stuff. I need you to trust me—"

"Of course I do." *Hello. Did we not just have sex?*

"—and I need to be able to trust you," he finishes.

I start to argue, but I'm embarrassed that he's even brought this up.

He nudges my chin with his, forcing me to face him, and speaks quietly against my mouth. "Listen to me, okay? What's between us? This is the best thing that's ever happened to me in my entire life, and I don't want it to end. Sometimes you feel so tricky, like fog over the ocean—like you just showed up at the beginning of the summer, and one day the sun will come out and you'll disappear and go back to your mom. And that scares the hell out of me. So that's why I tell you things about me, because I figure if I weigh you down with my baggage, then you'll be less likely to run."

My heart twists.

I press my brow against his. "Artful Dodger."

"Huh?"

"That's me. Or it used to be." That morning on the beach when Grace was mad at me ghosts through my thoughts. I need to do better. "I'm trying, Porter. I really am. I want you to trust me."

"That's all I ask." He leans back to look at me, smiles softly, and opens up his fingers to reveal the shark tooth again. "So . . . do you want it? People might talk."

I snatch it up with a grin. "Maybe they'll say that you're mine."

"Bailey, I've *been* yours. I've just been waiting for you to make up your mind."

Later that night, after Porter brings me back home, I'm too blissed out to be around people, especially my dad. So I put on my leopard scarf and sunglasses and take Baby out for a drive around the neighborhood. When I get to the big hill at the end of our street, I throw my hands up in the air, shouting, "I'm in love!" to the redwood trees.

"Pay no attention to that man behind the curtain."
—Frank Morgan, *The Wizard of Oz* (1939)

24

My dad's no cook, but the CPA in him can follow a recipe like no one's business. Together, however, we managed to ruin a roasted chicken, which was still raw two hours into cooking. That's when we figured out that something was wrong with one of our oven's elements. We dumped the chicken, gave it last rites over the garbage can—RIP—and called for pizza. And even though we were a little upset by the failure, our guests—Wanda, Grace, and Porter—didn't seem to mind.

It's been a week since Nude Beach, and it's the first time Porter's been invited inside my house, so I'm nervous anyway. I'm not sure why. Maybe it's because I've hung out at Porter's house several times, and it's so comfortable over there, and now I'm worried it won't be the same here. He already cracked a joke about hanging out with a cop, so there's that, too. Even though I don't think about Wanda as being some kind of intimidating authority figure, I can understand why Porter might feel that way. Now I feel defensive about her and want him to like both her and my dad, and that feels . . . stressful.

But when the pizza's delivered and Porter's thumbing through my dad's DVD collection, things start looking up. Turns out my dad and Porter like a lot of the same sci-fi movies. Porter has no idea what a huge mistake he's just made, because Dad is thrilled out of his ever-loving mind and will not shut up with the nerdery talk: Have you seen this space-pirate gem from 1977? What about this long-lost 1982 flick? If they start talking *Star Wars*, I'm going to have to shut it all down.

The entire time they're talking, I can't tear my eyes away from Porter. What I'm feeling for him now is like drowning and floating at the same time. When he gives me a quick glance, I'm overwhelmed. Does he feel like this too? This epic connection between us? It's thrilling and frightening. Like the rest of my life was just a series of bad B movies and we just walked onto the set of *Citizen Kane*.

"Lord, you've got it bad," Grace whispers near my ear. "Must have been good, huh?"

Ugh, I should never have told her what happened on the beach. I didn't give her any details, but maybe that's the problem. She's filling them in with her dirty little mind. I bat her arm away, and our discreet, playful slap-fest devolves into immature giggling. When my dad and Porter notice, something near hysteria rises up in me, and I herd Grace toward the sofa, ducking out of sight.

I'm trying so hard to be more open with him, to talk about . . . all of this. These chaotic feelings. About what happened in the back of the camper van. We haven't been together again, not like that. Haven't had time. We've had some lovely deep kisses in the front of the van after work and a lot of midnight phone calls about nothing much at all, really—we just needed to hear each other's voices. But every time I try to tell him how I really feel, how *much* I really feel, my chest feels like a hundred-pound fiery fist is squeezing my heart.

Sheer panic.

Once a coward, always a coward.

What if I can't change? If I can't be as honest and open as he needs me to be? As reliable a friend as Grace wants me to be? What if Greg Grumbacher ruined me forever? That's what scares me the most.

After all the male-on-male sci-fi talk, we all retire to the porch and sit around the patio table near the redwood tree that grows through the roof. Dad brings out the holy worn game box.

"Okay," he says very seriously. "What Bailey and I are choosing to share with you tonight is a Rydell family tradition. By taking part in this game—nay, this cherished and sacred ceremony—"

I snort a little laugh while he continues his speech.

"—you are agreeing to honor our proud family heritage, which extends as far back as . . . well, I think the price sticker on the box is from around 2001, so it's pretty ancient."

Wanda rolls her eyes. "I'll give it my attention for fifteen minutes, Pete."

"No, Sergeant Mendoza," he says dramatically, slicing his hand through the air as if he's some stern politician at a podium, commanding attention. "You will give Settlers of Catan your attention for a full hour or two, because the colonies deserve it."

"And because it will take you at least that long to build up your settlements," I tell her.

"Is there a dungeon master?" Porter asks.

Dad and I both chuckle.

"What?" Porter says, grinning.

"We have so much to teach you," I say, putting my hand on his. "And there's no dungeon master. Wrong kind of game nerd."

"Is this more or less boring than Monopoly?" Grace asks.

"Less," Dad and I say together.

"Monopoly is for losers," Dad informs her.

Porter frowns. "I love Monopoly."

"We have an entire chest full of old board games," I whisper loudly to him.

"I'm not going to like this, am I?" Wanda says on a heavy sigh.

"Now might be a good time to break out that expensive bottle of wine you guys brought back from San Francisco," I suggest.

Porter grins at me and rubs his hands together excitedly. "This looks super weird. I'm *so* in. Let's play."

God, I love him. I don't even know why I was so worried before. This is all fine now.

Dad unpacks the game and explains all the rules, confusing everyone in the process. We finally just start playing and teach as we go. They get the hang of it. I'm not sure if they like it as much as Dad and I do, but everyone seems to be having fun. We're laughing and goofing around a lot, anyway. Everything's going great, until about an hour into the game.

The pizza made me thirsty. I excuse myself to get some iced tea from the kitchen and ask if anyone else needs a refill. My dad does, so I leave to fetch tea for both of us. While I'm headed away from the table, my dad says, "Thanks, Mink."

Behind me, I hear Porter ask my dad, "What did you call her?"

"Huh? Oh, 'Mink'? That's just a childhood nickname," my dad says through the open doorway.

"I hear you call her that all the time," Wanda remarks, "but you never told me why."

"It's actually a funny story," Dad says.

I groan as I pour our tea, but my dad is already in storytelling mode, and I can hear him from the kitchen.

"This is how it came about. When Bailey was younger, fourteen years old, she was in the hospital for a couple of weeks." I glance back briefly to see him giving Wanda a lift of his brows that tells me they've had this conversation, so she knows about the shooting. "The entire time she was there, the TV was stuck on the classic movie station. You know, with all the old movie stars—Humphrey Bogart and Cary Grant, Katharine Hepburn. Night and day, that's all that was on. We were so worried about her, that by the time any-one thought to change the channel, she'd already started to actually like some of the movies and wouldn't let us change it."

I sigh dramatically as I walk back through the doorway onto the porch and set down our glasses of tea.

"Anyway, for a few days, after surgery, it was a little touch and go. And being a dad, I was worried, of course. I told her if she healed up and made it out of the hospital, I'd buy her whatever she wanted. Most girls her age would probably say, I don't know—a car? A pony? A trip to Florida with her friends? Not Bailey. She saw those glamorous actresses wearing all those fur coats before it wasn't PC to do so anymore, and she said, 'Daddy, I want a mink coat.'"

Wanda guffaws. "Did you get her one?"

"A fake fur," Dad says. "It was just the attitude I never forgot. And she still loves those old movies. Is everything all right, Porter?"

As I'm scooting my chair back under the table, I glance up and see that Porter has a peculiar look on his face. He looks like someone just told him his dog died.

"What's wrong?" I ask.

He's staring at the table and won't look at me. He was just laughing and clowning around a minute ago, now all of a sudden he's clammed up and his jaw looks as if it's made of stone and might break off.

Everyone's staring at him. He shuffles around in his seat and brings his hand up with his phone. "I got a text from my mom. Gotta go, sorry."

No way. The old *I got a text* trick? That's an Artful Dodger maneuver. He just pulled my own con on me?

334 • JENN BENNETT

"What's wrong?" I say again, standing up from the table with him.

"Nothing, nothing," he mutters. "It's no big deal. She just needs my help and it can't wait. Sorry." He seems agitated and distracted. "Thanks for dinner and stuff."

"Anytime," my dad says, worry creasing a line through his brow as he shares a look with Wanda. "You're always welcome here."

"See you, Grace," Porter mumbles.

I can barely keep up with Porter as he strides toward the front door, and when we're outside, he bounds down the steps without looking at me. Now I'm freaking. Maybe he really did get a text, but it wasn't from his mom. Because there's only one person that makes him this intense, and if he's avoiding my dad and Wanda, I'm worried it might have something to do with Davy.

"Porter," I call as he heads down the driveway.

"Gotta go," he says.

That just makes me mad. He can avoid my dad all he wants, but me? "Hey! What the hell is wrong with you?"

He spins around, and his face is suddenly livid with anger. "Was this some sick game?"

"Huh?" I'm completely confused. He's not making any sense, and his gaze is shifting all over my face. "You're scaring me. Did something happen?" I ask. "Is this about Davy? Did he do something again? Please talk to me."

"What?" Bewilderment clouds his face. He squeezes his eyes

closed and shakes his head, mumbling, "This is so screwed up. I can't . . . I gotta go home."

"Porter!" I shout to his back, but he doesn't turn around. Doesn't look my way again. I just stand helplessly, cradling my elbows in the driveway, watching as his van rumbles to life and disappears down the street around the redwood trees.

25

I text.

I call.

I text.

I call.

He doesn't respond.

Grace tries, too, but he doesn't answer her, either. "I'm sure it's some stupid misunderstanding," she assures me. But I'm pretty positive she doesn't believe that.

After Grace goes home, I continue to replay the entire porch conversation in my head, looking for clues, trying to remember exactly when I noticed something was wrong. I ask my dad, but he's no help. I'm so anguished, I even ask Wanda, and when I can tell by the expression on her face that even she feels pity for my desperate state, I nearly start sobbing in front of her, and that's when I know things have gone to hell in a handbasket.

"He claimed he got a text sometime during or after your dad was telling that story," Wanda says.

I rub the sockets of my eyes with the heel of my palms; my head's throbbing. On top of this, I think I'm getting sick. "But why wouldn't he tell me about it?"

"I hate to ask this," my dad says in a gentle voice, "but did you do anything that may have wounded his feelings? Lie to him in some way that he may have found out about?"

"No!" I say. "Like cheat on him or something?"

Dad raises both hands. "I didn't mean to imply that. Does he know about your online friend?"

"Alex?" I shake my head. "I haven't spoken to Alex online in weeks. And I never met him in person—or even found him. He blew me off because he found a girlfriend or something, I don't know. It doesn't matter. We never even really flirted. He was a sweet guy. We were just friends, honest."

"No sexting or dirty photos that could have been leaked online?" Wanda asks.

"God no," I say, and my dad practically wilts, he's so relieved. *Way to have faith, jeez.*

"Just checking," Wanda says. She's in total cop-interrogation mode. "And Porter was the hickey giver, right?"

"Yes," I snap. I don't mean to, but I can't help it.

I don't like where this conversation is going. Before long, she's going to ask me to submit to STD testing. And meanwhile, my dad, who's staring absently at his sci-fi movies, makes a choking noise, like he just realized something, but when I ask him what it is, he waves it away.

"It's nothing," he says, looking dazed and almost . . . amused. "Whatever's going on, I'm sure you'll figure it out, sweetie."

That just makes me even more frustrated, and a little angry, to be honest. None of this is really helping, so what's the point? I sneeze twice, and when Dad asks me if I'm coming down with a cold, I ignore him and go to my room. Then I plug in my phone and watch it as if the fate of the entire planet depends on one small, melodic chime emanating from its tiny speaker.

I wait until two a.m., and when that chime doesn't come, I turn on my side and stare at the wall, heart shattering, until I drift into restless sleep.

By the time my shift at the Cave rolls around the next day, I've made myself so sick with worry, I can't tell whether I want to see Porter or not. I've been trying so hard not to use Artful Dodger tactics lately, but I hesitate in the parking lot when I see his van, and take the long way around to the employee door. This must be how alcoholics feel when they fall off the wagon.

When I finally do see him, it's in the cash-out room at the exact same moment that Grace strolls in to count her drawer. My body tenses so hard at the sight of him, I'm in physical pain. Grace has taken on the role of peacemaker as she greets us, lightly complaining about how they've scheduled our lunch breaks, but neither Porter nor I say anything. It's awkward. Everyone knows it.

I can't do this. I've had no sleep. My mind is the consistency of wet sand. I'm pretty sure I'm running a fever, I've got chills, my nose won't stop running, and my eyeballs hurt. I'm not the only one; half the staff is out with some weird, mutant summer virus that Grace is calling "the lurgy." But I ignore how I feel physically, because I need to know what's going on with Porter. I have to!

"No," I tell Porter, blocking his way out of the room. "This isn't fair. I stayed up all night worrying. You need to tell me what's going on right now."

"Can we not do this right here?" Porter says, eyeing Grace.

"Where, then? I texted and called. How can I fix this if you won't tell me what I did wrong?"

"I needed to think." Now that I'm looking him directly in the eyes for the first time, I can see that he looks as bad as I feel. Dark circles band the undersides of his lower lashes, and his scruff looks unkempt. He looks exhausted. Good. "Maybe you need to do some thinking too."

"Think about what?" I ask, completely perplexed.

He glances at Grace again. "Look," he says in a lower voice, "I just . . . I'm really overwhelmed right now. I need a little space, okay?"

His words sting like a thousand hornets.

"Porter," I whisper.

The door to cash-out swings open, and Mr. Cavadini strolls inside with his clipboard. He opens his mouth to greet us, but whatever he starts to say is drowned out by my sneezing. Not polite sneezing either; I have to lunge for the box of tissues by the empty cash drawers afterward, and turn around while I clean myself up. I'm a disgusting mess.

"You've got it too?" Cavadini says, sounding horrified. When I turn around, he backs away and shakes his head. "Absolutely not. Grace, disinfect everything in cash-out that she's touched. Bailey, go home."

"Wha? I'm fine!" I say through a tissue.

"You're Typhoid Mary. Go home. Call in tomorrow and let me know how you are. We'll put you back on the schedule when you're not infectious."

No matter how I try, he won't let me argue. And when Porter and Grace are whisked away to the Hotbox, so are my chances of discovering why Porter needs "space." Miserable and feverish, I retreat home with no answers and crawl back into bed.

I will say one thing: Cavadini was probably right to boot me out of the Cave. A couple of hours later, I wake up and my entire body aches. I cannot stay warm. I call Dad at work after I take my temperature, and it's 101 F. He immediately rushes home and drives me to an urgent care facility, where I see a doctor who gives me something to reduce my fever, basically telling me what I already knew—*You've got the lurgy!*—and prescribes me a bunch of cold medicine.

The second day of my mutant illness, my dad changes the sheets on my bed, because I sweated through them all night like a beast. But at least my fever's broken. Which is good, because now I'm hacking up my lungs. He goes to work in the morning, but takes a half day, coming home at noon to feed me a lunch of soup and crackers. He also tries to lure me downstairs, but I'm content to stay in my narrow flight path of bathroom to bedroom. I have a paid online streaming account and a DVD player in my room. That's all I need to get me through this. I start watching a movie that reminds me of Alex, strangely enough, which makes me feel even worse than I already do.

Grace has checked in on me via text several times. The Cave is down to a skeleton crew, but she's managed to escape getting sick so far. I don't ask about Porter. She volunteers anyway: It's his day off, so she doesn't know if he's sick too—but would I like her to text him and ask? No, I would not. He wants space? Have the plains of Serengeti, for all I care. I'm beyond wounded now. I'm angry. At least, I think I am. It's hard to tell. I started taking cough syrup with codeine today, and it's giving me a little bit of a buzz.

Another kind of buzz lights up my phone midafternoon. I hit pause on the movie I'm watching. It's an alert from Lumière Film Fanatics. I have a new message? Maybe this syrup is making me hallucinate. But no. I click on the app, and there it is:

@alex: Hey. Mink, you there? Long time, no talk.

I stare at it for a minute, then type a reply.

@mink: I'm still here. Laid up sick in bed. Oddly enough, I was just thinking about you, so it's kind of freaking me out that you messaged me.

@alex: You were? Why? *is curious* (Sorry you're sick.)

@mink: I'm watching Key Largo. (Thanks. Me too. It's gross, trust me.)

@alex: Whoa. Bogie and Bacall Key Largo? I thought you said you couldn't stomach that? What about all the being-held-at-gunpoint?

@mink: It wasn't as bad as I thought it would be. I'm almost finished. It's so good. You were right.

@alex: Color me shocked. (I always am.) So . . . anything new happening? We haven't talked in so long. Fill me in on what's going on in the world of Mink. I've missed you.

I pause, unsure what to type. It would be weird to say *I've missed you too*, even though I have, because that feels like I'm betraying Porter. I'm so confused. Maybe he doesn't even mean it that way. Maybe he never did. Lord knows I'm not good at reading people.

@mink: The world of Mink has imploded. Do you have all day?

@alex: Funny, but I do.

I'm not sure whether it's the codeine streaming in my blood or the virus decimating my brain cells, but I settle back against my pillow and type the most straightforward message I've ever sent to Alex.

@mink: Actually, I'm sort of seeing someone—well, we kind of broke up. I think. I'm not sure. He won't talk to me. But I'm not over him. I just didn't want you to get the wrong idea. And maybe you wouldn't anyway, I don't know. But I used to think that there was something between us—you and me—or that there could be. And then this guy sort of just happened. I didn't expect it. So, anyway, I'm sounding like a complete idiot now, especially if you didn't feel that way about me. But I'm trying to turn over a new leaf and be more honest lately, so I just wanted you to know. In case you were still holding out hope for anything. I just can't. Not right now.

@alex: Wow. That's a lot to take in at once.

@mink: I know. I'm sorry.

@alex: No, I'm glad you said it. Truly. You have no idea how relieved I am to get things out in the open, actually.

@mink: Really?

344 • JENN BENNETT

@alex: Cross my heart. So . . . what's this guy like?

@mink: Honestly, he's kind of an ass. Cocky. Super opinionated. Always picking fights.

@alex: ??? And you like him why, again?

@mink: I'm trying to remember . . . Okay, he's also sweet and smart, and he makes me laugh. He's a surfer, actually. Like, stupid talented. And he geeks out about weather, which is sort of cute.

@alex: I see. But he makes you laugh?

I suddenly feel horrible. Here I am, spilling my guts about Porter, but I don't really know how Alex feels about it. About me. About this whole situation I just laid at his feet.

@mink: No one makes me laugh like you do.

@alex: That's all I ever wanted.

I laugh a little, then begin to cry.

@mink: I miss you too. I miss watching movies with you. And I'm sorry everything changed. I didn't know things were going to turn out this way. But I hope we can still be friends, because my life was better with you in it. And that's the truth.

@alex: I hope we can still be friends too. I need to go, though.

When the app tells me he's logged off, my soft crying turns into full-on sobbing. I'm not sure why, but I feel as though I've lost something important. Maybe it's because he didn't agree that absolutely, we should and will be friends—he said he hopes we can still be friends. Meaning what? He's not sure? Have I damaged not one, but two relationships?

My state of illness doesn't allow me to cry for long before my entire upper respiratory system clogs up and threatens to shut down. It's probably for the best. I force myself to calm down, try to blow my nose, and finish watching the last few minutes of *Key Largo*. At least I can count on Humphrey Bogart coming back for Lauren Bacall, though for a second there, it was touch and go.

When the credits roll, I hear noise in the stairwell, and then my dad appears in the doorway. "You— Hey . . . have you been crying?" he says in a hushed voice. "Are you okay? What's wrong?"

I wave a hand. "Nothing. It's fine."

His brow furrows for a second, but he seems to believe me. "You have a visitor, Mink. You feeling up for it?" He gives me a warning look, though how I'm supposed to interpret that look is beyond me.

I sit up straighter in my bed. Visitor? Grace is at work. "I . . . guess?"

Dad moves out of the way and motions for someone to come inside my room.

Porter.

"Hey," he says, gritting his teeth when he sees me. "Wow, you weren't faking, were you? Should I don one of those surgical masks?"

My dad chuckles. "I haven't caught it yet. But you might want to keep your distance and wash your hands on the way out."

Porter gives my dad a casual salute, and before I know it, we're alone. Just me and Porter. In my bedroom. A week ago, that would have been a fantasy. Now I'm stuffed into unflattering booty shorts and a faded T-shirt with an embarrassing, uncool band on it that I don't listen to anymore. My unwashed hair is shoved into one of those messy buns that's actually messy, not sexy messy. And I can't think straight because I'm high on cough syrup.

"So, this is your secret garden?" he says, strolling around as I stealthily try to shovel wads of used tissues off my bedcovers into a wastebasket. He stops in front of my dresser to inspect all the printouts I've taped around the mirror: vintage pin-curl instructions, retro nail-painting guides, and several close-up photos showcasing Lana Turner's hair. "Ah. I get it now."

I'm sort of wishing he didn't. I feel very exposed, as if he's peeking behind the Wizard of Oz's curtain. Why didn't I close my closet door? I hope there's nothing embarrassing in there.

He's made it to my stack of boxes. "What's all this? Going somewhere?"

"No, I just haven't unpacked everything yet."

"You've been in California for how long now?"

"I know, I know," I mumble. "I just haven't had the time."

He gives me an askance look before moving on to my shelves of DVDs. "But you had time to unpack fifty million movies? God, you are just like your dad, aren't you? Total film fanatic, and super organized. Are these alphabetical?"

"By genre, then alphabetical by title," I say weakly, feeling foolish.

He whistles. "We need you over at Casa Roth to reorganize the madhouse that is our DVD library, stat. Lana keeps forgetting to put the discs back in the cases after she watches something."

"I hate that," I say.

"I know, right? Criminal offense."

"Porter?"

"Yeah?"

"Why are you here?"

He turns around, hands in the pockets of his shorts. "I'm done with needing space. That was stupid. Just forget about it."

"Wait, what? How can I forget about it? What is 'it'? I need to know what I did."

"You didn't do anything. It was just a misunderstanding."

Still confused. "About me?" My cough-syrup-addled brain goes back to that night again, like it has a hundred times before, and all I can latch on to is . . . "You got a text from someone? You said it wasn't Davy, but were you lying? What does this have to do with me?"

He squints. "Are you drunk, or is this just how you are when you're sick?"

"Errmm," I moan, waving my hand at the bottle on my night-stand. "Codeine."

"Holy . . . You're on the purp? Glad Davy's not here, or he'd have stolen that and downed the whole thing in one gulp. Are you taking the right dose?"

I stick out my tongue and make an *ahh* sound. When both of Porter's brows slowly rise, I take that as a sign that my answer wasn't appropriate, and sigh deeply, pulling the bedspread higher over my chest. "Yes, I took the right dose," I say grumpily. "And if you're just trying to avoid answering my questions, I'd like you to leave."

He stares at me for entirely too long, like he's thinking things over, or hatching some sort of devious plan—I can't tell which. The keys that hang on the leather strap from his belt loop rock against his hip as he jangles his pocket change. Then, abruptly, he turns around and heads to my DVD shelves, runs his fingers along the cases, and plucks one out.

"What are you doing?" I ask.

"Where's your player? Here? Let's see, what do we have . . . *Key Largo*? Is that any good? Let me just put it back in the case. I don't want to pull a Lana. Is everything—"

"Porter!"

"—set, or do I have to switch the input? Where's your remote? If you've gotten your diseased crud on it, I'm not touching it. Scoot over. And don't cough on me." He's peeling off his HOT STUFF jacket and motioning to let him sit next to me in the double bed.

I'm suddenly well aware that my father is right downstairs. And wait—why do I care? I'm sick. And gross. And we're not even together.

Are we?

"Porter—"

"Scooch."

I scooch. He plops down next to me, long legs stretched out and ankles crossed on top of the covers. When he sees one of my snotty tissues next to his elbow, he makes a sour face.

I angrily toss the tissue onto the floor. "I'm not watching a movie with you until you tell me why you stormed out of my house that night."

"I'm being completely real with you when I say it was the misunderstanding of the century. And it's nothing you did wrong. I realize that now. Like I told you before, I needed some time to think about things, because it was . . . well, it doesn't matter. But"—he crosses his arms over his chest when I start to protest, like he's not budging—"let's drop the whole thing."

"What? That's—"

"Look, it's really nothing. It was stupid. I'm sorry for making you worry over nothing. Let's just forget it. Hit play, will you?"

I stare at him, flabbergasted. "No."

"No, what?"

"I can't accept that. I need to know what happened."

He leans back against the headboard and looks at me for a long time. A really long time. Now I'm uncomfortable, because he's smiling at me—this strange, slow smile that's hiding a secret. It makes me want to hide or hit him.

"Maybe I'll feel like talking after the movie starts," he says. "What's this flick about, anyway? I just picked something random."

Momentarily distracted, I glance at the menu on the screen. "*The Philadelphia Story*? You've never seen this?"

He shakes his head slowly, still smiling that funny smile. "Tell me about it."

That's weird, because it looked like he was choosing something particular on the shelf, but whatever. "It's one of my favorite movies. Katharine Hepburn is a society woman, an heiress, you see, who learns to love the right man—that's her pompous ex, Cary Grant, who she bickers with constantly—by kissing the wrong man, who's Jimmy Stewart."

"Is that so?"

"Your grandmother never watched it?" I ask.

"Don't remember this one. Do you think I'll like it? Or should I pick out something else?" He throws a leg over the side of the bed. "Because if you want, I could go ask your dad for suggestions—"

I clamp a hand around his arm. "Oh wait, it's wonderful. So funny. Like, brilliantly funny. Let's watch it."

"Hit play," he says, sinking back into my pillows. "You can fill me in on trivia as it goes."

"And then you'll tell me?" I insist.

"Hit play, Mink."

I narrow my eyes at his use of my nickname, unsure if he's

making fun of me, but I'll give him a pass. Because, hello! *The Philadelphia Story.* I could watch this a thousand times and never get weary of it. Watching with someone else who's never seen it is so much better. With Porter? I can't believe my luck. I hope he likes it.

We start the movie, and for the moment, I'm not caring that I'm sick anymore. I'm just happy that Porter's here with me, and that he's laughing warmly at the right lines. It would be perfect, really, if he wouldn't stop staring at me. He's watching my face more than the screen, and every time I look at him quizzically, he doesn't even glance away. He just smiles that same knowing smile. And that's creeping me out.

"What?" I finally whisper hotly.

"This is . . . amazing," he says.

"Oh," I say, brightening. "Just wait. The movie gets even better."

Slow smile.

I pull the covers up to my chin.

A quarter of the way through the movie, my dad comes up to remind me to take all my various cold medicines, at which point several jokes are made at my expense between the males in the room. They both think they're comedians. We'll see who's laughing when Porter gets the lurgy after lounging on my bed.

Halfway through, Porter suddenly asks, "What were your plans this summer?"

"Huh?" I glance at him out of the corner of my eyes.

"That time at work, you were telling Pangborn that you had

other plans this summer, and that I wasn't part of those plans. What were those plans?"

My heart pounds as I try to think up some plausible excuse, but the cough syrup is slowing down my thought process. "I don't remember."

His jaw tightens. "If you come clean about that, I'll tell you the reason I left your house on game night. Deal?"

Crap. No way am I confessing that I've been scoping out another guy half the summer—an anonymous guy who I've been chatting with online for months. That sounds . . . unstable. Psychotic. Porter would never understand. And it's not like Alex and I acted on any feelings. We never proclaimed our love for each other or sent heart-filled, dirty poetry.

"I have no idea what you're talking about," I tell Porter.

Even through my buzzy haze, I can sense his disappointment, but I can't make myself divulge my secrets about Alex.

"Think hard," Porter says in a quiet voice. Almost a plea. "You can tell me anything. You can trust me."

There it is again. The *T* word. My mind drifts back to our conversation in the back of the camper van. *I need to be able to trust you.*

I know he wants me to tell him. I just . . . can't.

I'm not sure when it happened, but the last thing I remember is Jimmy Stewart kissing Katharine Hepburn. The next thing I know, I'm waking up dopey several hours later.

Porter is long gone.

• • •

Two days later, Cavadini puts me back on the schedule, and I head into work. I don't see Porter in cash-out. It's just Grace and the new guard who replaced Pangborn. Porter is here today—I know, because I checked the schedule—so I search for him as we head out to the floor. That's where I spot him, handling the changing of the guard. He's letting the morning ticket takers out of the Hotbox—two stupid boys, Scott and Kenny. I step up to the back door before they can all walk away and hand Grace my cash drawer, motioning for her to go inside without me.

"You left my house without saying good-bye," I tell Porter.

"You were pretty sick. I'm kind of busy right now, so—"

"You also left without telling me about game night."

He glances at Scott and Kenny. "Maybe later," he says.

"That's what you said before."

"And my offer still stands." He leans closer and whispers, "Quid pro quo, Clarice."

Not that again. He's not *Silence of the Lambs*-ing me into confessing about Alex. No way, no how. I try another tactic. "You go first, then I'll consider telling you."

"Bailey," he says again, like it's some kind of coded warning I should understand. "You really don't want to do this here." He glances at the two boys.

It hits me like a physical blow that he's using evasion techniques against me. From the moment all of this happened on game night with the fake text message—because it was fake, wasn't it?—to the distraction of *The Philadelphia Story*, until right now, when conveniently he is surrounded by people and therefore cannot discuss the matter.

Is this what it feels like to be Artful Dodgered? Because it sucks, big-time.

Porter clears his throat. "I've, uh, got to get them to cash-out, but—"

"No," I say, cutting him off. I realize I sound unreasonable now, and I'm mildly embarrassed that I'm raising my voice in front of Tweedledee and Tweedledum—but I just can't stop myself. "I need to know what happened on game night."

"Hey. We'll talk later. Trust me, okay?"

"Oh, are we on your schedule now? If Porter deigns to dole out a crumb? I'm just supposed to wait around for you like some well-behaved puppy dog?"

His face darkens. "I never said that. I just asked you to trust me."

"Give me a reason to."

His head jerks back as if I've slapped him, and then his face turns stony. "I thought I already had."

My chest tightens, and I suddenly wish I could take it all back. I don't want to fight with him. I just want things to go back to how they were before that night, when everything changed. As he walks off with the idiots, I hear Kenny say, "Damn, Roth. You've always got hot girls chasing after you. I need to start surfing."

"Yeah, but they're always whiners, and who needs that drama?" Scott says. "Bitches are crazy."

Porter chuckles. Chuckles!

Suddenly, I'm Alice in Wonderland, falling through a rabbit hole, watching the beautiful memories from the last couple of months pass me by as I descend into madness. And walking away from me is the old Porter Roth, the stupid surfer boy that I loathed. The one who humiliated me.

I'm devastated.

I pound on the Hotbox door. Grace swings it open, her face pinched with concern. I don't have time to explain; the line is long, and she's inserted my cash drawer, readying everything for me to start.

Ugh. It's already a million degrees in here. My chest is swelling with confusion and hurt, emotions rising with each passing second.

"Two tickets." Some stoner boy with shaggy blond hair is standing outside my window with some girl, giving me an *I don't have all day* look. I stare back at him. I think I've forgotten how to use the computer. I'm beginning to go numb.

"What the hell is going on?" Grace whispers, tapping me on the arm. "Are you still sick? Are you okay?"

No, I'm not okay. I'm not okay at all. I can't get enough air though my nostrils. Part of me blames Porter for making me feel this way. But once the shock of him laughing at that sexist comment wears off, I'm still left with the sinking feeling that the root of our fight is actually my fault, and I can't figure out why.

What did I do wrong on game night? He said it was just a misunderstanding, but that feels like a cover-up. Because something upset him, badly, and he blamed me for it that night. And now

I feel so completely stupid, because I don't know what I did, and he won't tell me.

It's like I'm staring at a giant jigsaw puzzle and there's one piece missing, and I'm scrambling to find it—looking in all the sofa cushions, under the table, under the rug, checking the empty box. WHERE IS THAT PUZZLE PIECE?!

"Yo, I said two tickets," the boy at the window enunciates, like I'm stupid. Is that a surf company logo on his T-shirt? Is this . . . one of the trashy creeps who was hanging out with Davy at the posole truck? Who was being all disgusting, harassing those girls in front of my dad and Wanda? Oh, wonderful. Just freaking terrific. "Anyone home in there? I'm not standing here for my health, babe."

Camel's back, meet straw.

I'm not quite sure what happens next.

A strange heat rushes through my head—some sort of stress-induced overload, brought about through trying to determine what happened with Porter . . . heart hurting over our fight, over his reaction to Scott's sexist comment. And all of it is topped off with the rotting cherry that is this jerk standing here now.

Or maybe, just maybe, after a long summer, the Hotbox finally gets the better of me.

All I know is that something breaks inside my brain.

I switch on my microphone. "You want tickets? Here you go."

In a manic fit, I pop open the printer, rip out the folded pack of blank ticket paper, and begin feeding it through the slot—

shove, shove, shove, shove! It waterfalls from the other side like the guy just won a million Skee-Ball tickets at an arcade.

"Have all the tickets you want," I say into the microphone. "Bitches are crazy."

Creeper dude looks stunned. But not as stunned as Mr. Cavadini, whose face appears next to his. Cavadini is holding his clipboard, doing his rounds. His gaze shifts from the pile of bent-up tickets on the ground to me, and he's horrified. Customer service nightmare.

To Davy's friend, he says: "Let me take care of this, and comp your attendance today." And he gestures for someone to let the guy's party through and clean up the pile of blank tickets.

To me, he says: "What in blazes is the matter with you, young lady? Have you lost your mind?" His nose is pressed against the Hotbox's glass. His face is so red, his Cave tie looks like it might cut off circulation and strangle him.

"I'm really sorry," I whisper into the microphone, gripping it with both hands as ugly tears stream down my cheeks, "but I sort of *have* lost my mind."

"Well," Mr. Cavadini says, unmoved by my pitiful display of emotion, "you'll have plenty of time to find it in your free time, because you're fired."

"I hate to shatter your ego, but this is not the first time I've had a gun pointed at me."
—Samuel L. Jackson, *Pulp Fiction* (1994)

26

I don't make a scene. I just clean out my locker, clock out, and leave while everyone gawks at me in silence. When Porter calls my name across the parking lot, I refuse to turn around. Helmet on. Kickstand up. Keys in ignition. I'm gone. The Cavern Palace is now a "was." I no longer have a summer job.

I consider not telling my dad about getting fired for about five minutes, but I'm tired of being a coward. Besides, he'd find out sooner or later. I wonder if the Pancake Shack is hiring.

Grace comes over to my house after her shift and I tell her the whole thing, every bit of it and more. Before I know what I'm saying, I'm telling her about Greg Grumbacher and the CliffsNotes version of how I got shot. How Porter was the first person I really told, and now look—just *look!*—where that trust got me. And sure, I was talking to some guy online before I moved here, and yes, I had planned to meet him, but we don't talk anymore, and NOTHING HAPPENED, and that's none of Porter's business. It's no one's business but mine.

For a brief moment, I'm worried that I've freaked her out.

But she says very seriously, "It's a shame that I'm going to be forced to commit severe testicular trauma upon that boy."

After this, our shared appetite for vengeance quickly spirals out of control. She calls Porter a *C* word, which is apparently okay to do if you're English. She then asks if I want her to talk to him (I don't) or spread horrible rumors about him at work (I sort of do). When she starts getting creative about the rumor spreading, it just makes me sad, and I start crying again. My dad comes home from work in the middle of my sob session, and Grace gives him the lowdown. She should be a TV commentator. By the time she's finished explaining, I'm done with the tears.

My dad looks shell-shocked.

"Bet you're sorry you signed up for your teenage daughter to move in with you now, huh?" I say miserably. "Maybe this is why mom hasn't called all summer. She's probably thinking, *Good riddance.*"

He looks momentarily confused, but quickly disregards that last remark, comes up behind me, wraps his arms around my shoulders, and squeezes. "Are you kidding? I wouldn't miss any of this for one single second. And if there's one thing I know about, it's how to get over breakups. Or potential ones. Whatever this is. Get your stuff, girls. We're going out for lobster and laser tag."

Porter starts texting me the next day. Nothing substantial, just several short texts.

Text 1: *Hey.*

Text 2: *I'm so sorry about work. I feel awful.*

Text 3: *We need to talk.*

Text 4: *Please, Bailey.*

Dad advises me to ignore all of those texts and let him simmer. After all, Porter did the same thing to me. Time apart is healthy. Dad also quizzes me, asking me if I've realized why Porter walked out on game night. "You're a good detective, Mink. You can figure this out on your own."

Maybe I don't want to anymore. I've pretty much given up trying.

Besides, I have other things to think about, like looking for another job, one that doesn't mind that I've been sacked from my last place of employment. Dad offers to ask around at the CPA office. I politely decline.

When I'm looking through the classifieds in the local free paper we picked up during our million-dollar lobster feast the night before, Dad says, "What did you mean when you said your mother hasn't called all summer?"

"Just that. She hasn't called. All summer. Or texted. Or e-mailed."

A long moment drags by. "Why haven't you said anything?"

"I thought you knew. Has she called you?"

He rubs his hand over head. "Not since June. She said she'd be in touch with me later to see how we were doing, but she told me she'd mainly be communicating through you. I'm such an idiot. I should have checked in with you. I guess I was too busy being selfish about having you here with me that I let it slip. This is my fault, Bailey."

After a moment I say, "What if something's wrong?"

"I'm subscribed to her firm's newsletter. She's fine. She won a big court case last week."

"So . . ."

He sighs. "You know how long it's taking you to get over Greg Grumbacher? Well, it's taking her just as long. Because it may have hurt and scared you, but not only did it do those things to her, too, she's also living with the guilt that the whole thing is her fault. And she still hasn't forgiven herself. I'm not sure she ever will completely. But the difference between the two of you is that you're ready to try to move on, and she still isn't."

I think about this. "Is she going to be okay?"

"I don't know," he says, rubbing a gentle hand over my cheek. "But you are."

The following day, I decide I am finished letting Porter simmer. No more games. This whole thing has spun so far out of control. I am just . . . done.

At eight in the morning, I text Porter and tell him I want to meet and talk. He suggests the surf shop. He says his family is at the beach, watching Lana surf, and he is there alone opening the shop. It hurts my heart that he's not out there with them, but I don't say that, of course. Our texting is all very civil. And meeting in a public place sounds like a reasonable plan.

It takes me a little while to stoke up my courage. I cruise down Gold Avenue. Circle the boardwalk parking lots. Idle for a minute watching the fog-covered top of the Bumblebee Lifts. Speed down the alley to make sure Mr. Roth's van isn't parked out back.

Since I'm unsure where our relationship stands, I decide to park Baby in front of the shop, like a lot of the other scooters do along the boardwalk storefronts. No special privileges: I can walk through the entrance like any other Mary, Jane, or Sue.

Ignoring the compelling scent of the first churros being fried that morning, I spy movement in the shop and wait for Porter to let me inside. Surf wax wafts when the door swings open. But it's the sight of his handsome face that makes my throat tighten painfully.

"Hi," I say stoically.

"Hi," he answers gruffly.

I stand there for a second, and then he gestures for me to come inside. When I do, that big white fluffy cat I saw on the roof with Don Gato tries to sneak in the door with me. He shoos it away with his foot and says, "Scram."

He locks the door behind me before glancing at his red surf watch, changing his mind, and unlocking it again. "One minute until nine," he explains. "Time to open."

"Oh," I say. Doesn't really look like there's a line of people itching to get inside, so I guess we still have plenty of privacy. Then again, I don't know when his family's coming back. Better make this quick.

Ooaf. Why am I so nervous?

Porter looks in turns hopeful and worried and wary. He shoves his hands into his pockets and heads toward the back of the shop. I follow. When he gets to the counter, he walks around it and faces me like I'm a customer.

Okay, then.

"So . . . ," he says. "You mentioned that you were ready to talk."

Nodding, I reach inside my pocket and pull out the shark tooth. I've already removed my keys. I set it down on the counter and slide it toward him. "You gave this to me on the condition that I be more honest and open with you because you need to trust me. However, I've clearly done something that has hurt you, and must assume that I have broken your trust. Therefore, I am returning your tooth, and dissolving our . . . whatever it is we are—"

"Bailey—"

"Please let me finish. My mom's a lawyer. I know how important verbal contracts are."

"Dammit, Bailey."

The shop door opens behind me. Great. Can't people wait five stinking minutes for Mr. Zog's Sex Wax? I mean, come on.

Just when I'm ready to move aside and let Porter deal with the customer walking up behind me, Porter's expression transforms into something very close to rage. And it's at this exact moment that I recognize the pattern I'm hearing on the wooden floor. It's not the sound of someone walking: it's the sound of someone limping.

"Get the fuck out of here," Porter shouts.

I swing around, heart pounding, and see Davy heading toward me. He looks much rougher than the last time I saw him at Fast Mike's motorcycle garage, which is saying a lot. He's not only wearing a shirt, miracle of miracles, he's wearing a sand-colored trench coat, and it looks like he's still on at least one crutch, partially hidden behind the coat.

"Hello, cowgirl," he says in an emotionless, lazy voice that sounds like it got flattened by an eighteen-wheeler. He's high as hell—on what, I don't know. But his eyes are just as dead as his words, and his head's moving a little funny, bobbing and weaving.

Out of the corner of my eye, I see movement from Porter.

"Nuh-uh." Davy lifts his crutch and points it in Porter's direction.

Only, it's not a crutch. It's the shotgun from the bonfire.

I freeze. So does Porter; he was in the middle of bounding over the counter.

"Saw you riding around in the parking lot earlier," Davy says to me. "Thought maybe you were coming over to apologize. But you drove right past me."

Shit! How could I have not noticed Davy's big yellow truck?

"Put the gun down, Davy," Porter says in a casual voice that sounds a little forced. "Come on, man. That's insane. Where did you even get that thing? If someone saw you walking around with that, you could end up in jail. Don't be stupid."

"Who's going to see me?"

"Anyone who walks in here," Porter says. "Dude, we're open. My folks are on their way back from the beach. They just called. They'll be here in two minutes. And you know Mr. Kramer comes in here every morning. He'll call the cops, man."

Davy thinks about this a second and waves the gun toward me. *Breathe*, I tell myself.

"Cowgirl here can go lock the door. I want a private conversation, just the three of us. I've got a beef with the two of you. An apology is owed, and maybe a little cash out of the register while you're at it. Payback for pain and misery suffered. What you did to my knee."

I don't move.

"My parents are just down the street," Porter repeats, this time sounding angry.

Davy shrugs. "Guess you better hurry with the register, then. Go lock the door, cowgirl."

I flick a glance at Porter. He's breathing heavy. I can't read his face all that well, but what I do know is that he's absolutely miserable and conflicted. Funny thing is, for the first time in forever, I'm not. I'm scared and worried, yes. And I hate the sight of that goddamn gun with an unholy passion I can't measure.

But I am not afraid of Davy.

I am furious.

I just don't know what to do about him.

Eyes guarded, I plod to the front door and lock it. The windows are enormous; I can see his reflection in the glass, so I watch him the entire way there. Watch him watching Porter, because that's where he's pointing the shotgun now. And why wouldn't he? Porter's the one who kicked his ass. Porter's the one who nearly jumped the counter. Porter's an athlete, nothing but muscle. Even a rational, sober person would consider Porter the bigger threat.

Davy's not sober.

I take my time strolling back to them, and I think about my dad's warnings about oversteering, and about how I exploded in the Hotbox—twice. I think about all my Artful Dodger skills and how they're partly inherited from my CPA dad, and his love of details and numbers, and partly inherited from my attorney mom, and her love of finding loopholes. I think about how my dad said I'm going to be okay because I'm willing to try to get better.

But mainly I think about that day last month when those two punks tried to steal the Maltese falcon from the Cave. They underestimated me too.

Davy gives me a brief look, enough to see that I'm approaching but giving him a wide berth, head down. "Locked up tight?"

"Yep," I say.

"All right," he says, pointing the shotgun at Porter. "Register. Empty it."

Lowest of lows. Robbing your best friend's family. I know Porter's thinking it, but he says nothing. His jaw is tight as he presses a few buttons on the computer screen. "Haven't started it up yet," he explains. "Can't open the drawer until the program's running. Hold on a sec."

Bullshit. He must have put the drawer in himself, so the computer's on. He probably has a key to the drawer. But Davy's too stoned to realize this, so he waits. And while he does, Porter's eyes dart toward mine. And in that beautiful, singular moment, I know we're both linked up.

Trust is a golden gift, and this time, I'm not wasting it.

I shift my focus to Davy. The counter is in front of him, and behind him is a rack with some short, squat bodyboards on it—a third the size of a surfboard, but "way lamer," as Porter once joked.

I wait. *Come on, Porter. Give me an opening.*

As if he's read my mind, he suddenly says, "Oh, lookie here. The computer is finally waking up, Davy."

Davy's head turns toward Porter.

I step back, slip around, and slide one of the bodyboards off the stand. As I do, it makes a sound. *Crap!* It's also a lot lighter than I hoped. *Oh, well.* Too late now, because Davy's turning around, cognizant that I'm closer than he expected. I don't have a choice.

Right as his gaze connects with mine, I grip the board in both hands, rear back, and smack him in the side of the face.

He cries out as his head whips sideways. His step falters, and he stumbles.

The shotgun swings around wildly and clips me in the shoulder. I grab it and try to wrestle it out of his hand. It suddenly breaks free, and I fly backward with the gun—but that's because Porter has hurdled over the counter.

Porter slams Davy to the floor as my back hits the rack of

bodyboards, knocking them over. I scramble to stay on my feet and hold on to the shotgun, but fail.

I fall on my face.

"Porter!" I'm swimming in a sea of foam bodyboards. The boys are struggling on the floor, and all I can see is Porter's arm pounding like a piston and Davy's trench coat flapping and tangling around his legs.

And then—

A loud whimper.

Heart knocking against my rib cage, I shove the bodyboards aside and jump to my feet.

Porter is lying on the floor.

Davy is below him, facedown. One cheek is turned against the wood. One eye blinking away tears.

"I'm sorry," Davy says hoarsely.

"Me too," Porter says, pinning Davy's arms to the floor. "I tried, man. Someone else is going to have to save you now."

Porter looks up at me and nods. I set the gun on the floor and kick it out of the way. Then I dig my phone out of my pocket and dial 911.

"Uh, yeah," I say into the phone, out of breath, swallowing hard. "I'm at Penny Boards Surf Shop on the boardwalk. There's been an attempted armed robbery. We're okay. But you need to send someone to come arrest the guy. And you also need to call Sergeant Wanda Mendoza immediately and tell her to come to the scene right now."

"I may go back to hating you. It was more fun."
—Cary Grant, *North by Northwest* (1959)

27

Turns out, Davy's shotgun was stolen. He also had a hella bunch of heroin and other narcotics in his coat. Wanda says since he's a month from turning eighteen and he's been arrested before, he might be tried as an adult and serve some time in prison. Right now, he's being detoxed in a jail cell. Wanda says his attorney will try to persuade the judge to put him a state-run rehab facility for a couple of weeks while he awaits trial. No guarantee that will happen, though.

I get all this information the day after the events in the surf shop, so I relay it by text to Porter and let him know. We haven't really had any time to talk, what with all the chaos. His family showed up a few minutes after the cops and were understandably freaked. Mr. Roth was so angry at Davy, he had to be restrained until Mrs. Roth could talk him down. Wanda called my dad, who immediately left work and rushed over to the surf shop to make sure I was okay. It was a whole fiasco.

370 • JENN BENNETT

By the time we'd given statements and everyone cleared out, Porter had to go to work at the Cave, so I followed my dad home. It wasn't until he was ordering us lunch that I realized Porter had, at some point when I wasn't paying attention, slipped the shark tooth back into my pocket. I got a text from him a few minutes later.

All it said was: *We're not done talking.*

The next day after dinner, out of the blue, my dad asks to see my old map of the boardwalk. I'd almost thrown it away in a fit when Alex blew me off weeks ago. I have to dig it out from my desk drawer in my bedroom. Dad spreads it out on the patio table near our redwood tree and studies it, nodding slowly.

"What?" I say.

Dad sits back in his chair and smiles at me. "You know, you're tenacious and stubborn. You got that from your mom. It's what makes her a great lawyer. I love tenacious women. That's what attracted me to Wanda. It's what makes her a good cop."

I give him the side eye. *Where's he going with this?*

"However, this tenacity thing also has its downside, because it's all forward movement with blinders on. Like a horse, you know?" He holds his hands up on either side of his eyes. "You plow ahead, and you make a lot of progress that other people wouldn't make, but you can't see what's happening on either side of the road. You have blind spots. You ignore things that are right next to you. Your mom did that all the time."

"Is that why you got divorced?"

He thinks about this for a long moment. "It was one reason.

But this isn't about your mom and me. I'm talking about you. And your blind spots. Don't be too tenacious. Sometimes you've got to stop and look around."

"Why don't you ever just come out and tell me what you're trying to say, Master Yoda?"

"Because I'm trying to raise you to think for yourself, young Jedi. I can offer advice, but you've got to do the work. The whole goal of parenting is for you to become an independent young woman and come up with your own answers. Not for me to provide them for you."

"It sounds like you read that in a parenting book."

He holds back a smile. "Maybe I did."

"What a dork," I tease. "Okay, what's your advice, then? Lay it on me."

"Have you told Porter that you were talking to Alex before you moved out here?"

"Um, no."

"Maybe you should. People can sense when you're holding things back from them. I knew your mom was cheating on me with Nate for months before she told me. I had no proof, but I could sense something was wrong."

I'm so floored by this, I don't know what to say. Dad has never talked much about Nate—or that he knew Mom was cheating with Nate. It makes me uncomfortable. What's weird is that he's so blasé. But it's sort of weirder that we can talk about this together now. And wait just one stinking second—

"I wasn't cheating on Porter with Alex," I tell him. "Or cheating on Alex with Porter."

"What you actually did or didn't do doesn't matter," Dad says. "It's the secrecy that eats away at you. Just tell Porter. And maybe be honest with Alex while you're at it. You'll feel better, I promise."

"I don't know about that," I mutter.

"Like I said, it's not my job to do the work for you." He folds up the map in neat squares. "But my advice, dearest daughter, is that you settle up your boy problems in order, one at a time."

It takes me an entire day to think about everything Dad said, but I think I finally see the logic. Alex was a big part of my daily life for a long time. And, sure, he blew me off. But I should have told him I'd moved across the country. Maybe if I tell him now, he won't even care anymore, especially now that I've broken the ice about Porter in that last heart-to-heart messaging we had. I guess I won't know until I try.

@mink: Hey. Me again. Are you still out there?

His reply comes two hours later:

@alex: I'm here. What's up?

@mink: Since we were being all super honest in our last talk, I thought I'd do some more bean spilling. This one is a little bigger. Are you ready?

@alex: Should I be sitting? *is afraid*

@mink: Probably.

@alex: Sitting.

@mink: Okay, so here's the deal. I'm in town, living with my dad, and have been here for a while. Sorry I didn't say anything. Long story, but I was worried it might be weird, and I have a tendency to avoid confrontation. But better late than never? I was wondering if you wanted to get together and have lunch. Anyways . . . this is getting awkward, so I'll shut up. I just wanted you to know that I'm sorry I never said anything about being here, and I thought maybe I could apologize in person, since we're both in the same town and used to be friends. (And hopefully still are?) What do you say?

I wait and wait and wait for his reply. This is a mistake. I should probably delete my message. If he hasn't read it yet, I might still be able to . . .

@alex: What about your boyfriend?

@mink: This would be a nonromantic lunch. I'm sorry, nothing's changed since our last conversation. I'm still not over him.

@alex: Why don't we go with our original plan? Meet me Sunday

374 • JENN BENNETT

night on the beach under the California flag, half an hour before the film festival's showing of North by Northwest.

Oh, crap. I wasn't prepared for that! I tear my room apart searching for the film festival guide that Patrick gave me and look up the schedule for the free films they're showing on the beach. *North by Northwest* doesn't start until nine p.m. It will be dark by then. Should I meet a strange boy after dark? That doesn't seem advisable. Then again, it's a public place, and when I browse the film guide, there are photos from last year; all the concessions areas appear well lit. Surely the flag is somewhere around there.

Should I do this? The Artful Dodger definitely would not. But am I that person anymore?

@mink: Okay. I'll meet you there.

That's one boy problem taken care of. Now for the next. This one seems harder. I shoot off a quick text.

Me: *Hey, you busy? I was hoping we could meet somewhere and talk. I'm willing to do the quid pro quo thing now. You win.*

Porter: *Actually, I'm sort of booked until after Sunday. How about after that?*

Me: *Okay, it's a deal. Will text you then.*

Actually, I'm relieved. *North by Northwest* is on Sunday, so that gives me time to meet Alex and mend things with him before I talk to Porter. Who knew two boys could be so much trouble?

•   •   •

In *North by Northwest*, Cary Grant plays an advertising executive who's mistaken for a CIA agent named Kaplan. The thing is, Kaplan doesn't really exist. So throughout the film, Cary Grant is constantly being forced to pretend he's someone he's not—a fake of a fake. Nothing is what it seems, which is what makes the story so fun to watch. Alex and I have discussed the film's merits online, but it's strange to think about those conversations now. I definitely wish I could be seeing it under happier circumstances.

By the time Sunday night rolls around, I'm strangely calm. Maybe it's because this has been a long time coming, me meeting Alex. Or maybe it's because I don't feel the same way about him as I once did, now that Porter's in my life. I think back to the beginning of the summer, when I was so worried and nervous about everything Alex could or could not be—tall or short, bald or hairy, shy or chatty—and none of those things matter anymore.

He is who is.

I am who I am.

Exactly who those people are couldn't really be identified in an online profile or captured correctly in all our written communication, no matter how honest we tried to be. We were only showing one side of ourselves, a side that was carefully trimmed and curated. He didn't see all my hang-ups and screwy problems, or how long it takes me to pluck my eyebrows every night. He doesn't know I tried to pick up a gay whale-tour host because I thought it might be him. Or that I can't tell the difference between a male and a female cat . . . Or about all the dirty GIFs I've laughed at with Grace, or the number of churros I can put away in one sitting before it starts to get embarrassing for the churro cart vendor, because he knows I'm really not buying them for "a friend." (Five.)

God only knows what I haven't seen of him.

So, you know, whatever. If he's nice, great. If not, no big deal. In my head, I'm holding my head high and wearing a Grace-inspired T-shirt that says I'M JUST HERE FOR THE CLOSURE in big, bedazzled letters.

I arrive at the beach a little more than half an hour before the film starts. They're showing it, ironically enough, near one of the first places I remember when I came into town: the surfers' crosswalk. Only, the whole area is transformed tonight, with one of those huge rotating double spotlights that's pointed toward the sky, announcing to the world, *Hey, movie over here!* They've also lit up the palm trees along Gold Avenue and hung film festival banners in the parking lot across the street, which is jammed with cars. I manage to squeeze Baby into a space alongside another scooter before following a line of people who are swinging picnic baskets and coolers, heading toward the giant white screen set up in the sand.

Alex was right all those months ago when he first told me about this: It looks really fun. The sun's setting over the water. Families and couples are chilling on blankets, and closer to the road, a row of tents and food trucks are selling burgers and fish tacos and film festival merchandise. I head for those, looking for flagpoles. All the palms are lit up, so I figure a flagpole must be spotlighted too, right? But when I've walked the entire row of vendors, I can't find it. No flags near the movie screen either. It's a pretty big screen, so I check around back, just to make sure. Nope. Nada.

This is weird. I mean, Alex lives here, so he knows the place. He wouldn't just tell me to meet him somewhere so specific if it wasn't there. I check my film messages to make sure there isn't anything new from him, and when I don't see anything I head back the way I came, all the way back down to the end of the concession row to the back of the seating area. That's when I spot it.

The flagpole is all the way up a set of steps, on a wide natural stone platform—a lookout over the ocean, where the surfer's crosswalk ends.

Right in front of the memorial statue of Pennywise Roth.

I sigh, and then snort at myself, because really, no matter what I do, I can't escape him. And if Alex is the nice guy I'm hoping he is, we can both have a laugh about it later.

Weaving around blankets, I make my way to the lookout and climb the stone steps. I'm getting a little nervous now. Not much, but this is surreal. The lookout is fairly spacious. It's banded in a wood railing with some built-in benches around the ocean side, where one older couple is gazing out at the sunset. Not him, for sure. I gaze up at the Pennywise statue. I've seen the photo of this online, of course, and driven past it, but it's weird to see it up close in person. Someone's put a Hawaiian lei around his neck; I wonder if it was Mrs. Roth.

Someone's sitting on a bench behind the statue. I blow out a long breath, straighten my shoulders, and lumber around ol' Pennywise. Time to face the music.

"Hello, Mink."

My brain sees who's in front of me, hears the words, but doesn't believe. It recalculates and recalculates, over and over, but I'm still stuck. And then it all comes rolling back to me, out of order.

The video store.

Breakfast at Tiffany's.

Him caring about the Maltese falcon being stolen.

Roman Holiday.

White cat at the surf shop.

Churro cart.

Is it wrong to hate someone who used to be your best friend?

Cheating girlfriend.

The Big Lebowski.

Watching movies at work.

My coworker, the human blunt.

The Philadelphia Story.

Mr. Roth . . . Xander Roth.

Alexander.

Alex.

My knees buckle. I'm falling. Porter leaps up from the bench and grabs me around the waist before I hit the ground. I kick at the stone below my feet, like I'm swimming in place, trying to get traction. Trying to get control of my legs. I finally manage it.

When I do, I go a little crazy. It's that stupid coconut scent of his. I shove him away from me, beat him—hard—landing blows on his arms until he lets me go in order to shield his face. And then I just fall to pieces.

I sob.

And sob.

I curl up into a ball on the bench and sob some more.

I don't even know why I'm crying so hard. I just feel so stupid. And shocked. And overwhelmed. Sort of betrayed, too, but that's ridiculous, because how could that be? Then I stop crying and gasp a little, because I realize that's exactly how Porter must have felt when he found out.

He sits down on the bench and lifts my head onto his lap, sighing heavily. "Where are you at in the screwed-up-ness of it all? Because there are all kinds of layers."

"We basically cheated on each other with each other," I say.

"Yeah," he says. "That's pretty messed up. When I told my mom, she said we pulled a reverse 'Piña Colada,' which is some cheesy 1970s song about this couple who write personal ads looking for hookups, and end up meeting each other."

"Oh, God," I groan. "You told your mom?"

"Hey, this is some crazy shit. I had to tell someone," he argues. "But look at it this way. We ended up liking the real us better than the online us. That's something, right?"

"I guess."

I think about it some more. *Ugh.* My dad knew. He was trying to tell me with all that talk about blinders and horses. Another wave of YOU ARE THE WORLD'S BIGGEST IDIOT hits me, and this time, I let the wave wash over me, not fighting it. The older couple that was hanging around on the lookout has left— guess a bawling teenage girl was ruining their peaceful sunset view—so we have the area to ourselves for the moment, and for that, I'm grateful. Below the lookout, hundreds of people throng the beach, but it's far enough away that I don't mind.

"You didn't know until game night at my house, right?" I ask.

"No."

That makes me feel somewhat better, I suppose. At least we were both stupid about this until he heard my nickname. *Oh, God.* He watched *The Philadelphia Story* with me on purpose. He knew then, and he didn't tell me. My humiliation cannot be measured. "Why?" I ask in a small voice. "Why didn't you tell me?"

"I was bewildered. I didn't know what to do. I couldn't believe you'd been living out here the entire time. Couldn't believe you . . . were *her*—Mink. At first, I thought you'd been screwing with me, but the more I thought about it, I knew that didn't fit. I just freaked for a while. And then . . . I guess I wanted to hold on to it. And I wanted you to discover it on your own. I thought you would. If I dropped enough hints, I thought you would, Bailey—I swear. But then I started thinking about why you didn't tell me—Alex—you moved out here, and how it felt as though you'd been lying to me . . . and I wanted you to come clean."

"Quid pro quo." I close my eyes, fully aware of the irony now.

"I didn't mean for things to go sideways," he insists. "When you got fired . . . Grace told me what happened in the Hotbox. For the record, she also made some threats to my manhood that gave me a few nightmares."

I groan. "I don't blame you for what I did in the Hotbox. I was upset at the time, but I've moved past it."

"I just want you to know that what Scott and Kenny were saying that day . . . I didn't think it was funny. I'm not even sure why I laughed. I think it was just a nervous reaction. I felt awful afterward. I tried to text you and tell you, but you weren't speaking to me. And then Davy happened . . ."

I sigh shakily, completely overwhelmed. "God, what a mess."

After a second, he says, "You know, what I haven't been able to figure out is why you lied about where you lived before you moved out here."

"I didn't. My mom and her husband moved from New Jersey to DC a few months before. I just never told Alex. You. Alex You. Ugh. That's not a random screenname, is it?"

"Alex is my middle name."

"Alexander. Like your father?"

"Yeah. It was my grandfather's, too." He pushes a curled lock of hair behind my ear. "You do realize this whole mishegas could have been avoided if Mink You would have just told me from the beginning that you were moving out here . . . right?"

I use his hand to cover my face. And then I uncover it and sit up, facing him, wiping away tears. "You know what? Maybe not.

Let's say I'd arranged to meet up with Alex You at the Pancake Shack when I first moved here, and that I hadn't gotten that job at the Cave. Would we have hit it off? I don't know. You don't know that either. Maybe it was just the situation we were in at the Cave."

Porter shakes his head and winds his fingers through mine. "Nope. I don't believe that, and I don't think you do either. Two people who lived in two different places and found each other, not once but twice? You could stick one of us in Haiti and the other in a rocket headed to the moon and we'd still eventually be doing this right now."

I sniffle. "You really think so?"

"You know how I said you were tricky like the fog, and that I was afraid of you running back to your mom at the end of the summer? I'm not afraid anymore."

"You're not?"

He looks toward the ocean, dark purple with the last rays of light. "My mom says we're all connected—people and plants and animals. We all know one another on the inside. It's what's on the outside that distracts. Our clothes, our words, our actions. Shark attacks. Gunshots. We spend our lives trying to find other people. Sometimes we get confused and turned around by the distractions." He smiles at me. "But we didn't."

I smile back, eyes shining with happy tears. "No, we didn't."

"I love you, Bailey 'Mink' Rydell."

I choke out a single sobbed laugh. "I love you too, Porter 'Alex' Roth."

We reach for each other and meet in the middle, half kissing, half murmuring how much we've missed each other. It's sloppy and wonderful, and I've never been hugged so tightly. I kiss him all over his neck beneath his wild curls, and he cups my head in both hands and kisses me all over my face, then wipes away my cried-out makeup drips with the edge of his T-shirt.

Applause and cheers startle both of us. I'd nearly forgotten all about the movie. Porter pulls me up with him, and we lean over the railing together to peer into the dark. Flickering light fills the beach, and the old MGM logo appears with the roaring lion. The music starts. The opening titles dart over the screen. CARY GRANT. EVA MARIE SAINT. Chills zip up and down my back.

And then I realize: I get to share all of this with Porter. All of me. All of us.

I glance up at him, and he's emotional too.

"Hi," he says, forehead pressed to mine.

"Hi."

"Should we head down to the beach?" he asks, slinging an arm over my shoulder.

"I seem to remember hating the beach at some point or another."

"That's because you'd never been to a real one. East Coast beaches are trash beaches."

I laugh, my heart singing with joy. "Oh yeah, that's right. Show me a real beach, why don't you, surfer boy. Let's go watch a movie."

"I wanted it to be you. I wanted it to be you so badly."
—Meg Ryan, *You've Got Mail* (1998)

28

I blow out two quick breaths and stash my purse in the borrowed locker. Behind me, through a narrow passageway onto the main floor, I can see the crowds in the stands and the bright lights of the auditorium. Almost time to start. I twist my head to either side and crack my neck before checking my phone one more time.

Some people thrive in the spotlight; others prefer to work behind the scenes. You can't make a movie with nothing but actors. You need writers and makeup artists, costume designers and talent agents. All of them are equally important.

I'm not a spotlight kind of girl, and I've made my peace with that.

These days, I've pretty much given up my Artful Dodger leanings. Mostly. I relapsed a little when school started a couple of months ago in the fall. But that doesn't mean I'm ready to run for senior class president like Grace. It *does* mean that ever since our girl talk on the beach after I let her down, I've tried to make good on being a dependable friend, so I helped her with all her campaigning. She won, but that was no surprise. Everyone loves Grace. I just love her a little more.

After school, I work at Video Ray-Gun, which is much less pressure than the Hotbox—not to mention less sweaty. Plus, I get first pick of the used DVDs that come through. And since Porter's shifts at the Cave are only on the weekends now that school's in session, I get to see him on my work breaks, because the surf shop is only a five-minute walk down the boardwalk from the video store. Win-win.

And I have to see him whenever I get the chance, because next week, he's flying out to Hawaii with his mom. They're meeting up with Mr. Roth to watch Lana compete in Oahu for some special surfing competition. And to talk to someone in the World League about Porter surfing in a qualifying event in January in Southern California. He's already registered, and he's been practicing every chance he gets. There's crazy buzz online in the surfing community that the Roth siblings could be the next big thing; a reporter from Australia called the surf shop last week and interviewed his dad for a magazine.

It's all exciting, and I'm thrilled to pieces that Porter finally wants to surf. He was born to do it. At the same time, I'm glad he's not giving up on the idea of going to college. He says he can do both. I don't think he realized that before, but I can understand why. His family's been through a lot. It's hard to think about next week when you're not sure if you'll even make it through today.

But I don't worry about him now. And I don't worry about him going pro like Lana, and whether he'll be traveling all over the world for a week here and there, Australia and France, South Africa and Hawaii. Maybe sometimes I'll get to fly out with him. Maybe not. But it doesn't matter. Because he's right. Surfing the Pipeline or rocket to the moon, we'll find each other.

"Five minutes," my captain calls out to the team.

Several of the girls around me rush to finish last-minute adjustments to their makeup and pull up their black tights, kneepads, and shiny gold shorts. One girl is running late and just getting her skates on. If the team captain, LuAnn Wong, finds out, she'll have to sit out the first period. LuAnn doesn't take any crap.

I joined the local Roller Derby team, the Coronado Cavegirls, two months ago. We're part of a regional Rollergirls league, so we compete against three other teams in the area, including one from Monterey. That works out well for me, because I also volunteer every other Saturday at the Pacific Grove Natural History Museum. It's mainly cataloging shells in the stockroom, and I don't get paid or anything, but I love it.

At first, I was a little scared to join the derby. It seemed too "spotlight" for me, and most of the girls are a couple of years older. One skater is even in her late thirties. But Grace encouraged me, the uniforms were totally cool, and the more I thought about it, the more I liked the idea. When I'm out there skating, it's not about me, it's about the team. We work together as a group. I'm a jammer, which means I get to wear the helmet with the star on it, and my goal is to skate past the opposing team's blockers as fast as I can. My Artful Dodger skills are put to better use on the derby track than in my daily life.

Plus, it helps me blow off steam. When I was working the Hotbox, I overheated, figuratively and literally. Skating gives me an outlet for my frustrations. I don't have to jump punk kids who steal falcons from museums, throw tickets at customers, or wrestle shotguns away from junkies. I can knock around girls bigger than me and it's not only legal, it's encouraged.

I peek out through the passage and scan the stands for familiar faces, spotting them almost immediately. My dad is sitting with Wanda; they never miss my Roller Derby bouts. In front of them are Grace and Taran—who returned from India at the end of the summer, thankfully, so I didn't have to fly over there and kick his ass—and Patrick with his boyfriend, and then Mrs. Roth and Porter. He's wearing his HOT STUFF devil jacket, which makes me smile. (Note to self: Tear that jacket off later in the back of his van.)

"Three minutes, ladies," LuAnn calls out behind me. "Get ready to line up."

As my teammates zip around me, I whip out my phone and ask one of the girls to take a photo of me smiling over my shoulder with the crowd in the background. My skate name is printed in bold letters on the back of my jersey: MINK.

I text the photo, with the time, date, and precise geolocation, to my mother. I don't wait for a reply; I know it won't come. But

I haven't given up hope that one day she'll be ready to forgive herself. To forgive me for leaving her and moving out here. And when she is ready? She can come and visit me and Dad. Maybe we'll even take her out for posole, who knows.

After the last call, I stash my phone in the locker and line up with my teammates. Everyone's buzzing. It's always like this before we go out. It's such a rush. I shake out my arms and adjust the strap on my helmet. Everything's in place. I can hear the announcer riling up the crowd. They're cheering. It's almost time to go.

"Are you ready, girls?" LuAnn asks, skating down the line, making eye contact with each one of us.

She touches my shoulder, reminding me of how Pangborn used to, and I give her a little nod.

I'm so ready.

I am Mink. Hear me roar.

ACKNOWLEDGMENTS

Megaton thank-yous to:

10. My extraordinary agent, Laura Bradford, for the extremes she endured to deliver good news, which put the US Postal Service's "rain nor heat nor gloom of night" motto to shame.

9. My badass editor, Nicole Ellul, for being the best I've ever had, hands down.

8. My awesome US team at Simon Pulse—Mara Anastas, Liesa Abrams, Tara Grieco, Carolyn Swerdloff, Regina Flath, and all the names and faces I don't know yet—for championing this book and believing in its potential.

7. My amazing UK team at Simon & Schuster UK—Rachel Mann, Becky Peacock, Liz Binks, and everyone else who works tirelessly behind the scenes—for your infectious enthusiasm.

6. My foreign editors, Barbara König and Leonel Teti, for continuing to have faith in my books, and to Christina at LOVE-BOOKS for taking a chance on me.

5. My beta readers, Veronica Buck and Stacey Kalani, for their honesty and kindness.

4. My foreign rights agent, Taryn Fagerness, for tolerating my dumb questions.

3. My personal support team—Karen and Ron and Gregg and Heidi and Hank and Patsy and Don and Gina and Shane and Seph—for all their endless cheerleading. I don't deserve any of you.

2. My husband, for continuing to endure my Writing Madness. I don't deserve you most of all. Love you.

1. And to my readers, thank you for giving me a reason to believe in myself. I hope I can return the favor through the words in this book, even in a small way.

ABOUT THE AUTHOR

Jenn Bennett is an artist and RITA Award–nominated author of the Arcadia Bell urban fantasy series (for *Kindling the Moon*) and the Roaring Twenties romance series, including *Bitter Spirits*, which was chosen as a Publishers Weekly Best Book of 2014 and was the winner of the *RT Book Reviews* Choice Paranormal Romance Book of the Year, and *Grave Phantoms*, which was awarded the RT Book Reviews May Seal of Excellence for 2015. *The Anatomical Shape of a Heart* (titled *Night Owls* in the UK) was her first YA contemporary romance. She lives near Atlanta with one husband and two evil pugs.